Noli Me Tangere

by JOSE RIZAL

TRANSLATED BY LEON MA. GUERRERO

GUERRERO PUBLISHING

First published 1961 by Longman Group Ltd.
(formerly Longmans, Green & Co Ltd), London.

Worldwide rights assigned to The Estate of
Leon Ma. Guerrero, 1994.

First published in the Philippines 1995 by
Guerrero Publishing, Manila.

Exclusively distributed in the Philippines by Anvil Publishing Inc., 2/F,
Team Bldg., 14 P. Antonio St., Bo. Ugong, 1604 Pasig City, Philippines
Tel: (632) 671 1899/9235/6136. (632) 914 0155 Fax: (632) 671 1308.

ISBN 971-27-0436-6 Book Paper edition
ISBN 971-27-0439-4 Newsprint edition

Designed by Manny del Rosario

Printed in Manila by Capitol Publishing House Inc.
Typesetting by Tonio R. Ramirez

'What! No Caesar upon your boards, no mighty Achilles?
'Is Andromache gone? Does not Orestes appear?'

'No! But there are priests and shrewd commercial attachés,
'Subalterns and scribes, majors enough of hussars.'

'But, I pray you, my friend, what can such a laughable medley
'Do that is really great; greatness how can they achieve?'

Schiller: *Shakespeare's Ghost*
(Arnold-Forster Translation)

Table of Contents

TO MY COUNTRY:

IN the catalogue of human ills there is to be found a cancer so malignant that the least touch inflames it and causes agonising pains; afflicted with such a cancer, a social cancer, has your dear image appeared to me, when, for my own heart's ease or to compare you with others, I have sought, in the centres of modern civilisation, to call you to mind.

Now, desirous of your welfare, which is also ours, and seeking the best cure for your ills, I shall do with you what was done in ages past with the sick, who were exposed on the steps of the temple so that the worshippers, having invoked the god, should each propose a remedy.

To this end, I shall endeavour to show your condition, faithfully and ruthlessly. I shall lift a corner of the veil which shrouds the disease, sacrificing to the truth everything, even self-love—for, as your son, your defects and weaknesses are also mine.

THE AUTHOR

Europe, 1886.

INTRODUCTION
Two Novels That Made a Revolution

FEW novels, except perhaps the now much disparaged *Uncle Tom's Cabin*, have made a more shattering impact on the society in which they were conceived and read than the *Noli Me Tangere* and *El Filibusterismo* of the Filipino national hero, José Rizal. And surely no writer paid a higher penalty for self-expression; Rizal was executed by a firing squad mainly because of these two books, now revered by his country as the gospels of its nationalism and lately made by law required reading in its colleges.

It is usually not much fun to read gospels, but the *Noli* was meant to be enjoyed; at its best it is a delightful comedy of manners, an irreverent satire on the last years of the Spanish colonial regime in the Philippines. It has the melodramatic excitement of the elder Dumas's *The Count of Monte Cristo*, by which Rizal was influenced in his early years. The characters come to life with surprising ease and linger in the memory: the absurd Doña Victorina, the elegant Dominican hair-splitter, the peasants worriedly classifying Spanish insults into various degrees of danger, the bell-ringer Crispín, even the ham-fisted, oddly sympathetic Father Dámaso. Rizal was perhaps less fortunate with his plot and his protagonists, who tend to be plaster-cast in sorrowful Wertherian attitudes when they are not earnestly debating the desirability of reforms 'from above' and revolution 'from below', an issue, however, which has not yet entirely lost its topicality.

The *Noli* can be thus enjoyed as a novel even without its aura of historical significance. But, like its sequel, it was nothing if not political. When it was written (in Spanish) and published (in Berlin in 1887), the Filipinos were only beginning to think of themselves as Filipinos rather than as member of various tribes scattered among 7,000 islands between Borneo and Taiwan. Their segregation from their fellow Malays after the colonial wars of the East Indies were settled, and the consciousness that the Spanish oppression was suffered by all in common, had given rise to a feeling of separate nationhood, brought to a point by a dispute on the rights of the native clergy and the execution of three Filipino secular priests in 1872.

Rizal was eleven at the time; his elder and only brother, a protégé of one of the executed priests, feared he would be implicated in the alleged conspiracy and prudently went home to the provinces. Indeed Rizal did not have to go far from his family circle and home town to find his material. His father had become relatively affluent by leasing and working lands from the great estates of the Dominican Order: troubles over taxes, tithes, and rentals hounded the family throughout Rizal's life, and find their echo in both the *Noli* and the *Fili*. When he was still a schoolboy under the Jesuits his own mother was the victim of a false charge of attempted poisoning, and, like Sisa in his story, was marched to gaol along the highway in public degradation, only, like Ibarra's father, to be acquitted after long suffering and humiliation. When, upon the publication of the *Noli*, Rizal was accused by his critics of exaggeration, he could retort that he was ready to match every incident in his novel with one from life.

An extremely talented and versatile scholar with a gift for language, more sensitive than most of his contemporaries to racial discriminations, and aflame with impotent anger at the misgovernment of the Philippines, Rizal left for Spain at the age of twenty-one to continue his studies in Madrid. Like many another nationalist after him, he hoped to find in the metropolis a freer atmosphere and a readier audience than in the colony. By and large, he was disappointed. He found sufficient freedom of thought, speech, and the press in a Spain that scarcely a decade before, although only briefly, had been a constitutional republic.

But he also found his compatriots, with a few honourable exceptions, dissipating their time on women and cards; Rizal was not a prig but he sought his pleasures on other levels. A small Filipino review intended to promote Philippine interests died after a few issues. The Spanish Ministers, some of them liberals, were unapproachable, indifferent, or wary of challenging the religious Orders. Rizal tried to enlist the collaboration of his countrymen in writing a symposium on conditions in the archipelago, but found no response. It was then that he decided to write the book himself, choosing the form of a satirical novel that would open the eyes of his countrymen to their true condition, and of the Spaniards to the errors and injustices committed in their name. It was about two years in the writing; one-half was drafted in Spain, a quarter in France, the remainder, together with the final revision, in Germany, in the hours he could spare from his studies.

The *Noli* is unabashedly anti-clerical, or, more precisely, it is aimed at the

Spanish friars in the Philippines at that time. It had to be. In Rizal's view and that of most Filipino intellectuals, the excesses of authority and the denials of individual freedom in the Philippines could be traced to the mendicant and preaching friars (Dominicans, Augustinians, Franciscans and Recollects) who controlled the Philippine Church, because the hierarchy and most of the strategically located parish priests were drawn from their ranks. The Church in turn was the only element of stability and continuity in a colonial administration whose lay heads came and went with every change of government in unstable Madrid. Believing themselves secure in the loyalty and affection of a Catholic Filipino people, whose ancestors the first virtuous missionaries had protected from the abuses of the colonisers, these Orders were the true rulers of the Philippines, representing to the administration that only they could avert a popular rising, and to the people that only they could give protection as of old from official excesses.

Was the *Noli* also anti-Catholic or anti-religious? Rizal frankly explained his purpose to a friend: 'I am aiming at the friars, but since they were shielding themselves behind the rites and superstitions of a certain religion, I had to free myself from it in order to strike at the enemy hiding behind it… Those who abused its name must bear the responsibility.' The issue, let us fondly hope, has lost its original passion and importance. Rizal's ribald laughter should be heard as an echo, still amusing but no longer wounding, of a battle fought much too long ago. The contemporary reader of Honor Tracy's *The Straight and Narrow* or Bruce Marshall's *A Thread of Scarlet* will not be shocked by the *Noli*, and indeed Rizal anticipated many of the most effective gibes at superstition in the latter and in Peyreffite's *The Keys of St. Peter*.

Only 2,000 copies of the *Noli* were printed; Rizal had to borrow money from a friend to publish the novel at his own expense, and never made a penny out of it. At first the book was sold openly in Manila but, when Rizal's home-coming in the year of its publication brought matters to a head, it was unanimously condemned as 'heretical' and 'subversive' by a special jury of the Royal and Pontifical (Dominican) University of Santo Tomas, and subsequently the government board of censorship recommended the absolute prohibition of its importation, reproduction, and circulation in the Philippines. It came to be considered proof of disloyalty to possess a copy, and Rizal confided to his agent the fear that copies of the book were being bought in order that they might be destroyed.

For all that, the impact of the *Noli* was phenomenal among an illiterate population where public opinion, such as it was, was moulded by a handful of Spanish-speaking intellectuals. The best evidence of its success was the immediate recognition given to Rizal by both his own countrymen and the Spaniards, in the Philippines as well as in Spain, as the leader of the growing nationalist movement for the expulsion of the Spanish friars and other reforms. The official hostility towards himself and his family now assumed such proportions that, after a few months, he was compelled to leave the country again in the hope, quickly defrauded, of sparing his family from persecution. Indeed, already abroad, he learned that one of his brothers-in-law, like Ibarra's father, had been denied burial in consecrated ground because of their relationship.

For a year Rizal worked in the British Museum on annotations to a history of the Philippines that, he hoped, would establish the ancient dignity and culture of the pre-Spanish Filipinos, denigrated in the monkish chronicles as savages just down from the trees. A man of great and many talents, he won the esteem of the European scientists with whom he corresponded and conferred, and planned to organise an international association and congress of scholars on the Philippines. In the meantime a Filipino review had once again been issued in Spain by the small colony of expatriates there, and, a master of polemics, he assiduously contributed political articles of remarkable depth and prescience (in one of them he foresaw that within a century the Philippines would fall either to the North American Republic or to Japan, a prophecy which was fulfilled in both respects in less than half the time).

But the control of editorial policy became an issue of *émigré* politics, and Rizal withdrew once again to write the sequel of the *Noli*. After he had completed *El Filibusterismo*, the feeling grew on him that his place was in the Philippines, but his family opposed his return, which would place him within reach of his enemies. For a time he practiced his profession in Hong Kong, and negotiated with the British North Borneo Company for the establishment of a free Filipino colony there. But he lacked the necessary funds and finally returned to Manila, ostensibly in order to raise them by the liquidation of his family interests. He had a higher purpose. Before embarking he left two sealed letters with a friend in Macao to be opened and published after his death.

One was addressed to his family and revealed that he was exposing himself to danger 'to crown my life-work and bear witness with my example to what I have always preached'. The other was addressed to his countrymen and said that he could no longer live abroad 'knowing that so many suffer unjust persecution because of me', could no longer stand aside 'seeing my brother and sisters and their numerous families hounded like criminals; I prefer to risk death and willingly give my life to free so many innocent people from such unjust persecution.' He added: 'I also want to show those who deny our patriotism that we know how to die for our duty and our convictions.'

At first he was well received. The Governor General himself granted him a personal audience and a full pardon for his father and sisters. But he proved too popular. Friends and admirers carried him in triumph from province to province; he himself, with only rudimentary precautions, started to organise a national League for mutual assistance among all Filipinos. He was promptly arrested on the belated and transparently false charge that subversive pamphlets had been found in his baggage at Customs inspection. In confidential administrative proceedings he was then banished to the town of Dapitan on the distant and only half-explored island of Mindanao.

There is an uncanny foresight in the plot of the *Noli*, which should silence those who would dismiss it as implausible and contrived. The protagonist Ibarra, an intellectual recently returned to the Philippines from Spain, arouses the enmity of the friars, apparently because of an innocent programme for popular education, finds himself implicated in a revolt he never planned, refuses to flee when warned, and is finally seized and condemned to banishment while his fiancee is promised to a Spaniard. I am not of the common opinion that Rizal saw himself in Ibarra and spoke through him; there was always a curious ambivalence in Rizal, and in the end I believe that Elias prevailed over Ibarra in his own mind. But Rizal might have been re-living the vicissitudes of Ibarra when his own fiancee was prevailed upon to marry an English railway engineer, and when he saw his proposals for reform branded as subversive, was himself banished on false charges, refused an offer of rescue, and was eventually accused of inspiring the Philippine Revolution.

This broke out in 1896 when he had been four years in rustication. He had spent the time under surveillance, managing nevertheless to dabble in projects for the improvement of the town and for the rehabilitation of his family's fortunes in new surroundings. He had turned once again to farming (he was a licensed land appraiser) and trading. He had opened a small school, and practised his profession as a physician; his fame as an ophthalmologist brought him patients from all over the country and even from abroad. One of them came from Hong Kong attended by a pretty Irish girl, who returned to share Rizal's anti-climactic exile.

The death he had expected, the death to give witness, had not come; and it may be surmised that even unexpected love and domesticity after wandering over half of Europe had been insufficient compensation, and that a brilliant correspondence on religious issues with his old Jesuit mentors in Manila had not stilled his intellectual restlessness. Was he bored? In any case he had taken the strange decision to volunteer to serve as a doctor with the Spanish forces in Cuba.

His offer had been accepted; he was on his way to Barcelona aboard a Spanish warship, having once more turned away an opportunity to escape in Singapore, when he was suddenly arrested in mid-sea and sent back to the Philippines on the next mailboat. The Revolution had started after the premature discovery of the *Katipunan*, the Association of the Sons of the People, an outgrowth of Rizal's League, but under proletarian rather than intellectual middle-class leadership.

There was no Elias to rescue Rizal when he was brought to trial. The court-martial proceedings were a judicial farce, but a political necessity in the times. The charges were absurd on their face, but fundamentally they were a correct identification of the author of the *Noli* and the *Fili* as the 'soul', although not the actual military leader, of the nationalist revolution. Fifty years later, under a more realistic colonial administration of another race, Rizal would have gone on eventually from gaol to the Prime Ministership of his independent country. But the Spaniards are not a people who are given to accommodations. Rizal was condemned to death and executed publicly by a firing squad of Filipino colonial troops on the 30th December 1896.

The Spanish regime in the Philippines lasted less than two years more. Now that Asian nationalism is a force to be reckoned with, it would not be amiss to recall what the western world seldom realises: that the Filipinos, inspired by Rizal, made the first nationalist revolution in Asia in 1896, established its first democratic republic, which survived until 1901, and in

1946, exactly half a century after Rizal's execution, became the first Asians to win independence from western colonialism. It is not mere patriotic pride that leads Filipinos to acclaim the author of the *Noli* and the *Fili* as the first Asian nationalist and as one who in his way moved the world.

A NOTE ON THE TRANSLATION

THE *Noli* has been translated many times into many languages almost from the date of its publication. The present version is an attempt to make it palatable to a new generation of English-speaking Filipinos and give it, beyond them, a wider audience among other English-speaking peoples on the first centenary of Rizal's birth in 1961.

Personally I have never been at ease with any of the existing English translations of the *Noli*. When prepared by those whose native language is English, they lack a feeling or understanding of the Filipino *milieu*. When essayed by Filipinos, they suffer from an, it seems to me, exaggerated reverence for the original text which makes for tortured constructions. Both kinds are usually encumbered with numerous explanatory footnotes which are irritating and discouraging, although no doubt they are helpful to foreigners and even for many contemporary Filipinos who no longer have any idea of the customs of their forefathers.

Each generation, it has been said, needs its own translations, and I have tried in this version to provide a completely new one that would give the contemporary reader 'the ease of original composition,' the *Noli* as Rizal might have written it if he had been writing in English for the present generation of Filipinos. The thesis of Matthew Arnold in his essay 'On Translating Homer' is that a translation should affect us in the same way as the original may be supposed to have affected its first hearers; that was scarcely possible with the *Noli*, the condition of the Filipinos having largely, although not entirely, changed, but it was something to be aimed at.

With this in mind, though not without misgivings about purists, I have incorporated into the text the unavoidable explanations of historical, local, classical, theological, and other references and allusions which would otherwise remain obscure to a generation not so erudite as Rizal's or as familiar with the Philippines of his time. If this practice adds to the ease of the reader I shall count it worth the indignant protests that are bound to be made.

Rizal's style is often unlikely to appeal to the modern ear; Spanish, moreover, is a language that can afford to be more florid and sentimental than modern English. I have therefore allowed myself the further liberty of paraphrasing certain passages that might otherwise have provoked a sophisticated snigger, particularly the love-scene on María Clara's balcony which has been the delight of generations of Filipino sentimentalists. To them, both as a fellow addict and as a fancier of romantic Spanish, I offer my most abject apologies, and trust that I have made sufficient expiation by translating the verses in the original into English rhymes instead of rendering them, as has been usual, into prose.

Other passages had to be re-worked willy-nilly; thus, the ingenious exploration of the commanding officer and his wife into the proper pronunciation of *'Filipinas'* defies direct translation, whether free or literal, and I was compelled to invent similar difficulties with the pronunciation of 'Philippines'. Recognizable alternatives had to be provided also for Doña Victorina's fractured Spanish, which I have rendered into what is known as 'Filipino English', and her latter-day Andalusian accent, which I have transferred to the American 'Old South'.

In a number of cases I have thought it helpful to translate the original Spanish into modern Philippine equivalents, for example, *'convento'* into 'parish house' since the convent, properly speaking, would be the Order's mother-house in the capital; *'alférez'* into 'lieutenant' or 'commanding officer', which was in fact the post held by the *'alférez'* in the history; *'gobernadorcillo'* and *'teniente mayor'* into 'Mayor' and 'Vice Mayor', the *'Alcalde'* of the province into 'Provincial Governor', etc. The footnotes to the neglected Basa-Benitez translation of the *Noli*, the Catholic Dictionary, and unpublished papers on the organisation of the Spanish colonial administration in the Philippines provided me with useful glimpses into these recondite affairs.

I did not find it wise to translate the title. The words are taken from John XX, 17, and are spoken by the risen Christ to Mary Magdalen, but the incident would seem to have no connection with Rizal's story; indeed the late Monsignor Knox, in his translation of the Bible into modern English, renders the phrase as 'Do not cling to me thus', instead of 'Touch me not', a phrase which in any case is much too Victorian and demure for our more robust age to read without embarrassment. Rizal himself explained to a friend that he had chosen his title to suggest rather that he would write of things as yet unwritten because untouchable, and his Dedication expresses the same thought. Would 'The Untouchable' or 'The Untouchables' have conveyed Rizal's sense of the invulnerability of the Spanish friars? Perhaps, but a confusion with the Hindu pariahs, untouchables in an entirely opposite sense, would have been unavoidable. *Noli Me Tangere* will always be known to all Filipinos as the *Noli*, and translators should recognise their limitations.

L. Ma. G.

Embassy of the Philippines in London
Rizal Day, 1959.

PREFACE TO THE 1995 EDITION

I think somewhat like the Chinese. I honour the
father for his son, but not the son for his father.
Let each one receive his reward or punishment for
his own deeds, not for the deeds of others.

Tasio

   Many thanks are due to Stephen Troth of Longman Group Hong Kong for releasing the rights to my father's translation, helping it become more widely available in the Philippines. Innumerable kindnesses have also been shown by the Guerrero family, friends and all who have worked in producing this new edition of the *Noli*.

David Guerrero

Manila
The birth anniversary of José Rizal, 1995.

1 • *A Party*

DON SANTIAGO DE LOS SANTOS was giving a dinner party one evening towards the end of October in the 1880's. Although, contrary to his usual practice, he had let it be known only on the afternoon of the same day, it was soon the topic of conversation in Binondo, where he lived, in other districts of Manila, and even in the Spanish walled city of Intramuros. Don Santiago was better known as Capitan Tiago—the rank was not military but political, and indicated that he had once been the native mayor of a town. In those days he had a reputation for lavishness. It was well-known that his house, like his country, never closed its doors except, of course, to trade and any idea that was new or daring.

So the news of his dinner party ran like an electric shock through the community of spongers, hangers-on, and gate-crashers whom God, in His infinite wisdom, had created and so fondly multiplied in Manila. Some of these set out to hunt polish for their boots; others, collar-buttons and cravats; but one and all gave the gravest thought to the manner in which they might greet their host with the assumed intimacy of long-standing friendship, or, if the occasion should arise, make a graceful apology for not having arrived earlier where presumably their presence was so eagerly awaited.

The dinner was being given in a house on Anloague Street which may still be recognised unless it has tumbled down in some earthquake. Certainly it will not have been pulled down by its owner; in the Philippines, that is usually left to God and Nature. In fact, one often thinks that they are under contract to the Government for just that purpose. The house was large enough, in a style common to those parts. It was situated in that section of the city which is crossed by a branch of the Pasig river, called by some the creek of Binondo, which, like all rivers of Manila at that time, combined the functions of public bath, sewer, laundry, fishery, waterway, and, should the Chinese water-pedlar find it convenient, even a source of drinking water. For a stretch of almost a kilometre this vital artery, with its bustling traffic and bewildering activity, hardly counted with one wooden bridge, and this one was under repair at one end for six months, and closed to traffic at the other end for the rest of the year. Indeed, in the hot season, carriage horses had been known to avail themselves of the situation and to jump into the water at this point, to the discomfiture of any day-dreamer in their vehicles who had dozed off while pondering the achievements of the century.

On the evening in question a visitor would have judged the house to be rather squat; its lines, not quite correct, although he would have hesitated to say whether this was due to the defective eyesight of its architect or to earthquake and typhoon. A wide staircase, green-banistered and partly carpeted, rose from the tiled court at the entrance. It led to the main floor along a double line of potted plants and flower vases set on stands of Chinese porcelain, remarkable for their fantastical colours and designs.

No porter or footman would have asked the visitor for his invitation card; he would have gone up freely, attracted by the strains of orchestra music and the suggestive tinkle of silver and china, and perhaps, if a foreigner, curious about the kind of dinner parties that were given in what was called the Pearl of the Orient.

Men are like turtles; they are classified and valued according to their shells. In this, and indeed in other respects, the inhabitants of the Philippines at that time were turtles, so that a description of Capitan Tiago's house is of some importance. At the head of the stairs the visitor would have found himself in a spacious entrance hall, serving for the occasion as a combination of music-and dining-room. The large table in the centre, richly and profusely decorated, would have been winking delectable promises to the uninvited guest at the same time that it threatened the timid and naïve young girl with two distressing hours in close company with strangers whose language and topics of conversation were apt to take the most extraordinary lines. In contrast with these earthly concerns would have been the paintings crowded on the walls, depicting such religious themes as *Purgatory, Hell, The Last Judgment, The Death of The Just Man,* and *The Death of the Sinner,* and, in the place of honour, set off by an elegant and splendid frame carved in the Renaissance style by the most renowned woodworker of the day, a strange canvas of formidable dimensions in which were to be seen two old crones, with the inscription: *Our Lady of Peace and Happy Voyage, Venerated in Antipolo, Visits in the Guise of a Beggar the Pious and Celebrated Capitana Inés, Who Lies*

Gravely Ill. This composition made up for its lack of taste and artistry with a realism that some might have considered extreme, the blue and yellow tints of the patient's face suggested a corpse in an advanced state of decomposition, and the tumblers and other receptacles which were about her, the cortège of long illnesses, were reproduced so painstakingly as to make their contents almost identifiable. The sight of these paintings, so stimulating to the appetite, and so evocative of carefree ease, might have led the visitor to think that his cynical host had formed a very shrewd opinion of the character of his guests; and that indeed it was only to disguise his judgment that he had hung the room about with charming Chinese lanterns, empty bird-cages, silvered crystal balls in red, green, and blue, slightly withered air plants, stuffed fishes, and other such decorations, the whole coming to a point in fanciful wooden arches, half Chinese, half European, which framed the side of the room overlooking the river, and gave a glimpse of a porch with trellises and kiosks dimly lighted by multi-coloured paper lanterns.

The dinner guests were gathered in the main reception room which had great mirrors and sparkling chandeliers. On a pinewood platform stood enthroned a magnificent grand piano, for which an exorbitant price had been paid, and which this night seemed more precious still because nobody was presumptuous enough to play on it. There was also a large portrait in oils of a good-looking man in a frock coat, stiff and straight, as well-balanced as the tasseled cane of office between his rigid ring-covered fingers, who seemed to be saying: 'See what a lot of clothes I have on, and how dignified I look!'

The furniture was elegant; uncomfortable, perhaps, and not quite suited to the climate, but then the owner of the house would have been thinking of self-display rather than the health of his guests, and would have told them: 'Shocking thing, this dysentery, I know, but after all you are now seated in armchairs come straight from Europe, and you can't always do that, can you?'

The salon was almost full, the men segregated from the women as in Catholic churches and in synagogues. The few ladies were mostly young girls, some Filipinas, Spaniards the others, hastily covering their mouths with their fans when they felt a yawn coming on, and scarcely saying a word. If someone ventured to start a conversation it died out in monosyllables, not unlike the night-noises of mice and lizards. Did the images of Our Lady in her various appellations, which hung from the walls in between the mirrors, oblige them to keep this curious silence and devout demeanour, or were women in the Philippines in those times simply an exception?

Only one took the trouble of making the lady guests welcome; she was a kindly faced old woman, a cousin of Capitan Tiago, who spoke Spanish rather badly. Her hospitality and good manners did not extend beyond offering the Spanish ladies cigars and betel-nut chew on a tray, and giving her hand to be kissed by her compatriots, exactly like a friar. The poor old woman ended up by becoming thoroughly bored, and, hearing the crash of a broken plate, hurriedly seized the excuse to leave the room, muttering:

'*Jesús!* Just you wait, you wretches!'

She never came back.

The men, however, were already in higher spirits. In one corner a number of cadets were vivaciously whispering to one another, sharing scarcely muffled laughs as they glanced about the room, sometimes pointing openly to this or that person. On the other hand two foreigners, dressed in white, went striding up and down the salon, their hands clasped behind them, and without exchanging a single word, exactly like bored passengers pacing the deck of a ship. The centre of interest and liveliness seemed to be a group composed of two priests, two laymen, and an officer, who were at a small table with wine and English biscuits.

The officer was an ageing lieutenant, Guevara by name, tall, stern, with the air of a Duke of Alba left stranded in the lower ranks of the Constabulary roster. He said little, but what he said was heard to be sharp and brief. One of the friars was a young Dominican, Father Sibyla, handsome, well-groomed, and as bright as his gold-rimmed glasses. He had an air of premature gravity. Parish priest of Binondo, and formerly a professor at the Dominican College of San Juan de Letran, he had the reputation of being a consummate casuist, so much so that in other times, when members of his Order still dared to match subtleties with laymen, the most skilful debater among the latter had never succeeded in trapping or confusing him; the agile distinctions of Father Sibyla had made his antagonist look like a fisherman trying to catch eels with a piece of string. The Dominican seemed to weigh his words and they were few.

By way of contrast, the other friar, a Franciscan, was a man of many words and even more numerous gestures. Although his hair was greying, his robust constitution seemed well preserved. His classic features, penetrating look, heavy jaws, and Herculean build, gave him the appearance of a Roman patrician in disguise, and recalled one of those three monks in the German story who in the September equinox would cross a Tyrolean lake at midnight, and each time place in the hand of the terror-stricken boatman a silver coin, cold as ice. However, Father Dámaso was not so mysterious as that; he was a jovial man, and if the tone of his voice was rough, like that of a man who has never held his tongue and who thinks that what he says is dogma and beyond question, his frank and jolly laugh erased this disagreeable impression; one could even forgive him when he thrust out toward the company a naked pair of hairy legs that would have made a fortune at the freak-show of any suburban fair.

One of the civilians, Mr. Laruja, was a small man with a black beard whose only notable feature was a nose so large that it seemed to belong to an entirely different person. The other was a fair-haired young man, apparently a newcomer to the country, who was just then engaged in an excited discussion with the Franciscan.

'You'll see,' said the latter. 'A few more months in this country, and you'll be agreeing with me; it's one thing to govern from Madrid, and quite another to make-do in the Philippines.'

'But...'

'Take me, for example,' Father Dámaso continued, raising his voice to keep the floor, 'I've had twenty-three years of rice and bananas, and I can speak with authority on the matter. Don't come to me with theories and rhetoric; I know the natives. Listen, when I first arrived, I was assigned to a town, small it's true, but very hard-working in the fields. At that time I didn't know much Tagalog, but I was already hearing the women's Confessions; we understood one another, if you see what I mean. Well, sir, they came to like me so much that three years later, when I was transferred to a larger parish, left vacant by the death of a native priest, you should have seen all those women! They broke down and cried, they loaded me with presents, they saw me off with brass bands!'

'But that only goes to show...'

'Just a moment, one moment! Hold your horses! Now, my successor served a shorter time, and when he left, why, sir, he had an even greater escort, more tears were shed, more music played, and that in spite of the fact that he used to flog them more and had doubled the parish fees!'

'Permit me...'

'And that isn't all. Some time after, I served in the town of San Diego for twenty years; it's only a few months since I...left it.' The recollection seemed to depress and anger him. 'Well, twenty years! Nobody will deny that's time enough to know *any* town. There were six thousand souls in San Diego, and I couldn't have known each and every one of them better if I had given them birth and suck myself. I knew in which foot this little fellow limped, or where the shoe pinched that other little fellow, who was making love to that other dusky lady, and how many love affairs still another one had, and with whom, mind you, and who was the real father of this or that little urchin; all that sort of thing—after all, I was hearing the Confessions of each and every one of those rascals; they knew they had better be careful about fulfilling their religious duties, believe me. Santiago, our host, can tell you I'm speaking the honest truth; he has a lot of property there; in fact that is where we got to be friends. Well, sir, just to show you what the native is really like: when I left, there was scarcely a handful of old crones and lay members of our Order to see me off! That, after twenty years!'

'But I don't see the connection between this and the abolition of the tobacco monopoly,' complained the new arrival when the Franciscan paused to refresh himself with a glass of sherry.

Father Dámaso was so taken aback that he almost dropped the glass. He glared at the young man for some time, and then exclaimed with unfeigned shock:

'What? How's that? But is it possible that you can't see what's clearer than daylight? Don't you see, my dear boy, that all this is tangible proof that the reforms proposed by the Ministers in Madrid are mad?'

It was the young man's turn to be puzzled. Beside him Lieutenant Guevara deepened his frown, while Mr. Laruja moved his head ambiguously, uncertain whether to nod approval or shake disapproval of Father Dámaso. The Dominican, Father Sibyla, for his part, merely turned away from them.

'You believe...' the young Spaniard finally managed to blurt out, his face grave and inquiring.

'Believe it? Just as I believe in Holy Gospel! The native is so lazy!'

'Excuse me,' said the new arrival, lowering his voice and drawing his chair closer. 'What you have just said interests me very much indeed. Are the natives really *born* lazy? Or was that foreign traveller right who said that we Spaniards use this charge of laziness to excuse our own, as well as to explain the lack of progress and policy in our colonies? He was, of course, speaking of other colonies of ours, but I think the inhabitants there belong to the same race as these people.'

'Rubbish! Pure envy! Mr. Laruja here knows the country as well as I do; ask him, go on, ask him if the ignorance and laziness of these fellows can be matched.'

'Quite right,' Mr. Laruja agreed promptly, 'there is nobody lazier anywhere in the whole wide world than the native of these parts.'

'None more vicious, or more ungrateful!'

'Or so ill-bred!'

The fair-haired young man looked uneasily around him.

'Gentlemen,' he whispered, 'I believe we are in the house of a native. Those young ladies…'

'Nonsense! You have nothing to worry about. Santiago does not consider himself a native; and in any case he is not around—and if he were, so what? Only newcomers have these crazy ideas. Let a few months pass; you'll change your mind when you have been to enough of their parties and dances, so-called, and have slept on their bamboo cots, and eaten a lot of *tinola*.'

'Is this *tinola* you speak about a fruit? Something like the lotus which makes men—what shall I say? —forgetful?'

Father Dámaso burst out laughing. 'Lotus, balotus! You're talking through your hat. *Tinola* is just a stew of chicken and squash. How long have you been here, anyway?'

'Four days,' replied the young Spaniard, rather put out.

'Did you come out for a job?'

'No, sir. I came on my own account—to know the country.'

'Well, sir, you are a rare bird indeed!' exclaimed Father Dámaso, studying him with amusement. 'All this nonsense, and you're paying for it out of your own pocket too! You must be mad. There are so many books on the subject, and with a pinch of brains—let me tell you, sir, many famous books have been written with just that, a pinch of brains.'

At this point Father Sibyla, the Dominican, abruptly cut short the exchange. 'You were saying, Your Reverence, that you had served twenty years in the town of San Diego, and that you had left it. Was not Your Reverence happy there?'

The question was put in an easy, almost casual manner, but Father Dámaso lost his joviality immediately and stopped laughing.

'No,' he grunted shortly, throwing himself back heavily in his armchair.

The Dominican went on, with even greater detachment:

'It must be painful to leave a town after twenty years, a town one knows as well as the clothes on one's back. As for myself, I was sorry to leave Kamiling, and I had been there only a few months. But my superiors were acting in the best interests of the Order, and, of course, also in my own.'

Father Dámaso showed signs of being distraught. Unexpectedly, he smashed his fist on the arm of his chair and let out a great roar: 'Either we have the Faith or we don't! Mark me, either priests are their own masters or they are not! The country is going to the devil! By God, it's gone already!'

And he smashed his fist down again.

Everyone in the salon was startled and turned to the little group. The Dominican raised his head and stared at the Franciscan from under the rim of his glasses. The two foreigners paused briefly, exchanged looks, showed their teeth momentarily, and then continued their promenade.

Mr. Laruja whispered in the newcomer's ear. 'You've put him in a temper; you should have addressed him as Your Reverence.'

Then the Dominican and the lieutenant, each after his own fashion, asked: 'What does your Reverence mean? What has come over you?'

'I say,' cried the Franciscan, raising his heavy fists, 'that the cause of all our troubles is that the Government takes the side of heretics against the ministers of God!'

'What do you mean, sir?' The officer half-rose from his chair.

'What do you mean?' the Franciscan echoed, in an even louder voice and facing the lieutenant challengingly. 'I mean what I say, and I say what I like, and I say that when a priest throws the corpse of a heretic out of the parish cemetery, no one, not the King himself has the right to meddle, and even less to impose penalties. Don't tell me that a tin-soldier general, a General Calamity…!'

'Sir,' cried the lieutenant rising to his feet. 'His Excellency is the Viceregal Patron of the Church!'

'Excellency, Viceregal Patron! Bah!' replied the Franciscan, also taking to his feet. 'There was a time when he would have been dragged down the palace stairs; the Orders did it to that free-thinker Governor Bustamante! *Those* were the days of faith!'

'I must warn you that I cannot allow such language. His Excellency stands in the place of His Majesty King Alfonso himself.'

'King Thingumajigg! For us there is no King but the legitimate King!'

This reference to the Carlist pretender to the Throne of Spain was too much for the lieutenant.

'Enough!' he ordered in a parade-ground shout. 'Either, sir, you withdraw what you have said, or I shall be obliged to report it to His Excellency as soon as possible tomorrow.'

'Why don't you go now? Go on!' Father Dámaso challenged him, closing in with fists clenched. 'Do you think that under my cassock I am less of a man? Get going! I'll even lend you my carriage,' he added sarcastically.

The affair was becoming slightly ludicrous. Fortunately, the Dominican intervened.

'Gentlemen,' he said with a ring of authority, in that natal accent that suits friars so well. 'Matters should not be confused, or offences sought where none were given. We should distinguish between the statements of Father Dámaso as man, and his statements as priest. His statements as priest, by themselves, can never offend because, of course, they are based on absolute truth. In his statements as man we must make a sub-distinction; those which he makes *ab irato*, that is to say, in anger; those which he makes *ex ore* but not *in corde*, that is to say, from the mouth but not from the heart; and finally those which he makes *in corde*, from the heart. Only the last can constitute an offence, and even then it would depend on whether they were premeditated for some reason or other, or whether they only arose *per accidens*, that is to say, without essential cause, and merely in the heat of discussion. If there should be...'

'*Per accidens* or perdition, I for my part know the reasons for those statements, Father Sibyla,' the officer broke in. With all the growing jumble of distinctions, he was afraid he would end being the one who was really at fault. 'I know his reasons, and Your Reverence will perhaps be good enough to distinguish among them. Some time ago, when Father Dámaso was away from San Diego, his vicar allowed the Christian burial of a most honourable gentleman; a most

honourable gentleman, sir, whom I had the honour to know on various
occasions and whose hospitality I had enjoyed. But it was said he had never
gone to Confession—so what? I don't go to Confession myself. But to
announce that he was a suicide was, sir, a lie, a veritable calumny. A gentleman
like that, with a son who was the object of all his love and hope; a man like
that, who had faith in God, who knew his duties to society; a man honest
and just—a man like that does not commit suicide! That's what I say, and
I don't want to say here some other things I have in mind, for which,' and
here he turned to Father Dámaso, 'Your Reverence should be grateful.'

Then, turning his back on the Franciscan, he continued:

'Well, then, this priest, having returned to his parish and learning what
had occurred, first turned his anger upon his unfortunate vicar, and then
ordered the corpse of the gentlemen in question to be dug up, thrown out
of the cemetery, and buried I don't know where. The town of San Diego was
too cowardly to protest; well, perhaps the truth is, very few learned about it;
the dead man had no relatives, and his only son is in Europe. But His
Excellency heard of it, and because he is a man with a good heart, he asked
that the outrage be punished. It was: Father Dámaso was transferred—to a
better parish! That is the whole story. Now, may it please Your Reverence
to make your distinctions.'

Having said this, he left the group.

'I am very sorry,' Father Sibyla apologised to Father Dámaso 'that unwittingly
I touched on such a delicate matter. Anyway, when all is said and done, you
seem to have gained from the transfer...'

'What is to be gained from such transfers?' Father Dámaso stammered,
beside himself with rage. 'And what about the losses? Papers... this and
that... everything is mislaid... all sorts of things get lost...'

But slowly the company regained its old tranquility.

Other guests had arrived, among them an old Spaniard, lame, but with a
mild and gentle face, who was leaning on the arm of an equally old Filipina,
all curls and paint and European finery.

They were greeted cordially: Doctor de Espadaña and his wife Doña
Victorina, who by local custom shared his title and styled herself Madam
Doctor. They soon took their places in a circle of acquaintances. There were
also a number of journalists and merchants, who, after exchanging greetings,

were seen to wander about aimlessly, not quite knowing what to do.

'Tell me, Mr. Laruja,' said the fair-haired Spaniard. 'What's the owner of the house like? I still have to make his acquaintance.'

'They say he's gone out; I've not seen him myself.'

'Rubbish,' interrupted Father Dámaso. 'Don't worry about introductions in this house. Santiago is a good egg.'

'He didn't invent gunpowder, certainly,' added Mr. Laruja.

'You also, Mr. Laruja,' Doña Victorina reproached him archly, in her particular version of Spanish. 'How also can the poor dear invent gunpowder? They say,' she added, fanning herself vigorously, 'that it was invented by the Chinese many centuries yet.'

'The Chinese? Are you crazy?' exclaimed Father Dámaso. 'Don't be silly, ma'am. Gunpowder was invented by a Franciscan like myself, a certain Father Something-or-other Savalls, in the—the seventh century!'

'Oh, Franciscan! Well, maybe he was a missionary in China, this Father Savalls,' replied the lady, who did not let her ideas go so easily.

'Madam, you must be referring to Schwartz,' Father Sibyla observed distantly.

'But Father Dámaso said Savalls. I was quoting him only.'

'Savalls, Suavarts, what does it matter? One letter won't make him Chinese,' interjected Father Dámaso peevishly.

'And it was the fourteenth, not the seventh, century,' added the Dominican magisterially, as if to take his colleague down another peg.

'Give one century, take another, that still doesn't make him a Dominican.'

'Come now, Your Reverence should not lose his temper,' smiled Father Sibyla. 'So much the better that he should have invented it, he saved his brothers in your Order the trouble.'

'And you say, Father Sibyla,' asked Doña Victorina with a great show of interest, 'that this was happening in the fourteenth century yet? But the fourteenth century before or after Christ?'

Fortunately for the Dominican two newcomers now entered the salon.

2 • *Crisóstomo Ibarra*

IF all eyes, even Father Sibyla's, were turned on the new arrivals, it was not because they were a pair of elegant beauties and if the lieutenant was so shaken out of his reflections that he involuntarily took a step forward, while Father Dámaso sat frozen in his armchair, it was not because the Governor General himself had entered with his aides. In fact it was only the original of the portrait on the wall, leading by the arm a young man in deep mourning.

Capitan Tiago first greeted his guests, kissing the hands of the priests, who were still so taken aback that they forgot to reciprocate with the customary blessing. Then he introduced his companion as Don Crisóstomo Ibarra, the son of a lately deceased friend, whom he had gone to meet upon his return from Europe.

The name caused a certain excitement among those who heard it. The Dominican slipped off his glasses the better to see the newcomer. Father Dámaso, already staring openly, lost colour, while the officer, forgetting to pay his respects to his host, became engrossed in a thoughtful examination of the young man. The latter was then exchanging the usual courtesies with members of the company. There seemed to be nothing extraordinary about him except for his mourning clothes. However, his more than average height, his features, his movements, all gave the impression of youth and of health, equally developed in mind and body. Slight traces of Spanish blood could be distinguished in his frank and cheerful face, beautifully bronzed and somewhat rosy in the cheeks, due perhaps to a long stay in a cold climate.

'Well, look who's here,' he exclaimed happily. 'Father Dámaso! The parish priest of my home town, my father's intimate friend!'

But the Franciscan, now the centre of attention, did not raise a finger, and the young man murmured abashed:

'I beg your pardon. I mistook you for someone else.'

His voice noticeably altered, Father Dámaso managed a few words. 'You were not mistaken. But your father was never an intimate of mine.'

Ibarra had slowly withdrawn the hand he had extended, and now gave the friar a look full of wonder. When he turned away he found himself the object of the officer's sombre scrutiny.

'Young man, are you the son of Don Rafael Ibarra?'

The newcomer bowed.

As Father Dámaso searched the lieutenant's face, the latter continued in a voice trembling with emotion:

'Welcome to your country. May you be happier in it than your Father! I had the honour of his acquaintance, and I can say that he was one of the most honourable and honest men in the Philippines.'

'Sir,' replied Ibarra, visibly moved, 'the tribute which you pay my father will surely help to relieve my doubts about his fate, which even now I, his own son, do not know.'

The old man's eyes filled with tears, and he walked away, leaving Ibarra alone in the middle of the room.

His host was nowhere to be seen. Nobody else could be found to introduce him to the ladies, many of whom were looking at him with interest. After a momentary hesitation, however, he approached them with a simple and unaffected grace, and said, with an apology, that after seven years abroad he could not resist paying tribute to his country's fairest ornaments. Even these compliments failed to draw any response, and Ibarra had perforce to withdraw.

He had better luck with a group of gentlemen, to whom, in what he said was the German fashion, he introduced himself as Juan Crisóstomo Ibarra y Magsalin. The others gave their names in exchange, more or less insignificant, more or less obscure. Only one seemed familiar.

'Do I have the honour of speaking with the poet whose works have for so long kept alive my love of country?' The young man he addressed gave a reluctant bow. 'They say you have stopped writing, but nobody seems to know why.'

'Why? Because one does not write poetry in order to flatter and to lie. Someone I know was brought before a judge for putting a commonplace in rhyme. Well, they've called me a poet, but they'll never call me a fool.'

'And may I know what the commonplace was?'

'Why, that the son of a lion is also a lion. The man barely escaped exile.'

It may be doubted that the long-absent Ibarra understood the reference to a political slogan used in the past by Filipino sympathisers with the Spanish Revolution of 1868. In any case he lost the opportunity to make any further inquiry because a cheerful-looking man now came up to him almost at a run. He was dressed in the embroidered shirt usually worn by the natives, with the difference that his had diamond studs. Clasping Ibarra by the hand, he smiled: 'I have wanted to meet you so much, Mr. Ibarra. Capitan Tiago is a very good friend of mine, and I knew your father too. I am Capitan Tinong. I live in Tondo, where my house is at your disposal. I do hope you will pay me the honour of a visit. Come to luncheon tomorrow!'

Ibarra was won over by so much kindness; Capitan Tinong was grinning and rubbing his hands together. 'Thank you,' he replied gratefully, 'but tomorrow I must leave for San Diego.'

'What a pity! Then, perhaps when you are back?'

At this moment a waiter in the livery of the most expensive restaurant in the city announced that dinner was served, and the company began to file into the dining-room, although not before the ladies, especially the Filipinas, had hung back to be coaxed after the native custom.

3 • At Dinner
When 'no' means 'yes'

FATHER SIBYLA seemed well satisfied with himself; he moved at his ease, and the sneer had vanished from his thin pursed mouth. He even deigned to talk with the lame physician, Dr. de Espadaña, who stuttered and could therefore keep up his end of a conversation only with monosyllables. The Franciscan on the other hand was in a frightful temper. He let out kicks at the chairs in his way, and even elbowed a cadet aside. The rest of the company were talking with great vivacity, praising the splendours of the table, except for Lieutenant Guevara, who looked as grim as ever, and Doña Victorina, who was snobbishly wrinkling her nose until the officer trod on the train of her dress.

'Don't you have eyes also, sir?' she cried out with the air of a serpent that has been stepped upon.

'Yes, ma'am, perhaps better than yours, but I was distracted by those extraordinary ringlets of yours,' retorted the ungallant officer.

Meanwhile the two friars, by instinct or perhaps by habit, had gone to the head of the table, where, like competitors for a professorial chair, they proceeded to mouth praises of their rival while giving to understand the opposite.

'After you, Father Dámaso.'

'No, indeed, after you, Father Sibyla.'

'But you are the family's oldest friend, confessor to the deceased lady of the house, my superior in age, rank, and office.'

'Well, strictly speaking, in age, no, but on the other hand you are the parish priest of the district,' replied Father Dámaso sourly, keeping his grasp of the chair.

'Since you command it, I have no choice, I suppose, but to obey,' Father Sibyla sighed, as if to put an end to it, and made ready to sit down.

'Oh, I don't command it,' protested the Franciscan. 'I would not dream of commanding!'

Father Sibyla was about to ignore these expostulations and to take the seat when his eyes met those of Lieutenant Guevara. Now, the highest civil official in the Philippines was, in the opinion of the priests, much inferior to a convent cook. The sword must yield to the toga, Cicero had told the Roman Senate, and the friars in the Philippines thought a cassock was as good as a toga. But Father Sibyla was courteous, and now he offered:

'Sir, we are in the world, not in church. The seat belongs to you.'

But it was plain enough from his tone that he believed otherwise, world or no world, and the officer curtly refused, either because he could not be bothered, or because he did not relish being seated between two friars.

None of the candidates for the head of the table had given thought to their host. Ibarra saw him smiling satisfaction on the scene, and called out:

'What's this? Aren't you joining us, Don Santiago?'

But all the seats had already been taken. Lucullus does not eat in the house of Lucullus.

'No, no, stay where you are, don't get up,' he said, his hand firmly on the young man's shoulder. 'I am giving this dinner party precisely in thanksgiving for your safe arrival. Hey, there! Tell them to serve the *tinola*.' And he added to Ibarra: 'I ordered *tinola* tonight for you; I'm sure you haven't had it for a long time.'

A great steaming tureen now made its appearance. The Dominican being at the head of the table, served out the contents, after murmuring grace with scarcely an Amen from the rest.

Whether by oversight or otherwise, Father Dámaso's portion turned out to be composed of a lot of squash and broth with barely a chicken neck and wing, while his fellow guests were eating chicken legs and chicken breasts, and Ibarra had the luck of drawing the giblets. The Franciscan seeing this, mashed the squash violently, took a few spoonfuls of broth, and then loudly dropped his spoon and pushed his plate away. This apparently escaped the attention of the Dominican, who seemed to be engrossed in conversation with the newly arrived Spaniard.

'How long have you been away?' Laruja asked Ibarra elsewhere at the table.

'Almost seven years.'

'Well, you must have forgotten by now what the country's like.'

'On the contrary. Although I seem to have been forgotten myself, I have always remembered.'

'What do you mean?'

'I meant to say that I had not had news from here for the past year, and I now find myself a stranger who doesn't know to this day how and when his father died.'

'Ah,' sighed the lieutenant.

'And where were you also?' asked Doña Victorina. 'Why did you not telegraph? When we married we already telegraphed the Peninsula.'

'Madam, for the last two years I was in northern Europe: in Germany and Russian Poland.'

Dr. de Espadaña, who had not dared say a word heretofore, thought that the moment had come to say something.

'In Spain I made the acq-cq-cq-cquaintance of a P-p-p-pole from Warsaw by the name of Stadt-tadt-tadtnitski, if I remember rightly. I wonder,' he asked timidly, almost blushing, 'whether you ever came ac-c-c-cross him.'

'Possibly,' said Ibarra amiably, 'but I do not recall the name just now.'

'B-b-but you c-c-couldn't possibly have mistaken him,' protested the physician, who had gained a little confidence, 'he was a g-g-g-golden blond and spoke Sp-p-panish very badly.'

'That would seem to be a good description, but unfortunately I never had occasion to speak a word of Spanish in those countries, except in one or two consulates.'

Doña Victorina was struck with admiration. 'But how did you arrange?'

'I used the language of the country, ma'am.'

'Do you speak English too?' asked the Dominican, who had been in Hong Kong and had a command of pidgin.

'I spent a year in England among people who spoke only English.'

'And what country in Europe do you like best?' asked the newly arrived Spaniard.

'After Spain, my second home, why, any free country in Europe.'

'Since you have gone around such a lot, tell us, what did you find most remarkable?' put in Laruja.

'Remarkable in what sense?' Ibarra asked thoughtfully.

'For instance, with regard to the life of the people—their social, political, religious life, life in general, in its essence, as a whole.'

It was some time before Ibarra answered:

'Frankly, putting aside the element of national pride in each of them ... well, what would be remarkable in those countries...Let me put it this way. Before visiting any of those countries I would try to study its history, its Exodus, so to speak, and after that I found everything understandable. I saw that in all cases the prosperity or unhappiness of nations is in direct proportion to their liberties and their problems, and, by that token, to the sacrifices or selfishness of their ancestors.'

'Is that all?' The Franciscan, who had not said a word from the start of the dinner, distracted perhaps by the food, now let out a roar of mocking laughter.

'It wasn't worth throwing your fortune away to learn that! Any schoolboy knows as much.'

Ibarra was dumbfounded while the rest of the company exchanged apprehensive glances, fearing a scene. Ibarra was tempted to retort: 'Dinner is over, and Your Reverence has had his fill.' But he restrained himself and merely said:

'Gentlemen, do not wonder at the familiarity with which I am treated by our former parish priest. That was the way he dealt with me when I was a child, and the years have not changed His Reverence. But I thank him for it because he recalls vividly the days when His Reverence was a frequent visitor at our house and sat at my father's table.'

The Dominican stole a glance at the Franciscan and found him uneasy.

Ibarra rose and continued:

'And now you must allow me to take my leave. I arrived only a few hours ago, and I must be off again tomorrow. I must attend to many things. We have all had a most wonderful dinner, but I am afraid I am not very fond of lingering over the brandy. Gentlemen, in spite of everything, I give you Spain and the Philippines!'

Ibarra emptied the wine glass which he had not yet touched. The old lieutenant followed suit silently.

'Don't go,' whispered Capitan Tiago. 'María Clara will be here soon; Isabel went to fetch her. Our new parish priest, a saint if ever there was one, is coming too.'

'I'll come tomorrow before leaving for San Diego. Now I really must make a very important call.'

And Ibarra took his leave, followed after a time by the lieutenant. Meantime the Franciscan was giving vent to his feelings.

'Did you see that?' he asked the newly arrived Spaniard, gesticulating with the dessert knife. 'All out of pride! He couldn't stand being reproved by a priest. He thinks he's somebody. Of course, that's what comes from sending these youngsters to Europe. The Government should put its foot down and stop it.'

'And what about the Lieutenant also?' Doña Victorina chorused. 'All evening already he is frowning. Better that he left us. So old, only lieutenant!'

The good lady obviously could not forget her downtrodden skirts and the unkind allusion to her ringlets.

That night the fair-haired new arrival began a new chapter in his *Colonial Studies*: 'How a Chicken Neck and Wing in a Friar's Dish of Tinola Can Spoil a Party.' He made, among others, the following observations:

'In the Philippines the most useless person at a dinner party is the host. They might well start by throwing him out; everything would go on without a hitch.'

'In the present state of affairs, it would be doing the Filipinos a favour not to let them leave the country, and not to teach them how to read.'

4 • *A Subversive Heretic*

AFTER leaving the dinner party Ibarra hesitated at the threshold of Capitan Tiago's house. The night air, already chilly at that time of year in Manila, seemed to clear his head. He bared his brow to the breeze, sighed, and went off toward the square of Binondo, looking searchingly about him.

Private carriages dashed past hansom cabs, their horses at a walk while waiting for a fare, and pedestrians of all nationalities. The streets looked exactly the same as when he had seen them last, with the same white-washed stucco-faced houses trimmed with blue. The lighted clock on the church tower, the Chinese corner-stores with their grimy curtains and iron railings, were all the same—even to the rail he himself had twisted out of shape one night as a prank.

'We go slow,' he said to himself, turning down De la Sacristía Street.

Ice-cream pedlars were crying out their wares as of old, and the same kerosene lamps lighted the old fruit and vegetable stalls.

'Amazing,' he thought, 'why, that's the same Chinaman I saw there seven years ago, and that old woman… still there! It might've been last night, and I could have dreamed those seven years in Europe. And, good God, there's that cobblestone, just as I left it.'

There it was indeed, dislodged from the sidewalk at the corner of San Jacinto and De la Sacristía.

He was thus pondering the phenomenon of an unchanging city in a country of uncertainties, when he felt the gentle touch of a hand on his shoulder. He turned and found himself face to face with Lieutenant Guevara, whose habitually hard frown had now softened almost into amiability.

'Watch your step, young fellow,' he said. 'Learn from your father.'

'I beg your pardon, but you seem to have thought a lot of my father; could you tell me how and where he died?' asked Ibarra.

'What!' exclaimed the officer. 'Don't you know?'

'I asked Don Santiago, but he put off telling me until tomorrow. Do you yourself happen to know?'

'Of course. Like everybody else. He died in prison.'

The young man fell back a step, and stared astonished at the lieutenant.

'In prison? Who died in prison?'

'My dear sir, your father, of course.' The officer seemed puzzled.

'My father in prison? What are you saying? Do you realise who my father was?' The young man was so distraught that he had seized the officer by the arm.

'I think I know,' he replied. 'Don Rafael Ibarra. You told me so yourself earlier this evening.'

'Yes, Don Rafael Ibarra.'

'But I thought you knew,' Guevara protested pityingly, conscious of the turmoil in Ibarra's mind. 'I supposed that… But come now, face it! In this country it's an honour to have gone to prison.'

'You cannot be joking; I suppose I must believe you,' said Ibarra in a strangled tone after a short silence. 'Can you tell me why he was in prison?'

The old man reflected.

'Odd you should know so little about your family affairs.'

'In his last letter, a year ago, my father asked me not to worry if I didn't hear from him; he said he expected to be very busy. He commended me to my studies, and sent his blessing.'

'Then he must have written to you shortly before he died. It will be a year since he was buried in your home town.'

'But why was my father imprisoned?'

'For a very honourable cause. But I'm due at the barracks. Come with me, take my arm, and I'll tell you as we go along.'

This was the story he told.

'As you know yourself, your father was the richest man in your province, and, although he was loved and honoured by many, others hated or envied him. Unfortunately, those of us Spaniards who come to the Philippines aren't always what we should be. I mean not only your father's enemies, but one of your own grandparents, as you shall see. The continual changes in the administration, demoralisation in high places, favouritism, combined with the cheaper fares and shorter trip out here since the Suez Canal was opened, are to blame for everything; the worst elements of the Peninsula come here, and if a good man comes, he is soon corrupted by the present conditions of the country. It was among these Spaniards, including the friars, that your father had his enemies, and they were many.

'Some months after your departure your father began to have trouble with Father Dámaso; I don't really know why. The parish priest accused him of not going to Confession; but then, he hadn't gone to Confession before that, and it hadn't stopped them from being friends, as you yourself will remember. Anyway, Don Rafael was honest and just, more so than many who go to Confession, or hear Confessions, for that matter. He had his own strict code of ethics. When, for instance, we talked about his disagreements with Father Dámaso, he would ask me: "Mr. Guevara, do you believe that God forgives a crime, say, a murder, merely upon Confession to a priest, a man who, after all, is bound to secrecy? And what do you say to a confession made in fear of hell, which is an act of mere attrition rather than contrition? Does one

win forgiveness by being a coward and shamelessly playing it safe? I have a
different idea of God. For myself I think that one wrong does not right
another, and forgiveness cannot be won with useless tears or alms to the
Church. I put it to you: if I had murdered the father of a family, if I had
widowed some unhappy woman and turned happy children into destitute
orphans, would I have satisfied divine justice by allowing myself to be hanged,
or perhaps by confiding my secret to one sworn never to reveal it, by giving
alms to priests who needed it least, by making a cash settlement of any
penances imposed, or even by weeping night and day? What good would
this have done the widow and the orphans? My conscience tells me that I
should have taken in every possible way the place of my victim, dedicating
myself, for the whole of my life, to the good of that family for whose misfortunes
I was responsible, and even then, even then, who could make amends for the
loss of a loving husband and father?" That was the way your father reasoned.
He always acted in accordance with these exacting principles. One can truly
say he never did anyone a conscious injury; on the contrary, he tried to atone
with good deeds for certain injustices which, he said, had been committed
by his grandparents. But to return to his troubles with the parish priest;
things were beginning to look ugly; Father Dámaso was making allusions to
your father from the very pulpit, and, considering that anything might be
expected from a man like him, it was a miracle that he didn't name your
father outright. I could see that sooner or later things were going to end badly.

'At that time there was a former artillery-man going the rounds in your
province. He was so gross and stupid that he had been dismissed from the
service, and, since he had to make a living and could not be allowed to do
manual work, which would have hurt our prestige, someone gave him the
job of collecting the tax on vehicles. This oaf had no schooling at all, and
the natives soon found out. To them a Spaniard who didn't know how to
read and write was a freak. So they all took to making fun of the poor wretch,
who had to pay with humiliations for the taxes he collected. He knew he
was the butt of their jokes, which further soured his already rough and evil
temper. They would give him papers upside down; he would pretend to read
them, and then would sign on the most likely blank space—and when I say
sign, I mean he would make a series of clumsy squiggles. The natives paid
their taxes, but they had their fun; he swallowed his pride, but collected.

In this frame of mind he was in no mood to give anyone his due of respect, and he even had very harsh exchanges with your father. One day he was given an official paper in a shop, and he was turning it over and over trying to put it straight, when a schoolboy burst out laughing, pointing him out to his mates. Our man heard them laugh, and looking round him, he saw that people were trying hard to keep a straight face. He lost his temper and turned on the schoolboys. They ran away, mockingly reciting the alphabet as he chased them. He was blind with rage and, when he could not catch them up, he hurled his stick at them. It hit one of the boys on the head and knocked him down. The wretched tax-collector promptly ran up to him, and started kicking him; none of those who had been having fun now dared to step in. Unfortunately, your father happened to be passing by. He was shocked and, seizing the tax collector by the arm, was remonstrating with him when the latter, still in a rage, started a wild swing. Your father did not give him time to finish it and, with the strength of a true descendant of Basques... well, some say that he hit him, others, that he did no more than give him a push. In any case the tax-collector staggered and fell a few feet away, hitting his head against a stone. Don Rafael calmly lifted the hurt child in his arms and took him to the town-hall. The tax-collector was throwing up blood; he never recovered consciousness and died a few minutes later. Naturally, the police intervened, your father was imprisoned, and all his hidden enemies showed their heads. All sorts of lies began to pour in; he was accused of heresy and sedition. Heresy is always a very serious charge; more so in this case, because the governor of the province at that time was a man who made a great show of piety, even saying the Rosary in church in a loud voice and with his servants for a chorus, perhaps so everyone hearing him would start praying too. But subversion of the established order is even worse than heresy, or the murder of *three* tax-collectors capable of reading, writing and making philosophical distinctions. Your father was deserted by all; his papers and books were confiscated. He was accused of subscribing to the *Overseas Mail* and other newspapers from Madrid, of having sent you to the German—and therefore Protestant—part of Switzerland, of having in his possession a photograph and even letters from a native priest executed for complicity in rebellion—and I don't know what else. Everything they could think of was charged against him: even the fact that, being of Spanish blood, he dressed like a native. Perhaps, if your father had been someone else, he would have been released in a short time. One physician attributed the tax-collector's death to apoplexy. But your father's great wealth, his faith in justice, and his hatred of the illegal and the unjust, ruined him. I did all I could; I hate begging favours, but I went to see the Governor General himself, the predecessor of the present one, and submitted to him that a man like your father, who took into his own house and fed every Spaniard who was poor or homeless, and in whose veins there ran good Spanish blood, could not be guilty of subversion. I offered to stand surety for him. I swore to his innocence by my poverty and my military honour. But all I got was a cold reception, and even colder dismissal, and the reputation of being a crank.

'Your father asked me to take charge of his case. I first applied to a young but already famous Filipino lawyer. He refused to undertake your father's defence. "I would be ruined," he told me. "If I took the case, that very fact could be made into a new charge against him, and perhaps against myself." He suggested that I engage a Spanish lawyer, and named one who was a fluent and forceful orator and enjoyed an immense prestige. I did so, and renowned counsel accepted the defence, which he carried out masterfully, brilliantly. But your father's enemies were many, some of them hidden and unknown. There were plenty of false witnesses, and their lies, which in other cases would have been exploded with a jibe from counsel, were now given credit for solidity and consistency. If counsel succeeded in discrediting them by showing their contradictions not only with each other, but even in themselves, new charges soon took the place of the old ones. He was accused of illegal and inequitable usurpation of many of his properties; indemnities and damages were demanded; he was said to have connections with bandits to buy protection for his fields and his herds. In short, the case became so complicated that after a year nobody could make head or tail of it. The governor left his post; his successor had a reputation for justice, but, alas, did not stay in office for more than a few months; and his successor, in turn, was too fond of fast horses.

'Your father's sufferings and disappointments, the rigours of prison, or perhaps grief of such ingratitude, broke his iron constitution, and he fell ill, of such an illness as only death can heal. He died in prison, with nobody by his side, just when everything was coming to an end, when he was about to be acquitted both of sedition and of murder. I arrived in time to see him die.'

The old man fell silent. Ibarra had not said a word. They had reached the barracks gate. The officer paused and put out his hand.

'Ask Capitan Tiago for the details, my boy. And now, goodnight. I must go in and see what's new.'

Silently but with emotions, Ibarra gripped the withered old hand, and followed him with his eyes until he was lost from sight.

He turned slowly and hailed a passing carriage.

'Hotel Lala,' he ordered, in an almost unintelligible voice.

'This chap must be just out of gaol,' thought the coachman, whipping up his horses.

5 • *Star in the Night*

IBARRA went up to his room, which faced the river, and dropped into an armchair, his eyes on the prospect that the open window stretched before him.

The house across the river was brightly lighted, and he could hear the merry strains of string-music. If he had been less preoccupied with his thoughts, and more curious, he might have been tempted to turn a pair of binoculars on the brilliant scene on the opposite bank. He would have seen a dazzlingly beautiful girl, her slenderness enhanced by the picturesque native dress, in the centre of a semi-circle of Chinese, Spaniards, and Filipinos, officers and priests, old ladies and young men, all competing for attention with gesture and compliment. Beside her he would have seen Father Dámaso, a Father Dámaso now smiling beatifically; Father Sibyla himself was conversing with her; and Doña Victorina was arranging in the girl's magnificent hair a coronet of pearls and diamonds which reflected the most bewitching colours of the spectrum. The girl was fair of complexion, perhaps rather too fair; her eyes, almost always downcast, reflected the purest innocence when she raised them; and when she smiled and showed her small white teeth, a rose would have seemed the merest vegetable, and the purest ivory merely an alephant's tooth.

Around her white and graceful neck, underneath the transparencies of the native pineapple fabric, a diamond necklace, as the native phrase went, gaily winked its eyes. Only one man did not seem to feel her luminous influence, if one might call it that. He was a young Franciscan, thin, pale, drawn, who gazed at her from afar, motionless like a statue, almost without drawing breath.

But Ibarra saw none of this. His mind's eye saw something else: four naked grimy walls enclosing a narrow space; high up in one of them, a barred opening; on the filthy floor, a cot; and on it, an old man dying, gasping for breath, looking despairingly round him, and sobbing out a name. The old man was alone. From behind the walls there might be heard from time to time the sound of a chain or of a moan... And then, far away, another scene, one of merriment, almost bacchanalian, with a young man laughing, shouting, watering flowers with a glass of wine to the applause and drunken laughter of the company... In the old man he recognised his father; in the young man, himself; and the name which the old man cried out, weeping, was his own.

Even after the lights of the house across the river had gone out, and the music and the noise had stopped, still Ibarra heard the anguished voice of his father, crying out, in his last hour, for his son.

Silence had fallen over Manila, and everything seemed to sleep in the embrace of oblivion. Cockcrow alternated with tower chime and the mechanical all's well of the bored watchman. A slice of moon began to show. Everything seemed to rest; soon Ibarra himself fell asleep, fatigued, if not by grief, at least by the strain of his journey.

Only the young Franciscan did not sleep, and kept watch in his convent cell. His elbow on the window-sill, his pale thin face resting on the palm of his hand, he contemplated in silence a distant star sparkling in the dark sky. The star faded, and the waning moon. But the friar did not stir: his eyes were on the far horizon already blurred by the morning mists, toward the field of Bagumbayan and the sea which was sleeping still.

6 • *Capitan Tiago*
Thy Will be done on earth...

CAPITAN TIAGO looked younger than he really was; he would have been taken for thirty or thirty-five years old. He was short and rotund, thanks to an abundance of fat that, according to his friends, was a sign of heavenly favour and, to his enemies, came from battening on the poor.

Light-brown in complexion, his face wore at the time of this history an habitually amiable expression. It was said there was no lack of brains in his skull, which in outward appearance was small and round, and covered with ebony-black hair cut long in front and very short in the back. His eyes, small but not at all almond-shaped, never betrayed emotion. His nose was fine, not flat, and he would have been quite satisfied in believing and passing himself off for a handsome man if his mouth had not been distorted by the abuse of tobacco and betel-nut, for the cud of the latter, tucked away behind one cheek, altered the symmetry of his features. Nevertheless, that bad habit had not impaired the whiteness of his own teeth and two others furnished by the dentist at twelve pesos each.

He was considered one of the richest property-owners in the district of Binondo and one of the most important landowners in the province of Pampanga and along the Lake of Bai, principally in the town of San Diego where—be it said in passing—it was his custom to raise the land rents yearly. For all that, San Diego was his favourite town because of its pleasant baths, its famous cockpit, and the memories it had for him; he spent at least two months there every year.

Capitan Tiago had also many urban properties on Santo Cristo, Anloague and Del Rosario Streets, all in Manila's Chinatown. He and a Chinese shared the opium concession, with, as was to be expected, enormous profits. He had the concession for the prisoners' mess in Bilibid gaol, and horse-fodder contracts with many important firms in the city. On good terms with the authorities, clever, accommodating, and, at least in speculating on the needs of others, even daring, he had only one rival when it came to concessions and biddings for public works and offices which the Philippine Government at that time let out to private persons. At the time of our story, therefore, Capitan Tiago was a happy man, as happy as a man with a little brains could be in those parts; he was rich, he was at peace with God, with the Government, and with men.

That he was at peace with God cannot be doubted; it was almost dogma. There are no reasons to be on bad terms with the good God when one is well-off, has never had any dealings with Him, and has never lent Him money. Capitan Tiago had never addressed himself to God in his prayers, not even in his greatest difficulties; he was rich, and he let his money pray for him. God has created (he would have argued) aloof and powerful priests to say

Masses and prayers of intercession, while, as for Novenas and Rosaries, He had, in His infinite mercy, created for the benefit of the rich, needy substitutes who, for a peso, were quite capable of saying even sixteen decades of the Holy Rosary in a row and of reading all possible prayer books, including, at a suitable increase in fee, even the Bible in Hebrew. If in times of acute distress Capitan Tiago needed divine help, and could not put his hands on even one Chinese red candle, he called on the saints, both male and female, to whom he had special devotion, making them uncounted promises to persuade them that what he wanted from them was good. But most of his promises he made to the Virgin of Antipolo, Our Lady of Peace and Happy Voyage. What is more, he kept these promises, which is more than can be said of his behaviour toward certain saints of lower category, with whom he was rather remiss and even ungentlemanly; indeed, sometimes, having got what he wanted, he put them out of his mind. It is equally true, of course, that he never bothered them again either. Capitan Tiago felt that there were many unemployed saints in the calendar who did not know what to do with themselves in Heaven. But to the Virgin of Antipolo he attributed a greater power and efficacy than all the other Virgins, put together, whether they carried silver sceptres, or a Child Jesus dressed, or a Child Jesus naked, or scapulars, or rosaries, or girdles. Perhaps this was due to the Virgin of Antipolo's reputation for severity and concern for her prestige. According to the sacristan of her shrine, the Virgin, whom he claimed to be an enemy of the photographic arts, turned black as ebony when she was displeased, unlike other Virgins who were more indulgent and had softer hearts. It is well-known that certain people love an absolute monarch better than a constitutional one, and for proof there is the difference in fortunes between Louis XIV and Louis XVI, or Philip II and Amadeo I. For this reason, perhaps, people went on their knees up the length of the Virgin's shrine to the foot of her altar, even Chinese unbelievers and haughty Spaniards. What defied explanation was why, for all that, the custodians of the shrine sometimes ran off to America and got married on the money offered to the fearsome Virgin.

Capitan Tiago kept his own household gods in a small chapel or oratory, leading off from the main living-room in his house and screened with a silken curtain. He had never really understood monotheism, and was more inclined towards polytheism, as could be judged from the images in the chapel. There was a group of the Holy Family, their busts and limbs done in ivory, with glass eyes, long eyelashes and curly blond hair, first-rate examples of the work of the native image-makers of Manila. There were oil paintings, also by Filipino artists, depicting the sufferings of the holy martyrs and the miracles of the Virgin. Here was St. Lucy raising her eyes to heaven, and bearing on a plate another pair of eyes complete with brows and lashes, such as can be seen in representations of the Trinity and on the ancient Egyptian coffins. Here also was St. Paschal the Dancer, patron of pregnancy and hope of childless couples. And there was St. Anthony of Padua, in the Franciscan habit, tearfully contemplating a Child Jesus attired in the uniform of a Governor General, complete with three-cornered hat, sabre, and high boots, as for a children's costume party in Madrid. Capitan Tiago interpreted this as proof that, even if God were to acquire the powers of a Spanish Governor General in the Philippines, the Franciscans would still treat Him like a doll. There was also St. Anthony the Abbot with a pig by his side, a pig which Capitan Tiago considered as miraculous as the saint himself for which reason he never referred to it as a pig, but as 'the Blessed St. Anthony's pet'. Over there were St. Francis de Assisi with seven wings sprouting from his coffee-coloured habit, placed above a St. Vincent, who had only two wings but to make up for it was carrying a trumpet; a St. Peter Martyr, his skull being cleft by a kneeling Moor with an outlaw's blade, and beside him the other St. Peter, in turn chopping off the ear of another Moor, Malchus no doubt, mouth drawn, and body writhing with pain, while a fighting cock crowed and beat its wings upon a Doric column. This Capitan Tiago interpreted to show that to become a saint it was the same to be chopper or chopped. Finally there was a beautiful St. Michael in gilded and painted wood, almost a metre high. The archangel, lower lip between his teeth, eyes blazing, brow furrowed, and cheeks rosy, carried a Greek shield on one arm and with the other wielded a Malay *kris*, ready to smite the devotee, or, to judge from his attitude and look, anyone else who should approach him too closely, rather than the tailed and horned Devil who chewed his girlish leg. Capitan Tiago never went near the image for fear of a miracle. After all he had known more than one image, even the most clumsily carved ones from provincial workshops, to come alive to the confusion and punishment of sceptical sinners. It was well-known that a certain image of Christ in Spain, called as witness to a betrothal in a certain case, had given testimony by nodding its head in answer to the questions put by the learned judge; that another image had unfixed its right arm from the cross to embrace St. Lutgarda; and that, as Capitan Tiago himself had read in a newly published tract, an image of St. Dominic had preached a wordless sermon in the town of Soriano in Spain. The image had not said a word, but it was deduced from its gestures, at least by the author of the pamphlet, that it was announcing the approaching end of the world. Capitan Tiago had also heard it said that the Virgin of Luta, whose shrine was in the town of Lipa, had once been observed with a swollen cheek and mud on the hem of her skirts; did this not prove scientifically that sacred images also took walks without lifting their skirts, and even suffered toothache, perhaps for our sins? Had he not seen with his own little eyes the images of Christ, during the Good Friday sermons on the Seven Last Words, thrice raising and hanging their heads in unison, moving to tears and pious exclamations all the women in church and indeed all sensitive souls destined for salvation? Capitan Tiago, therefore, being a prudent and religious man, avoided coming too close to the *kris* of St. Michael. 'Let us take no chances,' he said to himself. 'I know he's an archangel, all right, but I don't trust him. I just don't trust him.'

But every year without fail he joined the traditional pilgrimage to Antipolo, attended by an orchestra which added to the pomp and splendour of the festivities. He would also pay the fees for two special Masses of the many that were sung during the three Novenas and in between. After the daily devotions he would bathe in the renowned spring where the sacred image itself was said to have bathed, and where devotees still professed to see in the hard rock the footprints of the Virgin, and the marks left by her hair when she had rinsed it like any other woman who uses coconut oil, as if, indeed, this hair had been made of steel or had been hard as diamonds and had weighed a thousand tons! Capitan Tiago would have his lunch close to this spring, eating roast pig, a sour stew of freshwater fish, and other native dishes more or less appetizing, reflecting perhaps that two High Masses would cost rather more than four hundred pesos each, but that this was cheap, considering the glory gained by the Mother of God with the firewheels, rockets, bombs, and petards that would be fired, and considering also the rich profits which, thanks to the Masses, he would be making the rest of the year.

But Antipolo was not the only scene of his ostentatious devotion.

In Binondo, in the province of Pampanga, and in the town of San Diego, when he planned to back a fighting cock with heavy bets, he would send the parish priest gold coins for propitiatory Masses and, like the Romans who read the omens for battle in the entrails of sacrificial fowl, Capitan Tiago, making due allowance for the change of times and the discovery of new truths, would note the way the candle flames flickered on the altar during Mass, the direction of the incense smoke, the voice of the priest as he chanted the prayers, and other such omens, in which he attempted to read his fortunes. Everybody knew that Capitan Tiago lost few bets, and these losses could only have been due to the fact that the officiating priest had had a hoarse throat, that not enough candles had been lighted, that the tapers had been too greasy, that Capitan Tiago had passed off a bad coin among the others, or some such cause. On the other hand an official of a certain sodality had assured him that these disappointments were trials to which heaven submitted him to test his faith and devotion. Beloved of the priests, respected by sacristans and acolytes, favourite of the Chinese waxworkers and the makers of fireworks and pyrotechnic displays, Capitan Tiago was happy in the religion of his country, and persons of good character and great piety attributed to him also a great influence in the Celestial Court.

That he was at peace with the Government, there is also no doubt, however improbable this may appear to be. Unable to conceive anything new, and satisfied with his way of making a living, he was always ready to obey the most insignificant bureaucrat, and to shower in the appropriate places gifts of hams, capons, turkeys, and fruits imported from China in season and out of season. If he heard anybody speaking ill of the natives, he would bid himself remember that he was not one of those, and raised the loudest voice in the chorus. If he heard criticism of the Chinese and Spanish half-breeds, he added his own, perhaps because he already considered himself of pure Iberian blood. He was the first to applaud any new assessment or tax, most of all when he scented behind them a new contract or concession. He always had orchestras ready to congratulate or serenade governors, mayors, prosecuting attorneys, and all classes of officials, on their saints' namedays, birthday anniversaries, birth or death of some relative, or indeed on any other occasion that was out of the ordinary. He commissioned laudatory verses and songs extolling 'our gentle and understanding governor', 'our courageous and hard-working mayor, for whom the wreath of the just is reserved in Heaven,' and similar compliments.

He had been chief of the rich guild of half-breeds despite the protests of many who did not consider him qualified. In his two years in office he had worn out ten frock coats, as many top-hats, and half a dozen walking sticks. He would put on frock coat and top-hat to call at the Governor General's palace, Malacañang, at the *Ayuntamiento* or City Hall, at military headquarters; he would put on top-hat and frock coat to go to the cockpit, the market, religious processions, the humblest Chinese store; and under the frock coat and top-hat, Capitan Tiago, sweating under the delightful strain of twirling his tasselled cane of office, would give orders, make arrangements, unmake them, all with an admirable activity and an imperturbability even more admirable. Thus the authorities regarded him as a good man, full of the best will in the world, peaceful, obsequious, obedient, and generous with his gifts, a man who never read a single book or periodical from Spain although he knew Spanish well. They looked on him with the same feelings that a poor student might have for an old and comfortable shoe, whose worn-out heel showed exactly how its owner walked. In him came true both the Christian and the worldly beatitudes: 'Blessed are the poor in spirit', but no less 'Blessed are they who have possessions'. One might even apply to him what is said to be an erroneous translation from the Greek of the Christmas message: 'Glory to God in the highest, and peace on earth to men of goodwill.' But, as will transpire later on, it is not enough that men should have goodwill to live in peace. Unbelievers took Capitan Tiago for a simpleton; his subordinates considered him a martinet and a tyrant; the poor thought him ruthless, cruel, and ready to profit from all their miseries. In their huts were also heard many stories, bordering on calumny, about his affairs with women, and there was talk of broken promises, tears, and abandoned children. Gossip pointed to more than one young woman as she passed by, cynical and slack-breasted. But no young woman gave Capitan Tiago nightmares or disturbed his peace of mind; on the contrary, it was an old one, an old widow who competed with him in piety, and had indeed merited from many priests more enthusiastic praises and compliments than he had ever received in his best moments. Between Capitan Tiago and this widow, the residual heiress of brothers and nephews, there was a holy rivalry which benefited the Church as much as the competition between the steamships then plying the Pampanga river served the public interest. No sooner would Capitan Tiago bestow upon some Virgin a silver sceptre set with emeralds and topazes than Doña Patrocinio would commission one in gold and diamonds from the best jeweller in the city. If, for the religious procession commemorating the Virgin of the Holy Rosary's miraculous victory over the Dutch in Manila Bay, Capitan Tiago raised a triumphal arch with two facades of quilted cloth hung with mirrors, crystal balls, lanterns and chandeliers, Doña Patrocinio promptly ordered another, two yards taller, with four facades, and double the number of decorations. At such times Capitan Tiago would play his best card, which was High Mass with fireworks in the churchyard, and then Doña Patrocinio had to bite her lips with her toothless gums because her nerves just could not abide the pealing of the bells and the explosions. Capitan Tiago might then smile with satisfaction, but she would be thinking of her revenge and, for some special holiday, would pay from her legacies the fees of the best preachers of all the five religious Orders in Manila, the most renowned canons of the Cathedral, and even members of the new-fangled Society of St. Vincent de Paul, to discourse on the most abstruse theological theses to poor sinners who could understand only pidgin Spanish. Capitan Tiago's admirers would point out on such occasions that Doña Patrocinio usually slept through the sermons, but her partisans would counter that after all she had paid for them and the important thing in this and other matters was who paid the bill. In any case she had lately put Capitan Tiago to rout by giving to a certain church in the city three silver floats trimmed with gold to carry the sacred images in procession; each one had cost her more than three thousand pesos, and Capitan Tiago could thereafter only hope that she would soon breathe her last or suffer five or six adverse court decisions. Unfortunately for him, she had taken the precaution of retaining the best counsel at the bar of the Supreme Court, and, as far as her health was concerned, she seemed to have left no visible opening to disease. She was as tough as steel wire, and clung to life with the tenacity of a skin disease; all this, no doubt, to give testimony to the rewards of virtue. In any case her admirers were sure that she would be canonised upon her death, and that Capitan Tiago would yet have to venerate her on the altars, a situation which he seemed prepared to accept provided only she came to an earlier death.

Such was Capitan Tiago in those days.

He had been born the only son of a sugar miller of Malabon, a town near Manila. His father had been rather well off, but so miserly that he had refused to spend a penny on his son's schooling. For this reason the boy had been brought up by a kind-hearted Dominican, a good man who tried to teach his ward all the good that he knew. But just when the boy was about to enjoy the pleasure of being called a 'logician' by virtue of entering the course in Logic, his guardian died, and then his father , which put an end to his studies and compelled him to go into business for himself. He soon married a good-looking girl from the district of Santa Cruz, who not only gave him social position, but also helped him make his fortune. Doña Pía Alba, for that-was the name of his wife, was not satisfied doing business in sugar, coffee, and indigo. She also wanted to manage a farm, and the couple bought lands in San Diego, at which time they had made friends with Father Dámaso and Don Rafael Ibarra, the wealthiest landowner of the town.

For six years the couple were childless, and this lack of an heir made their zest to make money an almost censurable ambition. Doña Pía was slender, healthy, well-formed. But in vain did she undertake Novenas, or, upon the advise of her pious friends in San Diego, appeal to Our Lady of Kaysaysay in the distant town of Taal, or give alms, or dance in the procession of Our Lady of Turumba in the town of Pakil in full midsummer sun. It was all in vain until Father Dámaso advised her to make a pilgrimage to the shrine in Obando, there to dance on the feast of St. Paschal and ask for a son. It was believed at that time that a triumvirate in Obando granted sons or daughters, at choice: Our Lady of Salambaw, St. Clare, and St. Paschal the Dancer. The advice was wise; Doña Pía soon afterwards knew she would become a mother. But like Shakespeare's fisherman, who stopped singing when he had found a treasure, she lost her spirits, turned melancholy, and was never again seen to smile. Everyone explained it as a caprice of pregnancy, even Capitan Tiago, but only a puerperal fever put an end to her sadness. Father Dámaso himself stood godfather to the lovely girl whom she left orphaned at birth. St. Paschal had failed to produce the boy they had asked him, and so the girl was named María Clara María, after Our Lady of Salambaw, and Clara after the second member of the triumvirate of Obando, thus punishing the honest St. Paschal with oblivion.

The little girl grew up in the care of her Aunt Isabel. For most of the years she lived in San Diego, not only because the climate there was thought to be healthier but also because Father Dámaso was so fond of her.

María Clara did not have the smallish eyes of her father; she had her mother's eyes, large, black, shadowed by long lashes, gay and sparkling when she was at play, thoughtful and deep otherwise. As a child her hair was almost fair; her nose, neither sharp nor flat, gave her a classic profile; her mouth recalled her mother's, small and winsome, with cheerful dimples; her skin was as fine as an onion's, and as white as cotton; anyway, so said her fond relations, who professed to find proofs of Capitan Tiago's paternity in her small well-shaped ears.

Her Aunt Isabel attributed the child's semi-European features to pre-natal influences; she said she had often seen Doña Pía in the first month of her pregnancy weeping before the image of St. Anthony. Another cousin of Capitan Tiago was of the same opinion, but she differed in the choice of the proper saint; she gave the credit to the Virgin or St. Michael. A cousin of Capitan Tinong, a famous scholar who had memorised a Spanish philosophical treatise in its entirety, sought an explanation in planetary influences.

María Clara, everybody's darling, grew up amid smiles and caresses. Even the friars made much of her; for the religious processions they dressed her up in white, plaited her rich curly hair with flowers, fixed two silver and golden wings to her frock, and tied two white doves to her hands with blue ribbons. The child was so gay, her chatter so charming, that Capitan Tiago, in a transport of parental love, lost no occasion to sing the praises of the saints of Obando, advising all and sundry to adorn their houses with suitable images and works of art.

In tropical countries a child of thirteen or fourteen turns woman overnight, a bud flowering suddenly. For this period of transition María Clara, upon the advice of the parish priest of Binondo, was put in the convent of St. Clare to receive from its nuns a strict religious education. She said goodbye with tears in her eyes to Father Dámaso, and to her only childhood friend, Crisóstomo Ibarra, who afterwards left for Europe. In the convent school, where communication with the outside world could be had only through a double grating, and even then only under the supervision of a nuncensor, María Clara lived seven years. Then, each for his own reasons but also because they were conscious of the mutual attraction between their children, Don Rafael and

Capitan Tiago made arrangements, some years after the departure of the younger Ibarra, for the betrothal of the two young people, each of whom, at opposite corners of the earth and in very different surroundings, welcomed the news with joy.

7 • *Love on a Balcony*
The Song of Songs

MARIA CLARA, stylishly dressed, with a blue rosary wound around her wrist like a bracelet, and her Aunt Isabel, equipped with reading glasses and a book of religious meditations to read during Mass, went to church that morning earlier than usual, for it was the day that Ibarra had promised to call.

Indeed, no sooner had the priest left the altar at the end of the Mass than the young girl made it clear that she wanted to go home, to the manifest surprise and annoyance of her good aunt who had thought her niece to be pious and as fond of prayer as a nun. The kindly old woman struggled to her feet, muttering and crossing herself repeatedly, but if her admonitions were sharp, they were also maternal, as if she had reflected that, after all, God would forgive María Clara, since He knew the hearts of young girls better than she did.

After breakfast María Clara whiled away the time knitting a silk purse, while her aunt took up a duster to repair the ravages of the dinner party the night before, and Capitan Tiago went over his papers.

But every street-noise, each carriage that passed, made the young girl start and sigh. How she wished she were back in the convent school among her friends; there indeed she could have faced him without a blush!

'I am beginning to think, María,' said Capitan Tiago, 'that the doctor's right. You should go to the provinces; you've lost colour; perhaps the country air will do you good. What do you say to Malabon... or San Diego?'

María Clara blushed when she heard the name of Ibarra's home town. But Capitan Tiago was absorbed in his papers and had not raised his head.

'Well then, that's settled,' he went on. 'Isabel and you had better go to the convent and pack your things. You're not going back and you might want to say goodbye to your chums.'

María Clara felt a pang of pain; she had been happy in convent school and now she was leaving it forever. But there were compensations. 'Then,' Capitan Tiago went on, 'in four or five days, after you have got some new dresses, we can be off to Malabon. Your godfather is no longer in San Diego, you know. His place has been taken by that saintly young priest who was here last night.'

'All the more reason, cousin, why we should go to San Diego,' remarked Aunt Isabel. 'Besides we have a better house there and it is almost time for the town fiesta.'

María Clara could have kissed her aunt for it, but then she heard a carriage stop outside their door, and she turned pale.

'That's true,' Capitan Tiago replied and then, hearing the carriage too, exclaimed: 'That must be Don Crisóstomo now!'

The knitting fell from María Clara's hands; she felt she could not move if she wanted to, listening to those steps coming up the staircase, and then to that fresh manly voice. Suddenly she sprang up and ran off to the oratory and all its saints. The two cousins burst out laughing while Ibarra, entering the room, was in time to hear the door close behind her.

She heard him ask about her, in that voice she had heard so often in her girlish dream, and promptly kissed the saint she found nearest, lucky Abbot Anthony, besieged, in flesh and in wood, with such charming temptations! María Clara had her eye to the keyhole when her aunt, interrupting this examination, found herself overwhelmed with kisses.

'Now, then, you silly girl,' said the old lady, brushing aside an unexpected tear in her tired eyes. 'Do tell me what on earth's the matter with you!'

María Clara covered her face with her hands.

'Come now, fix yourself up,' Aunt Isabel scolded her fondly. 'He's talking to your father about your... well, come along, and don't make them wait.'

María Clara let herself be pushed into her bedroom like a child.

Capitan Tiago and Ibarra were chatting amiably when Aunt Isabel returned, half-dragging her niece who looked everywhere except where she should.

But finally her eyes met Ibarra's; they exchanged smiles; and then, on the excuse of escaping the clouds of dust Aunt Isabel was raising, went out to the balcony.

Outdoors the sky was blue; there was a cooling breeze, although it certainly did not smell of roses, which stirred the leaves and flowers of the climbing vines, the air plants, the stuffed fishes and the Chinese lanterns. The splash of a paddle in the murky creek, the rumble of carriages and carts on the Bridge of Binondo, came faintly to them, although not the whisper of her aunt: 'Oh, there you are! So much the better; all the neighborhood can keep an eye on you.'

At first they only exchanged pleasantries. But women are the sisters of Cain and she was jealous.

'Did you think of me?' she asked. 'Always? Didn't you ever forget me? You've travelled so much; you've seen so many great cities, with so many beautiful women!'

'How could I forget you?' Men are, for that matter, also brothers of Cain, and know how to lie and to evade. 'How could I,' he asked, looking into her dark eyes, 'forget an oath, a sacred oath?'

He spoke of the stormy night when she had found him weeping by his mother's bier. She had come up to him, put her hand on his shoulder, that hand which for some time now had always been snatched away from him, and she had said: 'You've lost your mother, I never had one.' And they had wept together.

'You loved her,' he reminded her now. 'And she loved you like her own daughter.'

That night there had been rain and lightning, but, he said, there was music in his ears, and he could have sworn his mother smiled.

'If only they could see you now!' he cried. Did she remember, he asked, that he had held her hand and his mother's dead hand, and had sworn to love her, to make her happy, whatever happened?

'I have never regretted that promise,' he said now. 'I make it again.'

He swore, and she believed him, that he had never forgotten her during his travels. The Italian sun had not seemed warmer than her smile, the fields of Andalusia not brighter than her eyes, and, losing his way in the Black Forest or boating down the Rhine, he had remembered her in the romantic German legends of the Lorelei.

'I haven't seen as much of the world as you have,' she laughed. 'I know only Manila, Antipolo, and your home town. But I have remembered you too, ever since we said goodbye, and even though Father Confessor told me that I shouldn't and made me do penance for it.'

She began to tease him about their childhood games and quarrels. He had been such a cheat, and such a bad loser, and he had always wanted the best of everything. Once they had gone bathing in the river with his mother. He had already started school with the Jesuits in Manila, and had told her the Latin and Spanish names of the familiar plants and flowers on their way, but she had gone off chasing butterflies. Then he had made for her a wreath of orange leaves and flowers, but his mother had taken it and crushed the flowers into their native hair shampoo.

'You cried and said she didn't know anything about mythology,' María Clara teased. 'And your mother said not to be silly, and that our hair would smell all the better of it. I laughed at you, remember, and you went off in a huff and wouldn't talk to me the rest of the day until on our way back I picked some sage leaves by the roadside and gave them to you to put in your hat so you wouldn't get a headache.'

Ibarra smiled, opened his wallet, and pulled out a paper wrapped round some leaves, withered black but still faintly scented.

'Look, your sage leaves!'

She was not to be outdone and swiftly drew from her bosom a white satin purse. 'No, don't touch,' she tapped him lightly on the hand. 'It's a farewell letter.'

'The one I wrote to you before leaving?'

'And have you written me any other?'

'What did I have to say?'

'A number of lies, sir, and an equal number of excuses,' she laughed. 'Just a moment; I'll read it to you. Oh, don't be embarrassed, I'll skip the compliments.'

She started to read. 'My...I'll skip the next word; it's a lie.' Her eyes ran down the letter.

My father insists that I go abroad, and nothing I say will make him change his mind 'You are a man now,' he tells me, 'and should think of the future and your duties. You must learn something about life in order to serve your country. But you cannot learn it here; if you stay with me, under my care, sharing my worries from day to day, you will never be able to take a long view. And when I'm gone, you will be like the plant described by our poet Baltazar, "grown in water, withering the moment it is not tended, shrivelled by a touch of sun". Ah, you see, you're quite grown up,

*and yet you cry.' I was hurt by this reproach, and confessed that if I did not want
to go it was because I loved you. My father fell silent, and after reflection placed his
hand on my shoulder and said with emotion: 'Don't you think your father loves you
too, and hates to see you go? It isn't long since we lost your mother; I'm getting old;
I'm nearing that age when one seeks the help and the company of the young; yet I accept
loneliness, even though I don't know whether I shall ever see you again. But I must
think of more important things. Your future is before you, mine is coming to an end.
Love begins for you; it is dying for me. There is fire in your blood, mine begins to run
cold. But you cry, and are incapable of sacrificing the immediate present for your own
good and the good of your country!' My father's eyes filled with tears; I fell on my
knees before him, embraced him, asked his forgiveness, and said I was ready to leave...*

Ibarra had turned pale and was pacing up and down, visibly touched.

María Clara stopped reading. 'What is it? What's the matter with you?'

'You have made me forget my duties. I must leave for home right now.
Tomorrow is All Saints' Day.'

She fell silent, held him briefly with her great dreamy eyes and, plucking
some flowers, sighed: 'You're right. You must go; I shan't keep you. We
shall see each other in a few days. Put these flowers for me on their graves.'

Shortly afterwards, the young Ibarra went down the stairs, accompanied
by Capitan Tiago and Aunt Isabel. María Clara shut herself up in the oratory.

'Please tell Andeng, our housekeeper, to get the house ready for María and
Isabel,' Capitan Tiago asked Ibarra as the latter entered his carriage. 'Happy
voyage!'

Later he told María Clara, who knelt distraught before an image of the
Virgin: 'Come now, light two candles, the two-peso kind, one to St. Roch
and the other to St. Raphael: they are the patron saints of travellers. And
don't forget to light the lamp before Our Lady of Peace and Happy Voyage.
There are many bandits about. Better spend four pesos on candles and six
coppers worth of oil now than pay a heavy ransom later!'

8 • *Memories*

IBARRA rode off towards the square of San Gabriel, and was soon crossing
one of the busiest districts of Manila. What had depressed him the night
before, now, in full daylight, made him smile in spite of himself.

The hustle and bustle everywhere, so many carriages and cabs at a dash, Europeans, Chinese, and natives, each dressed after their own fashion, fruit pedlars, messengers, porters stripped to the waist, foodshops, inns, restaurants, shops, carts pulled by philosophical carabaos, the noise, the incessant movement, the sun itself, a certain smell, the riot of colours—he had almost forgotten what Manila was like.

The streets had still not been paved. Let the sun shine two days in a row, and they dissolved into clouds of dust that covered everything, blinding passers-by and sending them into fits of coughing; let it rain a day, and the streets became a marsh, gleaming at night with the reflected lanterns of carriages that splashed mud on the pedestrians on the narrow sidewalks as far as five metres away. How many women had lost their embroidered slippers in that sea of mud! In time the chain-gangs would show up to repair the streets; shaven-pated men wearing short-sleeved shirts and knee-length pants lettered and numbered in blue, chained in twos, grimy rags wrapped round their ankles against the friction of the fetters or perhaps the coldness of the steel, burnt by the sun, driven to exhaustion by the heat, their exertions, and the whips of the trusties who derived their peculiar pleasures from flogging their fellows. The prisoners were usually tall men with stern faces, whom Ibarra had never seen smile but whose eyes flashed when the whip fell whistling across their shoulders, or when a passer-by tossed them a cigar butt, damp and shredded, to be picked up by the nearest and hidden in his straw helmet while his fellows watched the other passers-by with unfathomable looks. Ibarra remembered the noise they made, the dull thud of rock being crushed to fill up the holes in the streets, mingling with the almost merry clank of heavy fetters round their swollen ankles. Once in his boyhood Ibarra had witnessed a scene that had struck his imagination. It had been high noon; the sun's rays fell mercilessly. Under the poor shade of a wooden cart lay one of these unfortunates, unconscious, his eyes staring wide. Two of his fellows were silently putting together a bamboo litter, without anger, without sorrow, without impatience—that, it was said, was what the natives were like. You today, our turn tomorrow, they seemed to be telling themselves. People hurried by without a glance; the women passed, looked and went on their way; the sight was common enough, so common that hearts had grown calloused. The carriages rolled by, their varnished bodies gleaming in the rays of a brilliant sun in a cloudless sky. He alone, a boy of eleven, newly arrived in town, had been touched; he alone, he felt sure, had slept badly because of it.

But that had been long ago. Turning his attention back to the city, Ibarra noticed that the honest old pontoon bridge was gone. It had been a good bridge for all its faults, rising and falling with the tides of the river Pasig, which more than once had battered and destroyed it.

The almond trees in the square of San Gabriel had not grown much, and were as thin as ever.

The Escolta, the main business street, seemed to him less attractive than when he had last seen it, in spite of a new building decorated with draped female figures, which had taken the place of a group of warehouses.

He found the new Bridge of Spain more worthy of note, while the houses on the right bank of the river, among bamboo clumps and groves, where the Escolta ended opposite the Island of Romero, reminded him of the chilly mornings when he had been paddled past them bound for the baths of Uli-Uli.

He met many carriages drawn by teams of magnificent ponies, carrying businessmen on their way to their offices, still half asleep, military men, Chinese in foolish and ridiculous postures, grave friars, canons, and, in an elegant open carriage, Father Dámaso himself, serious and frowning. But he had passed on before Ibarra could be sure, and in any case here came Capitan Tinong, greeting him jovially from the high native horse-cart in which he rode with his wife and two daughters.

At the foot of the bridge Ibarra's horses went at a trot towards the Drive of the Sabana. To his left, from the cigar factory at Arroceros, came the rattle and clatter of the women cigar-makers beating tobacco leaves. Ibarra could not help smiling when he recalled the strong smell of tobacco which saturated the old pontoon bridge at five every afternoon, and how it had made him sick as a boy. He imagined the women's lively chatter, the broad jokes, so reminiscent of the district of Lavapiés in Madrid, where other cigar-women rioted and put the despised policemen to rout with ribald laughter.

The Botanical Garden dispelled these pleasant recollections; an odious comparison put before his eyes the botanical gardens in Europe, in countries where it cost much money and determination to make a leaf grow or a bud flower, and even those in other colonies, where withal the gardens were flourishing, well-tended, and open to the public. Ibarra turned his eyes away and saw to his right the old city of Manila, surrounded still by its walls and moats like an under-nourished adolescent wrapped in her grandmother's finery.

Then, far away, the sea...

On the other side lay Europe, he thought, Europe with all its beautiful countries, never at rest, searching for happiness, dreaming at dawn and disenchanted by nightfall, contented in the midst of all disasters; over there, on the other side of the sea, were the truly spiritual nations, which, while not condemning material things, were yet more spiritual than those which boasted of placing spiritual things first.

But these reflections vanished at sight of a small hill on the field of Bagumbayan. The solitary eminence, beside the Drive of the Luneta, brought to his mind the man who had opened the eyes of his intelligence, and had made him understand the good and the just, giving him only a handful of ideas, yet these not commonplaces but convictions that had stood up well under the glare of all that he had learned later. That man had been an old priest, whose parting words still resounded in his ears. 'Do not forget that if wisdom is the patrimony of all men, only those of good heart can inherit it; I have tried to transmit to you what I in turn received from my teachers, adding to that legacy as much as I was able in handing it on to the next generation'. You must do the same with your own inheritance, increase it threefold, for you go to countries that are very rich.' And the priest had added with a smile: 'They come here seeking gold; go you to their countries in search of the treasures we lack. But remember all that glitters is not gold.' The priest had died on a scaffold on that hill.

But to the rebellion surging from this memory he opposed a whispered affirmation: 'No, in spite of everything, my country comes first—first the Philippines, daughter of Spain—first, Mother Spain. What was destined, what was unavoidable, cannot stain the honour of the Motherland.'

Thus, oblivious of his surroundings, he went by the village of Ermita, that phoenix of nipa that rose regularly from its ashes with blue and white houses with red zinc roofs; then the village of Malate with its cavalry barracks behind the screen of trees; and further on the scattered little huts with their pyramidal roofs hidden between banana groves and betel-nut trees, constructed like nests by the father of the family that lived in each of them.

The carriage rolled on. Once in a while it met a native horse-cart drawn by one or two ponies, whose hempen harness showed they came from the provinces; the driver would lean forward to stare at the passenger of the elegant carriage, without saying a word, without a single greeting. At other times a cart drawn by a slow-moving phlegmatic carabao would bring a touch of liveliness to the broad dusty road under the brilliant tropic sun. The timeless melancholy song of the driver astride the carabao would be accompanied by the strident whine of the bone-dry wheel against the enormous axle of the heavy vehicle, or else by the low rumble of the worn-out runners of a native sled dragging itself heavily over the dust or mud puddles of the road. Herds of cattle grazed in the wide fields around them; a white heron perched serenely on the back of an ox drowsily ruminating the grass of the meadow; in the distance young mares leapt and galloped, pursued by a vigorous stallion of long tail and abundant mane; the stallion neighed and the earth trembled under the beat of his powerful hooves.

Ibarra travelled thinking or dozing, oblivious to the poetry of the countryside, now gay, now quietly sad, with no eyes for the sun which made the tree-tops sparkle, the barefoot peasants run over the smoking earth, and the young farm-girl pause under the shade of an almond tree or a bamboo clump to savour vague and inexplicable thoughts.

The carriage moved on, rolling from side to side like a drunkard, over the bumpy road, now clattering across a bamboo bridge, now up a steep incline, now rapidly downhill.

9 • *Local Goings-on*

IBARRA was right; it was in fact Father Dámaso in the open carriage, headed for the very house he had just left. The friar arrived just as María Clara and her Aunt Isabel were entering their richly decorated carriage.

'Where are you going?' he asked, absently tapping the young girl's cheek.

'To the convent school to fetch my things,' she answered.

'Ah!' Father Dámaso muttered distractedly. 'Ah! Let's see who's going to have his way, we shall see...' And he went upstairs slowly, head bent, leaving the two women puzzled.

'He must be trying to memorise a sermon,' said Aunt Isabel, 'Get in, María, or we'll be late.'

Whether it was a sermon or not, serious matters indeed must have been on Father Dámaso's mind, for he neglected to offer his hand to Capitan Tiago, who as a result had to bend his knees halfway in order to kiss it.

'Santiago,' he said quickly, 'we have to speak about very important things. Let's go to your study.'

He made Capitan Tiago so uneasy he was unable to reply, and obediently followed the burly priest who closed the door behind them.

Meantime, in another part of the city the scholarly Dominican Father Sibyla, had left his parish house very early after Mass and had gone to the convent of his Order at the city gate which, depending on the ruling dynasty in Madrid, was called after either Isabel II or Magellan.

Paying no heed to the succulent smell of chocolate or the clatter of coins and drawers which came from the Procurator's office, and scarcely replying to his respectful and deferential greetings, Father Sibyla went up the stairs, crossed a number of corridors, and knocked at a certain door.

'Come in,' said a feeble voice.

'God restore Your Reverence to health,' was the young Dominican's greeting as he entered.

An aged priest was seated in a great armchair; he was gaunt and rather yellowish, like one of Ribera's saints. His eyes were buried deep in their sockets, under heavy eyebrows that, habitually contracted, emphasised the brilliance of the feverish eyes.

Father Sibyla gazed at him with emotion, his arms crossed under the venerable scapular of St. Dominic. Then he bowed his head without saying a word and seemed to be waiting.

'Ah', sighed the invalid, 'they advise an operation, Hernando, an operation at my age! This country, this terrible country! Profit from my experience, Hernando.'

Father Sibyla slowly raised his eyes, and fixed them on the invalid's face. 'And what has Your Reverence decided?' he asked.

'To die! What else can I do? I am in great pain but... I have caused pain to many, and I am paying my accounts: And you, how are you? What brings you here?'

'I came to report to you on the mission with which you entrusted me.'

'How has it gone?'

The young priest seated himself, turned away with annoyance, and said:

'They've been telling us stories. The young Ibarra is sensible enough; he doesn't seem stupid; I think he's all right.'

'You think so?'

'Hostilities broke out last night.'

'Ah, already? What happened?'

Father Sibyla described briefly what had happened between Father Dámaso and Crisóstomo Ibarra.

'Anyway,' he continued, 'he is marrying the daughter of Capitan Tiago. She has been brought up by nuns of our own Order. He for his part is wealthy and he will not want to risk happiness and fortune by making enemies.'

The invalid nodded approvingly.

'Yes, I agree with you. With such a wife, and such a father-in-law, he will be ours, body and soul. If not, then I would rather he openly declared himself an enemy.'

Father Sibyla looked astonished.

'For the good of our holy Order, that is to say,' the old man added, breathing with difficulty. 'I prefer attacks to stupid praises and the flatteries of friends, who, after all, are paid well enough.'

'Your Reverence believes...'

The aged priest looked at him sadly.

'Always keep in mind,' he said between painful gasps, 'that our power will last only as long as people believe in it. If we are attacked, then the Government will argue that it is because we are acknowledged to be an obstacle to any schemes for independence, and it will conclude that we must be kept in power.'

'But if the Government listens to our enemies? Sometimes the Government...'

'It won't.'

'Nevertheless, if out of greed the Government should come to desire for itself what we have acquired... If there should be some daring, some reckless man...'

'Then let him look out!'

Both fell silent.

'Moreover,' the invalid continued, 'attacks wake us up; we discover our weaknesses, and can improve ourselves. Exaggerated praises only fool us, lull us to sleep, while making us ridiculous to the outside world and, once we become ridiculous, then we shall fall as we fell in Europe. Money will no longer enter our churches; nobody will buy scapulars, penitential belts, or anything at all, and when we have ceased to be rich, we shall likewise cease to move conscience.

'But we shall always have our landed estates, our urban properties...'

'All will go as they went in Europe. The worst part of it is that we are working our own ruin. For example, take this unbridled desire to raise every year, and at our own discretion, the rentals on our lands; it will be our ruin. The native is forced to buy elsewhere lands that are as good as ours, if not better. I fear we are on the decline. Whom God would destroy, He first makes mad. That is why we should lighten our hand; already the people complain. I have thought it out well; let the others do what they will; let us for our part try to keep whatever prestige we have left; and since we shall soon appear before God, let us keep our hands clean. May the God of Mercy pity our weaknesses.'

'So Your Reverence believes that the rentals or tributes...'

'Let's stop talking about money,' the invalid interrupted wearily. 'You were saying that Lieutenant Guevara had promised Father Dámaso...'

'Yes, Father,' replied Father Sibyla with a smirk. 'But when I saw him this morning he told me he was sorry for what had happened last night, that the sherry had gone to his head, and that to his mind Father Dámaso was in a similar state. 'And the promise?' I asked him jokingly. 'Father,' he answered, 'I know how to keep my word when it does not stain my honour; but I am not and have never been an informer and that is why I still have only a lieutenant's stars.'

Father Sibyla then took his leave after speaking of other matters of no importance.

Lieutenant Guevara had indeed refrained from reporting the previous night's altercation to Malacañang, but the Governor General had heard of it nevertheless. Discussing with his staff certain allusions which the Manila newspapers were making to him, he had been told the story of Father Dámaso, in a version that was rather coloured although perhaps more in keeping with official form.

'Who told you this?' His Excellency asked with a smile.

'Laruja was telling the story this morning in a newspaper office.'

The Governor General continued smiling.

'From woman and friar take no offence. I intend to live in peace during the time that remains to me here and I want no more troubles with men who wear skirts. What's more, I know the Father Provincial made a mockery of my order. I ask the transfer of that friar as a punishment, and they go and move him to a much better parish. Typical friar's tricks, as we say in Spain!'

But when he found himself alone His Excellency stopped smiling.

'Ah,' he sighed, 'if these people weren't so stupid, they'd soon take the measure of these Reverences! But every people deserves its fate, and let us do what everybody else does.'

Meantime Capitan Tiago had finished conference with Father Dámaso, or rather the latter had finished with him.

'Well, now you're warned,' said the Franciscan when he took his leave. 'All this could have been avoided if you had only asked me first, if you hadn't lied when I asked you about it. Try not to make any more silly mistakes, and rely on her godfather.'

After the friar had left, Capitan Tiago took two or three turns in his drawing-room, reflecting and sighing, until, struck by a sudden idea, he ran to the chapel and snuffed out the candles and the votive lamp he had ordered to be lighted for the safety of Ibarra.

'There's still time,' he muttered. 'It's a long way to San Diego.'

10 • *The Town of San Diego*

THE town of San Diego lay near the shores of the Lake of Bai, surrounded by fields and meadows. It grew sugar, rice, coffee, and fruit, which were shipped directly to Manila, or else sold at throwaway prices to Chinese middlemen who exploited the credulity or vices of the farmers.

When on clear days the boys of the town climbed to the topmost story of the mossy, vine-covered church tower, they had below them a panorama of great beauty, although they were perhaps more interested in identifying their houses with rival shouts, in the jumble of nipa, tile, zinc and palm roofs, each to be recognised among their orchards and gardens by their own special signs, this one by a certain tree, that one by a light-leaved tamarind, a third by a coconut tree laden with nuts, or a bamboo clump, a betel-nut palm, a cross.

Beyond lay the river, like a great glass snake sleeping on the green fields, its back horned here and there by rocks.

From afar it glided narrowly between steep banks to which contorted trees clung with naked roots, with a little house, barely to be descried, poised on the edge of an abyss, defying the winds and looking on its slender stilts like a heron watching the snake before pouncing on it. Nearer town, the river widened and moved more peacefully down a slight descent. The trunks of palms and other trees, the bark still on them, served as shaky bridges between the two banks, but if they were bad bridges, they were on the other hand magnificent gymnastic machines on which to test a sense of balance, which was not to be sneezed at. The boys of the town, when they bathed in the river, found it amusing to watch some woman cross, balancing a basket on her head, or a tottering old man, feeling his way with a staff which more often than not slipped out of his grasp into the water.

But what always caught the eye was what might be called a peninsula of forest in that sea of cultivated fields. There might be found century-old trees with hollow trunks, which had died only when lightning struck their proud tops and set them afire; at such times, it was said, the fire had not spread, and had died on the spot. There also were enormous rocks which time and Nature had covered with velvety moss, and whose cracks the air had filled with layer upon layer of soil, packed in by the rains and fertilized by the birds. The vegetation of the tropics grew freely: bushes, thickets, interlaced creepers passing from tree to tree, hanging from the branches, clutching the roots on the ground and the ground itself. And, as if Nature were not yet content, plants grew on plants: moss and mushrooms in the crevices of tree-trunks, aerial plants side by side with the leaves of the trees they climbed.

It was a forest that commanded respect. There were strange legends about it.

The most credible, and by the same token the least-known and believed, was that when San Diego was only a miserable bunch of huts, and deer and wild pig roamed its grass-grown streets at night, there came to it one day an old Spaniard with deep-set eyes. He spoke Tagalog quite well, and, after going round the neighbourhood, he asked for the owners of the forest and acquired it, presumably because it was known to have some hot springs, in exchange for clothes, jewellery, and a certain amount of money, which he handed over to pretenders who really had no title.

Afterwards, no one knew how, he disappeared. The simple peasants were beginning to believe he had been the victim of an enemy's spell when a fetid odour from the forest called the attention of some herdsmen. They traced it to its source and found the body of the old man in a state of putrefaction hanging from the branch of a *balete* tree. If in life he had inspired fear with his deep cavernous voice, his sunken eyes, and soundless laughter, now, dead a suicide, he disturbed the sleep of the women. Some of the false vendors threw his jewellery into the river and burnt the clothes they had received from him, and after the corpse was buried at the very foot of the *balete*, nobody ever dared pass by. Once a herdsman in search of his animals said he had seen mysterious lights there; those whom he called to help went so far as to hear lamentations. An unlucky lover who, to win the favour of his disdainful mistress, promised to pass the night under the tree and to prove it by tying a length of rattan around its trunk, died of a swift fever the day after the dare.

Months after, a young man, a Spanish half-breed to all appearances, arrived and said he was the son of the deceased. He established himself in those parts, dedicating himself to agriculture, especially the growing of indigo. Don Saturnino was taciturn, of a rather violent character, sometimes cruel, but very active and hardworking. He walled in the grave of his father and visited it from time to time. When he was getting on in years, he married a girl from Manila, by whom he had Don Rafael, the father of Crisóstomo Ibarra.

Don Rafael from an early age made himself loved by the peasants; agriculture, introduced and encouraged by his father, developed rapidly; new settlers came, and behind them many Chinese. The hamlet soon became a village with a native priest; then the village became a town, and when the native priest died, Father Dámaso took his place. But throughout these changes the old man's grave and its surroundings remained untouched. Sometimes the boys of the town, armed with sticks and stones, ventured to pick fruits nearby. But in the midst of their fun, or as they stared silently at the ancient rope swinging from the fatal branch, one or two stones would fall, coming from nobody knew where, and then they would cry out: 'The old man, the old man!' and throw away fruits and sticks, jump down from the trees, scatter among the rocks and bushes, without stopping, until they were out of the forest, pale, some panting, others in tears, and very few in any mood for laughter.

11 • *The Bosses*
Divide and rule
(The New Machiavelli)

WHO ran the town of San Diego?

Not Don Rafael Ibarra in his lifetime, although he had the most money and lands, and almost everyone was under obligation to him.

A modest man who depreciated whatever he did for the town, he never had partisans, and, when he was in trouble, everyone had turned against him.

Capitan Tiago?

It is true that his debtors welcomed him with orchestras, gave banquets in his honour, and showered him with gifts. The best fruit might always be found on his table; when a deer or wild pig was caught, he was given a quarter; if he admired a debtor's horse, it was in his stables half an hour later. But people laughed at him behind his back and called him Sacristan Tiago.

The Mayor perhaps?

This wretch did not command, he obeyed; he dared not reprimand, but was himself reprimanded; he made no decisions, they were made for him; yet had to answer to the Provincial Governor for whatever he had been ordered to do by the real masters of the town as if it had all been his own idea. But let it be said to his credit that he had neither stolen nor usurped his office; it had cost him five thousand pesos and many humiliations, although, considering the income, it was cheap at that.

Was it God then?

Ah, the good God did not trouble the consciences or the sleep of the inhabitants of San Diego. At least He did not make them tremble, and, if they had been spoken to about Him in some sermon, they would surely have thought with a sigh: 'If only there were indeed a God!' They did not bother much about Our Lord; the saints, male and female, gave them enough to do. In their eyes God had become one of those weak kings whose people pay court only to their favourites.

The truth was that San Diego was a kind of Rome; not the Rome of the calculating Romulus tracing her future walls with his plough; nor that later Rome, stained with blood, her own and others', that dictated laws to the world; but the Rome with which it was contemporaneous, the Rome of the nineteenth century, with the difference that, instead of marble monuments and a Colosseum, San Diego's monuments were made of plaited bamboo and its people gathered in a nipa cockpit. The parish priest was the Pope in the Vatican; the commanding officer of the garrison, the King of Italy in the Quirinal; all of this, of course, in terms of rattan and bamboo, but, in San Diego no less than in Rome, there were continuous quarrels, for each authority wanted to be sole master and found the other superfluous.

The parish priest was Father Bernardo Salví, the young and taciturn Franciscan who had replaced Father Dámaso. In his habits and manners he was very different from the usual run of members of his Order, even more so from his pugnacious predecessor. Father Salví was thin, sickly, almost constantly immersed in his own thoughts, strict in the performance of his religious duties, and careful of his good name. He made such an impression on his parishioners that barely a month after his arrival almost everyone in San Diego had joined the lay auxiliary of the Franciscan Order, the Tertiaries, to the discomfiture of the rival Confraternity of the Most Holy Rosary sponsored by the Dominicans. The pious heart leaped with joy to see around so many necks four or five scapulars, around so many waists a girdle of knotted rope, and over coarse cotton habits so many long-drawn faces. The head sacristan made quite a tidy fortune selling—perhaps it would be more correct to say, furnishing for a fee—the necessary paraphernalia for the salvation of souls and the discomfiture of the Devil, who had once dared to contradict God face to face, doubting His very word, as may be found inscribed in the Book of Job, and who had carried Our Lord Jesus Christ across the skies, but who had now apparently become so susceptible that he shied away from a napkin painted with the crossed forearms of the Franciscan Order, and fled from its knotted cincture. But perhaps this proved only that progress had been made in such matters, and that the Devil was a reactionary, or at least a conservative like everyone who lives in darkness, the only alternative being that he had acquired the sensitivities of an adolescent girl.

In any case Father Salví was most assiduous; when he preached, and he was very fond of preaching, he caused all the doors of the church to be closed, like Nero who did not allow anyone to leave the theatre while he sang; but Father Salví did it for the good, and Nero to the destriment, of souls.

Father Salví punished the faults of his subordinates with fines, and flogged them only rarely, unlike Father Dámaso who had fixed everything with blows of his fist and stick, delivered with a guffaw and the best will in the world. One could not think badly of Father Dámaso because of this; he was convinced that one could deal with natives only with blows; a fellow-friar had said so in a book, and Father Dámaso believed it because he never contradicted the printed word, to the discomfort of many. Although Father Salví used his stick only a few times, he made up for quantity with quality; yet one could not think of him badly because of that, either; fasting and abstinence had impoverished his blood and frayed his nerves, and, as the common people said, had gone to his head. As a result it did not make much difference to the backs of the church sacristans whether the parish priest feasted like Father Dámaso or fasted like Father Salví.

Since, according to the womenfolk, the Devil himself was keeping out of the priest's way after the great tempter had been caught one day, tied to the foot of the bed, flogged with the knotted cincture, and set free only after nine days, the only rival of the spiritual power (with tendencies toward the temporal) in San Diego was the commander of the local detachment of the Constabulary, who had the rank of second lieutenant.

Naturally, anyone who, after the Devil's painful experience, still had the temerity to clash with such a man as the parish priest deserved a worse reputation than the poor imprudent Devil himself, and it was generally agreed that the commanding officer deserved whatever fate he should meet. His wife, an old Filipina much painted and rouged, called herself Doña Consolación; her husband and others had another name for her. The lieutenant, when he was not avenging his matrimonial misfortunes on his own person by getting drunk like a lord, did it by drilling his soldiers up and down in the noonday sun while he lolled in the shade, or, more often, by beating up his wife. Perhaps she was no Lamb of God taking away his sins, but she certainly gave him a foretaste on earth of the pains of Purgatory. They beat each other up with gusto, giving their neighbours a free show which might perhaps be described as a vocal and instrumental concert, a four-hand concerto with full pedal.

Whenever these scandalous happenings reached the ears of Father Salví, he smiled, crossed himself, and said an Our Father; when the couple called him a hypocrite, a Carlist, and a miser, he smiled again and prayed a little more.

The lieutenant in turn lost no opportunity to warn the few Spaniards who called on him:

'So you're going to the parish house to visit Father Wouldn't-Hurt-A-Fly! Look out! If he offers you chocolate, which I doubt, but anyway if he does offer it, keep your ears open. If he calls the servant and tells him, "So-and-so, make a pot of chocolate, hey," then you can rest easy; but if he says, "So-and-so, make a pot of chocolate, ha," then you'd better pick up your hat and get away at a run.'

'What!' his visitor would ask, taken aback. 'He wouldn't throw the pot at me would he? Good heavens!'

'My dear chap, he wouldn't go as far as that.'

'Well, then?'

'Chocolate, *hey*, means really good chocolate; chocolate, *ha*, means it will be very watery.'

But this may have been merely malicious gossip on the part of the commanding officer; the same story was told of many a parish priest; indeed it may have been a practice of the Order.

The lieutenant, prompted by his wife, had another trick up his sleeve to play against the parish priest; he imposed a nine o'clock curfew. Doña Consolación professed to have seen Father Salví, disguised in a native shirt and hat, stealing down the streets at all hours. Father Salví took a saintly revenge. Whenever he saw the lieutenant in church he unobtrusively ordered the sacristan to close all the doors; then he took the pulpit and preached until the very saints on the altar shut their eyes and the wooden dove above him, symbol of the Holy Ghost, begged for mercy. The commanding officer, like all reprobates, was not thus to be reformed; he left when he could, swearing, and at the first opportunity seized a sacristan or servant of the priest, arrested him, beat him up, and set him to washing down the floors of the barracks and his own quarters, which thus acquired a brief respectability. The sacristan, fined for his absence by the friar, would tell the story; Father Salví would hear him in silence, pocket the fine, and, while he pondered a new subject for another sermon that would be even longer and more edifying, would in the meantime let loose his goats and sheep to chew up the lieutenant's garden. But, of course, these things did not prevent the parish priest and the commanding officer from shaking hands when they met, and conversing politely.

As for Doña Consolación, when her husband was sleeping it off or having a siesta, and she could not pick a quarrel with him, she stationed herself at her window; she could not stand young girls and in a blue flannel blouse, a cigar in her mouth, she shouted out ribald nicknames for them as they passed by, frightened, embarrassed, with downcast eyes, and scarcely breathing. Doña Consolación had a great asset: to all appearances she had never looked into a mirror.

These were the bosses of the town of San Diego.

12 • All Saints' Day

PERHAPS the one thing that, beyond argument, distinguishes men from animals is the cult of the dead, a practice which, strangely enough, is all the more deeply rooted the more uncivilised a people may be. Thus the natives of New Guinea are said to keep the bones of their dead in boxes and to converse with them; in most of the countries of Asia, Africa, and America the natives give banquets for the dead, at which they serve the most exquisite foods from their kitchens or those dishes known to have been the favourites of the deceased in their lifetime; the Egyptians built them palaces; the Moslems, chapels; and so on. But the people who understand these things best and have truly read the human heart are surely the natives of Dahomey. They know that man is vengeful, so, they say, the best way to please a dead man is to sacrifice all his enemies on his grave; they know also that man is curious and will probably be bored in after-life, so each year they behead a slave and send him on to the dead with all the latest news.

The Filipinos at that time were different from all the rest. According to historians the ancient inhabitants of the Philippines had venerated their ancestors as tutelar deities; now the contrary was true, and the dead had to place themselves under the protection of the living. Epitaphs notwithstanding, hardly anybody believed that the dead were at rest, much less in peace. The greatest optimist imagined his great-grand-parents still roasting in Purgatory and, always provided that he did not end up in a worse place, expected to keep them company himself for a considerable time. A visit to the churches and cemeteries of the Philippines on All Saints' Day, which is there dedicated to the dead, would have sufficed to convince the sceptic that this frame of mind was not exceptional.

In San Diego the cemetery was located west of the town, in the middle of rice fields, and was reached by means of a narrow lane, dusty in the dry season, and what might be described as navigable when it rained. A wooden gate and a wall, made half of stone and half of bamboo and wooden stakes, served to separate it from the living, but apparently not from the parish priest's goats and a number of pigs of the neighbourhood, which came and went freely, exploring the graves and otherwise livening up the gloom.

A large wooden cross on a stone base marked the centre of the large enclosure. The wind had turned and twisted the tin scroll at its head, and the rain had washed away the traditional inscription, I.N.R.I., which on the True Cross had mocked at Jesus of Nazareth, King of the Jews. As on Golgotha itself, bones and skulls were heaped in confusion at the foot of the cross, tossed there by the indifferent grave-digger making room for new arrivals. There they awaited, not the resurrection of the dead, but the attentions of some animal to warm and wash their coldness and their bareness. Nearby grew a few flowers, their names, like the skulls, now known only to their Creator; their petals palely smiled, and their perfume was the perfume of the sepulchre. Along the outskirts of the cemetery there were recent excavations; over here a depression in the ground, over there a slight mound. Bramble bushes tore at the legs; the flowering *pandakaki* heightened the smell of desolation. Grass had crept into all corners, and climbing vines covered the walls and niches, clothing nakedness and disguising ugliness, filling up the cracks made by tremors and quakes, and hiding from the eye the venerable emptiness of old graves.

On this All Saints' Day the animals had been frightened away from the cemetery; only a pig or two stubbornly stuck its snout through the fence and seemed to beseech the mourner not to eat everything up.

Two men were digging a grave near a lopsided wall. One of them, the town grave-digger, worked impassively, tossing out vertebrae and bones with much the nonchalance of a gardener clearing away twigs and stones. His mate was visibly miserable, covered with sweat, incessantly smoking and spitting.

'See here,' he said in Tagalog. 'Wouldn't it be better to dig somewhere else? This seems to be a fresh grave.'

'Oh, one grave's as fresh as another.'

'But I can't stand it. Look at that bone you just split; I swear it bled. And that hair!'

'Don't be so squeamish. One would think you were a clerk. Now, if you'd dug up a twenty-day corpse, like I have, at night, in the dark, and raining too, with my light going out on me...'

His mate shivered.

'The coffin came apart, the corpse looked like jumping out, and smelled, and I had to take it on my shoulders; well, it was raining, and both of us got wet...'

'But for God's sake, why dig him up at all?'

'Why? How the devil should I know? Those were my orders.'

'Whose orders?'

The grave-digger stepped back and looked at his mate from head to foot.

'Man, you talk like a Spaniard! Why, a Spaniard himself asked me the same question afterwards; confidentially, of course. Well, I'll give you the same answer: the big friar told me to do it.'

'I see. And what did you do with the—the body?'

'Well, listen to that! If I didn't know you, I'd take you for a Spaniard; you're asking exactly the same questions as that other chap. Well, the big friar told me to bury the body in the Chinese Cemetery, but you know how far that is from here, and that coffin was heavy, let me tell you...'

'No! No! I'm through!' The grave-digger's mate dropped his shovel and jumped out. 'Look at that skull; I've split it. I won't get any sleep tonight!'

The grave-digger burst out laughing as his mate ran away crossing himself.

The cemetery was filling up with men and women in mourning clothes. Some seemed to be uncertain about the grave they sought; they disputed it with others, and then went off each their separate ways and knelt where they thought best; those whose parents had been buried in wall-niches lighted tapers before them and fell to praying devoutly; on all sighs and sobs were heard, either exaggerated or repressed amid a murmur of Latin prayers.

At this time a bright-eyed little old man entered the cemetery; he was bareheaded; many were heard to laugh when they saw him, and some women frowned. Unheeding the old man went to the pile of skulls, knelt, searched with his eyes among the old bones, carefully picking up one skull after another, frowning and shaking his head as if he had not found what he sought. He looked round him, and finally rose.

'You there!' he called out to the grave-digger.

The grave-digger raised his head.

'I am looking for a skull, a lovely skull, as white as coconut meat, with all its teeth. I kept it at the foot of the cross, under some leaves. Do you know where it is?'

The grave-digger shrugged his shoulders.

'Look,' the old man said, showing him a silver coin. 'This is all I've got, but I'll give it to you if you'll find it for me.'

The coin sparkled and it seemed to make the grave-digger think. He looked at the heap of bones and asked:

'Isn't it there? If it isn't, then I don't know where it is.'

'Look, when they pay me what they owe me, I can give you more,' the old man went on. 'The skull was my wife's, you see, and so, you understand, if you can find it for me...'

'If it isn't there, then I don't know where it is. I can give you another one, if you like.'

'You're like the grave you dig!' the old man cried out with passion. 'You don't know your own worth! Tell me, for whom do you dig that grave?'

'How do I know?' replied the other peevishly. 'For a dead man, I suppose.'

'Just like the grave you dig, exactly, exactly!' the old man cackled. 'You know neither what you swallow nor what you throw up! Dig away, dig away!'

And he turned towards the gate.

The grave-digger had finished his task; two heaps of fresh reddish earth rose at the edges of the new grave. He drew out some betel-nut from his straw hat, started to chew it, and looked round him blankly.

13 • Storm Signals

AS the old man was leaving, a carriage, which seemed to have come a long way to judge from the dust that covered it and from the sweat on its horses, pulled up at the entrance to the cemetery lane.

Ibarra alighted from it with an aged servant, dismissed it with a gesture, and went towards the cemetery in sombre silence.

'I couldn't come back; I was sick and very busy,' the servant explained timidly. 'Capitan Tiago said he would take charge of having a proper tomb made, and I did plant some flowers, and made the cross myself.'

Ibarra made no reply.

'Over there, sir, behind that large cross,' the servant continued, pointing towards a corner of the cemetery when they had passed the gate.

Ibarra was so engrossed in his own thoughts that he did not perceive the surprise caused by his arrival among a number of persons, who, recognising him, paused in their prayer to follow him with curious eyes.

The young man walked with care so as not to step on some old grave, slightly sunken in the grass; in other times he had not scrupled to walk over them, but now he had greater respect for the dead; his father was one of them. He stopped when he had passed the large cross, and looked everywhere around him; his companion, searching the ground for some vestige of the grave they sought, and seeing nowhere the cross he had made, stammered in confusion, half to himself:

'Was it here? No it was farther on. But the earth has been dug up!' Ibarra watched him, full of anguish.

'Yes,' he continued, 'I remember a stone beside it; the grave was rather cramped; the grave-digger was sick, and it had to be dug by some peasant from the fields. But perhaps that man can tell us what's become of the cross.'

They approached the grave-digger, who greeted them by taking off his hat with a quizzical look.

'Can you tell us which is the grave, thereabouts, that had a cross?'

The man threw a glance in the direction pointed by the servant, and fell to thinking.

'A large cross?'

'Yes, a large one,' the old man agreed eagerly, giving Ibarra a significant look. The young man's face lighted up.

'A cross tied with rattan? With carvings?'

'That's the one! It looked like this,' and the servant traced a Byzantine cross on the ground.

'Were there flowers planted around the grave?'

'That's it,' cried out the servant triumphantly, naming the flowers, and offering the grave-digger a cigar. 'Tell us where the grave is, and the cross.'

The grave-digger scratched an ear and yawned.

'The cross? Well, I burned it.'

'Burned it? But why?'

'Because the big friar told me to.'

'Who's the big friar?' asked Ibarra.

'The one who beats up people, Father Big Stick.'

Ibarra drew his hand across his forehead. 'But you can at least tell us where the grave is; you must remember that.'

The grave-digger smiled.

'The dead man isn't there any more,' he replied coolly.

'What do you mean?'

'I buried a woman in his place a week ago,' he smirked.

'Are you crazy?' asked the servant. 'Why, it's hardly a year since we buried him!'

'Well, that's the way it is. I dug up the body many months ago. Orders of the big friar. He wanted me to take it to the Chinese cemetery, but it was very heavy, and it was raining that night...'

He stopped short and fell back, frightened by the look on Ibarra's face. The young man seized him by the arm and shook him.

'Did you do it?' he asked in a voice beyond description.

'Don't be angry, sir,' the grave-digger replied, pale and trembling. 'I didn't put him in with the Chinamen. Better drown than lie with the heathen, I said to myself, and so I threw the body into the river.'

Ibarra held him tightly by the shoulders and fixed him with a piercing stare. After a long time he exclaimed: 'Poor fool, you didn't know what you were doing,' and rushed away blindly, trampling over graves and bones.

The grave-digger felt his arm and muttered:

'What a lot of trouble these dead men make! First it was the big friar. He beat me up for letting them bury that chap. I was sick at that time, too. Now this fellow comes along and nearly break my arm for unburying him. That's Spaniards for you. Bet I'll lose my job.'

Ibarra walked hurriedly, his eyes in the distance; the old servant followed him, weeping.

The sun was about to set; heavy clouds canopied the sky towards the east; a dry wind was shaking the tree-tops and whipping the bamboo clumps into a moaning. Head bare, eyes dry, without a sigh, he walked as if in flight, perhaps from the memory of his father, or perhaps from the approaching storm. He crossed the town and made for its outskirts, to the old walled house which he had not entered for so many years. From the distance it seemed to send him signals as the wind opened and closed the windows, and made the flowering bushes wave their branches merrily. In the garden doves fluttered around their cote.

But the young man had no eyes for the joys of homecoming; he was staring at a friar who was walking towards him. It was the parish priest of San Diego, the brooding Franciscan who was the commanding officer's enemy. The wind folded back the wide wings of his hat and pressed the cotton habit close to his body, outlining his thin curved flanks. He carried in his right hand a walking-stick with an ivory handle.

The two had not met before, and the young man stopped in his tracks and gave the friar a searching look. Father Salví turned his head and pretended not to notice.

After a moment's hesitation Ibarra approached him swiftly, grasped him by the shoulder, and asked in a voice so low that it was almost unintelligible:

'What have you done with my father?'

Father Salví, frightened by the terrible emotion in the young man's face, was unable to answer or even, he felt, to move.

'What have you done with my father?'

The heavy hand on the friar's shoulder was forcing him downward, and, making an effort, he answered:

'You are making a mistake, I have done nothing to your father.'

'Oh, no?' the young man insisted, forcing the priest to his knees.

'No, I assure you. It was my predecessor. It was Father Dámaso.'

The young man released him with an exclamation, struck his own forehead, and leaving poor Father Salví rushed towards his house.

Meantime the servant had come up and helped the friar to his feet.

14 • *Tasio*

AFTER leaving the cemetery the strange old man wandered aimlessly about the streets of the town.

He was a former student of philosophy who had given up his studies and his hopes of a career in obedience to his aged mother. It was not due to any lack of means or brains; on the contrary, it was precisely because his mother was rich and he, or so they said, was talented. The good lady had feared that her son might become too much of a scholar and forget God, and so had made him choose between becoming a priest and leaving college. He was in love and had chosen the latter alternative, marrying soon after. Left a widower and an orphan in less than a year, he had buried himself in his books, seeking release from sorrow, idleness, and the temptations of the cockpit; but he became so fond of his studies and of purchasing books that he neglected his estates completely and was gradually ruined.

Well-bred people called him by his real name, which was Don Anastasio, or Tasio the scholar; the ill-bred, who were in the majority, called him Tasio the fool for his unorthodox ideas and odd behaviour.

Now he seemed to have forgotten his dear skull, and smiled as he saw the dark clouds gathering above the town. A storm was brewing that afternoon; lightning flashes momentarily brightened the leaden sky; the atmosphere was oppressive and humid.

Near the church the scholar met a man in an alpaca jacket, carrying a brace of candles and a tasselled cane of office, who greeted him in Tagalog.

'Well, you're looking pleased with yourself.'

'Quite right, Mr. Mayor,' Tasio replied. 'I have something to look forward to.'

'And what may that be?'

'The storm.'

'The storm? You're thinking of taking a bath!' The Mayor cast a mocking glance at the old man's shabby clothes.

'A bath? Not a bad idea, especially after stumbling across garbage,' Tasio replied in the same vein, even more contemptuously in fact, and meeting the Mayor's eye. 'But I'm looking forward to something even better than that.'

'Well, what?'

'A lightning bolt or two that will kill and burn,' the scholar said gravely.

'Why don't you ask for the Deluge and be done with it?'

'We would all deserve it, including you and me. Take yourself, Mr. Mayor. You have there a brace of candles bought from a Chinaman's shop. For my part, I have suggested to every mayor this town has had in the last ten years the purchase of a lighting-rod, but everybody laughs it off, and would rather spend the money on fireworks and bell-pealing. You yourself went even further; the very day after I made my suggestion to you, you commissioned a Chinese foundry to cast a bell for St. Barbara, who is supposed to be our patroness in storms, although it has been scientifically established that it is dangerous to ring bells in stormy weather. Tell me, when a lightning bolt struck the town of Biñang in the year '70, why did it hit precisely the church tower, destroying the clock and an altar beneath it? What was St. Barbara's little bell doing then?'

There was a flash of lightning, and the Mayor paled and crossed himself: 'Jesus, Mary, Joseph! Blessed St. Barbara!'

Tasio let out a laugh.

'The name of your patroness suits you perfectly,' he punned in Spanish and went off towards the church.

Inside, sacristans were making a catafalque out of two large tables placed one above the other, covered with black linen with white stripes and painted skulls, and surrounded by large tapers in wooden candelabra.

'Are you doing it for the souls of the dead or the price of the candles?' he asked.

Then, seeing two boys about ten and seven years old, he went towards them without pausing for a reply.

'Coming with me, boys?' he asked them. 'Your mother has cooked you a dinner fit for friars.'

'The head sacristan won't let us go until eight, sir,' the older boy answered. 'I hope I can get my pay tonight for mother.'

'Ah. And where are you going now?'

'To the tower, sir, to toll for the Holy Souls in Purgatory.'

'Going to the tower, eh? Be careful, now, keep away from the bells if the storm breaks.'

He followed them with pitying eyes as they climbed the stairs leading to the choir loft, and then left the church.

Outside he rubbed his eyes, looked again at the sky, and murmured:

'Now I'd be sorry for any lightning.'

With bowed head, sunk in thought, he was walking towards the outskirts of the town when a voice called out to him in Spanish from a window, with an invitation to call. Raising his head, he saw a man, thirtyish in age, who was smiling down at him.

'What are you reading there?' asked Tasio, pointing to a book in the man's hand.

'Very suitable reading for this season. It's called *The Sufferings of the Blessed Souls in Purgatory,*' his friend replied good-humouredly.

'Man, man, man!' exclaimed the old man in rising tones of admiration as he entered the house. 'The author must be very clever indeed to be able to write about that.'

At the head of the stairs he was welcomed by the house-owner and his wife. His name was Don Filipo Lino; hers, Doña Teodora Viña. Don Filipo was the equivalent of a Vice Mayor in the town, and the head of a party that was almost liberal, if such a thing as a party, and a party of liberals at that, had been possible in a Philippine town in those times.

'The son of the late Don Rafael has returned from Europe. Did you see him in the cemetery?'

'Yes,' said Tasio. 'I saw him as he was leaving his carriage.'

'They say he was searching for his father's grave. It must have been a terrible blow.'

The scholar shrugged his shoulders.

'Then you feel no concern for him in his misfortune?' asked the young housewife.

'Madam, you know that only six people saw Don Rafael to his grave, and I was one of them. It was I who went to see the Governor General himself when everybody here, including the authorities, was keeping his mouth shut after the shocking profanation of his grave—all this despite the fact I have always preferred to honour a good man while he lives rather than when he is dead.'

'And so?'

'But for all that, ma'am, I do not believe in hereditary—monarchies. Perhaps because I have a little Chinese blood from my mother, I think somewhat like the Chinese. I honour the father for his son, but not the son for his father. Let each one receive his reward or punishment for his own deeds, not for the deeds of others.'

The woman changed the topic and asked: 'Have you had a Mass said for your deceased wife, as I advised yesterday?'

'No,' replied the old man with a smile.

'What a pity!' she exclaimed with real sorrow. 'They say that until tomorrow at ten o'clock the souls of the dead will wander freely, waiting for the living to pray for their release from Purgatory. They say that a Mass said at this time is worth five on other days, or even six, as the parish priest said this morning.'

'Well, now, it seems we must make the most of this special season, eh?'

'Doray!' Don Filipo intervened. 'You know that Don Anastasio does not believe in Purgatory.'

'Not believe in Purgatory, do you say?' protested the old man, half-rising from his seat. 'Why, I even know something of its history!'

'The history of Purgatory!' the couple showed surprise. 'Come now, you must tell it to us.'

'You don't know it, and yet you have Masses said for the benefit of souls there, and you speak of their sufferings! Well, since it has started to rain and it looks as if it will last for some time, we can at least try not to be bored.'

While Tasio collected his thoughts, Don Filipo closed his book and Doray seated herself at his side, determined not to believe a word.

'Purgatory,' began old Tasio, 'existed long before Our Lord Jesus Christ came into this world. According to Father Astete it must have been located in the very centre of the globe; on the other hand, according to a monk cited by Father Girard, it was to be found in the neighbourhood of the famous monastery of Cluny. However, for our purpose, the actual site doesn't matter. Now then, who were being roasted in these fires lighted at the very creation of the world? For they must date to the very beginning of time; according to Christian philosophy God created nothing new after He rested.'

'But Purgatory could have existed *in potentia*, that is to say, potentially, even if not *in actu* or actually,' objected the Vice Mayor.

'A very fine distinction! However, I must point out that there were those who knew it to exist actually. One of them was Zarathustra or Zoroaster, who wrote part of the Avesta and founded a religion with certain points of similarity to our own. Zarathustra, according to the scholars, lived at least eight hundred years before Christ; I say at least, because Gaffarel, after considering the opinions of Plato, Xanthus of Lydia, Pliny, Hermipus, and Eudoxus, judged him to have antedated our era by twenty-five hundred years. Be that as it may, the fact is that Zarathustra was already speaking in his time of a kind of Purgatory,.and taught the means of escaping from it. The living, he said, could redeem the souls of those who had died in sin by reciting passages of the sacred book, Avesta, and performing good works, on condition, however, that this be done by a relative within the fourth generation. This season of suffrage lasted five days every year. Later, when this belief had become deeply rooted among the people, the priests saw it could be made into a good business, and exploited those "prisons of impenetrable darkness where dwells remorse", to use Zarathustra's language. They laid down the rule that for a *derem* a coin said to be of little value, a soul could be saved a year of suffering; however, since there were sins against that religion which were punished by three hundred to a thousand years of suffering, such as lying, bad faith, the breaking of a plighted word, etc., the result was that the rascals pocketed millions of *derems*. Here you will observe something that already resembles our Purgatory, although, of course, we must keep in mind the difference in religions.'

A lightning flash, followed by a clap of thunder, brought Doray to her feet; crossing herself she exclaimed: 'Jesus, Mary, Joseph!' and left the room, explaining that she was going to burn a palm leaf blessed on Palm Sunday, the traditional protection in stormy weather, and to light votive candles.

The rain now started pouring down, and watching the young housewife out of the room with his eyes, the scholar continued:

'Now that she has left us, we can discuss this matter more philosophically. Doray may be rather superstitious but she is a good Catholic, and I hate to destroy anyone's faith. Pure intuitive faith differs as much from fanaticism as fire from smoke, or music from mere noise; those who confuse the two are like the deaf. Among ourselves we can say that the idea of Purgatory is good, uplifting, and reasonable. It links the living and the dead, and leads to a more honest life. The evil lies in the way the concept is abused. But now let's see how the idea of Purgatory, which is absent from both the Old and the New Testaments, became Catholic doctrine. Neither Moses nor Jesus Christ make the slightest mention of Purgatory, and the only text from the Bible that can be cited, one from the Second Book of Maccabees, Chapter Twelve, on prayers for the dead "for their guilt's undoing", is insufficient; furthermore, this book was pronounced apocryphal by the Council of Laodicea, and the Holy Catholic Church sanctioned it only much later. Nor did the pagans believe in anything like it. The much-quoted passage from the sixth book of Virgil's Aeneid on penances after death could not have been an expression of such a belief, even though it gave St. Gregory the Great an excuse to speak of "drowned souls," and was developed by Dante in his Divine Comedy. The Brahmins, the Buddhists, the Egyptians who gave Greece and Rome the idea of Charon and Avernus—none of them had anything like the concept of Purgatory. I do not even mention the religions of the northern European peoples; these were religions fit for warriors, troubadours, and hunters, but not for philosophers, and although their beliefs and rites still survive under Christian forms, the religions themselves could not follow the hordes to the sackings of Rome and found no place in the Capitol. They were religions born on the northern mists that vanished under the midday sun. Anyway, the early Christians did not believe in Purgatory. They died in the cheerful confidence that they would soon see God face to face. Apparently the first Fathers of the Church to make mention of Purgatory were St. Clement of Alexandria, Origen, and St. Irinaeus, and they were influenced perhaps by the religion of Zarathustra, which was still flourishing at that time throughout the Orient; indeed we come across frequent rebukes of Origen's Orientalism. St. Irinaeus gave as proof of the existence of Purgatory Christ's stay underground for three days after his death, three days, so to speak, in Purgatory, and from this he concluded that each soul would have to stay there until the Resurrection of the Body; but he would seem to be contradicted in this by Christ's promise to the Good Thief on Calvary: "This day thou shalt be with Me in Paradise." St. Augustine also speaks of Purgatory; while not affirming its existence, he does not, on the other hand, believe it impossible, on the supposition that the punishment which we receive in this life for our sins might well be continued in the next.'

'The devil take St. Augustine!' cried Don Filipo. 'Weren't our sufferings in this life enough for him? Why think of their extension?'

'Well, that's how the matter stood: some believed in Purgatory, others did not. Although St. Gregory went so far as to say that "it must be believed that any venial sins are subject to the penalty of the fires of Purgatory", nothing was done definitely until the year 1439, that is to say, eight centuries later, when the Council of Florence declared that there should exist a purifying fire for the souls of those who had died in the love of God but without having fully satisfied Divine Justice. Finally, the Council of Trent under Pius V, in its twenty-fifth session in 1563, issued the decree on Purgatory which starts with the words: "When the Catholic Church, inspired by the Holy Ghost", etc., and which states that the suffrages of the living, their prayers, alms, and other good works, were the most efficient means of liberating souls from Purgatory, second only to the Holy Sacrifice of the Mass. The Protestants, however, do not believe in Purgatory, and neither do the Greek Orthodox clergy. They do not find a basis for it in the Bible; they say that death puts an end to the time when a man can gain merit or suffer its loss; and they argue that the authority given to the Apostles to "bind on earth" does not include the authority to "bind in Purgatory". Of course, it may be countered that, Purgatory being the centre of the globe, it naturally falls under the jurisdiction of St. Peter. But I should never end if I were to repeat here everything that has been said on the subject. Some day when you feel like discussing it with me, come along to my house, and there we shall consult books and thresh it out freely and undisturbed. Now I must go; I don't know why a pious tradition gives license to robbery on the eve of All Souls'; you officials tolerate it; and I fear for my books. I wouldn't mind it if they were stolen to be read, but I know that there are those who want to burn them to do me a good turn, and that kind of good turn, worthy of the Caliph Omar who burned the famous library in Alexandria, is frightening. Some think me already damned because of my books...'

Meantime Doray had returned, carrying a little brazier with dry palm leaves that gave off a penetrating but pleasant perfume.

'All the same,' she asked with a smile, 'I suppose you do believe in damnation?'

'I really don't know, ma'am, what God will do with me,' replied old Tasio thoughtfully. 'When I am dying, I shall place myself in His hands without fear, to do with me as He will. But something occurs to me.'

'What's that?'

'If only Catholics can be saved, and of these only five per cent, according to many priests, and if we are to believe the statistics that Catholics are only one-twelfth of the population of the earth, it would seem that thousands upon thousands of human beings would have been damned during the countless centuries before the coming of the Redeemer, and that now, even after the Son of God Himself had died for us, only five out of every twelve hundred could be saved! Surely not! I prefer to believe and say with Job that God would "as well wrestle with a flying leaf, chase a wisp of straw!" No, the infliction of so much suffering is impossible; to believe it is to blaspheme!'

'What would you have, after all? God's justice, God's perfect goodness—'

'But God, All-Just and All-Good, could see the future before creation,' replied the old man with a shudder. 'Man is by definition a contingent, not a necessary, being; that is to say, he does not have in himself a sufficient reason for existence, and would not exist without God. God should not have created him at all if, to make one human being happy, it were necessary to send hundreds upon hundreds to eternal damnation, and all for inherited faults or a moment's weakness. If this were true, you had better strangle your child in his sleep. If this were not blasphemy against the God who should be All-Good, then the Phoenician Moloch, sanguinary deity, horrible idol, fed on human sacrifices and the blood of innocents, in whose brazen belly were burned babes torn from the bosom of their mothers, would be esteemed by comparison a timid virgin, a veritable friend, the Mother of Humanity!'

Distraught by these reflections, the old man, scholar or fool, rushed out of the house and down the streets in rain and darkness. Then a blinding flash and a terrible peal of thunder lighted the figure of the old man; his arms were raised to heaven as he cried:

'You protest! But indeed I know that You are not cruel, and that I should only call You by the name of the All-Good!'

15 • *The Bell-ringers*

AS lightning bolt and thunder peal followed one upon the other it seemed that God was writing His name in fire upon a trembling sky. The rain fell in torrents, hurled this way and that by a screaming wind. In the brief intervals of silence the overawed church bells could be heard tolling their melancholy prayers for the dead.

The two boys to whom the scholar had spoken were in the second story of the church tower. The younger one, Crispín, a timid boy with large black eyes, pressed himself as closely as he could to his brother, Basilio, who resembled him except that his eyes were more deeply set and his expression more determined. Both were dressed shabbily, their clothes patched and mended. They were seated on a length of lumber, each of them holding the end of a rope hanging from the darkness above them. The wind drove the rain against them and shook the flame of the candle set upon a great stone, which, on Good Fridays, was rolled on the floor of the choir loft to imitate the thunder that was said to have marked the Crucifixion.

'Pull on your rope, Crispín,' said Basilio to his brother.

The latter hung on it with all his strength, but could produce only a weak peal that was instantly drowned by an echoing thunder clap.

'If only we were home with mother,' he sighed, looking at his brother. 'I wouldn't be scared there.'

The older boy did not reply; he was watching the candle drip away with a worried look.

'Nobody calls me a thief there,' Crispín added. 'Mother wouldn't allow it. If she only knew they beat me!'

Basilio looked away from the candle, raised his head, and holding the end of the rope between his teeth pulled on it strongly. Overhead the bell rang loud and clear.

'We're not going to live like this all our lives, are we, brother?' Crispín went on. 'I wish I were sick at home. I wish I'd fall sick tomorrow. I wish I were sick a long time. Then mother would take care of me, and wouldn't let me come back here. Then they wouldn't call me a thief, and they'd have to stop beating me. You could fall sick too.'

'No,' answered Basilio. 'Then we'd all die. We wouldn't have anything to eat, and it would break mother's heart.'

Crispín fell silent; after a while he asked: 'How much will you make this month?'

'Two pesos. They've fined me three times.'

'Pay what they say I stole. Do pay it, brother.'

'Are you crazy, Crispín? Mother wouldn't have anything to eat. The head sacristan says you stole two ounces, and two ounces are thirty-two pesos!'

The younger boy counted thirty-two on his fingers. 'Six hands and two fingers,' he reckoned thoughtfully. 'One finger, one peso. One peso, how many coppers?'

'One hundred and sixty.'

'One hundred and sixty coppers! And how many are one hundred and sixty?'

'Thirty-two hands,' said Basilio.

Crispín stared at his fingers. 'Thirty-two hands,' he echoed. 'Six hands and two fingers, and each finger thirty-two hands, and each finger of the thirty-two hands a copper. So many coppers! You couldn't count them in three days. And if you really had them you could buy slippers, a hat to wear when the sun is high, an umbrella for when it rains, food, nice clothes for you and mother; I'm sorry I didn't steal it after all!'

'Crispín!' his brother reproved him.

'Don't be angry. The parish priest said he would beat me to death if the money wasn't found. Well, if I had stolen it, I could give it back, couldn't I? And if I didn't give it back, and they killed me, then at least you and mother could have some clothes, couldn't you? I wish I'd stolen it.' Basilio silently pulled on the rope, and then replied with a sigh: 'What I'm afraid of is what mother will say when she hears about it. She'll give you a scolding.'

'Do you think so?' asked the youngster taken aback. 'But you'll tell her they beat me up, and I'll show her my bruises, and look at my pocket! Why, it's full of holes. I've only had one copper, ever; I got it for Christmas, but the friar took it away from me yesterday. I've never seen a more beautiful copper. Mother won't believe it; she won't believe it!'

'If the friar tells her so...'

Crispín began to cry and sobbed:

'Then you go home by yourself. I won't go home. Tell mother I'm sick. I'm not going home.'

'Don't cry, Crispín,' said Basilio. 'Mother won't believe it, so don't cry. Old Tasio says there's a good supper waiting for us.'

Crispín raised his head and looked at his brother.

'A good supper! I haven't had anything to eat yet; they wouldn't give me anything to eat until the money was found. But suppose mother believes them! You must tell her the sacristan is lying, and the friar who believes him, they're all lying; they say we're thieves because our father is a bad man who...'

A head appeared at the head of the stairs and, like Medusa's, it froze the words on the boy's lips. . It was a long narrow face, framed with lank black hair, with smoked spectacles to conceal a blind eye; it belonged to the head sacristan, who made it a habit to move silently and without warning.

The two boys shivered.

'Basilio, I fine you two sovereigns for not ringing the bells in the proper timing,' he said in a voice so dead he might have lost the use of his vocal chords. 'And for you, Crispín, you are staying until what you have stolen has been found—the night if necessary.'

Crispín turned a beseeching look towards his brother.

'But we already have permission,' Basilio objected timidly, 'and mother will be waiting for us at eight.'

'Well, you're not going home at eight, either, but at ten.'

'But, sir, curfew's at nine, and it's a long way home.'

'Are you giving me orders?' the head sacristan asked peevishly, and seized Crispín by the arm to drag him away.

'Sir,' pleaded Basilio, holding on to his brother defensively, 'it's a week since we saw mother!'

The head sacristan slapped the boy's hand away and pulled at Crispín. The boy threw himself on the floor crying, and called to his brother. 'Don't leave me; they're going to kill me!' But the sacristan paid no heed and dragged him down the stairs into the shadows.

Basilio was left speechless as he heard his brother's body rolling down the steps, a sharp cry, a series of slaps, a sobbing that gradually faded away.

He was scarcely breathing, his eyes staring, his fists closed.

'When will I be old enough to work in the fields!' he muttered between clenched teeth and ran down the stairs to the choir loft. He listened to his brother's voice as it cried out even more faintly to his mother and his brother; then a door closed. He stood a moment still shaking, covered with sweat; he buried his teeth in his fist to muffle a cry from the heart as his eyes searched the shadows of the church. A votive lamp burned feebly; the catafalque could be discerned in the centre of the nave; the doors were closed and the windows barred.

Abruptly he turned and went up the tower stairs, past the second story where the candle still burned, and up to the third. He untied the ropes from the bell clappers, and went back; he was pale, but his eyes shone, not with tears.

The rain was slackening and the sky slowly clearing.

Basilio knotted the ropes together, tied one end to the balustrade, and, without bothering to put out the candle, let himself down into the darkness.

A few minutes later, along one of the streets of the town, a challenge was heard, and then two shots, but nobody took alarm and everything was silent again.

16 • Sisa

IN the dark night the townspeople slept. Having said the three parts of the Rosary with special litanies for the dead, prayed the Novena for the Holy Souls, and lighted candles before sacred images, the rich and well-to-do slept peacefully, well satisfied that they had performed their duties toward those who had bequeathed them their fortunes. The next day they would hear the three Masses that each priest was allowed to say on All Souls', make the offering of two pesos for one more Mass to be said for their intention, and perhaps make another contribution to win an indulgence. They found it easier to satisfy divine than human justice.

But the poor and the indigent, who scarcely made enough money to keep body and soul together, and had to bribe petty bureaucrats, clerks, and guards to let them alone, did not sleep in the peace which romantic poets ascribe to them; perhaps such poets have never been poor. This eve of All Souls' the poor were oppressed by their thoughts; they had said their prayers in their hearts, troubled by their ignorance of Novenas, ejaculations, psalms, and the pious formulas composed by friars for those would could not think or feel for themselves, or who, even if they could, would have been unable to understand them. The poor had prayed in their own language for themselves and for all those in whose love they had found happiness, and their language, while it may have sounded like an invocation, was in reality a lament and a complaint. Would He, Who had blessed poverty, and the suffering souls be content with simple prayers offered before a bad engraving by the light of a crude lamp, or would they perhaps look for tapers before images of the Crucified, artistically blood-stained, and Virgins with aristocratic mouths and eyes made of glass? Would they require Masses said mechanically in Latin by some priest? Had the Church, founded for suffering humanity, forgotten her mission to comfort the afflicted and the down-trodden and to humble the powerful in their pride; and were her promises now only for the rich, who could afford to pay?

A poor widow, watching over her sleeping children somewhere in the town that night, worried about the money for the indulgences which would shorten the sufferings of her parents and husband. Every peso, she considered, meant a week of comforts for her children, a week perhaps of laughter and of fun, a month's savings, a dress for her daughter who was fast becoming a woman. But it was necessary to make sacrifices: the Church would not save the souls of her dear ones for nothing; indulgences were not given away, they must be paid for. She must work nights, sleep less; her daughter must bare her legs a little longer; they must eat less, if necessary; the cost of salvation was high. These were the widow's thoughts as she lay on her straw mat on the floor, rocking the hammock which hung from the rafters and where her youngest slept. The baby breathed in restful ease; once in a while he grunted and chewed; it was his hungry stomach, unsatisfied with the leftovers of his elders, dreaming of food. It was hard indeed for the poor to enter the kingdom of heaven!

The cicadas sang monotonously in the night, joining their constant cry to the chirping of the crickets in the grass. The mole crept out of its hole in search of food. The gekko, reassured by the passing of the rain, thrust its head through a hole in a worm-eaten tree, and added to the concert his ominous discordant note. Dogs howled in the streets, convincing the superstitious that ghosts and spirits were about, but in truth neither dogs nor insects remarked the many sorrows of man.

Sisa, the mother of Basilio and Crispín, lived an hour away from the town. She had married a selfish and cynical man, a cockfight addict who had deserted her for a life of aimless wandering, and now she lived only for her sons. The rare meetings between husband and wife were always painful, for, having gambled away her few jewels, and finding that she no longer had any money left for his whims and vices, he fell into the habit of beating her. She had a weak character, with more heart than brains, and could only weep for her loves. Her husband was to her a god, just as her sons were angels in her eyes. He knew how much she loved and feared him, and, in the manner of all false gods, only became more cruel and capricious.

When Sisa had consulted him about putting Basilio in Church service he had asked noncommittally, his face darker than ever, and his hands scarcely pausing in their caresses of his fighting cock, whether the boy would make much money. She had not dared press for an answer; in any case, she was hard up, she wanted her boys to learn how to read and write in school, and she had gone ahead. Her husband had nothing to say about that either.

The eve of All Souls', at about half-past ten or eleven, when the stars were already shining in the sky which the storm had cleared, Sisa sat on a wooden bench watching a handful of twigs burning in her stove, a primitive tripod of raw rocks on which a little rice-pot was cooking. On the coals were three dried sardines of the kind that were then sold three for two coppers.

A melancholy smile on her face, her chin on the palm of her hand, her eyes on the weak yellowish flame of the bamboo so quickly consumed, she thought of the amusing riddle about the rice-pot and the fire which her son Crispín had once put to her.

Black sat down; and after
Red tickled him, bubbled with laughter.

She was still young; once she must have been pretty and charming. Her eyes, which, like her character, her sons had inherited, were beautiful, deep, and long-lashed; her nose was well-proportioned; her pale lips attractively drawn. Her complexion was what the Tagalog call *kayumangging kaligatan*, that is to say, a clear golden brown. In spite of her youth, sorrow, or perhaps hunger, had made her pale cheeks sunken; and if her abundant hair, once her greatest glory, was still well groomed, with a simple chignon unadorned with pins and combs, it was not out of coquetry but habit.

She had not left her hut for several days, working on a dress she had been told to finish as soon as possible. She needed the money so much she had missed Mass that morning; she would have lost at least two hours going to and coming back from town: poverty makes one sin! She had finished the dress, but she had not been paid with more than a promise.

All day she had rehearsed the pleasures of the night. Her sons were coming, and she planned a treat for them. She bought sardines, plucked the best tomatoes in her garden (they were Crispín's favourite dish), and begged her neighbour, Tasio the scholar, who lived half a kilometre away, for some dried wild boar and a wild duck's leg (Basilio's favourites). Full of expectations she cooked the whitest rice, which she herself had gardened. It was indeed a dinner fit for friars.

But, by an unfortunate coincidence, her husband had shown up; he had eaten the rice, the dried wild boar's meat, the duck's leg, five sardines, and the tomatoes. Watching him, Sisa had said nothing, although she felt he was eating her own flesh. Only when he was satisfied did he remember to ask after his sons; then Sisa was able to smile. The father had asked after his children; and that for her was more than eating. Happily she promised herself not to eat that night; there was not enough left for three.

He picked up his cock and made to leave.

'Don't you want to see them?' she asked tremulously. 'Old Tasio told me they would be a little late. Crispín can read now, and maybe Basilio will bring home his pay.'

On hearing this her husband hesitated, but his better nature prevailed.

'In this case, keep a peso for me,' he said and went off.

Sisa wept bitterly. But she remembered her sons and dried her tears. She cooked fresh rice and prepared the three remaining sardines; each of her sons could have one and a half.

'They'll be hungry,' she thought. 'They'll come a long way and they won't be choosy.'

She had her ears cocked to the slightest noise; they might be footsteps; strong and clear, that would be Basilio; light and uneven, Crispín.

The *kalaw* had called in the forest two or three times since the rains had stopped, but her sons had not yet come.

She put the sardines inside the rice-pot so they would not get cold, and went to the door of her hut to look down the road. To amuse herself she sang. She had a beautiful voice; indeed when her sons heard her sing a *kundiman* they wept without knowing why.

But that night her voice trembled and she stopped her singing and stared into the darkness. There was nothing from town except a wind shaking the rain-water from the broad banana leaves.

Suddenly she saw a black dog in front of her; the animal sniffed something along the path. Sisa was frightened, picked up a stone, and threw it. The dog ran off, howling.

Sisa was not superstitious, but she had heard so much said about presentiments and black dogs that she was frightened. She hurriedly closed the door and seated herself near the light; the dark breeds fancies and peoples the empty air with spectres.

She tried to pray, and asked God and the Virgin to protect her sons, especially her little Crispín, but remembering them distracted her, and her mind's eye lingered over their faces which had smiled so often on her dreams and vigils in the night. Suddenly she felt her hair rise, her eyes opened wide, as, illusion or reality, she saw Crispín beside the stove where they had so often sat and chatted: now he said nothing and looked at her with his great pensive eyes, smiling.

'Mother, open the door! Open up, mother,' said the voice of Basilio outside. Sisa shuddered and the vision disappeared.

17 • *Basilio*
Life is but a dream

BASILIO stumbled into his mother's arms. A chill seized Sisa's heart when she saw him alone. She tried to speak but made no sound, wanted to hold her son but could not find the strength, and could not even weep.

But the sight of blood on the boy's forehead made her cry out.

'Don't worry, mother,' Basilio said. 'And as for Crispín, he stayed behind in the parish house.'

'Stayed behind? Is he all right?'

The boy raised his eyes reassuringly, and Sisa wept at last, passing from an extremity of anguish to one of relief. She embraced her son and kissed his blood-stained forehead.

'Crispín is all right—you left him in the parish house! But why are you hurt, darling? Did you fall down and hurt yourself?'

She ran her hands over him.

'The head sacristan, when he took Crispín away, told me I couldn't leave until ten, and I ran away because it was so late. Then the sentries challenged me, I started to run, and they fired. A bullet must have grazed my forehead. I was afraid they'd catch me and make me wash down the barracks floor and beat me up; that's what they did to Pablo, and he hasn't got over it yet.'

As she thanked God for saving her son Sisa bustled about for towels, water, vinegar, and heron feathers.

'One finger's breadth lower and they would have killed you! They would have killed my son! Sentries never think of mothers!'

'You'd better say I fell off a tree. Don't tell anyone the guard went after me.'

After she had bound up Basilio's wound, Sisa asked why Crispín had stayed behind. Basilio threw her a quick glance, put his arms about her, and gradually broke to her the story about the missing money. But he was careful not to say anything about his brother being beaten.

'My good Crispín!' Sisa cried. 'How dare they say such things about my good Crispín! It's only because we're poor, and the poor have to stand for everything.'

They were silent for a while.

'Have you had anything to eat? No? There's some rice and dried fish.'

'I don't feel like eating anything. I'd like a drink of water, that's all.'

'You don't like dried fish; I know. I had something else ready for you, but your father came. You poor darling!'

'Father came?'

Instinctively Basilio looked at his mother's face and arms. Sisa felt a sudden pain in her heart as she heard the tone in which her son had put his question; she understood only too well what he had in mind, and she hastened to add:

'Yes, he was here, and he asked a lot about the two of you. He wanted so much to see you. And he was so hungry! He said that if you are always as good as you have been, he'll come back and live with us again.'

Basilio made a grimace that made his mother protest.

'I'm sorry, mother,' he said gravely. 'But aren't we better off, just the three of us, you, Crispín, and I? But you're crying. I'm sorry. Forget it.' She sighed. The oil in the lamp was running low.

'Are you sure you'll have nothing to eat? Then let's go to bed. It's getting late.'

Sisa closed up the hut and banked the handful of coals in the kitchen stove. Thus does man cover up with the ashes of outward indifference the burning emotions of his soul lest they be extinguished by careless exposure to one's fellows.

Basilio said his prayers and lay down near his mother, who was on her knees.

He was hot and cold by turns; with eyes closed he thought of his brother, who had looked forward so much to sleeping by his mother's side, and would now be sobbing and shivering with fear in some dark corner of the parish house. Crispín's cries echoed in his ears, just as he had heard them in the church tower; but he was tired, and so fell asleep and dreamed.

He saw a chamber lit by two candles. The parish priest, cane in hand, listened sombrely to the head sacristan, who spoke to him in an unknown language and with terrifying gestures. Crispín was there before them, trembling, his tearful eyes searching all around him for some friend, some hiding place. The friar now turned upon him and asked him exasperated questions. The cane whistled through the air. The boy ran to hide behind the sacristan but the latter seized him, held him tight, and offered him to the anger of the friar. The poor boy struggled, kicked, screamed, threw himself on the floor, rolled, rose, fled, slipped, fell, warding off the blows with his hands, hiding them when they were cut, howling. Basilio saw his brother writhing, beating his head against the floor; saw and heard the cane; saw his brother rise and, mad with pain, throw himself on his tormentors and bite the friar in the hand. The latter screamed and let fall the cane. The sacristan seized a stick, hit the boy on the head, knocking him senseless. The friar kicked Crispín again and again, but the boy no longer defended himself, no longer screamed. He rolled along the floor inertly, leaving a wet trail behind him.

The voice of Sisa called him back to reality.

'What's the matter? Why are you crying?'

'I was dreaming,' Basilio answered, raising himself, covered with sweat. 'Oh, God! Say it was a dream, mother, only a dream.'

'What did you dream?'

The boy did not answer. He sat up to dry his tears and sweat. The hut was in darkness.

'A dream, a dream,' Basilio repeated in a low voice.

'Tell me what you dreamed,' his mother said when he had gone back to bed. 'I can't sleep.'

'Well,' he whispered, 'I dreamed that we went harvesting, in a field full of flowers. The women had baskets full of grain, and the children too... I don't remember anything more, mother, really I don't.'

Sisa did not insist. She did not believe in dreams.

'Mother,' said Basilio after a few minutes of silence. 'I thought up a plan tonight.'

'What plan?' Sisa, humble in everything, was humble even with her children, whom she believed cleverer than she was.

'I don't want to work for the parish priest any more!'

'What!'

'Listen, mother. I was thinking; today the son of Don Rafael came back from Spain, and he's sure to be as good as his father. Well, then, mother, tomorrow, go fetch Crispín from the parish house, and collect my pay; tell them I don't want to work there any more. Then, as soon as I'm well again, I'll go and see Don Crisóstomo and ask him to please let me be his herdsman; I'm old enough now to take care of his oxen and carabaos. Crispín can take lessons from old Tasio. He doesn't flog, and he's a good man, even if the parish priest doesn't think so. Anyway, why should we be afraid of the friar? Can he make us any poorer? Believe me, mother, the old man is all right; I have seen him in church many times, when there was nobody else there; he gets down on his knees and prays; it's true. So, mother, it's all settled. I'm not going to work for the friar any more. One doesn't make much, and then they fine away everything you earn. Everybody complains about it. I'm going to be a herdsman instead, I'll take very good care of the herds, and so I'll make the owner like me. Maybe they'll let me milk a cow; Crispín likes milk a lot. Who knows, maybe they'll give me a calf if they see I'm behaving well; we'll take care of it and fatten it up like our hen. I'll pick fruits in the forest and sell them in town together with the vegetables from our garden, and then we'll have some money. I'll lay traps and snares to catch birds and wild goats, I'll fish in the river, and when I'm bigger I'll go hunting. I could also cut firewood; we could sell it or else give it to the owner of the herds; that way we'll keep him happy. When I'm old enough to plough, I'll ask him for a piece of land to grow sugar cane or corn and you won't have to sew any more until midnight. We'll have new clothes every holiday, and we'll eat meat and big fishes. Meantime I'll be my own master, we'll see each other and eat together every day. And since old Tasio says Crispín is very clever, we'll send him to Manila to study; I'll support him by working. Isn't that right, mother? He'll be a doctor yet. What do you say?'

'What can I say? Yes, darling,' answered Sisa embracing her son.

But she noted that her son did not include his father in his plans for the future, and she wept silently.

Basilio kept on talking about his plans with the confidence of that age which sees nothing more than what it wants to see. Sisa said yes to everything, everything looked good to her. Sleep fell once more on the tired boy's eyelids, and this time the good fairy of whom Andersen tells us opened up for him her beautiful parasol full of happy pictures.

He already saw himself a shepherd with his brother; they picked fruits in the forest, climbed from branch to branch, light as butterflies; they entered caves with glittering walls, bathed in springs where the sands were dust of gold and the pebbles like the stones in the Virgin's crown. The little fishes sang to them and laughed, the bushes lowered their branches, loaded with coins and fruit. Afterwards he saw a bell, hung from a tree, with a long rope to ring it; to the rope was tied a cow with a bird's nest between its horns, and Crispín was inside the bell... And so he dreamed on.

But his mother, who was not so young as he was, and had not been running for an hour, did not sleep.

18 • *The Faithful Departed*

IT must have been seven in the morning when Father Salví finished saying the last of the three Masses a priest is allowed to say on All Souls' Day; he had run through them in an hour.

'Father must be ill,' the devotees told one another. He had not moved with his usual deliberation and elegance.

Back in the sacristy Father Salví took off his vestments without saying a word, without looking at anyone.

'Look out,' the sacristans whispered among themselves. 'We're in for a bad time. It's going to rain fines, all because of the two brothers.'

He left the sacristy to go up to the parish house, in whose courtyard, which had been converted into a school, some seven or eight women were waiting for him, seated on the benches, while a man walked to and fro. When they saw him coming, the women rose and one came forward to kiss his hand, but the priest made such an impatient gesture that she stopped midway.

'Father Tightwad must have lost a sovereign!' she snickered, offended by this reception. Not give her his hand to kiss, she, the monitor of the Confraternity, Sister Rufa! It was unheard of.

'This morning he did not sit in the confessional,' added Sister Sipa, a toothless old woman. 'I wanted to make my Confession in order to go to Communion and gain indulgences.'

'Well, I am sorry for you,' replied a young woman with a candid face. 'This week I gained three plenary indulgences, and applied them all to the soul of my husband.'

'Badly done, Sister Juana,' said the offended Rufa. 'One plenary indulgence was enough to get him out of Purgatory; you should not waste the holy indulgences; do what I do.'

'I said to myself, the more the better,' answered the simple Sister Juana with a smile. 'But tell me, what do you do?'

Sister Rufa did not answer immediately. First she asked for some betel-nut, chewed it, looked at her audience, which listened attentively, spat to one side, and, still chewing, began:

'I do not waste a single day. Since I joined the Confraternity I have gained 157 plenary indulgences and 760,598 years of indulgences. I note down all that I gain because I like to have my accounts clear; I don't want to fool anyone, or to be fooled.'

Sister Rufa paused, chewing away. The women gazed on her admiringly, but the man who was walking to and fro stopped and told her a little disdainfully:

'Well, this year along I have gained four plenary indulgences more than you, Sister Rufa, and 100 years more, and that in spite of the fact that I have not been paying much this year.'

'More than I? More than 189 plenary indulgences and 994,856 years?' Sister Rufa repeated, rather put out.

'That is to say, eight plenaries and 115 years more, and that in a few months,' repeated the man, from whose neck hung grubby rosaries and scapulars.

'Well, it isn't strange,' said Rufa, admitting defeat. 'After all you are the prefect of the Confraternity.'

The man gave a flattered smile.

'Indeed it isn't strange that I should gain more indulgences than you; I could almost, almost, say that I gain indulgences even in my sleep.'

'And what do you do with them?' four or five voices asked together.

'Pschaw,' the man answered, making a grimace of supreme contempt, 'I give them away here and there.'

'Now that is something for which I cannot praise you,' Rufa protested. 'You'll go to Purgatory for wasting indulgences! You know what the parish priest says: for every wasted word, forty days of fire; for every wasted handsbreadth of thread, sixty; for every wasted drop of water, twenty. No doubt about it, you're going to Purgatory!'

Brother Pedro replied with supreme confidence.

'I'll know how to get out of there. I've rescued so many souls from the fire. I have made so many saints. Even on my death bed I could gain, if I wanted to, at least seven plenary indulgences, and I could save even more souls just by dying!'

And having said this, he moved away proudly.

'Nevertheless, you should do what I do. I never waste a day and I keep my accounts in order. I don't want to cheat or be cheated.'

'What do you do, then?' asked Juana.

'Well, for example, suppose I gain a one-year indulgence. I note it down in my book, and I say: Blessed St. Dominic, our Father and Lord, please find out if somebody in Purgatory has one year to go, not one day more or less. Then I flip a coin. If it's heads, then there's nobody. If it's tails, then there is. Let's say it's tails. Then I write down "Paid". Let's say that it comes out heads. Then I keep the indulgence in my credit account, and in this way accumulate groups of a hundred each, all of which are noted down carefully. It's a pity you can't use indulgences like money. Imagine if we could lend them out with interest. Why, we could save more souls. Believe me, do what I do.'

'I have a better way,' put in Sister Sipa.

'What?' Rufa exclaimed taken aback. 'Better?' Impossible. Nothing can be better than my system.'

'Now, one moment, listen, and you will be convinced, sister,' replied old Sipa peevishly.

'Well, come on, let's hear it,' said the others.

After a portentous cough the old woman began: 'You all know very well that by saying the prayers, Blessed be thy purity, and My Lord Jesus Christ, our most sweet Father, by the joy, etc., one may gain a ten-year indulgence for each and every letter.'

She was immediately interrupted by various voices. 'Twenty!' 'No, less!' 'Five!'

'Give one, take another, it doesn't matter. Now, when one of my servants breaks a dish, a tumbler, or a cup, I make them pick up the pieces, and for each piece, even the smallest one, they have to say either the Blessed be thy purity prayer or the My Lord Jesus Christ, our most sweet Father one. Well, all these indulgences which I gain I apply to the blessed souls in Purgatory. Everybody in my house knows that. Except the cats.'

'But,' Rufa objected, 'these indulgences are gained not by you but by your servants.'

'And who pays for my cups and saucers, may I ask? They're happy enough to pay me that way, and so am I. They save themselves a beating—except perhaps for a rap on the head, or a pinch.'

'I'll do it too!'

'Me too!'

'And I'

But Rufa objected stubbornly: 'What if the dish has broken into only two or three pieces? You don't gain much.'

'Huh!' old Sipa replied. 'They pay just the same, then I glue the pieces together, and there's nothing lost.'

Sister Rufa had run out of objections, but young Juana said timidly:

'If you'll allow me to ask you...I am rather uncertain about something. You ladies understand so much about these things concerning Heaven, Purgatory, and Hell, while I, I do admit it, know so little.'

'What is it?'

'Many times, in Novenas and other prayer books, I come across this instruction: Three Our Fathers, three Hail Marys, and three Glorias.'

'Well?'

'What I would like to know is how to say them. Shall I say three Our Fathers one after the other, then three Hail Marys, then three Glorias, or shall I say one Our Father, then one Hail Mary, and then one Gloria, three times?'

'Why, three Our Fathers...'

'Pardon me, Sister Sipa,' Rufa interrupted. 'They should be said the other way. Males are not to be mixed with females. The Our Fathers are males, the Hail Marys are females, and the Glorias are the children.

'Pardon me, Sister Rufa. Our Father, Hail Mary, and Gloria, are like rice, victuals, and sauce, a mouthful for saints...'

'Wrong. If that's the way you pray, no wonder you never get anything you ask for.'

'And you,' replied old Sipa, 'never get much good out of your Novenas because of the way you pray.'

'Who, me?' asked Rufa rising to her feet. 'Why, just a while ago I lost a little pig. I prayed to St. Anthony, and I found it. So much so that I even sold it at a good price. There!'

'Is that so? Maybe that's why your neighbour was saying you had sold a little pig of hers.'

'Who said that? The shameless liar! Do you think I'm like you?'

The prefect had to intervene and make it up. For a while everybody had forgotten about the Lord's Prayer, and was talking about pigs.

'Come now, come, don't quarrel about a little pig, sisters. The Holy Scriptures give us a model. Even the heretics and Protestants, whose herd of swine was sent by Our Lord Jesus Christ into the sea, did not rebuke him. Shall we who are Christians and, more, brothers and sisters in the Confraternity of the Holy Rosary, quarrel about a little pig? What will our rivals, the Tertiaries, say about us?'

Everyone fell silent, impressed by the profound wisdom of the prefect, and fearful of what the Tertiaries might say. Pleased by their submissiveness, he changed his tone and continued:

'Soon the parish priest will send for us. We shall have to tell him which preacher we have chosen from among the three he proposed yesterday: Father Dámaso, Father Martín, or the vicar. I don't know whether the Tertiaries have made their own choice yet, but we shall have to decide now.'

'The vicar,' Juana murmured timidly.

'Huh, the vicar doesn't know how to give a sermon,' said Sipa. 'Father Martín is better.'

'Oh, Father Martín! He hasn't got the voice for it,' another exclaimed disdainfully: 'Father Dámaso would be best.'

'That one, that one!' cried Rufa. 'Father Dámaso knows how to give a good sermon. He's an actor, that one!'

'But we don't understand him,' mumbled Juana.

'Because he is deep! Anyway, as long as he speaks well...'

At this point Sisa entered, a basket on her head. She greeted the women and went up the stairs.

'Well, if she can go up, we can too!' they told one another.

As she went up the stairs, Sisa felt her heart beating violently. She did not know what she could tell the priest to appease his anger or what she could say on behalf of her son. That morning, in the first light of dawn, she had gone down to her kitchen-garden and picked the best-looking vegetables, which she had then arranged in a basket lined with banana leaves and topped with flowers. The priest liked watercress in his salad, she knew, and so she had gone to search for it by the river. Then she had put on her best clothes, and, without waking her son, taken the road to town, the basket on her head.

Now she went up the stairs slowly, trying to make as little noise as possible, listening intently lest perhaps she might hear a familiar voice, a fresh, childish voice.

But, hearing nothing, and meeting no one, she went to the kitchen.

There she looked in every corner, and saw only servants and sacristans, who received her greetings coldly, hardly answering.

She took no offence, and asked: 'Where can I leave these vegetables?'

'There—anywhere,' said the cook, scarcely looking up from the capon he was plucking.

Sisa arranged the egg plants, the *amargosos*, the *patolas*, the *zarzalida*, and the tender sprigs of watercress on a table, covered them with flowers, and with an uncertain smile asked a servant, who seemed more approachable than the cook:

'Could I speak to the priest?'

'He's sick,' the man replied in a whisper.

'And Crispín? Is he in the sacristy, do you know?'

The servant gave her a surprised look.

'Crispín?' he asked, with a frown. 'Isn't he home? You're not going to deny it, are you?'

'Basilio is at home, but Crispín stayed here,' answered Sisa. 'I'd like to see him.'

'Oh, I remember! He did stay behind, but later...later he ran away. He stole a lot of things. The priest sent me to the barracks early this morning to notify the Constabulary. They must have gone to your house by now to look for the boys.'

Sisa covered her ears, opened her mouth; her lips moved soundlessly.

'What a pair of boys you have!' the cook added. 'One can see you were faithful to your husband; they've turned out just like him. Look out for that little one; he may go his father one better.'

Sisa broke into bitter tears and dropped on a bench.

'Now, don't you go crying here,' the cook shouted at her. 'Don't you know Father is sick? Go cry in the street!'

They almost pushed her down the stairs while the sisters of the Confraternity exchanged whispered guesses as to what was wrong with the priest.

The unfortunate mother covered her face with her shawl and choked back her tears.

When she reached the street, she looked uncertainly round her and then, as if she had taken a decision, walked away rapidly.

19 • *Adventures of a Schoolmaster*

> *At a play—that's all there is to it—*
> *The masses don't know if to cheer it or boo it,*
> *But they've paid for a seat*
> *You must give them a treat*
> *If you have to talk silly to do it.*
> —Lope de Vega

WITH the hypocrisy of Nature, the lake slept quietly among its mountains as if the night before it had not conspired with the storm. As the first rays of light awakened phosphorescent reflections in the water, greyish silhouettes were drawn afar, almost on the horizon: fishing nets being raised and gathered, the sails of barges and boats.

Two men dressed in deep mourning brooded silently upon the waters from an eminence. One of them was Ibarra. The other was a youth, humble in appearance, with melancholy features.

'It was here,' he said. 'Your father's body was thrown here. This is where Lieutenant Guevara and I were taken by the gravedigger.'

Ibarra gripped his hand gratefully.

'It's nothing to be thankful for,' the young man, a schoolmaster, said. 'I owed your father many favours, and the only one I could do him was to accompany him to his grave. I came here knowing no one, without recommendations, name, or fortune—as I am now. My predecessor had quit the school to go into the tobacco business. Your father befriended me, got me a house, and let me have what I needed to improve my teaching. He used to go to the school, and slip a little money to the boys who were poor but diligent; he gave them books and paper. But, like all good things, that didn't last very long.'

Ibarra uncovered himself and, for a long time, seemed to lose himself in prayer. Then he turned to his companion and asked:

'You said my father helped these poor boys. And now?'

'Now they do what they can, and study when they can.'

'What do you mean?'

'Their shirts are torn. They are ashamed to come to school.'

Ibarra fell silent.

Then, with a note of interest in his voice, he asked: 'How many students do you have now?'

'More than two hundred on the rolls. In class, twenty-five.'

'How can that be?'

The schoolmaster smiled sadly. 'That is a long and tiresome story.'

'Don't think I am asking out of mere curiosity,' Ibarra replied gravely, looking out at the far horizon. 'I have had better thoughts, and I believe that making my father's wishes come true is worth more than weeping for him, and much more than avenging him. Nature is his grave. His enemies were the people and a priest: I forgive the people because of their ignorance, and I respect the priest because of his office and because I desire respect for the religion which civilised human society. I seek inspiration in the man to whom I owe my being. That is why I am interested in education, and I should like to know the difficulties it meets with here.'

'Sir, the country will bless your memory if you bring to life your father's noble purposes,' said the schoolmaster. 'Do you want to know the difficulties encountered by education here? Well, then, in our present circumstances education will never be possible without the most powerful help, first, because the young have no inducement or encouragement to study, and secondly, because, even if they had, they would be stifled by poverty and other needs more pressing than education. They say that in Germany even the son of a peasant spends eight years in the village school. Here, who would spend half that time where there is so little to be gained from it? They learn to read and write, they memorise passages, whole books, in Spanish, without understanding a single word—how does school do any good to our village boys?'

'You see what's wrong. How is it that you have not tried to put it right?'

'Ah,' said the schoolmaster, shaking his head. 'A poor school teacher does not fight single-handed against prejudices, against certain influences. I would need, above all, a schoolhouse, a place to teach in; now I must do so on the ground-floor of the parish house, beside the carriage of the parish priest. The boys like to read out loud, and naturally, in such a place, they annoy the parish priest. Sometimes he comes down in a temper, especially when he is not feeling well, and he shouts at them, and sometimes insults me. You will understand that it is impossible, in that way, either to teach or to learn. The children lose their respect for their teacher when they see him badly used, and unable to assert his rights. If the teacher is to be listened to, if his authority is to be beyond question, he needs prestige, a good name, moral authority, a certain freedom. Allow me to give you details—sad ones. I have wanted to introduce reforms, and I have been laughed at. I have spoken of certain defects in the system. To correct them, I tried to teach the children Spanish; not only because those were our official instructions but also because I thought it would do everyone good. I used the simplest methods—I taught words and phrases without recourse to complicated rules, I planned to teach them grammar only when they were used to the language. After a few weeks the smartest ones could almost understand me, and they could even make up a few phrases.'

The schoolmaster hesitated; then he made up his mind and continued: 'I should not be ashamed of the story of my grievances. Anyone in my place would have done the same thing. As I was saying, I was making a good start. But, a few days later, Father Dámaso, who was the parish priest at that time, sent for me through the head sacristan. I knew his temper and I was afraid to keep him waiting. I went up right away and bade him good day in Spanish. For his part, by way of greeting, he had put out his hand to be kissed; he withdrew it, and without replying to me broke out into gales of laughter.

I was disconcerted; I did not know what to do. The head sacristan was present. I did not know what to say on the spur of the moment. I stared at him, and he kept laughing. I was beginning to lose my temper; I could see I was going to be imprudent; to be a good Christian and at the same time to have some dignity—these things are not incompatible. I was going-to ask him what he was laughing about when suddenly, passing from laughter to insult, he said slyly: *"Buenos días, is it? Buenos días!* That's a laugh. So you speak Spanish, do you?" And he started laughing again.'

Ibarra could not repress a smile.

'You smile,' said the schoolmaster, smiling himself. 'I admit that I did not feel like smiling at the time. I was standing. I felt the blood rushing to my head. I felt that lightning was playing round my brain. I saw the priest far away, very far away. I went up to him to answer him, not knowing what I was going to say. The head sacristan interposed himself between us. Then Father Dámaso rose and told me seriously in Tagalog: "Don't go around in borrowed clothes. Use your own native tongue and be happy with it. Don't go spoiling Spanish; it's not for you." Then he quoted a popular saying about a teacher who could not read and was a fool, yet ran a school. I wanted to stop him, but he went into his room and slammed the door. What could I do? I can barely live on my salary, and to collect it I must have his approval and go all the way to the capital of the province. What could I do against him, the chief moral, political, and civil authority in the town, supported by his Order, feared by the Government, rich, powerful, consulted, listened to, believed and obeyed always and by all? If I am insulted, I must swallow it; should I dare reply, I would be thrown out of my job, ruining my career for ever, and, for all that, the cause of education would not be advanced. On the contrary, everyone would take the side of the parish priest, and heap abuse on me, calling me presumptuous, proud, and haughty, a boor, a bad Christian, and, more likely than not, anti-Spanish and subversive. Neither learning nor zeal are expected from a schoolmaster; but only resignation, self-abasement, and passivity. God forgive me if I have betrayed my conscience and my reason, but I was born in this country, I must make a living in it, I have a mother to support, and I must go along with my fate like a drowned man borne by the tide.'

'And this incident made you lose heart completely? How have you managed since then?'

'I wish I had learned my lesson,' the schoolmaster replied. 'Then my misfortunes would have been *fewer. The truth* is that, from that time on, I grew to hate my work. I wanted to find another job, like my predecessor, because work becomes unbearable when it must be done unwillingly and with a sense of shame. Every day in school was a reminder of the insult I had suffered, and I spent very bitter hours. But what was I to do? I could not disappoint my mother; I had to tell her that her three years of self-sacrifice, which had made my career possible, had also given me happiness; I had to make believe that my profession was most respectable, the work delightful, and my path strewn with roses; that the discharge of my duties had won me friends, and only friends, that the people respected me and held me in high regard. Otherwise, without making myself any happier, I would only have made her unhappy, which would have been useless and wrong. So I stayed at my post, and did not want to lose heart. I wanted to fight back. From the day when I was so grossly insulted, I took a good look at myself, and I found that, really, there was much I did not know. I made myself study Spanish night and day, as well as everything connected with my work. The old scholar lent me books; I read whatever I could lay my hands on, and I analyzed whatever I read. The new ideas which I found here and there changed my outlook, and I saw many things quite differently. I saw errors where before I had only seen truths, and truths in what had seemed to me errors. For example, from time immemorial the rod had been the characteristic of the school. I used to believe, I had been made to believe, that it was the only efficient way of compelling study. Now I came to think that, far from helping the child to progress, it held him back considerably. I was convinced that it was impossible to think in the face of rod and whip; apprehension, fear, upset even the most self-possessed; a child's imagination, moreover, is all the more impressionable because it is more lively. And since it is necessary to have an outward and an inward calm, a serenity in the spirit, a material and moral tranquility and receptivity for the brain to receive ideas, I believed that, before everything else, I should inspire in the children confidence, a sense of security, and self-respect. Also, I realised that the sight of daily floggings killed the sense of pity, and stifled that of personal dignity, which moves the world; and with it the sense of shame, which once lost is difficult to recover. Observe that when a child is flogged he is consoled that others should be flogged in their turn, and he smiles with satisfaction when he hears the others howl, while, if a child is set to flog others, he may obey the order with repugnance the first time, but afterwards grows used to it, and even enjoys his sorry assignments. The past horrified me. I wanted to salvage the present by modifying the old system. I tried to make study pleasant and good-humoured; I wanted to make the primer not a black book bathed in the tears of childhood, but a friendly guide to marvellous secrets; I wanted to make the school not a torture-chamber but a playground of the mind. So, I cut down flogging gradually; I took the rod and the whip home, and replaced them with the spurs of competition and self-esteem. If a child did not learn his lesson, I blamed it on his lack of effort, never on his lack of brains. I made the children believe that they had more talent than they really had, and trying to live up to it they were compelled to study, just as self-confidence leads to heroism. At first it seemed that the change of method was impractical; many stopped studying altogether; but I persisted, and I saw that little by little spirits were rising, more children came to school more often; and any child who was praised before the whole class studied twice as much the next day. Soon it became known throughout the town that I was sparing the rod. The parish priest sent for me, and I, fearing another scene, greeted him drily in Tagalog. This time he took a very serious tone with me. He said that I was spoiling the children, that I was wasting time, that I was not doing my duty, that the father who spared the rod spoiled the child, according to the Holy Ghost, that "Knowledge maketh a bloody entrance", and so on. He put before me a helping of ancient sayings, as if it were sufficient for something to have been said by the ancients to put it beyond discussion; by this theory, we should believe in the existence of the gargoyles which those ages created and carved on their palaces and cathedrals. To cut matters short, he advised me to be diligent and to return to the old methods, otherwise he would have to speak to the Mayor. My misfortunes did not end there. Some days afterward the parents of the schoolchildren showed up in the parish house and I had to call on all my patience and resignation. They began by exaggerating the virtues of the past when teachers had character and taught as their grandfathers had taught. "They were wise men in those days," they said; "they straightened out the bent twigs all right. And those men were not youngsters, they were old and experienced, full of white hairs, strict. Don Catalino, the chief of them all and founder of his school, never gave less than twenty-five canings a day, that is how he brought up children to be wise, even priests. Ah, the old men were worth more than we; yes, sir, more than we." Others were not satisfied with these rude hints; they told me straight out that, if I followed my system, their children would learn nothing and would have to be taken out of school. It was useless to reason with them; since I was young, they did not want to listen to me. What I would have given for grey hairs! Their authority was the parish priest, John Doe and Richard Roe, even themselves, saying that they would have learned nothing if they had not been flogged by their teachers. Some were sympathetic, and sweetened a little the bitterness of these criticisms. But considering everything I felt I had to give up my methods, although after much effort they were beginning to bear fruit. In despair I took whip and cane to-school the next day and began anew my barbarous task. Serenity disappeared and sadness returned to the faces of the children, who were already beginning to love me; they were my only relatives, my only friends. I tried to be sparing in my canings and to give them as leniently as possible, but the boys felt deeply hurt and degraded, and they wept bitterly. That touched my heart, and, although I had a grudge against their stupid families, I could not avenge myself on these innocent victims of the prejudices of their parents. Their tears scalded me; I felt my heart suffocating me; and one day I left the class before time and went home to cry alone. Perhaps my sensitiveness may surprise you, but if you were in my place you would understand. Old Don Anastasio used to tell me: "So the parents wanted you to use the rod? Why didn't you use it on them?" As a result of all this I fell ill. Scarcely had I recovered when I returned to the school and found my pupils reduced to about a fifth of their former number. The best ones had quit upon the return to the old methods, and of those who remained, a few went to school to escape their household chores, and none showed any happiness or congratulated me on my recovery; it was the same to them whether I got well or not; perhaps they would have preferred it if I had stayed sick, because my substitute, although he flogged them more, on the other hand seldom went to class. My other pupils, whose parents were able to oblige them to go to school, simply played truant. The parents blamed me for having spoiled their children, and heaped reproaches on me. One, however, the son of a peasant woman who used to visit me when I was sick, has not come back because he went to work for the parish priest, and the head sacristan said that boys in the friar's household did not have to go to school, it was beneath them.'

'And you resigned yourself to your new pupils?' asked Ibarra.

'Could I do anything else?' he answered. 'However, many things had happened during my illness, and our parish priest was changed. I conceived new hope and tried again, so that the children should not lose their time completely and so that they might profit as much as possible from the floggings; let these humiliations have some fruit for them at least, I thought. Now that they could not love me, I wanted them at least to remember me afterward with less bitterness, retaining something useful from their schooldays.

You know that in the majority of the schools the textbooks are in Spanish, except for the Tagalog catechism which varies according to the religious Order to which the parish priest belongs. These textbooks are usually Novenas, three-day devotions, and the Catechism from which children learn as much piety as they would from the books of heretics. Finding it impossible to teach them Spanish directly or to translate so many books, I tried to replace them little by little with short extracts from useful works in Tagalog, such as the treatise on good manners and right conduct by Hortensio and Feliza, some pamphlets on agriculture, and others. Sometimes I myself translated short works like the history of the Philippines by Father Barranera, and then dictated the Tagalog version to my pupils so that they could copy it down in their notebooks, supplementing it sometimes with my own observations.

Since I had no maps with which to teach them geography, I copied one of the province which I saw in the capital, and with this reproduction and what I could draw roughly on the tiled floor, I gave them some notions of what our country was like. This time it was the women who raised an outcry; the men were content to smile, seeing in this another hare-brained experiment of mine. The new parish priest sent for me. Although he did not reprimand me, he told me that first of all I should take care of religion, and that, before teaching such things as geography and history, I should make sure by examinations whether or not my pupils already knew by heart the 15 Mysteries of the Rosary, the ejaculations to the Holy Trinity, and the Catechism of Christian Doctrine. As a result, I am now working to turn my boys into

parrots so that they will know by rote so many things about which they do
not understand a single word. I have already taught many the Mysteries and
the ejaculations, but I am afraid my efforts will be in vain as far as the
Catechism is concerned, for the greater part of the pupils still cannot tell the
questions from the answers, and what either are about. And so we shall do
until we die, and so will those who are still unborn, and in Europe they will
speak of progress!'

'Let us not be such pessimists,' replied Ibarra rising to his feet. 'The Vice
Mayor has invited me to attend the town meeting in the courthouse. Who
knows, there you may find an answer to your questions.'

The schoolmaster also stood up but, shaking his head in disbelief, answered:
'You'll see that the project they were telling me about will end up like my
own. You'll see if I am right or not.'

20 • *The Town Meeting*

IT was a hall twelve to fifteen metres long by eight to ten wide. Its
whitewashed walls were covered with charcoal drawings, more or less ugly,
more or less obscene, with words to match. Ten old-fashioned flintlocks were
in a corner, backed against the wall, together with rusty sabres, short swords,
and native knives: these were the weapons of the municipal policemen when
they were sent out on occasion in pursuit of outlaws and highwaymen.

At one end of the hall, which was decorated with dirty red curtains, was
hidden, hanging from the wall, a portrait of the Sovereign; under it on a
wooden platform a large old chair opened its splintered arms; in front of it
was a large wooden table, stained with ink, chipped and carved with inscriptions
and initials, like many of the tables in the German inns frequented by students.
Benches and rickety chairs completed the furniture.

This was San Diego's town-hall, court-room, torture chamber, etc. The
principal men of the town and its outlying communities were now gathered
there, conversing with one another although the old men did not mix with
the young: they could not stand one another. They represented the conservative
and the liberal parties, and their antagonism grew all the more extreme the
farther they were away from the capital.

'I don't like the way the Mayor is acting,' said Don Filipo, the head of the liberal faction, to two or three of his friends. 'He must be up to something when he leaves the discussion of the budget to the last hour. Note that we have scarcely eleven days left.'

'And now he has shut himself up with the parish priest, who, of course, is sick and can't come himself,' observed one of the young men.

'It doesn't matter,' replied another. 'We have everything ready. As long as the old men's plan does not get a majority.'

'I don't think it will,' said Don Filipo. 'I'll sponsor it.'

'What? What are you saying?' his hearers asked, surprised.

'I say that, if I get the floor first, I'll sponsor the project of our enemies.'

'What about our own?'

'You can take care of sponsoring that,' the Vice Mayor answered smiling and turning to the youthful head of a neighbourhood association. 'You will take the floor after I have been defeated.'

'We don't understand you,' said his hearers, looking at him doubtfully.

'Listen,' said Don Filipo, lowering his voice so that only two or three could hear him. 'This morning I met old Tasio.'

'Well?'

'The old man told me: "Your enemies hate you more than they hate your ideas. Do you want something not to be done? Then propose it, and, although it may be more useful than a bishop's mitre, it will be rejected. Once they have defeated you, make the humblest among your followers sponsor what you really want, and your enemies, to humiliate you, will approve it." But keep it secret.'

'But...'

'That is why I will sponsor the project of our enemies, exaggerating it to the point of absurdity. Quiet now. Here come Mr. Ibarra and the schoolmaster.'

Both these young men greeted the various groups without joining in their conversations.

A few minutes later the Mayor entered, looking out of sorts. He was the man who had been carrying the brace of candles the night before. At his entrance the murmuring stopped, each one took his seat, and silence fell gradually.

The Mayor seated himself in the armchair placed under the portrait of the Sovereign, coughed four or five times, ran his hands over his hair and face, placed his elbows on the table, withdrew them, coughed again, and repeated the entire procedure.

'Gentlemen,' he said at last in a faint voice. 'I have ventured to call all of you to this meeting...er...er... We are to celebrate the feast of our patron saint, St. Diego, on the 12th of this month...er...er... It is now the second...er...er...'

At this point he was overcome with a fit of dry deliberate coughing which reduced him to silence.

Then a man of about forty, with an arrogant aspect, rose from the conservative benches. He was the rich Capitan Basilio, an antagonist of the late Don Rafael, and a man who claimed that the world had not taken a step forward since the death of St. Thomas Aquinas, and that humanity had indeed begun to go backward since he himself had left San Juan de Letran, the Dominican college in Manila.

'Allow me, Your Honours, to take the floor on such an interesting subject,' he said. 'I speak first, although others here present have more preponderant rights, because it seems to me that in these matters the first speaker is not necessarily the most pre-eminent, just as the last speaker is not necessarily the most insignificant. Furthermore, what I have to say is of such transcendence that it cannot be left to the last, and that is why I should like to speak first in order to give it the necessary emphasis. Your Honours will therefore permit me to speak first even at a meeting like this, where I see personalities most notable indeed, such as the incumbent Mayor, the former Mayor who is also my distinguished friend Don Valentin, the former Mayor who is my childhood friend Don Julio, our renowned captain of municipal police, Don Melchor, and so many other honourables whom Your Honours see here present but whose names I will not mention for the sake of brevity. I ask Your Honours to give me the floor before anyone else. Am I fortunate enough to have the meeting grant my humble plea?' The speaker bowed respectfully, with an expectant smile.

'Go ahead; we are anxious to hear what you have to say,' said the friends alluded to and others who considered him a great orator. The old men coughed with satisfaction and rubbed their hands together.

Capitan Basilio, after mopping up his sweat with a silk handkerchief, continued:

'Since Your Honours have been so kind and condescending to my humble person, giving me the floor before anybody else here present, I shall avail myself of this permission, so generously granted, and will now in fact address you. I imagine with my imagination that I find myself in the bosom of the most honourable Roman Senate—*Senatus Populusque Romanus*, the Roman Senate and People, as we used to say in those beautiful times that unfortunately for humanity will nevermore return—and I shall ask the *patres conscripti*, as the wise Cicero would have said if he had been in my place, I shall ask our founding fathers, I say, for we do not have enough time, and time is gold, as Solomon said, that in this important matter every one should express his views clearly, briefly, and simply. Thank you.'

And satisfied with himself and with the attention of his audience, the orator sat down, not without directing a vainglorious glance at Ibarra, who was seated in a corner, and another significant look at his friends, as if to say: 'Ha! That was well put, eh?'

His friends reflected both looks and stared smugly at the younger men, as if waiting for them to die of envy.

'Now anyone who wants may speak... er...' said the Mayor, who was unable to complete the phrase, being again attacked by coughing and sighing.

To judge by the silence, nobody wanted to be called a founding father, for nobody rose; Don Filipo saw his chance and asked for the floor.

The conservatives exchanged winks and meaningful signs.

'I shall now propose my budget for the fiesta,' said Don Filipo.

'Out of the question!' a tubercular old man, an intransigent conservative, blurted out.

'We vote against,' others chimed in.

'Gentlemen,' said Don Filipo, repressing a smile. 'I have not yet explained the plans that we, the younger men, are submitting here. This great project, we are sure, will be preferred by all to that which our opponents are thinking of or any they can possibly think of.'

This insolent beginning antagonised the conservatives once and for all, and they swore inwardly to put up an inflexible opposition.

Don Filipo continued: 'We have 3,500 pesos at our disposal. Now then, with that amount we can put on a fiesta that will eclipse in magnificence all that have been seen so far, whether in our province or in neighbouring ones.'

'Hm!' exclaimed the incredulous. 'The next town had 5,000 pesos to spend, and its neighbour had 4,000. Hm! Pure humbug!'

'Hear me, gentlemen, and you will be convinced,' Don Filipo proceeded, undaunted. 'I propose that a great stage be erected in the centre of the town square. That should cost 150 pesos.'

'Not enough,' a stubborn conservative objected. 'Make it 160.'

'Mr. Secretary, put down 200 pesos for the stage,' said Don Filipo. 'I propose that the Tondo comedy troupe be contracted for performances on seven consecutive nights. Seven performances at 200 pesos each make 1,400 pesos. Write down 1,400, Mr. Secretary.'

Old and young looked at one another in surprise. Only those who were in the secret did not move.

'I propose also a great fireworks display. None of these piddling little lights and Roman candles fit for children and young girls. We want large firecrackers and colossal rockets. I propose therefore 200 super-firecrackers at two pesos each and 200 rockets at the same price. We shall order them from the fireworks-makers of Malabon.'

'Hm!' interrupted an old man. 'A two-peso firecracker wouldn't frighten me. I wouldn't even hear it. It must be the three-peso kind, at least.'

'Put down 1,000 pesos for 200 firecrackers and 200 rockets.' The conservatives could no longer restrain themselves; some got up and conferred with one another.

'Moreover, to show our neighbours that we are lavish hosts and that we have money to spare,' continued Don Filipo, raising his voice and looking swiftly at the conservative faction, 'I propose, first, that we have four sponsors for the two feast days, and, secondly, that every day 200 fried chickens, 100 stuffed capons, and fifty roast pigs be thrown into the lake, as used to be done by Sulla, a contemporary of that Cicero of whom Capitan Basilio has just spoken.'

'That's it, like Sulla,' the flattered Capitan Basilio repeated.

The astonishment of the audience was growing by leaps and bounds.

'Since many wealthy people are coming, and they will be loaded with thousands and thousands of pesos, their best gamecocks, playing cards, and whatever you use to play the Chinese games, I propose fifteen days of cockfighting, permission to open all the gambling houses...'

But the young men interrupted him by rising to their feet; they thought the Vice Mayor had gone mad. The old men were engaged in a heated discussion.

'And lastly, so as not to neglect the pleasures of the soul...'

The muttering and even shouts that rose from all the corners of the hall covered his voice completely. It was nothing less than a riot.

'No!' cried an uncompromising conservative. 'I don't want him to flatter himself that he has made the fiesta, no! Let me speak, let me!'

'Don Filipo has fooled us,' said the liberals. 'We shall vote against. He has gone over to the old men. Let us vote against.'

The Mayor, more downcast than ever, did nothing to restore order; he waited for the assembly to re-establish it themselves.

The captain of municipal police asked for the floor; but when he was given permission to speak he did not open his mouth and returned to his seat in confusion and embarrassment.

Fortunately Capitan Valentín, the most moderate among the conservatives, stood up and said: 'We cannot accept what has been proposed by the Vice Mayor. His ideas seem rather extravagant. Only a young man like the Vice Mayor, who can stay up nights in a row and listen to so much noise without going deaf, can want so many rockets and so many stage shows. I have consulted sensible people and they unanimously reject the plans of Don Filipo. Is that agreed, gentlemen?'

'Yes, yes,' young and old said with one voice. The young men were enchanted to hear an old man speak thus.

'What are we to do with four sponsors for the fiesta?' the old man continued. 'What is the meaning of all these chickens, capons, and roast pigs thrown into the lake? Our neighbours will say we are just showing off, and afterwards we shall fast half the year. What are this Sulla and the Romans to us? Have they ever invited us to their fiestas? I at least have never received an invitation from them, and I've been around a long time.'

'The Romans live in Rome, where the Pope is,' Capitan Basilio whispered.

'Now I understand,' said the old man, not in the least discomposed. 'They probably held their celebrations during fast days, and the Pope must have ordered the food thrown into the sea to avoid the commission of sin. But anyway your plans for the fiesta are unacceptable, impossible, sheer madness!'

Don Filipo, opposed so vigorously, had to withdraw his proposals. The

most uncompromising conservatives, satisfied with the defeat of their greatest
enemy, had no misgivings when the young neighbourhood association leader
asked for the floor.

'I ask Your Honours to forgive me if, young as I am, I presume to speak
before so many persons distinguished as much by their age as by the prudence
and discernment with which they judge affairs, but since the eloquent orator,
Capitan Basilio, has invited all to express their opinion, let his word supply
authority to my insignificant person.'

The conservatives nodded with satisfaction.

'This young man speaks well. He is modest. He reasons admirably,' they
told one another.

'It's a pity he doesn't know how to gesture,' Capitan Basilio observed. 'You
can tell he hasn't studied Cicero. But he's still quite young.'

'If I submit to you a programme or a project,' the young man continued,
'I do so not in the expectation that you will find it perfect, or even that you
will approve it; but only, while submitting myself once more to the will of
all, to prove to our elders that we always share their thoughts, since we make
our own all the ideas so elegantly expressed by Capitan Valentín.'

'Well put, very well put,' said the flattered conservatives. Capitan Basilio
was making signs to the young man, to show him how to wave an arm or
thrust a foot elegantly forward. Only the Mayor remained indifferent—
distracted or pre-occupied with other thoughts.

The young man continued with more assurance:

'My plan, gentlemen, can be reduced to this: we must think up new
entertainments that are out of the common run, something we don't see every
day, and we must see to it that the money that has been raised does not leave
our town or is spent vainly on fireworks, but employed in something useful
to all.'

'That's it,' the young men agreed. 'That's what we want.'

'Very good,' the conservatives granted.

'What do we get out of the week of stage shows proposed by the Vice
Mayor? What do we learn from watching these kings of Bohemia and Granada
who order the heads of their daughters to be chopped off, or who load them
into cannon upon which they sit enthroned? We are neither kings nor
barbarians, and we have no cannon, and if we followed their example we

would be hanged in Bagumbayan. What to us are these princesses who go into battle, laying about them with broadswords, fighting princes in single combat, or else wandering forlorn in mountain and vale as if under the spell of a sorcerer? Our tradition is to admire sweetness and tenderness in a woman, and we would be afraid to hold a maidenly hand stained with blood, even though this blood were the blood of a Moslem or a giant; our people despise and consider vile the man who lifts his hand against a woman, whether he be prince, lieutenant, or unlettered peasant. Would it not be a thousand times better to present a picture of our own customs and traditions, so that we may thus understand and correct our vices and defects, and extol our virtues?'

'That's it,' the liberals agreed again.

'He's right,' some conservatives muttered thoughtfully.

'I never thought of that,' Capitan Basilio murmured.

One old man, however, would not give in. 'But how are you going to do it?' he objected.

'Very easily,' the young man replied. 'I have brought with me two comedies, which the good taste and well-known discernment of our distinguished elders gathered here will surely find most acceptable and entertaining. One is entitled *The Mayor's Election*, a comedy in prose, in five acts, written by one of the gentlemen here present. The other has nine acts for performance on two nights; it is a satirical fantasy written by one of the best poets in this province, and is entitled *Mariang Makiling*. When we saw that the discussion of the arrangements for the fiesta was being delayed, we were afraid that we would be short of time. So we quietly chose the cast and asked the actors to start learning their roles. We hope that with one week of rehearsals they will have more than sufficient time to give a successful performance. This plan, gentlemen, in addition to being novel, useful, and reasonable, has the great advantage of being economical too: we shall not need costumes, our own everyday clothes will do.'

'I'll pay for the stage,' Capitan Basilio exclaimed with enthusiasm.

'If you need any policemen for the play, I'll lend you mine,' said the captain of municipal police.

'And I, I,' another old man stammered, drawing himself up dramatically. 'If you have a part for an old man...'

'Approved, approved!' The sentiment of the meeting was unmistakable.

The Vice Mayor was pale with emotion; his eyes were filled with tears.

'He weeps out of spite,' the intransigent conservative thought, and cried out: 'Approved, approved without further discussion.'

Satisfied with his revenge and the complete defeat of his adversary he began to praise the project of the young man. The latter continued:

'A fifth part of the money raised could be utilised to award prizes: for instance, to the best schoolboy, to the best herdsman, farmer, fisherman, and so on. We can organise boat-races on the river and the lake, run horse-races, put up greased poles, and hold other games in which the country folk can join. In deference to tradition, a fireworks display may be conceded. Firewheels and illuminations make very attractive and entertaining spectacles, but I don't think we need the rockets proposed by the Vice Mayor. Two bands will be sufficient to liven up the fiesta. Thus we will avoid those competitions and quarrels among the poor musicians who come to cheer us up but who perforce turn into veritable fighting cocks that go home not only badly paid and badly fed, but badly bruised, and sometimes even wounded. With the remainder of the money we can begin a small building to serve as a school, for we should not expect God Himself to come down and build it for us. It is depressing that, while we have a first-class cockpit, our children must learn their lessons in, of all places, what is practically the stable of the parish priest. I have sketched out the programme for you. We must all work to carry it out.'

A murmur of satisfaction rose in the hall. Almost everyone agreed with the young man. Only a few muttered: 'Novelties, novelties! In our youth..;'

'Let's approve it for the time being,' said others. 'Let's put the Vice Mayor in his place.'

When order was re-established, everyone was in agreement. Only the concurrence of the Mayor was lacking.

The latter was in a sweat, fidgeting uneasily. He drew his hand across his forehead, and at last stammered with lowered eyes:

'I too agree, but...er...'

The meeting listened in silence.

'But?' asked Capitan Basilio.

'Very much in agreement,' the Mayor repeated. 'That is to say, I do not agree... I say yes, but...'

And he wiped his eyes with the back of his hand.

'But the parish priest,' the wretch continued, 'the parish priest wants something else.'

'Does the parish priest pay for the fiesta or do we? Has he contributed a single penny?' a penetrating voice inquired. It was Tasio the scholar.

The Vice Mayor was motionless, eyes fixed on the Mayor.

'And what does the parish priest want?' asked Capitan Basilio.

'Well, the parish priest wants... six processions, three sermons, three High Masses... And if there is any money left over, the Tondo stage troupe, and musical numbers during the intermissions.'

'Well, we don't want that,' said the young men and a number of the conservatives.

'The parish priest wants it,' the Mayor repeated. 'I have promised him that his wishes will be followed.'

'Then why did you call this meeting?'

'Precisely to inform you.'

'Why didn't you say so from the start?'

'I wanted to, gentlemen, but Capitan Basilio took the floor, and I didn't have the time... The parish priest must be obeyed.'

'He must be obeyed,' some of the old men echoed.

'He must be obeyed; otherwise the Mayor will throw us all in gaol,' other old men added darkly.

'Well, then, obey, and arrange the fiesta yourselves,' the young men exclaimed, taking to their feet. 'We withdraw our contributions.'

'Everything has already been collected,' said the Mayor.

Don Filipo approached him and said with a touch of bitterness: 'Sacrifice your self-esteem for a good cause. You sacrificed it before for a bad one, and you ruined everything.'

Ibarra was telling the schoolmaster:

'Do you have anything for the provincial capital? I am leaving at once.'

'Do you have any business there?'

'I have something in hand,' Ibarra answered mysteriously.

On the way back the old scholar told Don Filipo, who was bemoaning his failure:

'The fault is ours. You did not protest when they gave you a puppet for a leader, and I, fool that I am, had forgotten it!'

21 • *A Mother's Story*

Uncertain wandered
In restless quest
All ways meandered
No moment's rest
                              —Alaejos

SISA ran to her house in the grip of that panic which seizes the mind when in misfortune we find ourselves forsaken by all, and hope flees elusive before us. Then, seemingly surrounded by darkness, we chase even the merest glimmer of a light in the distance, no matter if an abyss opens in our path.

She wanted to save her sons, and mothers do not stop to ask how when it comes to helping their flesh and blood.

She ran headlong, pursued by fears and sinister premonitions. Had they already arrested Basilio? Where had Crispín gone?

Nearing her house she recognised, over her orchard fence, the helmets of two Constabulary soldiers. Her feelings were indescribable; her mind went blank. She knew these men were ruthless; they gave short shrift even to the riches men in town—what was to become of her and her children, already presumed to be common thieves? Soldiers were not human beings, they were soldiers; they were deaf to pleas and blind to tears.

Instinctively, Sisa raised her eyes to the sky, which seemed to smile back inscrutably; a few white fragments of cloud floated in the transparent blue. She stopped to suppress the trembling that shook her body. Now the soldiers had left her house; they had no one with them! They had caught no one except the hen Sisa had been fattening. She breathed again and her spirits soared.

'What good men they are, and how kind-hearted!' she whispered, almost weeping for joy. Had the soldiers burnt down her house but left her sons alone, she would still have heaped blessings on them.

Gratefully she looked up again; a flock of herons was flying by, light passing clouds in her native skies, and she went on, confidence reborn in her heart.

As she came nearer to the men she feared so much, Sisa pretended to be carefree, looking everywhere but at them, carefully deaf to her hen, which was squawking for help. Once past them, she wanted to break into a run, but prudence held her back.

She had not gone far when she heard them call her imperiously. She shuddered, but pretended she had not heard, and went on walking. They called her again, this time shouting an insult. In spite of herself, she turned, pale and trembling. One of the soldiers was beckoning to her.

Sisa approached them mechanically, feeling her tongue stiffen and her throat dry up with fear.

'Tell us the truth,' said one of them in a threatening voice, 'or we'll tie you up to that tree and shoot you!'

She stared vacantly at the tree.

'Are you the mother of the thieves?' the other asked.

'Mother of the thieves,' Sisa echoed mechanically.

'Where's the money your sons brought you last night?'

'Money...'

'Don't deny it or it'll be all the worse for you,' added the other. 'We've come to arrest your sons, but the elder got away from us. Where have you hidden the younger one?'

Sisa breathed a sigh of relief.

'Sir,' she answered, 'I have not seen my son Crispín for many days. I expected to see him this morning in the parish house, but there they only told me...'

The two soldiers exchanged a meaningful look.

'All right,' one of them snapped. 'Give us the money, and we'll leave you alone.'

'My sons, sir,' the wretched woman sobbed, 'wouldn't steal if they were starving! We're used to being hungry. Basilio didn't bring me a single penny. You can search the house, and, if you find a single sovereign, you can do what you want with us. We poor people are not all thieves.'

'In that case,' the soldier answered slowly, catching Sisa's eyes and holding them, 'you must come with us. Then your sons will have to give themselves up, sooner or later, and hand over the money they have stolen. Come along.'

'I? Follow you?' the woman whispered, falling back and looking with horror on their uniforms.

'Well, why not?'

'Have pity,' she begged, almost on her knees. 'I am very poor; I can't give you any money or jewels; you've already taken the only thing I had, the hen I was fattening for the market. Take everything else you can find in my hut, but leave me alone. I'd rather die here.'

'Come on! You must come with us, and if you don't come peacefully, we'll tie you up.'

Sisa broke into bitter tears. She knew she could not move them.

'At least,' she pleaded, when they seized her roughly and pushed her forward, 'at least let me go ahead of you.'

Something in her touched the two soldiers and they exchanged whispers.

'All right,' said one. 'You may try to run away before we get to town, so you'll have to stay between the two of us until we get there. But once in town you can go about twenty paces ahead. Mind now, don't go into any shop, and don't be stopping anywhere. Now, come along, and hurry.'

Her pleas and arguments were all in vain; useless, all her promises. The soldiers said they had already exposed themselves enough, as it was, and had made her too many concessions.

When she found herself flanked by them, she felt she would die of shame. True, there was nobody in the road, but the sun itself, the wind itself—true modesty imagines eyes everywhere. She covered her face with a shawl, and walking almost blindfolded she bewailed her humiliation in silence. She knew she was wretchedly poor, forsaken by all, even by her own husband, but until now she had treasured her good reputation and looked with pity on the women, scandalously dressed, who were known to the town as camp followers. Now it seemed to her that she had fallen even lower than they in human society.

She heard hoofbeats and recognised them. They belonged to one of the little caravans of men and women who carried fish to the inland towns in baskets slung on the flanks of their flea-bitten ponies. Passing by her hut these people had often asked her for drinking water and made her presents of fish. Now, as they went by, she imagined that they were insulting, scorning her, and that their stares, pitying or disdainful, penetrated through her shawl and struck her in the face like arrows.

At last they drew away, and Sisa sighed. She raised her shawl for an instant to see if it was still far from town. They were still a few telegraph poles away from the guard-house or check-point. The distance had never seemed so great to her.

On the edge of the road there was a leafy bamboo grove; in its shade she had taken her ease in other days, while her sweetheart made pleasant conversation; afterwards he would help her carry her basket of fruit and vegetables. Those days had vanished like a dream. Her sweetheart had become her husband; her husband, a tax-collector; it was the beginning of her misfortunes.

The heat of the sun was becoming oppressive, and the soldiers asked her if she wanted to rest.

'No, thank you,' she answered with a shudder.

She was horror-struck when they neared the town. She looked round her, distraught; the flat unending ricefields, the shallow ditches, the puny trees—what she would have given for an abyss to swallow her, or a rock on which to dash herself! She was in despair that she had followed the soldiers so far; so near her hut ran a deep river, its steep banks jagged with rock, in which she might have found sweet death. But the thought of her sons, of Crispín—what had become of him?—was a light in the darkness.

'When this is all over,' she sighed, 'we'll go live in the forest—in the very middle of it.'

She made an effort to calm herself and dried her eyes.

'Here we are, in town,' she told the soldiers in a low voice that defied definition: complaint, reproach, lamentation, all in one, prayer and cry of pain.

The soldiers, who were visibly moved, answered her with a gesture. Sisa walked rapidly ahead, trying to look unconcerned.

At that moment the church bells began to peal, announcing the end of High Mass. Sisa hastened her steps in order, if possible, not to meet any of the people leaving the church. In vain; there was no way to avoid them.

She greeted two acquaintances with a smile, but they looked at her quizzically. After that, to escape such vexations, she kept her eyes on the ground, but, strangely enough, stumbled over the stones in the road.

People were staring, they were whispering, they were following her with their eyes; she knew this, she felt it, although her eyes were on the ground.

Behind her she heard a woman shout coarsely:

'Where did you nab her? Did you get the money back?'

The woman wore a green and yellow skirt, without the customary overskirt, and a blue muslin blouse. It was plain from the way she dressed that she was a camp follower.

Sisa felt as if she had been slapped. That woman had stripped her naked before the crowd. She raised her eyes for a moment in order to swallow her humiliation to the dregs; she saw the people round her as if from a distance, an infinite distance, yet felt the coldness of their eyes, heard their whispers. The wretched woman walked without feeling the ground under her feet.

'Here, this way!' shouted one of the soldiers.

She turned quickly on her heel, like a mechanical toy about to run down. Blindly, incapable of thought, she only wanted to get away and hide herself. She saw a door; there was a sentry before it but she tried to enter; a voice, more imperious still, stopped her. Stumbling, she sought the voice, felt a shove at her back, shut her eyes, tottered forward and, her strength suddenly gone, collapsed on the ground, on her knees, and then on her haunches, shaken by a tearless, soundless weeping.

She was in the barracks of the Constabulary; around her were soldiers and their women, pigs, and chickens. Some soldiers were darning their uniforms; here a concubine lay stretched out on a bench, her head on her lover's thigh as she smoked, staring bored at the ceiling; there, another helped her man to wash his clothes and clean his weapons, humming a lewd tune.

'The chick's must've got away; you've only got the hen with you,' one of them called out to the new arrivals. Did she mean Sisa or her hen, which was still squawking?

The soldiers made no answer;

'Oh, well,' she continued, 'the hen is always better than the chicken.'

'Where's the sergeant?' asked one of the soldiers in exasperation. 'Have they notified the C.O. yet?'

He was answered with a shrugging of shoulders. Nobody really cared to find out what was to be done with Sisa.

She spent two hours in the barracks yard, half in a stupor, huddled in a corner, her head hidden in her hands, her hair in wild disorder. The lieutenant was notified at noon and he immediately dismissed the friar's charges. 'What will that skinflint friar think of next!' he said, and ordered Sisa to be released and the case closed.

'If he wants to get his money back,' he added, 'let him ask that famous St. Anthony of his or complain to the Nuncio. Now, clear out!'

So it was that Sisa was thrown out of the barracks; they had to throw her out because she did not want to move.

When she found herself in the middle of the street, she mechanically headed home, walking quickly, her head uncovered, her hair undone, her eyes fixed on the distant horizon. The sun was at its height, scorching, with no cloud to soften its dazzling light; a feeble wind stirred among the tree-tops in whose shade the birds lay hidden; the road was dust under her feet.

At last Sisa reached her hut, silently entered it, went from corner to corner, and left again, walking here and there. She ran over to old Tasio's house and knocked at the door, but there was no one there. Distressed she returned to her house.

'Basilio, Crispín!' she called out, pausing for an answer. But the only sounds in that solitude were the echoes of her cries, the sweet whisper of the nearby stream, and the music of the bamboo leaves. Call again, climb here, hasten there to gorge and river—her eyes darted to and fro, now sinister, then sparkling, still later darkened like a stormy sky—the light of reason, it seemed, flickered and was about to die.

Once again she went up the ladder of her hut and squatted on the mat where they had lain only the night before; she raised her eyes; caught on the sharp edge of the bamboo siding facing the precipice was, she saw, a shred of Basilio's shirt. She stood up, took it in her hand, and held it up to the sun. There was blood on it. But perhaps Sisa did not see the stains. She went down from her hut, studying the rag in the scorching sunlight, peering through it, and then, as if feeling a need for more light in a darkening world, lowering it and staring wide-eyed at the sun itself.

She walked aimlessly about, uttering strange cries, howls to frighten whoever might have heard her, inhuman sounds. In stormy nights, when the wind whips with invisible wings its following shadows, there is a moaning and a wailing to be heard in lonely ruins, which fill the heart with fear and shake the stoutest with an involuntary trembling, reason though one might that it is only the wind beating against the high towers and broken walls. Yet more dismal still than these inexplicable lamentations in the dark nights of storm was this mother's keening.

So did night overtake her. Then perhaps Heaven granted that in her sleep
an unseen angel's wing brushed against her pale face and cleared her memory
of its accumulated sorrows; perhaps such sorrows were beyond the strength
of that weak humanity and Providence prescribed with motherly affection
the sweet remedy of oblivion.

Be that as it may, Sisa rose on the following day and wandered with a smile
to sing and talk to every living thing.

22 • *Lights and Shadows*

IT was three days later, three days and nights which the town of San Diego
had spent in preparing, commenting, and gossiping about the fiesta.

While anticipating future pleasures some criticised the Mayor, others, the
Vice Mayor, still others, the young liberals; and there were not lacking those
who blamed everything on everybody.

They talked about María Clara, who had arrived accompanied by her Aunt
Isabel. They were glad she had come because they liked her but, even as they
praised her beauty, they remarked on the change in Father Salví. 'He's often
distracted at Mass,' his parishioners reported. 'He doesn't have much to say
to us any more.' Anyone could see, they said, that he was losing weight and
spirit. His cook observed that the priest was becoming thinner by the minute,
and complained that he did not do honour to his dishes. But what caused
the most gossip was the fact that more than two lights were seen burning at
night in the parish house while Father Salví visited a certain house, the house,
in fact, of María Clara! The pious women crossed themselves, but it did not
stop them from gossiping.

Juan Crisóstomo Ibarra had telegraphed from the capital of the province,
presenting his compliments to Aunt Isabel and her niece, but without
explaining his absence. Many thought he had been arrested because of his
treatment of Father Salví on the evening of All Saint's Day. But the talk of
the town reached its peak when in the afternoon of the third day he was seen
alighting from a carriage in front of his fiancee's house and courteously
greeting the friar, who was going there too.

Nobody bothered about Sisa and her sons.

Orange and *ilang-ilang* trees made a lovely nest for María Clara's house.

One afternoon she and Ibarra stood together by a window overlooking the lake. The window was framed by flowers and creepers, which were trained on bamboo and wire and scattered a subtle perfume, but the words they whispered were softer than the rustle of leaves and sweeter than the garden's perfumed air.

Ibarra was saying to María Clara: 'You'll have your wish before dawn. I'll get everything ready tonight.'

'I must let all our friends know at once. But do manage to leave out the parish priest.'

'Why?'

'I feel he's always watching me. Those deep, sad eyes of his—they make me uncomfortable; he scares me. And then when he speaks to me, his voice is so strange—and he says such odd things, things I can't understand—once he asked me if I hadn't dreamed of my mother's letters. I think he must be half mad. Sinang and Andeng say that he must be half out of his wits; he doesn't eat or wash himself and spends his time in the dark. Do make sure he doesn't come.'

'We can't help inviting him,' answered Ibarra thoughtfully. 'He's your guest, and besides he has been damned decent to me. When the Mayor talked to him about that thing I was telling you about, he had only praises for me and did not seek to make the slightest objection. I can see you're annoyed; don't worry—at least, we'll put him in another boat.'

They heard light footsteps, the priest's, who was approaching them, a strained smile on his lips.

'There's a chill in the wind,' he said. 'Aren't you two afraid of catching cold? If you do, you won't shake it off until the hot season.'

There was a tremor in his voice and his eyes were on the far horizon; he did not look at the young couple.

'On the contrary, it seems to be a pleasant evening. The breeze is delightful,' answered Ibarra. 'These months are both our autumn and our spring—a few leaves fall but there are always flowers.'

Father Salví sighed.

'I find it wonderful to have these two seasons running into each other without a cold winter in between,' continued Ibarra. 'In February the fruit-bearing trees will begin to bud, and by March the fruits will be ripe. When the hot months come we shall go somewhere else.'

Father Salví smiled. They turned to safer topics: the weather, the town, the fiesta. María Clara found an excuse to withdraw.

'And since we are talking of fiestas, let me invite you to one we are giving tomorrow. It is a country outing we and our friends are having.'

'Where is it going to be?'

'The young ladies want it by the creek, the one which runs through the forest nearby, near the *balete* tree. We must be up early so the sun won't bother us.'

After a moment's reflection, the friar answered:

'The invitation is very tempting. I accept if only to show you that I hold no grudge against you. But I shall have to go later, after attending to my duties. You're lucky you're free, absolutely free!'

A few minutes later, Ibarra took his leave in order to make the arrangements for the next day's picnic. Night had already fallen.

Out on the street someone approached and greeted him respectfully.

'Who are you?' asked Ibarra.

'Sir, you do not know my name,' answered the unknown. 'I have been waiting for you two days.'

'Why?'

'I have lost my children, my wife has gone out of her mind, and everyone says I deserve it. They say I'm a crook. Nobody had shown any sympathy.'

Quickly looking the man over, Ibarra asked:

'What do you want now?'

'Pity my wife and children!'

'I can't stop here,' answered Ibarra. 'If you want to come along, you can tell me what has happened to you while we're walking.'

The man thanked him, and soon they disappeared in the darkness of the poorly lighted streets.

23 • *A Fishing Expedition*

THE stars were still shining in the blue dome of heaven, the birds still asleep in the trees, when a merry party walked through the streets of the town by the festive light of pitch torches, heading for the lake.

In the van were five light-footed girls, hand in hand or with arms about each other's waists, followed by a number of elderly ladies and by serving-maids carrying on their heads baskets full of provisions, plates, and kitchen utensils. Their faces gay with youth and alight with expectation, their abundant black hair and the wide folds of their dresses streaming in the wind, they might have been divinities of the night fleeing the light of day; they were in fact María Clara with four friends, her cousin the jolly Sinang, grave Victoria, lovely Iday, and the pensive Nenang, a shy and modest beauty, all chattering away now, giggling, pinching each other, whispering, breaking into peals of laughter.

'Hush, most people are still in bed—you'll wake them up,' Aunt Isabel reprimanded them. 'We weren't half as noisy when we were young.'

'Then you weren't up as early as we are,' retorted little Sinang, 'or maybe old people weren't such slugabeds.'

Nevertheless they stopped their chatter, but only for a moment; they lowered their voices but soon forgot and were off again, their fresh young voices and their laughter echoing down the street.

'Make believe you're offended and don't speak to him,' Sinang advised María Clara. 'Pick a quarrel with him so he won't take you for granted.'

'Don't be so exacting,' said Iday.

'Go on and be exacting; don't be foolish. Man should obey woman before marriage; after marriage he will be doing whatever he pleases,' little Sinang counselled.

'What do you know about such things?' her cousin Victoria rebuked her.

'Sh, they're coming!'

True enough, a group of young men was approaching, carrying great bamboo torches and walking quite sedately to the strumming of a guitar.

'Sounds like a beggar's guitar, doesn't it?' Sinang laughed.

But when the two groups met, it was the girls who assumed a grave and proper demeanour, and looked as if they did not know what it was to laugh. On the other hand the young men talked, bowed, smiled, and asked six questions to get half an answer.

'Is the lake calm? Do you think we shall have good weather,' asked the mothers.

'Now don't you ladies worry; I'm a very good swimmer,' answered a tall thin young man, Albino by name.

'We should have gone to hear Mass first,' sighed Aunt Isabel, clasping her hands.

'It's not too late, ma'am,' suggested another young blood. 'Albino here studied in a seminary and can say Mass aboard.'

The latter thereupon slyly made a sanctimonious face like Father Salví's.

Ibarra, without losing his dignity, joined in the merriment.

When they reached the shore the women cried out at a happy surprise. They saw two large boats joined together and picturesquely decorated with garlands of flowers and varicoloured embossed cloths. From the makeshift awnings hung tiny paper lanterns among roses and carnations, and pineapples, *kasuy*, bananas, guavas, *lanzones*, and other fruits. Ibarra had brought carpets, rugs, and cushions, and fashioned them into comfortable seats for the women. Even the paddles and the punting poles were decorated. In the more lavishly accoutred boat were a harp, guitars, accordions, and a carabao-horn trumpet; the other had native earthen stoves in full blast, brewing tea, coffee, and ginger tea for breakfast.

'All the women here, all the men there,' commanded the older ladies as they embarked. 'Be still there, girls, don't move around so much or we'll capsize.'

'First make the sign of the cross,' said Aunt Isabel, promptly doing so.

'Are we going to be here by ourselves,' pouted Sinang. 'All by ourselves— ouch!'

The 'ouch' was due to a timely pinch administered by her mother.

The boats were slowly drawing away from the beach, the light of their paper lanterns glimmering reflected in the mirror-like surface of the lake. The East was beginning to glow with the dawn.

The party was rather subdued; the young people seemed to be brooding on the separation of the sexes decreed by the mothers.

'Look out,' said Albino the seminarian in a loud voice to another young man. 'Better be sure you keep your feet on that plug.'

'Why?'

'It's liable to come out and let the water in. This boat is full of holes, you know.'

'We're sinking!' shrieked the women.

'Have no fear, ladies,' the seminarian reassured them. 'The boat is quite safe, there are only five holes in it, and not very big ones either.'

'Five holes! Jesús! Do you want us all to drown?' exclaimed the women in a fright.

'Only five, ladies, and only this big,' said the seminarian, making a circle with his thumb and forefinger. 'Just make sure you keep your feet firmly on the plugs and keep them down.'

'My God! Most Holy Mary! The water is coming in already,' cried an old lady who was quite sure she was getting wet.

There was a little panic, some of the ladies were screaming, others seemed about ready to take to the lake.

'Keep your feet on the plugs there,' continued Albino, pointing to the place where the girls were.

'Where? Where did you say? We haven't the faintest idea... Oh do please come and show us where,' begged the frightened women.

Five young men had perforce to transfer to the other boat in order to reassure the frightened mothers. By an odd coincidence it seemed that there was a danger-point beside each girl; stranger still, Ibarra found himself beside María Clara, Albino beside Victoria, and so on. Tranquility was soon restored among the careful mothers, but not among the younger people.

As the waters were absolutely calm, the fish-traps not very far away, and there was plenty of time, it was agreed to stop and have breakfast. The lanterns were put out, as day had dawned by now.

'There is nothing like ginger-tea in the morning before going to Mass,' said Capitana Tica, the mother of jolly Sinang. 'Take ginger-tea with rice-cake, Albino, and you'll see that you'll even feel like praying.'

'That's exactly what I'm doing,' he answered. 'In fact I now feel like going to Confession.'

'No,' said Sinang, 'take coffee. It stimulates happy thoughts.'

'Right away. Actually, I was feeling rather depressed.'

'Don't do it,' advised Aunt Isabel. 'Take tea and biscuits. They say tea calms the mind.'

'Then I shall also take tea and biscuits,' said the accommodating seminarian. 'Fortunately, none of these beverages, unlike Catholicism, claims to be the only way of salvation.'

'But how can you?' asked Victoria.

'Take chocolate too? I should say so. So long as lunch is not too far behind.'

It was a beautiful morning. The light shining from the skies and that reflected in the waters combined to produce a clarity that was almost without shadow, a cool revealing clarity, alive with colour, which has been captured in some seascapes.

Almost everyone was in good spirits. They breathed in the light breeze that was just rising. Even the mothers, who had been so full of instructions and warning, now laughed and joked among themselves.

'Do you remember,' one of them asked Capitana Tica, 'when we went bathing in the river before we were all married? More often than not we would find little boats made from banana trunks floating down toward us. And they carried all kinds of fruit and flowers, each little boat with a pennant with one of our names on it.'

'And on the way,' interrupted another, 'we would find the bamboo bridges broken and then we would have to wade across the streams... the rascals!'

'Yes,' confirmed Capitana Tica. 'But I always preferred to get my skirts wet rather than show my feet. I knew they were watching us from the bushes along the banks.'

The young people who heard these things exchanged winks and smiles; the others were engrossed in their own conversations and paid no attention.

Only one man, who acted as steersman, remained silent and indifferent to all the merrymaking. He was a youth with an athlete's body and a face made interesting by great sad eyes and a stern mouth. His long unkempt black hair fell to his strong neck. The creases of his coarse dark shirt suggested the powerful muscles that helped his bare sinewy arms handle, as though it were a feather, the enormous oar that served as a rudder for the two boats.

María Clara had surprised him more than once studying her. He would then instantly turn his face away and look out into the distance, to the mountains, to the shore. She took pity on his loneliness and offered him some biscuits. The steersman gave her a startled look, but it lasted only for a second. He took one biscuit and thanked her briefly in a voice that was scarcely audible.

No one troubled about him after that. The merry laughter and the sallies of the young people did not move a single muscle in his face. He did not smile even when the gay Sinang grimaced with every pinch and was soon all smiles again.

After breakfast the party went on to the fish-traps.

There were two of these, set some distance apart, both belonging to Capitan Tiago. From afar a few herons could be seen perched contemplatively on the bamboo stakes of the traps, while the white birds which the Tagalog called *kalaway* flew here and there, their wings brushing the surface of the lake, their strident cries filling the air.

María Clara followed the herons with her eyes as they flew off toward the neighbouring mountain upon the approach of the boats.

'Do those birds nest on the mountain?' she asked the steersman, more perhaps to make him speak than to know the answer.

'Maybe, ma'am,' he replied. 'But no one has ever seen their nests.'

'Then haven't they any?'

'I suppose they have. Otherwise they would be very unhappy.'

The sadness in his voice escaped María Clara.

'And so?'

'They say, ma'am, that the nests of these birds are invisible and can make their possessors equally invisible; that, like the soul which can be seen only in the clear mirror of the eyes, these nests can be seen only in the mirror of the waters.'

María Clara fell musing.

In the meantime they had arrived at the fish-trap, and an old boatman tied up the boats to a bamboo pole.

'Not yet!' Aunt Isabel called out to the boatman's son, who was getting ready to go up the fish-trap with a landing net set at the end of a bamboo pole. 'We must get the *sinigang* ready first so the fish can go directly from the water to the broth.'

'Good old Aunt Isabel!' exclaimed the seminarian, savouring the stew in advance. 'She does not want the fish to be out of water for a moment.'

Andeng, María Clara's foster sister, was reputed to be an excellent cook, notwithstanding her clean and jolly face. She prepared rice water, tomatoes, and *kamias*, helped or hindered by some who perhaps wanted a place in her affections. The other girls peeled squash, shucked peas, or cut spring onions into pieces the size of cigarettes.

To while away the time for those who waited impatiently to watch the fish taken live from the trap, the lovely Iday took up the harp. She played it well, and besides had fingers well worth showing off.

When she had finished, the young people clapped and María Clara kissed her. The harp was the most popular musical instrument in the province and was indeed most suitable for the occasion.

'Victoria, please sing *The Marriage Song*,' requested the mothers.

The men protested and Victoria, who had a good voice, complained of a bad throat. *The Marriage Song* was a beautiful Tagalog elegy which described all the misery and sadness of this state without mentioning any of its pleasures. Then they asked María Clara to sing.

'All the songs I know are sad.'

'No matter, never mind!'

She did not wait to be coaxed and took up the harp. After a few opening notes she sang in a vibrant voice, pleasing and full of feeling:

Sweet are the hours in one's own country
Where all is friendly underneath the sun,
Sweet are the breezes from native ricefields,
Death less bitter, and love more sweetly won!
It is sweet there for the babe to waken
In his mother's bosom; without guile
To seek her kisses and embrace her
While their eyes meet in a smile.
Sweet is death for one's own country
Where all is dear 'neath the sun above,
Bitter the wind for those who have not
Country, Mother, and one true Love!

The voice died away, the song was finished, the harp was mute, yet still they listened and no one clapped. The girls felt their eyes fill up with tears. Ibarra seemed vexed. The impassive steersman kept his eyes in the distance.

Suddenly a thunderous noise was heard. The women screamed and stopped their ears. It was Albino, the ex-seminarian, who with all the strength of his lungs had blown a blast on the carabao-horn trumpet. Laughter and liveliness returned and the eyes, which had filled with tears, turned playful once again.

'What do you want to do, you heretic?' Aunt Isabel shouted. 'Split our eardrums?'

'Madam,' answered the ex-seminarian gravely, 'I have heard tell of a poor trumpeter who lived on the banks of the Rhine and who by playing his trumpet won the hand of a rich and noble maiden.'

'True,' confirmed Ibarra, who could not but join in the renewal of merriment. 'It was the trumpeter of Sackingen.'

'Do you hear that?' asked Albino. 'Well, I want to see if I can be as lucky as he was.'

And he blew another resounding blast with even greater strength, directing the horn particularly toward the ears of the girls who had been most affected by María Clara's song. There was, naturally, a bit of a hubbub, and he was finally silenced by the mothers, who went after him with their slippers.

'What a far cry are the Philippines from the banks of the Rhine!' he cried, massaging his arms. '*O tempora, o mores!* What times, what customs!' And then, quoting a well-known verse on the vicissitudes of fortune: 'Some get concessions, others contusions!'

Everybody was laughing now, even Victoria herself, but Sinang of the merry eyes whispered to María Clara: 'How lucky you are! I wish I had your voice!'

Andeng at last announced that the broth was ready to receive its contents.

The fisherman's son climbed over to the end of the fish-trap, to which the narrowing stake-fences led. Here might well have been inscribed Dante's 'Abandon all hope, ye who enter here', if the poor fish could have read and understood Italian, for fish that entered there came out only to die. The trap proper formed almost a circle, measuring approximately a metre in diameter, and made so that a man could stand on top and scoop the fish out with a small net.

'Now there's one place where I wouldn't be bored fishing with a rod,' said Sinang, shivering with excitement.

Everybody was watching intently; some saw already silver scales flashing, fish wriggling and struggling in the net. But when the young man dipped the net, no fish jumped up.

'It should be full,' muttered Albino. 'The trap hasn't been drawn from for five days.'

The fisherman raised the pole with its net, but it was empty. The water streaming out brightly in the sun made a mocking sound. There were exclamations of surprise, disappointment, and annoyance.

The operation was repeated, with the same result.

'You don't know your business,' Albino protested, climbing up to the enclosure and snatching the net from the fisherman's hands. 'Now watch this! Andeng, have the pot ready!'

But Albino apparently did not know the business either; the net remained empty and everyone laughed at him.

'Don't make so much noise; the fish can hear you and won't let themselves be caught,' he said. 'The net must be torn.' But upon examination the net was found to be whole.

'Let me try,' said León, Iday's suitor.

Having made sure that the pallisade was in good condition and checked the net, he asked: 'Are you sure the trap has not been drawn from for five days?'

'Absolutely! The last time was the eve of All Saints'.'

'Then either there is a spell on the lake or I'm going to get something.'

León dipped the pole in the water and paused astonished. He explored the water with the pole. Then, without withdrawing it, he whispered:

'Crocodile.'

'A crocodile!'

The word passed from mouth to mouth amid general consternation and astonishment.

'What did you say?' they asked him.

'I say there's a crocodile caught in the trap,' said León and, plunging the pole into the water up to the handle, he continued: 'Hear that? That's not sand; that's tough hide, the crocodile's back. Do you see those stakes shaking? It's struggling but it's all coiled up. Wait...it's a big one. Must be a yard thick all round.'

'What to do?'

'Catch it, of course,' said one.

'*Jesús*, and who's going to do that?'

No one offered to dive into the pool. The water was deep.

'We ought to tie him up to our banca and drag him about in triumph,' said Sinang. 'Eating up all our fish!'

'I have never seen a live crocodile,' said María Clara.

The steersman stood up, took a long rope, and climbed nimbly to the platform. León made way for him.

Only María Clara had noticed him so far; now everyone admired his splendid figure.

Then to everyone's surprise he dived into the trap, ignoring all the cries of warning.

'Take this knife!' Crisóstomo shouted, drawing a wide Toledo blade.

But he was already gone in a fountain of water, and the pool enclosed him in its secrets.

'Jesus, Mary, Joseph!' exclaimed the women. 'Something awful's going to happen! Jesus, Mary, Joseph!'

'Don't worry, ladies,' the old boatman said. 'If there's anybody in this province can do it, he can.'

'Who is he?'

'We call him the pilot. He's the best one I've ever seen, but he doesn't like his work.'

The water boiled and bubbled; it was evident that a struggle was taking place in its depths; the pallisade was shaking. Everyone watched in tense silence. Ibarra clutched his sharp knife with nervous hand.

The struggle ceased. The young man's head broke the surface to a chorus of cheers; the women were tearful with emotion.

The pilot drew himself up to the platform, holding the end of the rope, and started to heave at it, dragging up the crocodile.

It had the rope tied around its neck and under its forelegs. It was as big as León had surmised; on its back grew green moss, which is to crocodiles what grey hair is to a man. It was bellowing like a bull, trashing the bamboo fencing with its tail, gripping the stakes, and opening its great black jaws with their long teeth.

The pilot was lifting it up all alone; no one thought of helping him.

Once the crocodile was out of the water and on the platform, he squatted on top of it and snapped its great jaws shut with his powerful hands. He was trying to tie the jaws together when the crocodile, in one last effort, tensed its body and, striking the platform with all the strength of its tail, succeeded in leaping into the lake outside the fish-trap, dragging his captor behind him. The pilot was as good as dead! There was a cry of horror.

Then, with lightning speed, another body struck the water; they had hardly time to recognise Ibarra. María Clara did not faint because Filipina women do not know how.

Bloodstains spread through the waters. The young fisherman dived in, his native blade in hand, followed by his father. But they had scarcely disappeared when Crisóstomo and the pilot emerged, clinging to the reptile's dead body. Its white belly had been ripped open and the knife was stuck in its throat.

The joy was indescribable; countless arms were stretched out to lift the young men from the lake. The old ladies went wild with joy, laughing and breaking out into pious ejaculations. Andeng forgot that her stew had come to a boil three times: all the broth had spilled over and put the fire out. Only María Clara was speechless.

Ibarra was unscathed; the pilot had only a slight scratch on one arm.

'I owe you my life,' he said to Ibarra who was wrapping himself up in woollen blankets and rugs.

There was a note of regret in his voice.

'You are too daring,' answered Ibarra. 'Next time don't tempt God too far.'

'If you had not come back,' whispered María Clara, still pale and trembling.

'If I had not come back and you had followed me,' he replied, completing the thought, 'I should have been in the bottom of the lake with all my family.'

Ibarra had not forgotten that the mortal remains of his father were resting there.

The elder ladies no longer wanted to go to the other fish-trap; they were for going straight home, saying that the day had started badly and many other misfortunes might be in store.

'It's all because we didn't hear Mass,' one of them sighed.

'But what misfortune have we suffered, ladies?' asked Ibarra. 'Only the crocodile was out of luck.'

'Which proves,' concluded the ex-seminarian, 'that throughout its sinful life this wretched reptile never heard Mass. I really don't remember ever seeing it among the numerous crocodiles that frequent the church.'

So the boats went on, after all, to the other fish-corral, and Andeng had to prepare another *sinigang*.

The day wore on; a breeze was blowing gently; the freshening waves rippled around the body of the crocodile, raising, in the language of a contemporary Filipino poet, 'foamy mountains, gleaming, clear, enriched with the colours of the sun'.

Once again came the sound of music. Iday played the harp while the men played accordions and guitars more or less dexterously, but the most amusing was Albino, who really went to work on his guitar, went out of tune and off time or, more often than not, lost track completely and shifted to an entirely different melody.

The other fish-trap was visited with misgivings; many expected to find there the crocodile's mate, but Nature is a joker, and the net was full every time it came out of the water.

Aunt Isabel took command and assigned the various kinds of fish to different native dishes: 'The *ayungin* is good for the *sinigang*. Leave the *bia* for the *escabeche*. The *dalag* and the *buan-buan* for the *pesa*, the *dalag* will last longer. Put them in the net so they can stay in the water. The lobsters to the frying pan! The *banak* is to be roasted, wrapped in banana leaves and stuffed with tomatoes. Leave the rest for decoys; it's bad to empty the corral completely.'

Then they set out for the shore, at the edge of the ancient wood belonging to the Ibarras. There they would lunch in the shade, among the flowers, or under improvised awnings, by the crystalline stream.

There was music in the air; smoke rose in gay and tenuous whirlwinds from the earthen stoves; in the boiling pot the broth sang words of comfort to the poor fish, or perhaps jeered and taunted them; the body of the crocodile slowly revolved in the water, sometimes showing its white wounded belly, sometimes its moss-covered back; but man, Nature's favourite, felt no compunction over what a Brahmin or a vegetarian would have called so many fratricides.

24 • In the Wood

FATHER SALVI had said Mass very early and heard a dozen Confessions in a few minutes, which was not his usual practice.

Afterwards, with the reading of some letters, which had arrived carefully sealed with wax, the good friar seemed to have lost his appetite, and let his morning chocolate become stone cold.

'Father is falling sick,' said the cook as he prepared another cup. 'He hasn't been eating for the last few days, hardly touches two out of six dishes I serve him.'

'It's because he doesn't sleep well,' answered a servant. 'He has had nightmares since he changed bedrooms. His eyes are getting more and more sunken, and he's getting thinner and yellower by the day.'

Really, Father Salví was a pitiful sight. He had pushed away the second cup of chocolate and a dish of pastries from Cebu. Now he paced a large hall in deep thought, crumpling in his bony hands some letters which he read from time to time. Finally, he ordered his carriage, tidied himself up, and drove to the forest, where, near the haunted tree, the picnic was being held.

He dismissed his vehicle on the edge of the forest and entered it alone. A gloomy path, cleared at great effort through the thick wood, led to a stream fed by several hot springs, like those on the slopes of Mount Makiling. Its banks were bright with wild flowers, many of which had not yet been given Latin names, but which were no doubt already known to the golden insects in the wood, to its brilliant butterflies of every size and hue, blue and yellow, black and white, crimson and blue, bearing rubies and emeralds on their wings, and to the thousands of beetles gleaming with enamel and fine gold.

Only the humming of these insects, the chirping of crickets fussing night and day, a bird's song, or the dry snap of a rotten branch falling through the underbrush, broke the eerie silence.

Father Salví wandered for some time among the thick creepers, trying to avoid the thorns which caught at his cotton habit as if to hold him back, and the exposed roots which made him stumble continuously. Suddenly he stopped, hearing merry laughter and fresh voices coming from the stream and growing nearer.

'I'll see if I can find one of those herons' nests,' cried a melodious voice which he knew well. 'Then I could see him without his seeing me, and I could follow him everywhere.'

Father Salví hid himself behind a large tree and pricked up his ears.

'In other words, you want to do to him what the priest is doing to you— watching you everywhere you go?' asked a teasing voice. 'Better look out, jealousy makes people lose weight and get circles under their eyes.'

'No, it isn't jealousy at all. Just curiosity,' protested the silvery voice, but the merry one insisted: 'Oh, yes, it's jealousy, jealousy!' and broke out into laughter.

'If I were jealous, instead of making myself invisible, I would make him invisible, so no one could see him.'

'But then you couldn't see him yourself, and what fun would that be? What we had better do if we find the heron's nest is give it to the priest. Then he could watch us all he wanted, but we wouldn't have to stand the sight of him, don't you think?'

'I don't believe that heron's nest story,' a third voice remarked. 'But if I ever get jealous I'll know how to watch and be invisible.'

'And how? How would you do it? Would you be like Sister Eavesdropper?' This reminiscence of schooldays provoked new peals of laughter.

'You know how Sister Eavesdropper can be outwitted.'

From his hiding place Father Salví could now see María Clara, Victoria, and Sinang wading in the brook. The three moved with their eyes fixed on the mirror of the waters, searching for the mysterious heron's nest. They were wet up to the knees and the billowing folds of their bathing skirts outlined the graceful curves of their legs. Their hair was undone and their arms bare. They wore striped blouses of bright colours. They were picking the flowers and wild roots that grew on the river bank as they went on their quest of the impossible.

The priestly Peeping Tom was pale and motionless. His eyes, shining in their sunken sockets, devoured María Clara's white and finely moulded arms and the graceful neck ending in a suggestion of the bosom. The small rosy feet playing in the water aroused strange sensations in his starved body and unfamiliar thoughts and fancies in his feverish mind.

When the girls had moved out of sight beyond a turn in the stream and behind a thick bamboo clump, and their unkind insinuations could no longer be heard, Father Salví left his hiding place; he moved unsteadily, as if inebriated, and was bathed in sweat. He turned about with a lost look, hesitated, took a few steps as though he meant to follow the girls, then turned in the opposite direction and walked along the river bank in search of the other picnickers.

Farther on he saw in the middle of the stream a sort of bathing house, closely fenced in, from which rose the gay chatter of women. A thick bamboo clump served as its roof and it was hung about with palm leaves, flowers, and pennants. Beyond it he saw a bamboo bridge and the men bathing, while a crowd of male and female servants bustled about improvised stoves, plucking chickens, washing rice, roasting pig, and busying themselves with other culinary tasks.

On the opposite shore, in a clearing made for the purpose, many men and women were gathered under an improvised canvas awning, hanging partly from the branches of hoary trees and partly from newly-driven stakes. Among them were the commanding officer, the vicar, the Mayor, the Vice Mayor, the schoolmaster, and many former mayors and vice mayors, including Capitan Basilio, the father of Sinang, an old adversary of the deceased Don Rafael in a long-standing law suit. Ibarra had invited him to the picnic, saying: 'We are on opposite sides on a matter of law, but that doesn't mean we should be enemies.' The famous spokesman for the conservatives had then accepted the young man's invitation enthusiastically, sending along three turkeys and placing his servants at Ibarra's disposal.

The parish priest was received with respect and deference by everyone, even the commanding officer.

'But where does Your Reverence come from?' asked the latter, seeing the friar's face all scratches and his habit all leaves and twigs of dry branches. 'Did Your Reverence have a fall?'

'No, I lost my way,' answered Father Salví lowering his eyes and inspecting his habit.

Around and about them bottles of lemonade were being opened, and green coconut split for the bathers, who gulped down the cool coconut water and the tender meat, whiter than milk. Each of the young ladies was also given a collar of *sampaguita* flowers interspersed with roses and *ilang-ilang* to perfume her flowing hair. They sat or reclined in tree-hung hammocks or amused themselves at games around a great slab of stone on which could be found playing-cards, chessboards, pamphlets, and the cowries and pebbles used for native games.

They showed the priest the crocodile, but his mind seemed to be elsewhere, and he showed interest only when he was told that Ibarra had inflicted the gaping wound in the reptile's belly. In any case the now famous but anonymous pilot was nowhere to be seen; he had disappeared even before the arrival of the lieutenant.

María Clara emerged from the bathhouse at last, accompanied by her friends. She was as fresh as a rose the morning it opens, with the dew shining like diamonds on its petals. Her first smile was for Crisóstomo, her first frown for Father Salví, who noticed it but remained impassive.

When lunch was served, the parish priest, his vicar, the commanding officer, the Mayor, some former mayors and the Vice Mayor sat down at the table presided over by Ibarra. The mothers did not allow any man to sit down at the ladies' table.

'This time, Albino, you cannot invent holes in boats,' said León to the ex-seminarian.

'What's that? What are you saying?' asked the elder ladies.

'The boats were as whole as this plate,' explained León.

'*Jesús,* you rascal,' chuckled Aunt Isabel.

'Have you any news, Lieutenant, of the criminal who manhandled Father Dámaso?' Father Salví asked.

'What criminal, Your Reverence?' asked the commanding officer, looking at the parish priest through the wine-glass he had just emptied.

'Who else? The man who day before yesterday beat up Father Dámaso on the street, of course.'

'Beat up Father Dámaso?' asked a number of voices.

The vicar seemed to smile.

'Exactly. Father Dámaso is now in bed. They say it was one Elias, the same man who threw you into a mud-hole, Lieutenant.'

The officer flushed with shame, or perhaps it was the wine he had drunk.

'Well, I must say that all the time I thought you knew all about the incident,' continued Father Salví somewhat sarcastically. 'After all, I said to myself, the commanding officer of the garrison...'

The lieutenant bit his lip and stammered some stupid excuse.

At this point the company's notice was attracted by a pale, thin, poorly-clad woman; she had approached them so quietly that no one had seen her, made so little noise that had it been night they would have taken her for a ghost.

'Give that poor woman something to eat,' said the elder ladies. 'Listen, come here.'

But the woman went on to the table where the friar was sitting. He turned, recognised her, and dropped his knife.

'Give her something to eat,' ordered Ibarra.

'The night is dark and children vanish,' mumbled the beggar. But when the lieutenant tried to speak to her, she took one look at him and fled in panic to the wood.

'Who is she?' asked Ibarra.

'An unfortunate woman who has been driven out of her mind by shock and sorrow,' answered Don Filipo. 'She has been that way for the last four days.'

'Is her name Sisa?'

'Your soldiers arrested her,' the Vice Mayor told the commanding officer rather bitterly. 'They marched her through the town because of something having to do with her sons—I don't know what—it isn't quite clear yet.'

'What?' asked the lieutenant turning to the friar. 'She isn't the mother of your two sacristans, is she?'

The parish priest nodded.

'They've disappeared. Nobody knows where they are,' added Don Filipo sternly, looking at the Mayor, who dropped his eyes.

'Go after that woman,' Crisóstomo ordered the servants. 'I have promised to help find her children...'

'Disappeared, you say?' asked the lieutenant. 'Have your sacristans disappeared, Father?'

The priest gulped down the glass of wine before him and nodded.

'Well, well, Father!' exclaimed the officer with a jeering laugh, pleased to get his own back. 'Your Reverence loses a few pesos and my sergeant is routed out of bed to look for them; then Your Reverence loses two sacristans and not a word said. And you, Mr. Mayor... You must admit that you...'

Without bothering to continue he broke into a laugh, sinking his spoon into the red meat of a wild papaya.

The priest lost his head and blurted out in confusion:

'But I'm accountable for the money!'

'That's a fine answer, Father, for a shepherd of souls,' interrupted the lieutenant, his mouth full. 'A fine answer, indeed, for a man of religion!'

Ibarra made as if to intervene but Father Salví, controlling himself, replied with a strained smile:

'And do you know, Lieutenant, what they say about the disappearance of those boys? You don't? Well, then, ask your men.'

'What?' asked the officer, dropping his smile.

'They say that on the night of their disappearance several shots were heard.'

'Several shots?' repeated the lieutenant looking round at the company, who nodded confirmation.

Then Father Salví replied slowly and with biting sarcasm:

'Come now, I see that not only are you unable to do your duty for arresting malefactors but you don't even know what your own men are doing. Yet you set yourself up as a preacher and seek to teach others how to do their job. Surely you know the saying: the fool knows more about his own household than the wise man about his neighbour's.'

'Gentlemen,' broke in Crisóstomo, seeing the lieutenant pale. 'This reminds me. Now, what do you say to a little plan I have? I would like to put that madwoman in the hands of a good doctor, and in the meantime search for her children with your help and advice.'

The return of the servants, who had not been able to find the madwoman, put an end to the quarrel, and conversation turned to other subjects.

After the meal and while tea and coffee were being served, young and old separated into various groups. Some took to the chessboards, others picked up the playing-cards. The girls, however, chose to have their fortunes told through a device called *The Wheel of Fate*.

'Come over here, Mr. Ibarra,' shouted Capitan Basilio, who was a little high. 'We have a litigation fifteen years old, and no judge on the Supreme Court seems to be able to decide it. Shall we try and end it with a game of chess?'

'With great pleasure!' answered the young man. 'I'll be with you in a moment; the lieutenant is saying goodbye.'

Upon hearing of the contest all the elders who knew chess gathered round the board. The game was interesting and attracted even the uninitiated. But the ladies surrounded the priest to talk to him about spiritual matters. Father Salví probably did not find the place or the occasion suitable, for he gave vague answers and his sad and somewhat annoyed look fixed itself everywhere but on his interlocutors.

The game began with much gravity.

'It's understood, of course,' said Ibarra, 'that if the game ends in a draw we'll ask for the dismissal of the case.'

In the middle of the game Ibarra received a telegram. His eyes lighted up and he turned pale, but he put the message unread into his wallet, with a glance at the group of young people who were still cross-examining Fate amid shouts and laughter.

'Check the king,' said the young man.

Capitan Basilio had no other alternative than to hide his king behind his queen.

'Check the queen,' Ibarra rejoined, threatening it with a rook, which was protected by a pawn.

As he could neither cover the queen nor move it back because of the king, which was behind it, Capitan Basilio asked for time to think.

'With pleasure,' said Ibarra. 'It so happens that I had something urgent to say to our friends over there.'

He stood up and granted his opponent a quarter of an hour.

Iday was holding the cardboard disk with its forty-eight questions while Albino had the book of answers.

'It's a lie, it's not true, no,' Sinang was saying, midway to tears.

'What's the matter?' asked María Clara.

'Just imagine, I ask when I will grow up and be sensible. I throw the dice, and this nightbird of a priest reads the answer from the book: "When frogs grow hair." What do you think of that?'

Sinang made a face at the ex-seminarian, who could not hold back his laughter.

'What made you ask such a question in the first place?' her cousin Victoria asked. 'Serves you right for asking it.'

'Your turn,' they told Ibarra, giving him the wheel. 'We've agreed that the one who gets the best answer shall have a present from the rest. We have all asked our questions already.'

'And who has had the best answer?'

'María Clara, María Clara,' answered Sinang. 'Like it or not, we made her ask the question: "Is he faithful and true?" and the book answered—'

But María Clara, all blushes, covered Sinang's mouth with her hands and would not let her go on.

'Then give me the wheel,' smiled Crisóstomo. 'I ask: "Shall I be successful in my present undertaking?"'

'What a dull question,' complained Sinang.

Ibarra threw the dice and looked up in the book of answers the page and line indicated by the number on the dice.

'Dreams are but dreams,' read out Albino.

Ibarra drew out the telegram and opened it. His hands were shaking.

This time your book is wrong,' he exclaimed happily. 'Read this.'
'SCHOOL PROJECT APPROVED CASE DECIDED YOUR FAVOUR.
What does that mean?'

'Didn't you say that a prize was to be given to the one getting the best answer?' he asked in a voice shaky with emotion, as he carefully divided the telegram into two.

'Yes, we did.'

'Well, then, this is my gift,' he said, giving María Clara one half of the message. 'I am going to build a school for boys and girls in the town. The school will be my gift.'

'And the other half?'

'It's for the one who got the worst answer.'

'Then it's for me,' shouted Sinang.

Ibarra gave her the paper and walked away quickly.

'And what does this mean?'

But the happy young man was already far away and had returned to his game of chess. María Clara dried a happy tear.

Father Salví, as if casually, now joined the gay group. On his approach the laughter and chatter died down. He looked at the young people and could not find anything suitable to say; they were silent, waiting for him to speak.

'What's this?' he asked at last, picking up the book and glancing through it. '*The Wheel of Fate*, a book of game,' answered León.

'Don't you know it's a sin to believe in these things?' he cried out and angrily tore up its pages.

There were cries of surprise and anger.

'It's a greater sin to dispose of what belongs to someone else without the owner's consent,' rejoined Albino, rising. 'Your Reverence, that is equivalent to robbery and forbidden by God and men.'

María Clara clasped her hands and looked in dismay on the remnants of the book that a moment ago had made her so happy.

Father Salví, contrary to expectations, did not reply to Albino. He watched the torn pages scatter in the breeze, some to be lost in the forest, others in the water. Then he stumbled away, his head between his hands. He stopped a few seconds to speak to Ibarra, who accompanied him as far as one of the carriages which were waiting to take the guests away.

'At least that killjoy knew enough to go away,' muttered Sinang. 'He's got a face which seems to say: "Don't laugh so much; I know all your sins."'

After he had made his present to his fiancee, Ibarra was so happy that he began to play carelessly, without thinking out his moves or pausing to study the position of the pieces on the board.

The result was that, although Capitan Basilio had previously been hopelessly on the defensive, the game ended in a draw due to Ibarra's many subsequent mistakes.

'Case dismissed, case dismissed!' said Capitan Basilio gaily.

'Yes, we'll ask for its dismissal,' repeated the young man, 'whatever the decision of the judges may have been.'

They shook hands effusively.

While those present were celebrating the end of a suit which had driven both parties to exasperation, four Constabulary soldiers led by a sergeant, all fully armed and with fixed bayonets, suddenly interrupted the merrymaking and threw the ladies into a panic.

'Stand still, everybody!' shouted the sergeant. 'We'll shoot anyone who moves.'

Disregarding this stupid bravado, Ibarra rose to his feet and went up to the sergeant.

'What do you want?' he asked.

'We want the instant surrender to us of a criminal named Elias who served you as pilot this morning,' answered the sergeant in a threatening manner.

'A criminal? The pilot? You must be mistaken,' replied Ibarra.

'No, sir. That man Elias has been lately charged with laying hands on a priest...'

'Oh, was he the pilot?'

'The same one, according to reports. You admit people of ill repute to your parties, Mr. Ibarra.'

The latter looked at the sergeant from head to foot.

'I don't have to account to you for my actions. Everyone is welcome to our parties. You yourself, if you had come earlier, would have been given a seat at the table, like your C.O., who was with us two hours ago.'

Ibarra turned his back on the sergeant.

The sergeant chewed his moustache and, judging that his was the weaker side, ordered his men to search the wood, everywhere, for the pilot whose written description he had with him.

Don Filipo warned him: 'Now, look here, that description would fit nine-tenths of the natives. You might be making a mistake.'

When at last the soldiers returned, they said they had seen neither anyone nor any boat to arouse suspicion. The sergeant muttered shortly to himself and left as he had come, in Constabulary style.

Gradually spirits rose again amid questions and comments.

'So that was the Elias who threw the lieutenant into a mud-hole,' said León thoughtfully.

'How did it happen?'

'They say that one very rainy day in September, the lieutenant met a man carrying a load of firewood. The street was full of mudholes and there was only a narrow pathway along the edge, just wide enough for one person. Apparently the lieutenant, who was on horseback, did not stop but instead dug in his spurs, ordering the man with a shout to give way. But the latter was obviously unwilling either to carry his heavy load all that way back or to step aside into the mud, so he went ahead. The lieutenant lost his temper and tried to ride the man down, but the latter seized a stick of firewood and hit the lieutenant's horse such a blow on the head that it lost its footing and fell with its rider into the mud. They say that the man then went on his way, serenely indifferent to the raging lieutenant who fired five times at him from the mud. The man was a complete stranger to the lieutenant, so they guessed it was the famous Elias, who had shown up in this province a few months ago, nobody knew where from, and had made himself known to the Constabulary of certain other towns by similar feats.'

'Is he a bandit?' asked Victoria with a shudder.

'I don't think so. They say that once he even fought off some housebreakers.'

'He certainly doesn't look like a criminal,' added Sinang.

'No, he doesn't,' replied María Clara thoughtfully. 'But he has a brooding look. I didn't see him smile the whole morning.'

The afternoon went by and it was time to go back to town. They left the wood at sunset, falling silent as they passed the ghostly grave of Ibarra's ancestor, but were soon engrossed again in their warm and lively chatter under those branches so little used to their gaiety. The trees brooded over them and the air plants swayed above them as if mourning the swift passage of youth and its dreams for a day.

So let us leave them, going home by the light of torches, huge and crimson in the night, to the strumming of guitars. The company scatters, the lights go out, the song dies, the guitars grow silent, as they approach the habitations of man. Put on your masks; you are again among your brothers!

25 • *Elias and Salomé*

THE stout constables would have found their man if, after having thrown the outing into an uproar, they had proceeded before sunset that same evening to a small but picturesque cottage by the lakeside.

It lay amid luxuriant bamboo clumps and palm groves, on a slight eminence that made it safe from any rise in the waters. Red-flowering bushes grew at the foot of its rough rustic walls, which, like a flight of steps leading down to the lake, were cut from raw stone. The upper walls of the cottage were made of palm and wooden slats held together with split bamboo strips, and decorated with wreaths blessed on Palm Sunday, and artificial flowers from China. An *ilang-ilang* tree thrust an inquisitive branch through an open window, saturating the air with perfume. Cocks and hens strutted tentatively on the ridge of the roof, while others stayed on the ground to dispute with ducks, turkeys, and doves the last remaining grains of rice and corn which had been scattered in a kind of yard.

On an open bamboo porch a girl in her teens was sewing a transparent blouse of brilliant colours by the last rays of the sun. Her clothes were plain but becoming and clean; her blouse, skirt, and overskirt, well-mended. She carried no adornment or jewel other than a tortoise-shell comb, which served to fix the simple arrangement of her hair, and a rosary of black beads which hung from her neck over the front of her blouse.

She was attractive because she was young, because she had nice eyes, a pretty nose, and a small mouth, and because her features were harmonious and enlivened by a sweet expression; but she was not a beauty to strike the eye at first glance; she was like a flower in the fields, pale and without noticeable fragrance, which is carelessly stepped underfoot, and whose beauty can be appreciated only after a careful examination, one of those nameless flowers of almost imperceptible perfume.

From time to time she looked out on the lake, whose waters were rather troubled; she stopped her sewing and listened attentively, but, hearing nothing, returned to her task with a slight sigh.

When she finally heard the sound of steps, her face lighted up. She put aside her sewing, stood up, smoothed down her dress, and waited smiling beside the hut's small bamboo ladder.

Amid a flurry of doves and the honking and clunking of ducks and hens the taciturn steersman appeared, carrying a bundle of firewood and a bunch of bananas which he deposited wordlessly on the floor as he handed to the girl a milkfish that was still squirming and trashing its tail.

She looked at him anxiously, placed the fish in a basin full of water, and then resumed her sewing, sitting down beside the still silent Elias.

'I thought you would be coming by way of the lake,' she ventured to open the conversation.

'I could not, Salomé,' Elias answered quietly. 'The police launch is here and is patrolling the lake. There is someone aboard who knows me.'

'Lord, Lord,' she sighed apprehensively.

There was a long pause as he silently watched the pliant bamboo swaying from side to side and waving their lance-like leaves.

'Did you enjoy yourselves very much?' asked Salomé.

'*They* did, they enjoyed themselves.'

'Tell me how you spent the day. It will be almost as nice as having been with you.'

'Well, they went out on the lake... they fished... they sang songs, and... well, they enjoyed themselves,' he answered, his mind elsewhere.

Salomé could not restrain herself and exclaimed, with a searching look:

'Elias, you're so gloomy.'

'Gloomy?'

'Oh, I know!' she cried. 'Your whole life is gloomy. Are you afraid they'll catch you?'

Something like a smile moved his mouth.

'Do you need anything?' she went on.

'I have your friendship, haven't I?' he replied. 'And we are both equally poor.'

'Then what is the matter with you?'

'You have told me yourself often enough, Salomé. I am not one for talking.'

She bent her head and went on sewing. Then, trying to sound indifferent, she asked again:

'Were there many of you?'

'There were many of them.'

'Many women?'

'Many.'

'Who were the... young ones... the pretty ones?'

'I didn't know all of them. There was one...the fiancee of the rich young man who has just come back from Europe,' answered Elias indistinctly.

'Oh, I know, the daughter of the rich Capitan Tiago! They say she has turned out a real beauty!'

'Oh yes, very beautiful and very kind,' he replied, stifling a sigh.

Salomé gazed at him briefly and then lowered her head.

If Elias had not been so busy studying the fanciful shapes that clouds take at sunset he would have seen that Salomé was crying, and that two tears had fallen from her eyes on to her sewing. This time it was he who broke the silence, saying as he rose to his feet:

'Goodbye, Salomé. It's almost sunset, and, as you say, it will not do to have the neighbours saying that night overtook me here. But,' he added, in a different tone and with a frown, 'you have been crying! Now, don't try to deny it with that smile. You have been crying.'

'Well, yes, I have,' she answered smiling through fresh tears. 'It's only that I am gloomy too.'

'Dear friend, and why should you be gloomy?'

'Because soon I shall have to leave this place where I was born and brought up,' she answered drying her tears.

'But why?'

'Because it isn't right that I should live by myself. I shall go and live with some relatives of mine in Mindoro. Soon I shall be able to pay the debts my mother left when she died; the town fiesta is coming, and my hens and turkeys are well fattened up. But leaving the house where I was born and brought up will be more than leaving behind half of myself... the flowers, the garden, my doves! The next storm, the next flood, and it will all go down the lake!'

Elias grew thoughtful and, taking her by the hand and looking into her eyes, he asked her:

'Have you heard any talk against you? No? Have I ever tried to take advantage of you? You know I haven't. Then it must be because you have grown tired of our friendship and you want to avoid me...'

'Don't say that! If only I could grow tired of our friendship!' she interrupted. *'Jesús, María!* I spend the whole day and night thinking of the hour in the afternoon when you will be coming. You know, before I knew you, when my poor mother was still alive, I thought the morning and the night were the best times God had made. I loved the morning because of the sun rising and brightening the waters of the lake where my father lies; I loved to see my flowers freshened up, their leaves, which had seemed almost withered the day before, greener than ever. My doves and my hens greeted me so cheerfully, as if they were saying good morning; I did love the morning because, after tidying up the house, I would go off in my little boat to sell their midday meals to the fishermen, and they would give me fish, or let me have the ones I could find in their nets. The night I loved because I would rest from the work of the day, and dream in silence underneath these bamboo, to the music of their leaves, forgetting reality. I loved the night also because it brought me back my mother, who was away gambling all day. Well, ever since I have known you, morning and night have lost all their charms for me, and I find only the afternoon beautiful. Sometimes I think the morning was made only to prepare the way for the enjoyment of the delights of the afternoon, and the night only to dream and to enjoy the remembrance of feelings I never knew before. If it were left to me to live like this forever...! God knows I am happy as I am, I want nothing more than to be able to go on working like this, I do not envy rich girls their money, but...'

'But?'

'Nothing. I envy them nothing so long as I have your friendship.'

'Salomé,' Elias replied bitterly, 'you know my cruel past and you know that my misfortunes are not of my own making. If it were not for the tragic destiny that sometimes makes me regret my father and mother ever loved each other, if it were not because I do not want my children to suffer what my sister and I suffered, and what I still suffer, you would have been my wife in the eyes of God many months ago, and we would now be living in the depths of our forests, far from mankind. But by this very love I bear you, by this family which is to be, I have sworn to end with me that fate which has passed in my family from father to son; and this must be so, because neither you nor I would want to hear our children bewailing our love, which had brought them only misery. You do well in going to your relatives. Forget me. Forget a love that is foolish and useless. Perhaps over there you will meet someone different…'

'Elias!' she cried reproachfully.

'Do not misunderstand me. I am telling you what I would have told my sister if she were alive. I have no complaint against you, no hidden thought. Why should I hurt you with a complaint? Believe me, go to your relatives, forget me. Your forgetfulness will make me less unfortunate. You have nobody here except me, and the day I fall into the hands of those who are after me, you will be alone, and, if it is ever known that you were the friend of Elias, alone for the rest of your life. Make the most of your youth and your beauty and find yourself a good husband; you deserve one. You still do not know what it is to live alone, alone in the midst of mankind.'

'I was hoping you would come with me.'

'Ah, that is impossible,' answered Elias with a shake of the head, 'and now more than ever. I still haven't found what I came here to seek. Impossible. And today I lost my freedom.'

He told her briefly what had happened that morning.

'I didn't ask him to save my life; I am not grateful for what he did; but I am grateful for the spirit that moved him and I must pay this debt. For the rest of it, in Mindoro as anywhere else the past will always remain and will be discovered.'

'Then at least,' Salomé told him lovingly, 'stay here when I have gone, live in this cottage. It will make you remember me, and from far away I shall not fear that my house has gone with the wind or the waves. And when I think of this place, the memory of you and the memory of my home will be one. Sleep here, where I have slept and dreamt. It will be as if I myself were living here with you, as if I were at your side…'

'Oh,' cried Elias twisting his arms in despair, 'you are making me forget!' His eyes flashed, but only for an instant, and freeing himself from the girl's arms he fled and was lost in the shadows of the forest.

Salomé followed him with her eyes and listened motionless to the sound of his feet growing fainter.

26 • *In the Scholar's House*

NEXT morning, Ibarra toured his estate briefly and then went to old Tasio's house.

There was perfect calm in the garden; the swallows fluttering about the eaves could scarcely be heard. With its old walls covered with moss and a climbing vine that curled around its windows, the house seemed like the abode of silence.

Ibarra tied his horse carefully to a post and, almost on tiptoe, crossed the neat and scrupulously well-kept garden. He went up the stairs and, as the door was open, entered.

The first thing he saw was the old man, bent over a book in which he seemed to be writing. Collections of insects and leaves were hung on the walls among maps and old bookcases crammed with printed volumes and manuscripts.

The scholar was so absorbed in his task that he noticed the young man's arrival only when the latter, not wishing to disturb him, was on the point of withdrawing.

'Oh, you're here, are you?' he asked, giving Ibarra a puzzled look.

'I beg your pardon,' the latter answered. 'I see that you're very busy...'

'Well, I was doing a little writing, but there's no hurry. I need a break anyway. Can I help you?'

'Very much!' answered Ibarra drawing closer. His eyes fell on the book on the table and he exclaimed:

'What's this? Are you engaged in deciphering hieroglyphics?'

'No,' answered the old man, offering him a chair. 'I do not understand Egyptian, nor even Coptic, but I know something of writing systems and I am using my own symbols.'

'But why should you bother to write in code?' asked the astonished Ibarra.

'So no one can read what I write.'

Ibarra stared at the old scholar, wondering if he was really mad after all and if he was telling the truth. He leafed through the book and saw very well drawn animals, circles, semicircles, flowers, feet, hands, arms, and other symbols.

'But why do you write at all if you don't want to be read?'

'I am not writing for this generation but for those yet to come. If this one could read what I have written, it would burn my books, my whole life's work. But the generation that deciphers these characters will be a learned generation; it will understand me and say: "Not everyone slept during the night of our forefathers!" These strange characters—the sense of mystery they will create—will save my work from the ignorance of men, just as strange rites and the sense of the unknown have preserved many truths from destruction at the hands of priests.'

'And in what language do you write?' asked Ibarra, after a pause.

'In our own, in Tagalog.'

'Can it be written in hieroglyphics?'

'If it were not for the difficulty involved in drawing, which requires time and patience, I would almost say they are more useful than the Latin alphabet. The ancient Egyptians used the same vowels that we do in Tagalog. For example, the sound "o" is only used at the end of a word, and is not equivalent to the Spanish "o" but is midway between the Spanish "o" and "u". Also, like us, the ancient Egyptians did not really have the sound of the Spanish "e". But they had our "ha" and "kha" which cannot be truly written with the Latin alphabet used in Spanish. Take this word *mukha*,' he said, pointing to his book. 'I can transcribe the syllable "ha" more accurately with this drawing of a fish than with the Latin "h", which in any case is pronounced in a number of ways in Europe. Where the aspirate is not so strong, as for example in the word *hain*, where the "h" sound is weaker, I transcribe or symbolise it with the torso of a lion or these three lotus flowers, according to the strength of the vowel. One thing more: I can also transcribe the nasal sound which does not exist in the Spanish-Latin alphabet. I repeat that were it not for the difficulty of drawing the symbols, which must be perfect, it might even be more expedient to use these hieroglyphs in writing Tagalog. In any case this very difficulty compels me to be concise and to write only what is strictly necessary. The work also serves to amuse me when my guests from China and Japan go away.'

'Guests?'

'Don't you hear them? My guests are the swallows. This year one was missing, probably caught by some naughty Chinese or Japanese youngster.'

'How do you know they come from those countries?'

'Simply because for some years now I have been tying to their legs, just before it was time for them to go, pieces of paper with the name of the Philippines written there in English. I guessed they would not be flying very far away, and English is spoken in almost all these parts. For many years my little paper brought no answer, but lately I had them written in Chinese characters. Then the following November the swallows returned with messages other than mine. I had a Chinaman read them for me. One was in Chinese and conveyed greetings from the banks of the Hwang-ho. Another was apparently in Japanese. But I'm wasting your time with these stories. I still don't know how I can help you.'

'I came to talk to you about a matter of some importance,' answered the young man. 'Yesterday afternoon...'

'Have they arrested the unfortunate man?' interrupted the old man with much interest.

'Do you mean Elias? How did you know?'

'I saw the Muse of the Constabulary.'

'Who's that?'

'The lieutenant's wife. You didn't invite her to your party, but everybody in town knew the story of the crocodile by yesterday morning. She is as shrewd as she is mean, and guessed that only a man as foolhardy as the pilot could have thrown her husband into a mud-hole and manhandled Father Dámaso. She reads her husband's official reports and instructions, and when he returned blind-drunk, she lost no time in sending the sergeant and his squad out to your picnic, to spoil it and to get even with you. Be careful. Eve was a good woman, and she was made by God Himself. Doña Consolación is a bad woman, or so they say, and nobody knows where she came from! To be good, a woman must have been, at least some time, a virgin or a mother.'

Ibarra smiled slightly, then, drawing some papers from his wallet, he said:

'My late father was in the habit of asking your advice on certain matters, and I remember that he had reason only to congratulate himself on following it. I have in hand a little plan which I must make sure will succeed.'

Ibarra told him briefly of his plan for a school, which was to be a gift to his fiancee, and put before the impressed scholar the building plans he had received from Manila.

'Now I should like you to tell me whom in town I should win over to make my plan as successful as possible. You know everyone here. I have just arrived and I am almost a stranger in my own country.'

Old Tasio carefully examined the plans before him with eyes moist with tears.

'You're going to do what I once dreamed of doing, a poor madman's dream!' he exclaimed greatly moved. 'And my first advice is never to ask my advice!'

Ibarra looked surprised.

'Sensible people,' he continued bitterly, 'will take you for a madman too. People believe that those who don't think as they do are crazy and that's why they think me crazy. I'm grateful for it because the day I regain my reason according to their standards they'll take away the small measure of freedom I have purchased with my reputation as a rational being. And who knows? They may be right, I don't think or live according to their laws. My principles and my ideals are different. They think the Mayor is smart because he has never learned to do anything except serve chocolate to the parish priests and suffer Father Dámaso's bad temper, but now he is rich, can trouble the petty dreams of his fellow-citizens, and sometimes even talks of justice. "There's a man with brains!" the masses think. "See—he started with nothing and he has become great!" But look at me. I inherited wealth and rank; I spent my life in study; and now I am a poor man, unfit even for the most ridiculous office. They all say: "He's a fool. He doesn't know what it's all about." The priest nicknames me a pseudo-intellectual and suggests that I'm really a charlatan who is showing off what he learned in the university, although that is what is least useful to me. Maybe I'm really crazy and they are the sane ones. Who can tell?'

The old man moved his head as if to shake off a thought and continued:

'My second piece of advice is to consult the parish priest, the Mayor, and all other persons of rank. They will give you bad advice, foolish, worthless, but, of course, you don't have to follow it just because you asked for it. Pretend to do so as far as possible; make them believe you're doing what they want you to do.'

After a moment's reflection Ibarra replied:

'Your advice is good but difficult to follow. Must I carry out my plans under cover? Can't what is good be done in spite of everything? Truth does not have to dress up like Error in order to prevail.'

'But no one loves the naked Truth!' cried the old man. 'What you say is good in theory but it is feasible only in the dream-world of youth. Take the schoolmaster. He was fighting in a vacuum. He wanted to do good, with the sincerity of a child, and all he got was jeers and laughter. You told me you were a stranger in your own country; I believe you. You made a bad start the very day you arrived. You humiliated a friar reputed saintly by the masses and wise by his brethren. I hope to God you have not compromised your future! Just because the Dominicans and the Augustinians look down on the coarse habit of the Franciscans, their rope girdles and their open sandals; and just because a famous professor of the University of Santo Tomas once recalled that Pope Innocent III had described the Rule of the Augustinians as more fit for pigs than for men, don't imagine that all these friars will not join hands when the time comes to confirm what one of their procurators declared: "The lowest lay-brother is more powerful than the Government with all its soldiers." *Cave ne cadas.* Beware lest you fall! Money talks, and the golden calf has many times ousted God from His altars, even in the days of Moses.'

'I am not so pessimistic and life in my own country doesn't seem to me to be that dangerous,' smiled Ibarra. 'I believe your fears are a little exaggerated, and I hope to be able to achieve all my objectives without meeting any serious opposition from that quarter.'

'You will, if the friars help you. You won't, if they don't. The friar will only have to hitch the rope round his waist or shake the dust from his habit for you to break your head against the walls of the parish house. On the slightest pretext, the Mayor would then refuse you tomorrow what he granted today; no mother would allow her child to go to your school; and so, for all your pains, you would have been working against all you desire because you would only have discouraged anyone who might later wish to be equally generous.'

'For all that,' argued Ibarra, 'I can't believe the friars are so powerful as you make them out to be. Even supposing, even admitting, that what you say is true, I should still have on my side all sensible people, and the Government, which has the best of intentions and high objectives, and openly seeks the good of the Philippines.'

'The Government! The Government you say!' muttered the scholar, and raised his eyes to the ceiling. 'However desirous it may be of improving the country for its own sake and that of the Mother Country, however much this or that official may remember the generous spirit of Ferdinand and Isabella and pledge himself to it, the Government itself sees nothing, hears nothing, and decides nothing except what the parish priest or the head of a religious Order makes it see, hear, and decide. It is convinced that it rests on them alone; that it stands because they support it; that it lives because they allow it to live; and that the day they are gone, it will fall like a discarded puppet. The Government is intimidated with threats to raise the people against it, and the people cowed with the Government's armed forces. This is the basis of a strategy that is quite simple, but it works for the same reason that cowards in cemeteries take their own shadows for ghosts and the echoes of their own voices for calls from the dead. So long as the Government does not deal directly with the people it will not cease to be a ward, and will live like those idiots who tremble at the sound of their keeper's voice and curry his favour.

The Government does not plan a better future; it is only an arm, the convent is the head. Because of the inertia with which it allows itself to be dragged from failure to failure, it becomes a shadow, loses its identity, and, weak and incapable, entrusts everything to selfish interests. If you don't believe me, compare our governmental system with that of the countries you have visited...'

'Oh,' interrupted Ibarra, 'that's asking too much! Surely it's enough to satisfy us that our people do not complain or suffer like those of other countries, thanks to the Church and the benevolence of our rulers.'

'The people do not complain because they have no choice; they do not move because they are in a stupor; and you say that they do not suffer because you have not seen how their hearts bleed. But some day you will see and hear! Then woe unto those who draw their strength from ignorance and fanaticism, who take their pleasure in fraud, and who work under cover of night, confident that all are asleep! When the light of day reveals the monstrous creatures of the night, the reaction will be terrifying. All the forces stifled for centuries, the poisons distilled drop by drop, all the repressed emotions, will come to light in a great explosion. Who shall then settle the accounts, such accounts as the peoples of the world have presented from time to time in those revolutions that history records in bloodstained pages?'

'God, the Government, and the Church will not allow such a thing to happen!' replied Crisóstomo, greatly moved in spite of himself. 'The Philippines is religious and loves Spain, and she will realise how much the Mother Country is doing for her. Of course there are abuses; I won't deny there are shortcomings;

but Spain is working out reforms to remedy them; she is developing a programme; she is not selfish.'

'I know it, and that's the worst of it. The reforms which come from above are annulled below by the vices of all, by, for example, the get-rich-quick madness, and the ignorance of the people who let everything pass. Abuses cannot be corrected by royal decree if zealous authorities do not watch over its execution, and while freedom of speech against the excesses of petty tyrants is not granted. Otherwise plans will stay plans, the abuses will continue, which will not prevent the cabinet member in Madrid from enjoying the sleep of one who has done his duty. Furthermore, if a high official comes with great and generous ideas, he soon hears such advice as this, while behind his back he is taken for a fool: "Your Excellency does not know the country, and the character of the natives; Your Excellency will spoil them; Your Excellency will do well to trust So and So, and so on." And as His Excellency really does not know the country, which heretofore he had thought was somewhere in America, and besides, has weaknesses and faults of his own like any other mortal, he finally allows himself to be convinced. His Excellency also keeps in mind that he has worked hard and endured even more to obtain his office, that he will hold it only for three years, and that he is getting old and must think of his future rather than quixotic enterprises—a modest house in Madrid, a little country lodge, a good income on which to make a show at Court, those are the things he must work for in the Philippines. Let us not ask for miracles; let us not expect the foreigner who comes only to make his fortune and then go home, to take an interest in the welfare of the country. What does he care about the blessings or the curses of a country which he does not know and where he has no memories or loved ones? To be satisfying, glory must ring in the ears of those we love, within the walls of our homes, in the air of our native country where we shall be laid to rest. We want glory to warm our graves, so that we may not be reduced to nothing and something of ourselves may yet endure. We cannot promise any of these things to those who come to guide our destinies. And the worst of it is that, just when they have begun to learn what their duty is, it is time for them to leave. But we are getting away from our subject.'

'Before returning to it, I must first get something clear,' interrupted the young man excitedly. 'I grant you that the Government does not understand the people, but I also think that the people understand the Government even less. There are officials who are useless, even bad, if you will, but there are also good ones, and, if the latter can do nothing, it is because they are faced with an inert mass, the people, who take scant interest in the matters which concern them. However, I did not come here to argue with you on this point; I came to ask your advice. You say I should bow my head before grotesque idols...'

'Yes, and I repeat it because in this country you have either to bow your head or... lose it.'

'Bow my head or lose it,' repeated Ibarra thoughtfully. 'It is a hard dilemma. But why should it be so? Is my love of country incompatible with love for Spain? It is necessary to humiliate oneself to be a good Christian, and to betray one's conscience to achieve a good objective? I love my country, the Philippines, because I owe her my life and happiness, and because every man should love his country. I love Spain, the country of my forefathers, because, after all, the Philippines owe and will owe to Spain both happiness and future. I am a Catholic and keep pure the faith of my fathers. I don't see why I should bow my head when I can hold it high, or place it in the hands of my enemies when I can defeat them.'

'The reason is that the field in which you want to work is in the power of your enemies, and you cannot prevail against them. You must first kiss the hand that—'

'Kiss it!' Ibarra interrupted him passionately. 'You forget that between them they killed my father and then threw his body out of the grave. But I am his son and do not forget it, and, if I do not avenge him, it is to protect the good name of the Church.'

The old scholar bent his head.

'Mr. Ibarra,' he replied slowly, 'if you remember such things, and indeed I cannot advice you to forget them, you had better renounce the enterprise you plan and look for some other way to promote the welfare of our countrymen. The undertaking needs another man, because, to put it through, money and goodwill are not enough. In our country abnegation, tenacity, and faith are also required; the field is not ready for sowing, it is full of weeds.'

Ibarra realised the value of this advice, but could not allow himself to be discouraged. The memory of María Clara was in his mind, and it was necessary to keep his promise.

'Does not your experience suggest a way out that would be less painful?' he asked in a subdued voice.

The old man took him by the arm and led him to the window. A chilly wind, forerunner of the north wind, was blowing. Before them was the garden stretching out to the dense wood that served the house as a park.

'Why shouldn't we do as that weak stem loaded with roses and buds?' asked the scholar, pointing to a beautiful rose bush. 'The wind blows and shakes it and it bows down as if to hide its precious burden. If the stem were to stay straight it would break, and the wind would scatter the flowers, and the buds would die unopened. But the wind passes on, and then the stem straightens up again, proud of its treasure. Who will blame it for having bowed to necessity? Take that giant tree. The eagle builds its nest in those swaying stately branches. I transplanted it from the forest as a weak sapling. For months I had to prop it up with bamboo stakes. But if I had transplanted instead some full-grown vigorous tree, I am sure it would not have survived. The wind would have blown it down before its roots could have taken a firm grip, and before the ground had settled round it and given it the sustenance proper to its size and height. So might you come to an end, a tree transplanted from Europe to this stony soil, unless you look for support and make yourself small. You are in a bad situation, alone, high up. The earth shakes; there are storm signals in the skies; your family tree has been known to attract lightning. To fight alone against the world is not courage but foolhardiness. No one blames a pilot who takes refuge in port when the storm begins to blow. It is not cowardice to duck under a bullet; what is wrong is to defy it only to fall and never rise again.'

'But would this sacrifice have the fruits I expect?' asked Ibarra. 'Would the priest believe in me and forget his grievance? Would they sincerely help me to spread the benefits of an education that would compete with the convents for control of the country's wealth? Can they not feign friendship, pretend to protect me, while fighting and undermining me in the dark, under cover, wounding me where I am vulnerable, and thus defeat me sooner than if they attacked me openly? Given the antecedents you have assumed, anything could happen.'

'If that were to happen, if the enterprise should fail, you would be comforted by the thought that you had done everything in your power. In any case something would have been gained. The cornerstone would have been laid, the seed would have been sown. After the tempest some grain might perhaps sprout, survive the catastrophe, save the species from annihilation, and serve as grain seed for the children of the perished sower. The example of others can encourage those who only fear to begin.'

Ibarra weighed these arguments, saw his predicament, and realised that for all his pessimism the old man was right.

'I believe you!' he exclaimed, shaking his hand. 'I did not expect good advice in vain. This very day I shall put all my plans before the parish priest. After all, he has done me no wrong. He may be a good man, for not all of them are like my father's persecutor. Besides, I must win his sympathy for that unfortunate madwoman and her children. I have trust in God and men.'

He took leave of the old man and, mounting his horse, rode away.

'We shall see,' muttered the pessimistic scholar, following the young man with his eyes, 'how Fate develops the little play which opened at the cemetery.'

This time he was mistaken; the play had begun long before.

27 • *The Eve of the Fiesta*

IT was the tenth of November, the day before the fiesta.

Breaking out of the routine of everyday life the townspeople went into action in house, street, church, cockpit, and field. Flags and multicoloured hangings flew from the windows; music and the noise of rockets filled the air with merriment.

In the houses the girls busied themselves arranging native sweetmeats on gaily coloured dishes which they set out on little tables covered with white embroidery. In the yards chickens cheeped, hens cackled, pigs grunted, terrified by human rejoicing. Servants went up and downstairs carrying gilded dishes and silver tableware. Here, a broken plate provoked a scolding; there, a simple country wench raised a laugh; everywhere voices were heard commanding, gossiping, shouting, criticising, speculating, encouraging, in a confusion of noise and activity. All this anxiety and toil was spent for the coming guest, known or unknown, whom perhaps these generous hosts had never seen before and would never see again, stranger, foreigner, friend and foe, Filipino or Spaniard, poor man, rich man, who must be made happy and content without any expectation of gratitude. He was not even expected to have any regard for the family of his hosts before or after digesting their bounty.

Those who were rich, or who had been in Manila and had seen a little of the world, put in stocks of beer, champagne, liquors, wines, and European delicacies, of which they would hardly taste a drop or a mouthful. Their tables were set with elegance. The centrepiece was usually a large artificial pineapple, an excellent imitation, bristling with toothpicks exquisitely fashioned into the shape of a fan, a nosegay, a bird, a rose, a palm leaf, or a chain, each worked out of a single piece of wood by convicts in prison workshops—the artists had been felons; their instruments, dull knives; their only inspiration, the harsh command of their foreman. Around this pineapple were placed crystal trays bearing pyramids of oranges, *lanzones, ates, chicos,* and even mangoes, although they were out of season in November. Next there were platters covered with brightly coloured lace-paper on which rested hams, cured in the European or the Chinese manner, a huge meat-pie in the shape of the Lamb of God or the Holy Ghost, stuffed turkeys, and jars of native pickles decorated with fanciful designs made from the flower of the *bunga*, and other vegetables and fruits, cut in artistic shapes and stuck with syrup to the glass.

Elsewhere in the house, glass lamp shades, handed down from father to son, were being cleaned, and their copper rims polished; kerosene lamps were stripped of the protective red covers, which had kept out flies and mosquitoes and made them useless the rest of the year; crystal drops and ropes of pendants swung from chandeliers, striking musically against one another as they were dusted, joining their notes to the gaiety and sprinkling the white walls with the colours of the rainbow. The children at play amused themselves by chasing the reflections on the walls, or tumbled over one another; even when they broke a lamp chimney or two, the good humour of the fiesta was unimpaired, although at any other time of year tears in their round eyes would have told a different story. Like the venerable lamps, the needlework of the daughters of the house was now brought forth from its hiding places: crocheted veils, little pieces of tapestry, artificial flowers. Antique crystal trays, depicting miniature lakes with tiny fish, crocodiles, molluscs, weeds, coral, and rocks, all of brightly coloured glass, made an appearance, and were

piled up with cigars, cigarettes, and dainty betel-nut chew twisted into shape
by the delicate fingers of young girls. The floors shone like mirrors; hangings
of hemp or pineapple-fibre decorated the doors; from the windows hung glass
or paper lanterns in rose, blue, green, or red; the houses were filled with
flowers and flowerpots set on china pedestals; even the images of the saints
were decked with finery, and the reliquaries dusted, their glass covers polished,
their frames hung with garlands of flowers.

Fanciful bamboo arches fashioned in a multitude of ways, and decorated
with curled wooden shavings, rose in the streets at regular intervals, and the
mere sight of them was enough to lift up childish hearts. Around the courtyard
of the church a great and costly canopy had been erected on bamboo poles
to shelter the procession.

Now the boys of the town played under it, running, climbing, jumping,
and tearing the new shirts they should have saved for the day of the fiesta.

In the town square a stage had been built of bamboo, nipa, and wood; there
the stage troupe from Tondo would perform its wonders and compete with
the gods in the working of impossible miracles; there the most renowned
performers from Manila would sing and dance. The Filipino of that time
liked the theatre and was passionately fond of the drama. But he listened to
the songs, or admired the dancing and the acting, in silence; he neither hissed
nor applauded. Did the performance bore him? He quietly chewed his betel-
nut or went away without disturbing those who might be enjoying it. Some
boor might howl when the actors kissed or embraced the actresses; that was
all. In older times only plays had been staged; the town poet would write
one with the necessary ingredients of a clown, sword fights every two minutes,
and frightening changes of identity. But the Tondo troupe had killed the
provincial theatre by putting on a sword fight every fifteen seconds, employing
two clowns, and inventing even more fantastic situations in their plays. The
Mayor was very fond of these plays and, in agreement with the parish priest,
had selected for performance *The Prince Villardo*, or *Slaves Snatched from the
Infamous Cave*, a play which featured magic and fireworks.

Meanwhile the bells pealed merrily now and again, the same bells that only
ten days before had tolled so sombrely. Firewheels and petards filled the air
with explosions. The Filipino pyrotechnist, who learned his art from no
known master, would soon be showing off his skills, and was busy preparing

towers with Bengal lights, paper balloons inflated with hot air, pinwheels, giant firecrackers, and rockets.

Distant blasts of music were now heard, and the children went running pell-mell to the outskirts of the town to meet the brass bands. Five had been engaged for the fiesta, as well as three orchestras. The Pagsanhan band, which belonged to the clerk of court, could not be left out, or that from San Pedro de Tunasan, famous at that time because it was conducted by 'Professor' Austria, the vagabond 'Corporal Mariano', who was said to carry fame and harmony at the tip of his baton. Musicians praised his funeral march, *The Willow*, and deplored his lack of formal training, because with his native genius he might otherwise have brought glory to his native land.

The brass bands entered the town playing lively marches, followed by children dressed in rags, half-naked, this one in his brother's shirt, that one in his father's trousers. No sooner had a tune been played than they knew it by heart, imitated it, and whistled it with rare accuracy, and gave judgment on its merits.

All the while, rigs, coaches, and carriages had been streaming into town with relatives, friends, and strangers—gamblers with their roosters and money-bags, ready to risk their fortunes on the card table or in the cockpit.

'The commanding officer is getting fifty pesos a night,' a small fat man would whisper in the ears of new arrivals. 'Capitan Tiago is coming; he will run the *monte* game. Capitan Joaquín is bringing eighteen thousand pesos. There's going to be *liampo* too; Carlos the Chinaman will be the banker with ten thousand pesos. There are big gamblers coming from Tanawan, Lipa, Batangas, and even Santa Cruz. This is going to be big-time gambling, I tell you. But here, have some chocolate. This year Capitan Tiago will not clean us out as he did last year; he has only paid for three Masses of petition. I have a good-luck charm made of *cacao*. Oh, and how is the family?'

'Very well, thank you,' the visitors would reply. 'And Father Dámaso?'

'Father Dámaso will preach in the morning and play cards with us at night.'

'That's fine. Then there's no danger?'

'Oh, we're safe, absolutely safe. Besides, Carlos the Chinaman is passing out—you know.' And the fat little man made as if counting out money with his fingers.

Outside the town, the country people, the tenants, were putting on their best clothes in order to take fattened hens, wild-pig meat, venison, and fowl to the houses of their capitalist partners; some were loading their heavy carts with firewood, others with fruits and the forest's rarest orchids; still others, with broad-leaved *biga* and *tikas-tikas* with flame-coloured flowers to decorate the doors.

But the greatest activity was taking place in a flat wide elevation a short distance from Ibarra's house. There pulleys were squeaking and the air was filled with shouts and the metallic sounds of picks breaking stones, hammers driving nails, hatchets fashioning beams. A great number of men were digging, opening a wide and deep excavation; others were laying out stones from the town quarry in orderly rows, unloading carts, heaping up sand, arranging capstans and winches.

'That goes here, and that there! Lively now!' shouted a little old man with a quick intelligent face, who was leaning on a metre-stick with brass ends, from which hung a plumb string. This was the overseer of the construction. Master Juan, architect, master builder, mason, carpenter, whitewasher, locksmith, painter, stone-cutter, and, on occasion, sculptor.

'We've got to finish this today. No work tomorrow—it's a holiday of obligation—and the day after is the grand opening. Lively now!' Then, turning to some stone-cutters who were working on a great stone slab, he ordered: 'Make the hole just right for this cylinder—our names will be in it.'

To every stranger who came by he made exactly the same speech he had made a thousand times.

'Don't know what we are building, eh? Well, sir, it's a school, and it's going to be a model one, just like those in Germany, or even better! A famous architect drew up the plans, and I'm in charge of the project. Yes, sir, this is going to be a palace: two wings, one for the boys and the other for the girls; large garden in the centre—three fountains; line of trees along the sides, and small orchards so the kids can grow something between classes—no time wasted, every minute put to use. Now look at this—ever seen such deep foundations? Three metres and sixty-five centimetres. This building is going to have store-rooms, cellars, and punishment cells for naughty kids— right next to the playing yard and the gym, so they can hear what a good time the others are having. See that open space there? That's going to be an athletics field, where the kids can run and jump around in the open air. Garden for the girls over there, with benches, swings, walks for rope-skipping, fountains, birdcages, anything you can think of! This is going to be stupendous!'

Master Juan rubbed his hands; he was going to be famous! Foreigners would come to see the school and they would ask: 'What great architect built this?' And people would answer: 'Why, don't you know? It's unbelievable that you have never heard of Master Juan! You must come from very far away.'

With these thoughts he went to and fro, inspecting everything to the last detail.

'That's too much timber for a hoist,' he told a sallow-faced man who was in charge of a gang. 'I should have enough with three large pieces for a tripod and three more to hold them together.'

'Come now,' answered the sallow-faced man, smiling oddly, 'the more elaborate we make it, the more spectacular the effect. The whole thing will look better and more impressive, and people will say: "Now that must have taken a lot of work." You'll see, you'll see what a hoist I'll make. Afterwards I'll pretty it up with pennants and bunches of flowers and leaves, and you'll admit you were right to take me on with the other men, and that Mr. Ibarra couldn't ask for more.'

He grinned and chuckled, and Master Juan could not help smiling himself and nodding his head.

Some distance away the schoolmaster and about thirty boys were making wreaths and tying flags to the slender bamboo poles, covered with quilted white linen, which supported two pavilions joined by a trellis of banana leaves.

'Try to fashion the letters well,' he told those who were writing inscriptions. 'The Provincial Governor is coming, and many priests, and perhaps even the Governor General himself. They say he's in the province. If they see you have made a good job of these signs, they may have a word of praise for you.'

'And give us a blackboard?'

'Who knows? Anyway, Mr. Ibarra has already ordered one from Manila, and some other things are coming tomorrow which will be given out to you as prizes. Now leave those flowers in water; tomorrow we'll make the bouquets. You are to bring more flowers; the table must be absolutely covered with them; flowers make a cheerful sight.'

'My father's bringing water-lilies and a basket of sampaguitas tomorrow.'

'Mine brought three cartloads of sand free.'

'My uncle has promised to pay a teacher's salary,' added the nephew of Capitan Basilio.

Ibarra's plan had indeed found support from practically everybody. The parish priest had asked to sponsor the project and personally bless the laying of the cornerstone, a ceremony which was to take place on the last day of the fiesta as one of its principal features. The vicar himself had approached Ibarra shyly, offering to turn over to him all the offerings for Masses he might receive from the faithful until the completion of the building. Even more, the rich but thrifty Sister Rufa had volunteered, if the money should run out, to raise funds in other towns, provided only that her travelling expenses and meals were paid.

Ibarra thanked her and replied: 'We would not raise very much that way. I am not so rich that I can afford to pay your expenses, and anyway this building is not a church. Besides, I did not promise to build it at the expense of others.'

The young men, students who had come from Manila for the festivities, admired Ibarra and took him for a model but—as almost always happens when we want to imitate exceptional men, and only succeed in copying their little idiosyncrasies and even their defects because we are incapable of doing more—many of these admirers noticed only how Ibarra tied the knot of his cravat, others the shape of his shirt-collar, and not a few the number of buttons on his jacket and waistcoat.

The sinister forebodings of old Tasio seemed to have been dispelled forever. Ibarra remarked on it one day, but the old pessimist answered: 'Remember what our greatest Tagalog poet, Baltazar, who was as good a thinker as a poet, said:

'If you are greeted with smiling face and loving eye,
Be all the more on guard against a hidden enemy.'

These, and other things which are now to be related, were taking place on the eve of the fiesta.

28 • At Nightfall

VERY great preparations had also been made in the house of Capitan Tiago. Those who knew him understood that his love of ostentation and his pride as a Manilan required that he should put the provincials of the town to shame with his lavishness. But he had another reason for outshining the others; he had his daughter María Clara with him; and his future son-in-law, who had made himself the talk of everyone, was in town.

Indeed one of the most serious newspapers in Manila had devoted to Ibarra a front-page article entitled 'Imitate Him,' lavishing advice on him and a few praises. It had called him 'the cultured youth and wealthy businessman'; two lines below that, 'the distinguished philanthropist'; in the next paragraph, 'the pupil of Minerva who went to the Motherland to greet the true home of the arts and sciences'; a little farther on, 'the Filipino Spaniard', and so forth. Capitan Tiago, without begrudging him this success, burned to surpass him, and wondered if he too should build something at his own expense, perhaps a convent.

Some days before the fiesta a great number of cases had arrived at the house where María Clara and her Aunt Isabel were staying: food and drink from Europe, enormous mirrors, paintings, and the girl's piano.

Capitan Tiago himself arrived the very day before the fiesta. When his daughter greeted him by kissing his hand, he presented her with a handsome gold reliquary set with diamonds and emeralds, containing a splinter from the very same fishing-boat of St. Peter where Our Lord had sat when He filled the nets of the Apostles.

The meeting between Capitan Tiago and his future son-in-law could not have been more cordial. Naturally they spoke about the school, which Capitan Tiago wanted named after St. Francis.

'Believe me,' he said, 'St. Francis is a good protector. What do you get out of calling it the "Primary Instruction School?" Who is this "Primary Instruction"?'

At this point some friends of María Clara arrived and invited her to go for a walk.

'But don't be long,' Capitan Tiago told his daughter when she asked his permission. 'You know that Father Dámaso is just back, and is having dinner with us tonight.'

Then, turning to Ibarra, who seemed to have something on his mind, he added:

'Why don't you come to dinner too? You'll be all by yourself in your house.'

'I would have loved to come,' stammered the young man, avoiding María Clara's eyes, 'but I must stay home in case anyone calls.'

'Bring your friends along,' Capitan Tiago answered nonchalantly. 'There's always enough to eat at my house. Besides, I should like to see you and Father Dámaso come to an understanding.'

'Oh, there will be time enough for that,' answered Ibarra with a forced smile, and made ready to escort the young ladies.

They went downstairs, María Clara between Victoria and Iday, with Aunt Isabel bringing up the rear.

People made way for them in the street: María Clara's beauty was so striking. Her pallor had vanished, and, if her eyes remained pensive, her mouth on the contrary seemed to know only how to smile. With the affability of a girl who is happy she greeted the old acquaintances of her childhood, now the admirers of her fortunate youth. In less than fifteen days she had recovered the frankness, the self-confidence, the easy speech, which seemed to have languished behind the confining walls of the convent school. It was as if a butterfly, leaving the chrysalis, were making friends with the flowers all over again; a moment of flight and of being warmed by the golden rays of the sun had been enough to shake off the stiffness of the cocoon. This new sense of life suffused the girl's whole being; she found everything beautiful and good; she showed her love with that innocent grace which, knowing only the purest thoughts, does not know the reason for the simulated blush. True, when she was teased, she covered her face with her fan, but her eyes were smiling, and a shiver of pleasure ran through her body.

Houses were already being lighted up, and, in the streets where the brass bands went playing, chandeliers of bamboo and wood, imitations of those in the town church, were burning.

From the street, through the open windows, people could be seen bustling about their houses in an atmosphere of light and perfume and the music of piano, harp, and orchestra. The streets themselves were full of people, Chinese, Spaniards, Filipinos, some of the latter in European, others in native dress, all mixed up with one another, elbowing and shoving, servants carrying meat and fowl, students dressed in white, men and women in danger of being run over by the carriages and buggies which, despite the cries of the drivers to stand aside, could only make their way with difficulty.

In front of Capitan Basilio's house María Clara's party was greeted by some young men, who invited them to call. Sinang's merry voice as she ran downstairs put an end to any argument.

'Come up for a while so I can go out with you afterwards,' she cried. 'I am so bored with all these strangers who can only talk of fighting cocks and playing cards.'

They went up.

The room was full of people. Some came forward to greet Ibarra, whose name was known to all. They gazed enraptured on María Clara's beauty; one or two old women mumbled as they chewed their betel-nut: 'She looks like the Virgin!'

They had to stay for a cup of chocolate. Capitan Basilio had become Ibarra's intimate friend and champion ever since the day of the outing. He had learned from the telegram, which had been his daughter Sinang's prize, that Ibarra had known all along of the verdict in his favour, and, unwilling to be surpassed in generosity, Capitan Basilio had tried to call off their bargain that they would ask for the dismissal of the case between them if the chess game ended in a draw. When Ibarra had not agreed to it, Capitan Basilio had proposed that the money which would have gone to the costs of the suit be used instead to pay the salary of a teacher in the proposed town-school. The upshot of it all was that this well-known speaker now employed his oratory to convince other claimants against him to abandon their extravagant pretensions.

'Believe me,' he told them, 'even the winner in a lawsuit loses his shirt.'

But he persuaded nobody, even when he appealed, as usual, to the authority of the Romans.

After taking their chocolate the young people had to listen to the town organist playing the piano.

'When I hear him in church,' said Sinang with a mocking finger, 'I want to dance. Now that he's playing the piano, I feel like praying. That is why I'm going with you.'

'Do you want to sit in with us tonight?' Capitan Basilio whispered in

Ibarra's ear as the latter was leaving. 'Father Dámaso is going to be banker in a small game.'

Ibarra smiled and answered with a movement of the head that might have meant a yes as much as a no.

'Who is that?' María Clara asked Victoria, pointing with her eyes to a young man who was following them as they continued their walk.

'He—he's a cousin of mine,' replied Victoria, somewhat uneasily.

'And the other one?'

'He's no cousin of mine,' put in Sinang breezily. 'He's a son of my aunt.'

They went by the parish house, which was certainly not among the least lively. Sinang could not restrain a gasp when she saw that the antique lamps, which Father Salví would never allow to be lighted to save oil, were now burning brightly. Shouts and loud laughs could be heard, and friars seen, pacing ponderously up and down, moving their hands in rhythm, huge cigars in their mouths. The laymen with them tried as best they could to imitate what the good priests were doing; judging from their European dress they appeared to be provincial government officials or employees.

María Clara made out the rounded shape of Father Dámaso next to the correct silhouette of Father Sibyla. The mysterious and taciturn Father Salví was rooted in his place.

'He's depressed,' remarked Sinang. 'He's wondering how much so many guests will cost him. But you'll see; he won't pay for it; he'll take it out on the help. His guests always eat at someone else's expense.'

'Sinang!' Victoria reproved her.

'I can't endure him ever since he broke that *Wheel of Fortune*. I don't go to Confession to him any more.'

Among all these houses one stood out because it was unlighted, even its windows were shut. It was the house of the commanding officer. María Clara thought it strange.

'Oh, that witch!' exclaimed the irrepressible Sinang. 'The Muse of the Constabulary—that's what the old scholar calls her. What has she got to do with our fun? She must be furious. But wait for an outbreak of cholera, and you'll see that she gives a party.'

'Really, Sinang!' came another reproof from her cousin.

'I could never stand her, and even less after she spoiled our outing with those stupid soldiers of hers. If I were the Archbishop, I'd marry her off to Father Salví. Their children would be something to see! Just fancy, having that poor steersman arrested who threw himself into the water just to please—'

But she cut herself short: in a corner of the square, where a blind man was singing a fisherman's song to the tune of a guitar, a rare sight was to be seen.

This was a man covered with the wide round palm-leaf hat of the native peasants and wretchedly dressed in the shreds of a tail-coat, loose Chinese trousers torn here and there, and a pair of sandals about to come apart. The great brim of the hat left his face in shadow, but from the darkness two eyes flashed fiercely now and then, only to be extinguished instantly. He was tall, and, judging, from his movements, young. He would put down a basket on the ground, then move away, making strange incomprehensible sounds, and stand apart, completely isolated, as if he and the crowd were avoiding each other. Then a number of women would approach the basket, put in it fruit, fish, rice, and other things to eat. When it seemed that no one else would come up, other sounds would emerge from the darkness, sadder sounds, but less piteous, perhaps meant to be words of thanks; and the man would take up his basket and move away to do the same in another place.

María Clara sensed a tragedy and asked about this strange unfortunate.

'He's a leper,' answered Iday. 'He caught the disease four years ago. Some say he got it from his mother; he was nursing her. Others say he got it because he was kept too long in a damp cell in gaol. He lives out in the fields, near the Chinese cemetery. He has no contact with anyone; they all run away from him because they are afraid of catching it from him. You should see his hut! Wind, rain, and sun go in and out like a needle through cloth. He is forbidden to touch anything that belongs to anybody. One day a small boy fell into a ditch; the ditch wasn't deep, but the leper, who was passing by, helped the child out. The boy's father learned of it and complained to the Mayor. He had the leper flogged six times in the middle of the street, and then had the lash burned. It was horrible! The leper running away, the flogger running after him, and the Mayor screaming: "Let that be a lesson to you! Better to drown than catch your sickness!"'

'True,' María Clara whispered.

Scarcely knowing what she was doing, she went up quickly to the wretch's basket and dropped in it the reliquary which her father had just given her.

'What have you done?' her friends cried out.

'I had nothing else to give,' she answered, disguising with a smile the tears in her eyes.

'But what can he possibly do with your locket?' asked Victoria. 'One day they gave him money, but he pushed it away with a stick. Why should he want it? Nobody takes anything from him. Now if your locket could be eaten!'

María Clara looked enviously at the women who were selling food, and shrugged her shoulders.

But the leper went to his basket, took the glittering jewel in his hands, and falling on his knees kissed it. Then, uncovering himself, he buried his face in the dust that the girl had trodden.

María Clara hid her face behind her fan and raised a handkerchief to her eyes.

Meantime a woman had approached the unfortunate, who seemed at prayer. Her long hair was loose and unkempt; the lamplight revealed the terribly gaunt face of mad Sisa.

When he felt her touch, the leper cried out and leapt to his feet. But the madwoman clutched him by the arm to the horror of the people and urged:

'Let us pray, let us pray! This is the day of the dead! Those lights are human lives. Let us pray for my sons.'

'Get them apart! She'll catch it!' came voices from the crowd, but nobody dared to approach them.

'Do you see that light in the tower? That is my son Basilio going down a rope. Do you see the other light in the parish house? That is my son Crispin. But I do not go to see them because the parish priest is ill, and he has many golden coins, and the golden coins keep getting lost. Let us pray, let us pray for the soul of the parish priest! Once I took him the fruits of my orchard; my garden was full of flowers; and I had two sons. I had a garden, I grew flowers, I had two sons!'

Letting the leper go, she went away singing:

'I had a flowering garden, I had sons and a flowering garden!'

'What have you been able to do for that poor woman?' María Clara asked Ibarra.

'Nothing. She could not be found in town these last days,' the young man answered with embarrassment. 'Besides, I have been very busy. But cheer up. The parish priest has promised to help me, although he has advised much tact and secrecy; apparently the Constabulary is involved. The parish priest takes great interest in her.'

'Didn't the lieutenant say he would order a search for the boys?'

'Yes, but when he said it he was a little... high.'

He had scarcely said this when they saw the madwoman being not so much led as dragged along by a Constabulary soldier.

'Why have you arrested her? What has she done?' asked Ibarra.

'What? Haven't you yourselves seen her creating a disturbance?' replied the custodian of public peace.

The leper hurriedly picked up his basket and went away.

María Clara wanted to go home; she had lost her good humour and high spirits.

'Not everyone is happy,' she sighed.

Her sadness grew when, upon reaching her door, her fiancé refused to go up and took his leave.

'It can't be helped,' he said.

María Clara went up the stairs thinking that the holidays, when people had to stay home to wait for unexpected visitors, were a bore.

29 • *Letters*
Everyone speaks of the fair as he fared in it

NOTHING of importance to the characters of this story took place the night before the fiesta or the next day. But the foreigner might wish to acquaint himself with the way that the Filipinos held their fiestas at that time and for this purpose various letters may be useful. One of them was from the correspondent of a serious and distinguished Manila newspaper; worthy of respect both because of its style and uncompromising loftiness. Some light and natural inaccuracies may be forgiven.

The worthy correspondent of the high-minded newspaper wrote:

'San Diego, 11 November

'The Editor, etc.

'Distinguished friend:

'I have never witnessed, nor do I hope to witness in the provinces, a religious festival as solemn, as magnificent, and as moving as the one celebrated in this town by the very reverend and virtuous Franciscan friars.

'Attendance is of the greatest. Here I have had the happy opportunity of greeting almost all the Spaniards resident in this province, as well as three Reverend Augustinians from the province of Batangas, and two Reverend Dominicans, one of them the Very Reverend Father Hernando de la Sibyla who has honoured this town with his presence, something that its worthy inhabitants should never forget. I have also seen a great number of prominent people from the provinces of Cavite and Pampanga, and many men of wealth from Manila. There are many brass bands, among them that most skillful band from Pagsanhan which is owned by the clerk of court, Don Miguel Guevara, as well as a great concourse of Chinese and natives, who, with the curiosity that characterises the former, and the religious devotion of the latter, awaited with eagerness the day on which the fiesta was to be celebrated, in order that they might witness the comico-mimico-lyrico-choreographico-dramatic spectacle for which a great and spacious storage had been raised in the middle of the town square.

'At nine o'clock on the night of the tenth, the eve of the fiesta, after the succulent dinner which the sponsor of the celebration gave in our honour, the attention of those of us Spaniards and friars who were in the parish house was aroused by the music of two brass bands, that, accompanied by a thick crowd led by the principal men of the town, were coming, to the noise of firecrackers and rockets, to fetch and lead us to the places prepared and reserved for us at the stage show.

'We felt compelled to accept such a courtly invitation for all that I myself would have preferred to rest in the arms of Morpheus and give delightful rest to my limbs which were aching, thanks to the jogging and jolting of the vehicle furnished to us by the mayor of the neighbouring town.

'So we descended, and went in search of those of our compatriots who were dining in the house which is owned here by the pious and opulent Don Santiago de los Santos. The parish priest of the town, the Very Reverend Father Bernardo Salví, the Very Reverend Father Dámaso Verdolangas (who, by special grace of the All Highest, has by now recovered from the injuries which an impious hand inflicted upon him), the Very Reverend Father Hernando de la Sibyla, and the virtuous parish priest of Tanawan, as well as other Spaniards, were the guests of the Filipino Croesus. There we had the happiness of admiring not only the luxurious good taste of the host (uncommon in a native) but also the exquisite, most beautiful and wealthy heiress of the house, who proved that she is a consummate pupil of St. Cecilia by playing on her elegant piano the best German and Italian compositions with a mastery that recalled La Galvez to my mind. What a pity it is that such a flaw-less young lady should be so excessively shy and should conceal her accomplishments from a society that has for her only a profusion of admiration. Nor should I forget to mention that our host pressed champagne and the finest liqueurs on us in that profusion and abundance which characterise this famous businessman.

'Now for the stage show. You already know our artists, Ratia, Carvajal, and Fernandez; their witticisms were understood only by us; the uneducated classes did not get the point of a single joke. Chananay and Balbino: good but a little hoarse, the latter's voice suffered a tiny break, but all in all, and giving credit for willingness, admirable. The natives, above all the Mayor, greatly enjoyed the Tagalog play. The Mayor told us, rubbing his hands, that it was a pity the princess had not been made to fight the giant who had kidnapped her, more so if the giant had turned out to be invulnerable except in the navel, like one Ferragus who is mentioned in the *Tale of the Twelve Peers*. The Very Reverend Father Dámaso, with that goodness of heart which distinguishes him, shared the Mayor's opinion, and added that, in such a situation, the princess would know how to get the giant to uncover his navel and to deal him there a fatal stroke.

'Needless to say the thoughtfulness of the Filipino Rothschild allowed nothing to be wanting during the stage show; sherbets, aerated drinks, refreshments, sweetmeats, wines, and so forth were lavished among those of us who were present. Noteworthy, and with reason, was the absence of the well-known and cultured youth Don Juan Crisóstomo Ibarra, who, as you know, is scheduled to preside tomorrow at the blessing of the cornerstone of the great monument which with such philanthropy he is causing to be built. This worthy descendant of the Pelayos and Elcanos (for, I am in formed, one of his paternal grandfathers came from our heroic and noble northern provinces of Spain; it might even be that he was one of the companions of Magellan or Legaspi) has not shown himself the whole day because of a slight indisposition. His name runs from mouth to mouth, and it is pronounced only to be praised, praises which cannot but rebound to the glory of Spain and of genuine Spaniards like ourselves, who never belie our blood no matter how mixed it may be.

'Today at eleven o'clock in the morning we witnessed a highly moving sight. As is well known to all this is the feastday of Our Lady of Peace, which is commemorated by the Confraternity of the Holy Rosary, sponsored by the Dominicans. Tomorrow is the feast of the town's patron saint, St. Diego of Alcala, which is celebrated primarily by the Venerable Third Order of laymen and laywomen following the Franciscan rule. Between these two confraternities there exists a pious competition in the service of God, and it goes to such lengths that they have saintly quarrels, as happened lately when they had a tug-of-war over the oft-mentioned Very Reverend Father Dámaso, who will take the seat of the Holy Ghost tomorrow and deliver a sermon which, in the general expectations, will be a religious and literary event.

'Well, as I was saying, we witnessed today a highly moving and edifying sight. Six young religious, three who were to sing Mass, and three who were to assist them, emerged from the sacristy and prostrated themselves before the altar. Then the celebrant, who was the Very Reverend Father Sibyla, in that magnificent voice and with that religious unction which all the world knows and which make him so worthy of general admiration, intoned the *Surge Domine,* which was the signal for the procession to begin inside the church. The *Surge Domine* over, the Mayor, in formal morning dress, began the procession bearing the tall silver cross, followed by four acolytes swinging censers. Behind them came the bearers of the silver candelabra, the St. Dominic, St. Diego, and Our Lady of Peace, the latter with a magnificent blue mantle set with gilded silver plates, the gift of the virtuous ex-Mayor, that worthy model never too often named, Don Santiago de los Santos. All these images were borne on silver floats. Behind the Mother of God came we Spaniards and other religious; the celebrant was under a pallium carried by native headmen. The procession was closed by the meritorious corps of Constabulary. I believe it needless to mention that a great number of natives formed the two lines of the procession, carrying lighted candles with remarkable piety. The bands played religious tunes, and there were repeated salvoes of rockets and firewheels. Admirable indeed are the modesty and fervour that these rites inspire in the hearts of the faithful, the pure and profound faith that they have in Our Lady of Peace, the solemnity and fervent devotion with which these observances are held by those of us who had the happy fortune of being born under the sacrosanct and untarnished Spanish flag.

'The procession being over, the Mass was sung, to the accompaniment of an orchestra and a choir composed of the stage performers. After the Gospel, the Very Reverend Father Manuel Martin, of the Order of St. Augustine, who had come for the purpose from the province of Batangas, ascended the pulpit, and had the entire congregation hanging on his every word, especially the Spaniards with his introduction (which he gave in Spanish) delivered so trenchantly and in such felicitous phrases that our hearts were filled with fervour and enthusiasm. Enthusiasm is the right word for our feelings for Our Lady and our beloved Spain, above all when mention can be appropriately made of the sentiments, surely shared by all Spaniards, of that Prince of the Church, Cardinal Monescillo, who opposed the proposal of freedom for all religions in the Spanish Constitution.

'When the Mass was finished we all went to the parish house, together with the municipal officials and other important persons. There we were very well entertained with that courtesy, thoughtfulness, and prodigality which characterise Father Salví; we were given cigars and a substantial buffet which the sponsor of the festival had prepared on the ground floor of the parish house for all who felt the need of satisfying the needs of their stomachs.

'Nothing was lacking to make the celebration gay throughout the day and to keep up those high spirits typical of Spaniards, who cannot restrain themselves on such occasions, and show, in song and dance and other simple and merry amusements, that their hearts are strong and noble, that sorrows do not drown them, and that three Spaniards together are enough to banish sadness and depression.

'So it was that homage was paid to Terpsichore, the goddess of the dance, in many houses, principally in that of the cultured Filipino millionaire, where we were all invited to dinner. I need not tell you that the banquet, delicious and exquisitely served, was a second edition, revised and enlarged, of the Wedding of Cana and the nuptials of Camacho in *Don Quixote*. While we were enjoying the pleasures of the table, prepared for us under the supervision of a cook from a famous Manila restaurant, the orchestra played harmonious melodies. The very beautiful young lady of the house, displaying a shower of diamonds and wearing the native town costume, was, as always, the queen of the occasion.

We all deplored, from the bottom of our hearts, the slight sprain in her pretty ankle which deprived her of the pleasures of the dance, for, to judge from her other accomplishments, Miss de los Santos must dance like a sylph.

'The Provincial Governor arrived this afternoon to dignify with his presence the ceremony to be held tomorrow. He has expressed regret at the indisposition of the distinguished landlord, Mr. Ibarra, who, we have been informed, is already recovering, thank God.

'Tonight there was another solemn procession, but I will leave it for my letter tomorrow because, rattled and deafened by fireworks as I am, I am also very tired and so sleepy I can hardly hold my head up. The while, therefore, that I recover strength in the arms of Morpheus, that is to say, on a cot in the parish house, I wish you, distinguished friend, goodnight until tomorrow which will be the great day.

'Your most affectionate friend who kisses your hand, etc.'

The foregoing was the letter of the correspondent: follows now what Capitan Martín wrote to his friend Luis Chiquito.

Dear Choy:

'If you can, come at a run; the fiesta is very gay; fancy, Capitan Joaquin is almost broke; Capitan Tiago doubled his bets three times, and won three times on the first card; Manuel, the head man, who owns the house where we play, is so happy about his share of the kitty that he is losing weight. Father Dámaso smashed a lamp with a blow because he has not won a game yet; the Consul has lost on his fighting cocks and at the card-table all the money he won from us at the fiesta in Biñang and at the fiesta of Our Lady of the Pillar in Santa Cruz.

'We had expected Capitan Tiago to bring his prospective son-in-law, Don Rafael's rich heir, but it seems he wants to imitate his father; he has not put in an appearance. Pity! Seems he will never be much good to us.

'Carlos the Chinaman is making a fortune out of the *liampo;* I have a suspicion he has something hidden on him, a magnet maybe; he keeps complaining about a headache and wears a bandage around his head; and when the dice are coming to a stop he leans over them, to the point of almost touching them, on the pretext that he wants to watch closely. I don't trust him, because I have heard stories like this before.

'So long, Choy; my fighting cocks are doing well, and my wife is happy and enjoying herself.

> 'Your friend,
> 'Martín Aristorenas.'

Ibarra too had received a letter, a perfumed note delivered to him the night of the first day of the fiesta by Andeng, the foster sister of María Clara. The note read:

'Crisóstomo:

'I have not seen you for more than a day. I have heard you don't feel very well. I have prayed and lighted two votive candles for you, although Papa says there is nothing seriously wrong with you. Last night and today were tedious; they kept asking me to play the piano and dance. I didn't know there were so many bores in this world! If it hadn't been for Father Dámaso, who tries to amuse me with stories and gossip, I would have locked myself up in my room and gone to bed. Tell me what is wrong with you, and I shall ask Papa to go and see you. Meantime I am sending Andeng, so she can make you some tea; she is very good at it, better perhaps than your servants.

> 'María Clara

'P.D. If you don't come tomorrow, I shall not go to the ceremony. Goodbye for now.'

30 • *The Day of the Fiesta*

AT the first light of dawn the bands struck up a reveille, awakening the tired townfolk with lively tunes. Life and high spirits were reborn; once again the church bells went pealing and the fireworks cracking.

It was the last day of the fiesta; in fact it was the holiday proper. Much was to be expected, much more than the day before. The Tertiaries, members of the Venerable Third Order, were more numerous than those of the Confraternity of the Holy Rosary, and they went about smiling smugly, sure of humiliating their rivals. They had brought a greater number of candles, for one thing; the Chinese candle makers had reaped such a harvest that in pure gratitude they were thinking of getting themselves baptised, although it was asserted by some that the Chinese would do it for love not of Catholicism but of good Christian women, whom otherwise, they could not marry. To this devout women replied:

'Even so; it would still be a miracle for so many Chinamen to get married, and afterwards their wives would see to converting them.'

People put on their best clothes, jewel cases were emptied of their contents. Even the gamblers and cockfighters put on embroidered shirts with great diamond studs, heavy gold chains, and white straw hats. Only the old scholar remained the same as always, in his coarse-fibred, dark-striped shirt, buttoned up to the neck, comfortable shoes, and ash-coloured, broad-brimmed felt hat.

'You look gloomier than ever,' the Vice Mayor told him. 'Don't you want us to have a good time once in a while? We have so much to moan and groan about the rest of the year.'

'Having a good time doesn't mean making fools of ourselves!' answered the old man. 'It's the same senseless orgy every year. And all for what? Throwing away all that money when there is so much misery and need! But of course! I understand. The orgy, the bacchanal, serves to drown out the general lamentation.'

'You know I am of the same opinion as yourself,' replied Don Filipo, half serious, half smiling. 'I have advocated it myself. But what could I do against the Mayor and the parish priest?'

'Resign,' said the scholar and moved away.

Puzzled, Don Filipo followed the old man with his eyes.

'Resign,' he muttered, going toward the church. 'Resign! Yes, I would resign if this job were an honour and not a burden.'

The churchyard was full of people: men and women, young and old, dressed up in their best clothes, indistinguishable one from the other, went in and out of the narrow church doors. The smell of burnt powder, flowers, incense, perfume, filled the air; firecrackers, rockets, and petards that slithered unpredictably along the ground made the women run and shriek to the children's laughter. A brass band was playing in front of the parish house; another was escorting the municipal officials; still others marched along the streets under a multitude of waving and fluttering flags. The motley colours in the sunshine dazzled the eye, and tunes and explosions deafened the ear. The bells never stopped ringing; coaches and buggies got in one another's way, and when the horses took fright, reared up on their hind legs, and pawed the air, it made for a free show, which was one of the most interesting although it was not on the programme.

The sponsor of the day's celebrations had sent his servants out into the streets to search for guests, like the rich man in the Gospel; people were invited, almost by force, to take chocolate, tea, sweetmeats, and so forth. Not a few times such an invitation led to a squabble.

High Mass was about to begin, with the officiating priest wearing the dalmatic for greater solemnity, as the worthy correspondent had noted in the previous day's rites, only this time the celebrant would be Father Salví, and among the congregation would be the Provincial Governor with many other Spaniards and educated people who wanted to hear Father Dámaso, a preacher of great renown in the province. The commanding officer himself, made wary as he was by Father Salví's preaching techniques, had decided to be present to give evidence of his goodwill and, if possible, make up for the bad time the parish priest had given him in the past. Such was the fame of Father Dámaso that the correspondent had anticipated events and had written the following to his editor:

'What I forecast to you in my humble report yesterday has come true. We have had the rare pleasure of listening to the Very Reverend Father Dámaso Verdolangas, former parish priest of this town, now transferred to a larger one as a reward for his good services. The illustrious sacred orator took the seat of the Holy Ghost, and delivered a most eloquent and profound sermon which edified and held spellbound all the faithful who had anxiously awaited the salutary fountain of eternal life to gush from his fecund mouth. Sublimity of thought, boldness of imagination, novelty of phrase, elegance of style, spontaneity of gesture, grace of speech, nobility of idea—these are the qualities of the Spanish counterpart of the immortal French preacher Bossuet, and he is worthy indeed of the lofty reputation he has not only among the educated Spaniards but even among the unlettered natives and the shrewd sons of the Celestial Empire.'

The self confident correspondent, however, was almost compelled to discard what he had written. Father Dámaso was complaining of a slight cold he had caught the night before when, after singing some popular Andalusian songs, he had taken glasses of sherbet and stayed for some time out doors to see the stage show. As a result he had been on the point of renouncing his role as the interpreter of God to mankind, but since there was nobody else to be found who had learned the life and miracles of St. Diego (the parish priest had done so, it is true, but he had to sing the Mass) the other religious arrived at the unanimous verdict that Father Dámaso's voice had never sounded better, and that it would be a great pity if he should fail to deliver such an eloquent sermon as he had already written and learned by heart.

So his old housekeeper made him gallons of lemonade, smeared all sorts of oils and ointments on his chest and neck, wrapped him up in hot towels, massaged him, and subjected him to every imaginable treatment. Father Dámaso had taken some raw eggs beaten up in wine, and that morning had said not a word and taken almost nothing for breakfast; he scarcely tasted a glass of milk, a cup of chocolate, and a dozen biscuits, heroically giving up the fried chicken and half a cottage cheese from Laguna which he had every morning, because, according to the housekeeper, chicken and cheese contained salt and fats which provoke an excess of coughing.

'All this for Heaven and for our salvation!' the lady members of the Venerable Third order exclaimed, deeply moved, when they learned of these sacrifices.

'Our Lady of Peace is punishing him,' mumbled in turn the sisters of the Confraternity of the Holy Rosary, who could not forgive him for going over to the side of their enemies.

At eight-thirty in the morning the procession started under cover of the canvas canopy. It was similar to the one the day before, although with one novelty: the Venerable Third Order. Old men and women, and a number of old maids, had clad themselves in long habits: the poor wore them in coarse cotton cloth, the rich in silk, known as Franciscan 'cotton', because it was more often worn by the reverend Franciscan friars. All these sacred habits were genuine; they came from the Franciscan convent in Manila where people could acquire them in exchange for a donation in cash at a fixed rate, if such a commercial phrase is permissible. This fixed rate might be raised but not lowered. Besides these, other habits were also sold in the same convent, and in the monastery of St. Clare, which had not only the special quality of gaining many indulgences for the dead enshrouded in them but the even more special quality of being all the more expensive the older, more tattered, and more unwearable they were. This is mentioned for the benefit of any pious reader who should feel the need of such sacred relics, as well as of any smart tag-picker in Europe who wants to make a fortune by bringing to the Philippines a shipment of darned and greasy habits which could fetch as much as sixteen pesos apiece or even more, depending on how tattered they are.

St. Diego of Alcala went on a float decorated with embossed silver plates; he was rather slender, with head and shoulders in ivory, and an expression that was severe and majestic in spite of the heavy hair-ring of his tonsure, which was as kinky as the hair of the Negritos. His robes were of gold-embroidered velvet.

He was followed by Our Venerable Father St. Francis, and then by the Virgin, as in the procession the day before, only this time the priest under the pallium was Father Salví, and not the elegant Father Sibyla of the distinguished manner. But if the former lacked a handsome carriage, he had more than enough devotion: he kept his hands joined in a mystic attitude, his eyes were lowered, and he walked with shoulders bent. Those who bore the pallium were the same native headmen, in a happy sweat at seeing themselves practically the same as sacristans as well as tax-collectors, saviours of poor errant humanity, and by the same token other Christs who were giving their blood for the sins of others. The vicar, wearing a surplice, went from one float to the other swinging a censer, and from time to time regaled with its smoke the nostrils of the parish priest, who thereupon grew even more serious and grave of aspect.

In this manner the procession went on slowly and with deliberation to the sound of firecrackers, hymns, and the religious tunes with which the brass bands behind each float rent the air. Meantime the sponsor of the day's festivities was distributing tapers with such enthusiasm that many of those in the procession went home with enough light for four nights of gambling. As the float carrying the Mother of God passed by, the onlookers would fall on their knees and fervently pray the Apostles' Creed and the Hail Holy Queen.

Abreast of the house at whose windows, decorated with lavish draperies, could be seen the Provincial Governor, Capitan Tiago, María Clara, Ibarra, and a number of Spaniards and young ladies, the float stopped, and it chanced that Father Salví raised his eyes. But he did not make the slightest movement of greeting or recognition; he only drew himself erect so that the cope fell from his shoulders with a certain grace and with more elegance.

In the street, under the windows, there was a young girl with a pleasant face, luxuriously dressed, who carried in her arms a child of tender age. She was probably its nurse, for the child was fair and golden-haired while she was brown with hair blacker than jet.

When it saw the parish priest, the infant stretched out its tiny hands, gurgled in that childhood laughter which neither causes nor is caused by pain, and was heard to babble in a brief moment of silence: 'Pa—pa, pa—pa!'

The young woman shivered, hastily covered the child's mouth with her hand, and ran away in great embarrassment. The child broke into tears.

The evil-minded winked at one another, and the Spaniards who had witnessed the brief scene smiled. Father Salví's natural pallor turned a violent red.

And yet these people were wrong. The parish priest did not even know the woman, who was from out of town.

31 • In Church

THE barn which men had given for a house to the Creator of all things was packed from one end to the other. People pushed, squeezed, crushed one another amid the groans of the few who were leaving and the many who were coming in. An arm would be stretched from afar to dip a finger-tip in holy water; more often than not, a new wave of humanity would sweep the hand away from the font; a growl would be heard; a woman would scold as someone stepped on her toes; but the pushing and pulling went on. A few oldsters who managed to wet their fingers in the consecrated water (now the colour of mud after the whole town, not to mention its visitors, had washed itself in it) daubed themselves devoutly though with difficulty on the nape, pate, forehead, nose, chin, chest, and navel, in the conviction that they were thus sanctifying all these parts of their bodies and immunising themselves from stiff necks, headaches, tuberculosis, or indigestions. The younger people, whether because they were less sickly or because they did not believe in this pious preventive treatment, scarcely moistened a fingertip (and only so the devout would have nothing to say against them) and made the sign of the cross on the forehead, but without touching it, of course.

'It may be holy water and all that,' some young lady would think, 'but with that colour...!'

It was difficult to breathe; the heat was suffocating; there was a stench of the human animal; but the preacher was worth all these vexations; his sermon was costing the town two hundred and fifty pesos.

Old Tasio had exclaimed: 'Two hundred and fifty pesos for a sermon! To hear one man once! That is only a third of what all the stage players put together will be paid for working three nights. No question about it, you must be very rich.'

What does the sermon have to do with the stage show?' replied the indignant prefect of the Venerable Third Order. 'The stage show sends souls to Hell, the sermon sends them to Heaven. If he had asked a thousand, we would have paid him that, and we would still have been in his debt.'

'You're right, after all,' countered the scholar. 'As far as I am concerned at least, the sermon is funnier than the stage show.'

'As for me,' the other shouted in a rage, 'I don't even find the stage show funny.'

'I believe it. You understand the one as little as the other.'

And the impious old man had gone off, ignoring the insults and dire prophecies which the irritable prefect made about his future life.

Waiting for the Governor to arrive, the people sweated and yawned; fans, hats, and handkerchiefs tried to raise a bit of air; children squalled and cried, and gave the sacristans a busy time throwing them out of the church.

This led the conscientious and phlegmatic director of the Confraternity of the Most Holy Rosary to reflect:

'It is true that our Lord Jesus Christ said, 'Let the little children come unto Me', but in this case it should be understood to mean little children who don't cry.'

Old Sister Pute, who was in a religious habit, was telling her granddaughter, a little girl of six, who was kneeling by her side:

'Pay attention, you wretch, you're going to hear a sermon like the one on Good Friday.'

And to awaken her piety she pinched the girl, who made a grimace, pouted and scowled.

A number of men, squatting by the confessionals, were dozing off. One old man, whose head kept nodding while Sister Pute was mumbling her prayers and running the beads of her rosary rapidly through her fingers, finally led her to believe that his was the more reverent way of accepting the designs of Providence, and little by little she fell to imitating him.

Ibarra was in a corner. María Clara was kneeling near the main altar; the parish priest had courteously ordered the sacristans to clear a place for her. Capitan Tiago, in full formal dress, was seated in the pews reserved for officials; the boys who did not know him took him for a mayor, and did not dare come too close to him.

At long last the Governor, accompanied by his staff, entered from the sacristy and took one of the magnificent armchairs placed on a great carpet. He was in full gala attire, with the sash of the Grand Cross of Charles III and four or five other decorations.

The townspeople could not make out who he was.

'Look,' cried a peasant. 'A constable dressed up like an actor!'

'Idiot,' his neighbour replied. 'That's the Prince Villardo whom we saw last night on the stage.'

The Governor promptly rose in the estimation of the masses, being promoted thereby into a fairy prince, a conqueror of giants.

The Mass began. Those who were seated got up; those who were dozing were awakened by the ringing of the altar bells and the sonorous voices of the choir. Father Salví, although maintaining his gravity, seemed to be very satisfied with himself for he was being assisted by a deacon and sub-deacon who were nothing less than Augustinians.

Each of these sang well in his turn, more or less nasally, and more or less unintelligibly, but the celebrant's voice was rather tremulous and he was off-key not a few times, to the great surprise of those who knew him. However, he moved with precision and elegance; he gave the *Dominus vobiscum* with unction, tilting his head slightly and raising his eyes to the ceiling. Anyone who had seen him receiving the homage of the censer would have agreed with the famous physician of antiquity, Galen, that smoke can reach the brain from the nasal cavities through the ethmoidal sieve at the root of the nose. For Father Salví would draw himself up, throw back his head, and afterward walk to the centre of the altar with such pomposity and gravity that Capitan Tiago found him more imposing than the stage player of the night before who had appeared as a Chinese emperor, profusely painted, with a line of banners stuck on his back, a horsehair beard, and high-soled slippers.

'No doubt about it,' he said to himself, 'any one of our parish priests is more impressive than all the emperors put together.'

At last the long desired moment came when Father Dámaso was to be heard. The three priests seated themselves in their armchairs in an edifying posture, as the reputable correspondent would have said; the Governor and others who were privileged to carry staffs and canes of office imitated them; the music was silenced.

The transition from noise to silence awoke old Sister Pute, who had begun to snore under the influence of the music. The first thing she did on waking up was to give her grand-daughter, who had also fallen asleep, a sharp rap on the back of the neck. The child cried out, but was soon engrossed in watching a woman who was striking herself on the breast with conviction and enthusiasm.

All tried to settle down in comfort. Those who had failed to get a seat in the pews squatted; women sat on the floor on their haunches.

Father Dámaso went through the crowd preceded by two sacristans and followed by another friar, who was carrying a large notebook. He was lost to sight when he began to climb the spiral staircase of the pulpit, but soon his round head reappeared, followed by the thick neck and the rest of his body. He looked round him with self-assurance, half-coughing; saw Ibarra, and a certain blinking made it clear that he would not forget the young man in his prayers; and then gave Father Sibyla a look of contempt. Having finished this survey he turned surreptitiously to his companion, whispering: 'Ready, brother!' The latter opened his notebook.

But the sermon deserves a chapter to itself. A young man who was then studying stenography and who idolised great orators recorded the sermon; thanks to this a sample can now be had of sacred oratory in the Philippines of that time.

32 • The Sermon

FATHER DAMASO began slowly, intoning in a hushed voice: '*Et spiritum tuum bonum dedisti, et manna tuum non prohibuisti ab ore eorum, et aquam dedisti eis in siti.* And thou gavest thy good Spirit to teach them, and thy manna thou didst not withhold from their mouth, and thou gavest them water for their thirst.

'Words which the Lord spoke through the mouth of Esdras, in the second book, ninth chapter, twentieth verse.'

Father Sibyla threw the preacher a surprised look; Father Manuel Martín grew pale and swallowed hard: this text was better than his.

Whether it was because Father Dámaso noticed the impression he had made or because he was still hoarse, the fact is that he coughed several times. His hands clasped the sill of the pulpit. Over his head was the Holy Ghost, newly painted: white, neat, with rosy little claws and beak.

'Excellency (this to the Governor), most virtuous priests, Christians, brothers in Jesus Christ!'

Here he made a solemn pause, his eyes roaming over the congregation, whose attention and concentration satisfied him.

The first part of the sermon would be in Spanish; the rest in Tagalog: as the Gospel said of the Apostles, *'loquebantur omnes lingues,* they shall speak in all tongues.'

After the salutation and the pause, he raised his right hand in the direction of the altar, keeping his eyes on the Governor, then he slowly crossed his arms without uttering a word; but jumping into activity from this calm he threw back his head and pointed to the main door of the church, his hand sawing the air with such violence that the sacristans interpreted his gesture to be an order to shut the doors, and did so, while the lieutenant grew uneasy and wondered if he should leave or stay. But the preacher was already speaking with a voice that was strong, full, and resonant. No doubt about it: the old housekeeper was a good doctor. 'Radiant and resplendent is the altar, and spacious the portals of this church; but between them is the air that will transport the holy and divine message that will spring forth from my lips. Listen, then, with the ears of the soul and the heart so that the words of Our Lord may not fall on stony ground and be eaten up by the birds of Hell, but rather that you may sprout and thrive like holy seed in the field of our Venerable and Seraphic Father St. Francis. Ye great sinners, captives of those Moro pirates of the spirit who prowl the seas of eternal life in the powerful vessels of the flesh and the world, and you who, bound with the shackles of lust and concupiscence, row in the galleys of infernal Satan, behold with reverend remorse one who rescues souls from the devil's thrall, an intrepid Gideon, a valiant

David, a victorious Roland of Christianity, the Constable of Heaven, braver than all the Constabulary put together; present and future [then, noticing that the commanding officer was frowning]—yes, Lieutenant, braver and more powerful, one who with only a wooden cross for a gun dauntlessly puts to rout the eternal bandits of darkness and all the hordes of Lucifer, and would have annihilated them for ever had these spirits not been immortal! This marvel of Divine Creation, this unimaginable prodigy, is the blessed Diego of Alcala, who, to use a comparison—for comparisons, as someone has said, are a great help in comprehending the incomprehensible—who, I say, for all that he was a great saint, is only a soldier in the ranks, a mess steward, in that most powerful army which Our Seraphic Father St. Francis commands from Heaven and to which I have the honour to belong as corporal or sergeant, by the grace of God.'

The unlettered natives, who, according to the correspondent, got nothing from this paragraph except the words 'Constabulary', 'bandit', 'St. Diego', and 'St. Francis', remarked the lieutenant's sour face, and the preacher's pugnacious gesture, and concluded that the latter was upbraiding the former for not going after the bandits. St. Diego and St. Francis, on the other hand, would take the matter in hand, and very well indeed, as could be seen in a painting in the Order's convent in Manila, which showed St. Francis with his cincture alone repelling the Chinese invasion during the first years after the Spanish discovery of the Philippines. The faithful were pleased, therefore, and thanked God for this assistance, not doubting that, having annihilated the bandits, St. Francis would next destroy the Constabulary. It was with twice the attention they had given him that they heard Father Dámaso continue. 'Excellency, what is great is always great even beside the small, and what is small is always small even beside the great. History records this, but since History hits the mark once for every hundred misses, being the work of man, and man being prone to make mistakes—to err is human, as Cicero says, and, as they say in my own country, whoever has a tongue can be wrong—the conclusion is that there are deeper truths than can be found in History. These truths, Excellency, have been revealed by the Divine Spirit in His supreme wisdom, which has never been grasped by human intelligence, from the times of Seneca and Aristotle, those wise religious of antiquity, to our sinful present, and these truths are that what is small is not always small but is great, and is great not only beside the minuscule, but beside what is greatest on land and in the sky and in the air and in the clouds and in the waters and in space and in life and death.'

'Amen,' interjected the prefect of the Venerable Third Order, and crossed himself. With this rhetorical figure, which he had learned from a great preacher in Manila, Father Dámaso had planned to astound his audience, and indeed his prompter, struck dumb by so many truths, had to be prodded with the foot to recall him to his duties.

'Patent to your eyes...' the ghost said from below.

'Patent to your eyes is the conclusive and shattering proof of this eternal philosophic truth. Patent to your eyes is the sun of virtues—and I say sun, not moon, because there is no great merit in the moon shining at night; in the kingdom of the blind, the one-eyed man is king, and at night even a little star can shine; but what greater merit it is to shine in the middle of the day like the sun does—so does our brother Diego shine even in the midst of even the greatest saints! There you have patent to your eyes, to your impious incredulity, the masterpiece of the All Highest which will confound the greatest of the earth, yes, my brethren, patent, patent to all, patent!'

A man rose pale and trembling and hid in a confessional. He was a liquor dealer who had dozed off and dreamed that a patrol was asking him for the patent or license that he did not have. It is said he never left his hiding-place while the sermon lasted.

'Humble and retiring Saint, your wooden cross [actually, the image had a silver one], your modest habit, honour the great Francis of whom we are the sons and imitators. We multiply your holy breed throughout the world, in every corner, in the cities, in the towns, without distinction between white and black [here the Governor held his breath], suffering privations and tortures, all for your holy breed of faith and armed religion [the Governor sighed with relief], which maintains the world in equilibrium and prevents it from falling into the abyss of perdition!'

The congregation, even Capitan Tiago himself, was beginning to yawn. María Clara was not paying attention to the sermon; she knew that Ibarra was near by and her thoughts were on him as, fanning herself, she stared at the bull which symbolised one of the Evangelists and which had all the appearances of a small carabao.

'We should all know the Holy Scriptures by heart, the Lives of the Saints too; if you did, I would not have to preach to you now, ye sinners; you should know things as important and necessary as the Lord's Prayer, but many of you have already forgotten it, and you live like Protestants or heretics, like the Chinese who do not respect the ministers of God. But you will be damned, all the worse for you, ye damned!'

'Whassa matta Fale Lamaso!' muttered Carlos the Chinese with an angry look at the preacher, who went on improvising, unloosing a series of apostrophes and imprecations.

'You will die unrepentant and unshriven, ye race of heretics! Already God is punishing you on this earth in dungeons and prisons. Your families, your women, should flee from you; your rulers should send you all to the gallows so that the seed of Satan may not spread in the Lord's vineyard. Jesus said: "If a member of your body lead you into sin, cut it off and throw it into the fire..."'

Father Dámaso was nervous; he had forgotten his sermon and his rhetoric.

'Did you hear that?' a young student from Manila asked his companion. 'Well, are you going to cut it off?'

'Fat chance. Let him do it first.'

Ibarra was growing uneasy. He looked round for a secluded corner, but the church was full. María Clara heard and saw nothing; she was studying a painting of the Holy Souls in Purgatory, souls in the shape of men and women, naked, or with mitres, cardinal's hats, or hoods, being roasted in fire and clinging to the girdle of St. Francis which yet did not break under so much weight.

The friar-ghost had lost the thread of the sermon in the long improvisation, and jumped three long paragraphs when he next prompted Father Dámaso as the latter was trying to recover his breath after his apostrophe.

'Who among ye sinners who hear me would lick the wounds of a poor and ragged beggar? Who? Let him answer and raise his hand. No one! Exactly what I thought. Only a saint like Diego of Alcala could do it. He licked all the rottenness away, telling an astounded brother: "So shall this man be healed." Oh Christian charity! Oh unexampled compassion! Oh virtue of virtues! Oh inimitable model! Oh flawless wonder-worker!'

And he continued with a long list of exclamations, raising his arms to make a cross, and lifting and lowering them as if he wanted to fly or scare birds away.

'Before he died he spoke in Latin without knowing Latin. Marvel, ye sinners! You, in spite of all your books, and in spite of the blows you get to

make you study, will not speak Latin, you will die without speaking it.
Speaking Latin is a grace of God, that is why the Church speaks in Latin. I
speak Latin myself. What, was God to deny this boon to his dear Diego?
Could he die, could God allow Diego to die, without speaking Latin?
Impossible! God would not be just, He would not be God. Diego, then,
spoke Latin, and the authors of that age beat testimony to it.'

And he concluded his introduction with the passage that had cost him the most
effort and which he had in fact plagiarised from a great writer, Sinibaldo de Mas.

'I salute you, then, illustrious Diego, honour of Our Order. You are a
model of virtues, modest but honoured, humble yet noble, submissive but
upright, moderate in your ambitions, trustworthy even to your enemies,
compassionate and forgiving, zealous and scrupulous, combining faith and
devotion, credulous because guileless, chaste but loving, discreet in secrets,
long-suffering but patient, brave yet prudent, continent by choice, bold and
resolute, obedient to your superiors, sensitive of your honour, careful of your
interests but detached from them, fortunate and able, punctilious but well-
mannered, shrewd and foresighted, merciful for the love of man, circumspect
through modesty, fearless in righting wrongs, in poverty industrious but
resigned, generous though destitute, diligent yet relaxed, thrifty but not
miserly, innocent yet subtle, reformer within reason, eager for knowledge but
above it—God created you to feel the raptures of spiritual love! Help me
now to sing your glories and to praise your name, higher than the stars and
more refulgent than the very sun that turns beneath your feet! And you too,
my brethren, give me your help, beseech from God the inspiration that I
need by saying a Hail Mary.'

All fell on their knees, raising a murmur like the buzzing of a thousand
bumble-bees. The Governor bent one knee laboriously, his head shaking
with annoyance. The lieutenant was pale and contrite.

'To the devil with this priest,' muttered one of the young men from Manila.

'Quiet,' answered the other. 'His woman may be around.'

Meantime Father Dámaso, instead of saying a Hail Mary, was scolding his
ghostly prompter for skipping three of his best paragraphs, and was taking two
meringues and a glass of Malaya wine, certain of finding there more inspiration
than in all the holy ghosts, whether wooden doves or inattentive friars.
Sister Pute gave her grand-daughter another slap in the nape. Awakened she

asked sullenly:

'Is it time to cry?'

'Not yet, but don't fall asleep, you wretch,' her good grandmother answered.

There are only a few notes of the second part of the sermon in Tagalog. Father Dámaso improvised in this language, not because he had a greater command of it, but because he considered the Filipinos in the provinces to be ignorant of rhetoric and was not afraid of committing absurdities in their hearing. With Spaniards it was another matter; he had heard about the rules of oratory, and among his hearers there might be somebody with a nodding acquaintance with books, perhaps the Governor, so he wrote out his sermons, corrected and polished them, and then memorised and rehearsed them for two days.

It is well known that none of those present understood the sermon in Tagalog as a whole, the hearers were so dense, and the preacher so profound, as Sister Rufa said, so that they waited in vain for an opportunity to shed tears, and the wretched grand-daughter of the pious old woman went to sleep again.

Nevertheless this part of the sermon produced more results than the first part, at least with regard to certain hearers, as will be seen later. Father Dámaso spoke Tagalog with a heavy Spanish accent, and began by addressing the natives with what might be roughly rendered as my 'diar bradders in Hesoos Christ'. This was followed by an avalanche of untranslatable phrases; he spoke of the soul, of Hell of the 'belobbed pahtron sent' of the sinful natives, and of the virtuous Franciscan fathers.

This is all Greek to me,' said one of the two irreverent Manilans to his companion. 'I'm going.'

And seeing the church doors shut, he went out openly through the sacristy, to the great scandal of the congregation and the preacher, who turned pale and stopped in the middle of a phrase. There were some who expected a violent denunciation, but Father Dámaso was content to follow the young man with his eyes and continued his sermon.

He let loose maledictions against the age, against the lack of proper respect, against the nascent irreligiousness. This theme seemed to be his strong point, for he appeared inspired and expressed himself with vigour and clarity. He spoke of sinners who did not go to Confession, who died in prison without the Sacrament, of accursed families, of proud and vain half-breeds, of young know-it-alls, of pseudo-intellectuals, pseudo-lawyers, pseudo-students, and so on. Many have this well-known habit of ridiculing their enemies by describing them as pseudo-that; their brains do not suggest any other form of abuse, and it makes them happy.

Ibarra heard everything and understood the allusions. Under an outward composure, his eyes sought help from God and the authorities, but he found nothing except images of saints and the nodding Governor.

Meantime the enthusiasm of the preacher was rising by degrees. He spoke of the old times when every Filipino, upon meeting a priest, uncovered himself, bent his knee to the ground, and kissed the priest's hand. 'But now,' he added, 'you only take off that felt hat which you wear tilted anyway so as not to disarrange your hair. You are satisfied with saying: "Good day, Father". And there are vain intellectuals who think that because they have gone to school in Manila or in Europe they have the right to shake our hand instead of kissing it. Ah, the Day of Judgment is coming soon, the world is coming to an end, many saints have foretold it, fire and stone and ashes will rain down to punish your pride!'

And he exhorted the people not to imitate those whom he called savages, but instead to flee from them and abhor them because they were excommunicate.

'Listen,' he said, 'to what the Holy Councils say. When a native meets a priest on the street, he shall bend his head and offer his neck so that the Father may lean on it; if the priest and the native are both on horseback, then the native shall stop and shall take off his hat reverently; and finally if the native is on horseback and the priest on foot, the native shall get off his horse and will not remount until the priest tells him to be off, or has gone out of sight. That is what the Holy Councils say, and whoever does not obey shall be excommunicate.'

'And when the native is on a carabao?' a conscientious peasant asked the man next to him.

'Then, full speed ahead,' replied the latter, obviously a quibbler.

But in spite of the shouts and gesticulations of the preacher, many had fallen asleep or grown inattentive, for this was the king of sermon everyone always gave; in vain did some devout women try to sigh and snivel over the sins of the impious; they had to abandon the enterprise for lack of partners. With Sister Pute it was just the opposite. A man seated beside her had gone to sleep in such a manner that he had fallen against her, crumpling her habit.

The good old woman grabbed her wooden slipper and set to waking him up with blows.

'Get off me, you savage, you animal, you devil, you carabao, you dog, you damned fool!'

The preacher stopped and raised his eyebrows, taken aback by so great a scandal. Indignation choked down the words in his throat and he could only bellow, hitting the pulpit-sill with his fists. This had its effect; the old lady let go her wooden slipper with many a grumble, and crossing herself repeatedly fell on her knees.

'Aaaaah! Aaaaah!' the shocked priest at last managed to exclaim, crossing his arms and shaking his head. 'For that I spend the whole morning preaching to you, you barbarians! Here, in the very house of God, you quarrel and blaspheme. You have lost all sense of shame! You no longer respect anything. This is the fruit of the lust and incontinence of the age! Exactly what I was saying!'

And on the this theme he continued to preach for half an hour. The Governor was snoring, María Clara was nodding, having no more paintings or images to study or to amuse herself with. Neither word nor allusion had an effect any longer on Ibarra; he was dreaming now of a little house on a mountain-top, and he saw Maria Clara in its garden. Let humanity drag along in its wretched towns in the valley below!

Father Salví had had the altar bell rung twice, but this was merely adding fuel to the fire. Father Dámaso was stubborn and made his sermon even longer. Father Sibyla was biting his lips and fingering his gold-rimmed rock-crystal glasses. Only Father Manuel Martin seemed to listen with pleasure, for there was a smile on his lips.

At last God said enough; the orator had exhausted himself and went down from the pulpit.

All knelt to give thanks to God. The Governor rubbed his eyes, stretched out an arm, sighed profoundly and yawned.

The Mass went on.

When everyone knelt and the priests lowered their heads at the *Incarnatus est*, a man whispered in Ibarra's ear: 'At the blessing ceremony, stay close to the parish priest, don't go down the excavation, and don't go near the corner-stone. Your life depends on it.'

Ibarra saw Elias who, having said this, was losing himself in the crowd.

33 • The Derrick

THE sallow-faced man had been as good as his word. To lower the heavy granite cornerstone into the open pit of the foundations, he had prepared more than a simple derrick or the tripod for a block pulley which Master Juan had wanted; it was a showpiece as much as a machine, a superb showpiece.

The intricate scaffolding was more than eight metres high; four heavy logs sunk into the ground were the main supports, held together by thick cross-beams with great nails only half driven in, perhaps, the structure being only provisional, to facilitate dismantling it. Big cables stretched on all sides gave it a solid and impressive air; the whole was crowned by multicoloured flags, fluttering pennants, and large garlands of leaves and flowers artificially intertwined.

High above, in the shadow of beams, garlands, and banners, and held by ropes and iron hooks, was a huge block-pulley. The three heaviest cables of all rode the grooved rims of its three wheels, carrying suspended the huge stone, hollowed out in the centre to match the identical hole in another stone already lowered into the pit. The confined space thus to be formed was designed to keep souvenirs of the time: newspapers, manuscripts, coins, medals, and so forth, for the benefit of distant generations. The cables led to another pulley of equal size, set at the bottom of the structure, and were then wound about the cylinder of a windlass held firmly to the ground with heavy timbers. By means of this windlass, operated by two cranks and working through cogged wheels, the strength of a man could be multiplied a hundredfold, although what was gained in power was lost in speed.

'Look here,' said the sallow-faced man, turning the crank handle of the windlass. 'Look, Master Juan, how by myself I can raise and lower this enormous mass. It's all so well arranged that at will I can regulate its ascent or descent inch by inch so that a man in the pit can align the two stones at his leisure while I operate the machine here.'

Master Juan could not help but praise the man with the odd smile.

Bystanders were already commenting on the machine and complimenting him on it.

'Who taught you how to put this up?'

'My father, my late father,' he answered with his curious smile.

'And who taught your father?'

'Don Saturnino, Don Crisóstomo's grandfather.'

'I didn't know that Don Saturnino...'

'Oh, he knew a lot. He handled the whip well, and he knew how to punish his men by staking them out in the sun; but he knew more than that. He could liven up the sleepy and put the live ones to sleep. You'll see in time what my father taught me, you'll see.'

And the sallow-faced man smiled again his extraordinary smile.

On a table near by, covered with a Persian rug, was a lead cylinder and the objects which were to be preserved in the hollow of the cornerstone. A heavy glass case would contain the mummified presents which would provide the future with a reminder of the past.

Old Tasio the scholar thoughtfully muttered to himself.

'Perhaps some day, when the work begun today, grown decrepit after many vicissitudes, finally crumbles into ruins, whether by the forces of Nature or by the destructive hand of man, and moss and ivy cover the rubble; perhaps even later, when time shall have scattered moss and ivy and rubble equally like ashes into the wind, wiping out from the pages of history all vestige of the world and of those who built it, long since gone by then from human memory; perhaps later still when the present races of men shall have been buried and vanished in the layers of the earth; the pick of some miner, striking a chance spark from the granite, will discover, and bare these mysteries and enigmas from the heart of the rock. Perhaps the wise men of the nation that shall inhabit these regions will then set to work in the manner of our Egyptologists, who decipher the relics of a great civilisation obsessed with eternity and all unsuspecting of the long night that was to fall over it. Perhaps some wise teacher shall tell his five or seven-year-old pupils, in what will then be the universal language: "Gentlemen, having carefully studied and examined the objects found beneath our soil, having deciphered certain symbols and translated certain words, we can without hesitation assume that these objects belonged to man's barbaric age, to that dark age which we can only describe as quasi-mythical. Indeed, gentlemen, to give you a rough idea of the backwardness of our ancestors, I need only say that those who formerly inhabited this land not only gave their homage to kings but, even to resolve problems of their domestic government, had to appeal to the other end of the world, which is as if a body, in order to move a finger, had to consult its

head in another part of the globe, perhaps even in that part now covered by
the sea. This incredible weakness of character, hard as it may be for you to
believe it, can be understood if we consider the situation of those beings
whom I scarcely dare to call human. In those primitive times these creatures
still had (or at least they believed they had) direct relations with their Creator,
for they had His ministers among them, beings different from the rest, and
always identified with the mysterious letters 'V.R.' Our scholars are not in
agreement on the interpretation of these letters. We have only a mediocre
language teacher here; he speaks only one hundred of the rudimentary
languages of the past; his opinion is that 'V.R.' would stand for 'Very Rich'
since these ministers were a kind of demi-gods, most virtuous, most eloquent
orators, most accomplished scholars, who, in spite of their great power and
prestige, never committed the slightest mistake. This reinforces my belief
that they were of a different nature from the others; and there is, in addition,
my argument, which is not denied by anyone and which daily receives greater
confirmation, that these mysterious beings could make God come down to
earth merely by pronouncing certain words, that God could not speak except
through their mouths, and that they ate God and drank His blood and not
seldom gave Him also to common men to eat..." '

These and other things were put by the sceptical scholar into the mouths of the
corrupt spokesmen of posterity. Perhaps old Tasio was wrong; it is very likely.

An appetising and abundant luncheon was being prepared in the pavilions
where the schoolmaster and his pupils had worked two days before. On the
table set aside for the schoolboys, however, there was no wine, but instead a
great quantity of fruit. Under the trellis joining the two pavilions there were
seats for the musicians, and a table covered with sweetmeats and confectionery
and jugs of water, decorated with leaves and flowers, for the thirsty public.
The schoolmaster had ordered preparations to be made for popular games:
greased pole to be climbed, hurdles for obstacle races, pots and pans to be hit
blindfolded.

The crowd, wearing gaily coloured clothes, sought shelter from the blazing
sun in the shade of trees or under the trellis. Boys perched themselves on
branches or on boulders to make up for their lack of height and get a better
view of the ceremony; they looked with envy on the pupils of the school who,
neat and well-dressed, occupied the seats reserved for them. The parents of

the latter were elated; poor peasants themselves, they would watch their children eat from a white tablecloth like the parish priest and the Governor. It was enough to make them forget their hunger, a story to be handed on from father to son.

Soon the distant strains of music were heard. The brass band was preceded by a motley crowd of all ages dressed in all colours. The sallow-faced man grew uneasy and gave his machine one last look. A curious peasant was following his eyes and all his movements: it was Elias, who was also attending the ceremony, almost unrecognisable in his wide-brimmed straw hat and nondescript clothes. He had the best place of all, almost beside the windlass at the edge of the excavation.

With the band came the Governor, the municipal officials, all the friars except Father Dámaso, and the Spanish employees. Ibarra was conversing with the Governor, who had become very friendly after the young man had complimented him on his decorations and sashes. These aristocratic vanities were His Excellency's weakness. Capitan Tiago, the commanding officer, and a number of wealthy men were in the golden company of young ladies who twirled silken parasols. Father Salví was as silent and thoughtful as always.

'You can count on my support whenever it is a good cause,' the Governor was telling Ibarra. 'I shall let you have what you need, and, if I cannot, I shall have others do so.'

As they approached the site, the young man felt his heart beat faster. Instinctively he stole a look at the strange scaffolding raised there; he saw the sallow-faced man salute him respectfully, eyes fixed on him for an instant. He was surprised to see Elias, who reminded him with a significant wink of what he had been told in church.

The parish priest put on his vestments and the ceremony began. The one-eyed head sacristan carried the books of rites, and an acolyte the hyssop and the holy water. The rest, standing uncovered round them, kept such a complete silence that, although Father Salví read in a low voice, its trembling was noticeable.

In the meantime manuscripts, newspapers, medals, coins, and whatever else was to be preserved for prosperity had been placed in the glass case, and the whole inserted in the lead cylinder and hermetically sealed.

'Mr. Ibarra,' the Governor whispered in the young man's ear, 'would you put the cylinder in its place? The parish priest is waiting.'

'With pleasure,' he answered, 'but I would be usurping the honourable duties of the notary who must attest to this event.'

The notary took the cylinder gravely, went down the carpeted steps to the bottom of the pit, and with all due solemnity deposited the cylinder in the hollow of the stone. The parish priest then took the hyssop and sprinkled the stone with holy water.

The moment had come for each to spread a ceremonial trowelful of mortar on the surface of the lower half of the cornerstone, which was in the pit, so that the upper half might, on being lowered, adhere firmly.

Ibarra offered the Governor a silver trowel on whose broad blade the date had been engraved. But His Excellency wished first to deliver a speech in Spanish.

'Residents of San Diego,' he said ponderously, 'we have the honour to preside over a ceremony whose importance you will understand without our telling you. This is the foundation of a school, and the school is the foundation of society, the book on which is written the future of nations. Show us the schools of a nation, and we shall tell you what kind of a nation it is.

'Residents of San Diego, praise God, who has given you virtuous priests, and praise the Government of the Motherland, that untiringly spreads civilisation throughout these fertile isles, sheltered under her glorious mantle! Praise God who has taken mercy on you and sent you these humble priests who enlighten your minds and teach you the word of God. Praise the Government that has made, is making, and will make so many sacrifices for you and for your children.

'And now that the cornerstone of this building, of such transcendental importance, is being blessed, we, governor of this province, in the name of His Majesty the King, whom God keep, King of all the Realms of Spain, in the name of the illustrious Spanish Government, and under the protection of its untarnished and ever victorious flag, officially dedicate and open the construction of this school.

'Residents of San Diego, long live the King! Long live Spain! Long live the Friars! Long live the Catholic Religion!'

'Long live! Long live!' replied many voices. 'And long live the Governor!'

The latter went down the steps majestically to the strains of the band, which had struck up a march, deposited a few trowelfuls of mortar on the stone, and with the same dignity went up again. The employees applauded.

Ibarra offered another silver trowel to the parish priest, who, after looking him in the eyes for a moment, went down slowly. Midway down the steps he raised his eyes to the stone that hung from the thick cables overhead, but it was only for a second, and he continued on his way. He did what the Governor had done, but this time there was more applause: the friars and Capitan Tiago had joined the employees.

Father Salví looked round for someone to whom to pass on the trowel, gazed hesitantly at María Clara, but, changing his mind, offered the trowel to the notary. The latter gallantly approached María Clara, but she declined with a smile. Friars, employees, and the commanding officer, all then took their turn, one after the other; nor was Capitan Tiago forgotten.

Only Ibarra had not participated in the ceremony, and orders were about to be given to the sallow-faced man to lower the stone when the parish priest remembered the young man and asked him jestingly and with assumed familiarity:

'Aren't you going to take your turn, Mr. Ibarra?'

'I don't eat what I cook,' the young man replied in the same tone.

'Go on,' said the Governor, giving him a slight push. 'Otherwise I shall forbid the lowering of the stone, and we shall stay here till doomsday.'

Ibarra had to yield to this mock-terrible threat. He changed the small silver trowel for a large iron one, which made a number of those present smile, and calmly went down the steps. Elias watched him with an indescribable expression; anyone who had seen him then would have said that his whole soul had come to a point in his eyes. The sallow-faced man stared at the pit open below his feet.

Ibarra, after looking up quickly at the stone hanging over his head and then at Elias and the sallow-faced man, told the overseer in a voice that trembled slightly:

'Give me the pail, and go up and get me another trowel.'

The young man was left alone. Elias no longer looked at him; his eyes were fixed on the hand of the jaundiced man who, leaning over the pit, eagerly followed Ibarra's movements.

Through the hushed murmur of the employees who were congratulating the Governor on his speech came the noise of the trowel mixing the sand and lime.

Suddenly there was a tremendous crash; the pulley at the base of the scaffolding broke loose, followed by the windlass, which, revolving wildly, struck the base of the structure like a battering ram; beams wavered, cables snapped and flew apart, and everything collapsed in a second of terrible sound. A cloud of dust rose together with a cry of horror from a thousand throats. Almost everyone ran away; a very few dashed to the pit; only María Clara and Father Salví remained in their places, unable to move, pale and speechless.

When the dust had partly settled they saw Ibarra standing among beams, poles, and cables, between the windlass and the great stone slab which, in its swift fall, had shaken down and crushed everything beneath it. The young man still had the trowel in his hand and stared with horrified eyes at the dead body which lay at his feet, half-buried underneath the timbers.

'You're not killed? You're still alive? For God's sake, say something!' a number of the employees cried out with fear and anxiety.

'A miracle, a miracle!' cried others.

'Come down and get the body of this unfortunate clear,' said Ibarra, as if awakening from a dream.

It was only on hearing his voice that María Clara felt her strength go, and she fell, half-fainting, into the arms of her friends.

A great confusion reigned. Everyone was speaking, gesticulating, running from one side to the other, going down into the pit and up again, stunned, in consternation.

'Who is the dead man? Is he still alive?' the commanding officer asked.

They recognised the sallow-faced man who had stood beside the windlass.

'Arrest the supervisor of the construction and charge him,' was the first thing that the Governor could say.

They examined the body, but a hand on his chest could no longer feel the heart beating. The man had been hit on the head, and blood flowed from his nose, mouth, and ears. On his neck they saw strange marks; four deep depressions on one side, and a single one, rather larger, on the opposite side, as if a steel hand had clutched him by the neck.

The priests were warmly congratulating the young man, shaking his hand. The Franciscan of humble aspect, who had served as prompter to Father Dámaso, said with tearful eyes:

'God is just, God is good.'

'When I think that I was down there myself a few moments before it happened,' one of the employees told Ibarra. 'I mean, if I had gone down there last of all, Jesus'.

'My hair stands on end,' said another one, who was half-bald.

'Much better that it happened to you rather than to me,' an old man mumbled in a shaky voice.

'Don Pascual!' protested some Spaniards.

'Gentlemen, I say so because Mr. Ibarra was not killed; if it had been me, even if I had not been crushed to death, I would have died just thinking about it.'

But Ibarra was already beyond hearing, inquiring after María Clara.

'This should not interrupt the fiesta, Mr. Ibarra,' the Governor was saying. 'Thank God, the dead man is neither a priest nor a Spaniard. Besides, we must celebrate your escape. If that stone had caught you underneath.'

'No use laughing at hunches now,' the notary exclaimed. 'I could see it; Mr. Ibarra was reluctant to go down there; I could feel it.'

'Well, anyway, the dead man was just a native.'

'On with the fiesta! Music! Long faces won't bring the dead back to life. Captain, hold the investigation right here. Call the Municipal Secretary. Arrest the supervisor of the works.'

'To the stocks with him!'

'Yes, to the stocks. Hey, there, music, music! And the master builder to the stocks.'

'Mr. Governor,' Ibarra intervened earnestly, 'if long faces will not bring the dead back to life, even less would the imprisonment of a man of whose guilt we know nothing. I stand surety for him and ask that he be free at least for the time being.'

'Very well, but he must not do it again!'

All kinds of comments went round. The idea that a miracle had taken place was already accepted, although Father Salví did not seem to rejoice at a wonder that was attributed to his Order and his parish.

Nor was there lacking someone who added that, when the whole of the scaffolding was collapsing, he had seen a figure, dressed in a habit that was dark like a Franciscan's, go down into the pit. Undoubtedly that had been St. Diego himself. It was also learned that Ibarra had heard Mass, and the jaundiced man had not: that made everything as clear as the noonday sun.

'Do you see?' a mother upbraided her son. 'And you did not want to go to Mass! If I hadn't spanked you and made you go you would be like that man now, carried to the courthouse in a cart!'

The sallow-faced man was indeed being carried to the courthouse wrapped up in a mat.

Ibarra was hurrying home to change.

'A bad beginning,' muttered old Tasio, as he walked away.

34 • Free Thought

IBARRA had almost finished dressing when a servant informed him that a peasant was asking for him.

Assuming that the caller was one of his workmen, Ibarra ordered him to be shown into his study, which combined a library with a chemical laboratory. But, to his great surprise, he found himself face to face with the grim and mysterious figure of Elias.

The latter, interpreting correctly a movement of Ibarra, told him in Tagalog:

'You saved my life. I have repaid you by half. You have nothing for which to be grateful. On the contrary, I have come to ask you a favour.'

'Say it,' Ibarra answered in the same language, surprised by the peasant's gravity.

Elias looked Ibarra in the eyes briefly and replied:

'When human justice seeks to clear up this mystery, I ask you to tell no one of the warning I gave you in church.'

'Don't worry,' Ibarra answered in a tone of disappointment. 'I know they are looking for you, but I am no informer.'

'Oh, it isn't for my sake, not for my sake at all,' Elias exclaimed quickly' and with a certain haughtiness. 'It is for yours. I myself fear no man.'

The young man's amazement grew. The tone of voice used by this peasant, erstwhile steersman, was new to him and did not seem to be in keeping either with his class or his means.

'What do you mean?' he asked, searching this enigmatic man with his eyes.

'I do not speak in riddles. I am trying to express myself clearly. For your greater safety, it is necessary that your enemies should think you careless and over-confident.'

Ibarra drew back.

'My enemies? Do I have enemies?'

'Sir, we all have them, from the smallest insect to man, and from the poorest to the richest and most powerful. Enmity is the law of life.'

Ibarra looked at Elias in silence. 'You are neither a peasant nor a boatman,' he murmured.

'You have enemies in the upper and the lower classes,' Elias continued, paying no heed to the young man's words. 'You plan a great enterprise. You have a past: your father, your grandfather, had enemies because they had passions, and in life it is not the criminal but the honest man who arouses the greatest hatred.'

'Do you know who my enemies are?'

Elias did not answer immediately and fell into thought.

'I knew one,' he replied, 'the one who died. Last night I discovered that he was plotting against you from some words he exchanged with an unknown man whom I lost in the crowd. "you'll see tomorrow." These words caught my attention not only because of their meaning but also because the one who had said them had, a few days before, offered his services to the master-builder for the express purpose of supervising the lowering of the cornerstone; he had not sufficient motive to believe him ill-intentioned, but something in me told me that my hunch was right, that is why I chose for my warning to you a time and a place where you could not ask me any questions. You know the rest.'

Elias had finished for some time and Ibarra had not yet answered or said a word. He was sunk in thought.

'I am sorry that man was killed,' he said at last. 'Something more might have been learned from him.'

'If he had lived, he would have escaped the uncertain hand of human justice, which is blind. God judged him, God executed him, may God be our only judge!'

Crisóstomo asked with a smile:

'Do you believe in the miracle too? Here, I think, right before me, is the miracle everyone is talking about!' His eyes were on the bruises and contusions on the pilot's muscled arms.

'If I believed in miracles, I would not believe in God. I would believe in a man-made god; I would believe that in truth man had made God in his own image and likeness,' Elias answered gravely. 'But I do believe in Him. I have felt His hand upon me more than once. When everything was falling to pieces today, threatening annihilation to anyone in the pit, I held the villain beside me; he was struck down, and I am whole and safe.'

'You? So it was you?'

'Yes, I held him fast when he wanted to run away once he had put his plan in motion; I saw him commit the crime. I say to you: let God be the only judge among men, let Him be the only one with right over life, let no man ever think of taking His place.'

'Yet, this time, you...'

'No,' Elias interrupted, forestalling the objection. 'It was not the same thing. When one man condemns others to death, or destroys their future forever, he does it without danger to himself, and uses the strength of others to execute his orders, which after all may be mistaken. But I, in exposing the criminal to the same danger which he had prepared for others, shared the same risk. I did not kill him, I let the hand of God strike him down.'

'Don't you believe in chance?'

'Believing in chance is like believing in miracles. Both things must assume that God does not know the future. What is a chance? It is something that absolutely no one can foresee. What is a miracle? It is a contradiction, a subversion of the laws of Nature. Both contradiction and lack of foresight imply imperfection in the Intelligence that governs the machinery of the world.'

'Who are you?' Ibarra asked again with a certain fear. 'Have you studied?'

'I have had to believe much in God because I have stopped believing in men,' Elias answered evading the question.

Ibarra thought he understood this wanted man: he denied human justice, he repudiated the right of one man to sit in judgment on his fellows, he protested against the power and the superiority of some classes over others.

'But you must admit the need for human justice, however imperfect it may be,' he countered. 'No matter how many ministers He may have on earth, God cannot, or rather does not, make His judgments clear enough to settle the millions of conflicts roused by our passions. It is necessary, it is just, that man should sometimes sit in judgment over his own kind.'

'Yes, if it is to-do good, but not to do evil; yes, if it is to correct and improve, but not to destroy; because if his verdicts are wrong, he is powerless to undo the wrong he does. But,' he added, changing his tone, 'this discussion is beyond my powers. They are waiting for you, and I am delaying you. Do not forget what I have just told you. You have enemies. Take care of yourself — for the sake of your country.'

He took his leave.

'When shall I see you again?' asked Ibarra.

'Whenever you want, and whenever I can be useful to you. I am still in your debt.'

35 • *The Banquet*

THE great men of the province were eating in one of the decorated pavilions. The Governor was at one end of the table, Ibarra at the other, with María Clara on his right and the notary on his left. Capitan Tiago, the commanding officer, the Mayor, the friars, the employees, and the few young ladies who had stayed were seated not according to their rank but as they wished.

The gathering was lively and gay enough, but in the middle of the meal a messenger arrived with a telegram for Capitan Tiago. The latter asked the company's leave to read it, and, having been granted it, frowned, raised his eyebrows, and, changing colour, folded the message hurriedly and rose to his feet.

'Gentlemen,' he stammered, 'His Excellency the Governor General honours my house with a visit this afternoon.'

And he trotted away with both napkin and telegram, but without his hat, pursued by exclamations and questions. If the arrival of a band of high-waymen had been announced, it could not have had a greater effect.

'But listen here!'

'When is he coming?'

'Do tell us!'

'His Excellency!'

Capitan Tiago was by now beyond hearing.

'Really! His Excellency no less, and he chooses to stay with Capitan Tiago!' someone protested, regardless of the presence of his daughter and prospective son-in-law.

'He would not have made a better choice,' the latter replied.

The friars exchanged looks whose meaning was clear. *The Governor General is up to his old tricks. It's an insult to us. He should have stayed at the parish house.* But since each of them was thinking the same thing nobody bothered to say it out loud.

'I was told about it yesterday,' said the Governor, 'but His Excellency had not yet made up his mind.'

'Do you know, Mr. Governor,' the Mayor, and the commanding officer asked uneasily, 'how long the Governor General plans to stay?'

'I don't know for certain. His Excellency likes to spring surprises.'

'Here come more telegrams!'

They were for the Governor, the Mayor, and the commanding officer, and they carried the same announcement. The friars did not fail to remark that there was none for the parish priest.

'His Excellency arrives at four o'clock this afternoon, gentlemen,' the Governor said solemnly. 'We can eat at our leisure.'

The doomed Spartan king, Leonidas, could not have said with greater style at Thermopylae: 'Tonight we dine with Death.'

The conversation returned to its usual channels.

'I see that our renowned preacher is not with us,' one of the employees timidly remarked. He was an inoffensive character who had not opened his mouth until it was time to put food in it, and who had not said a word the whole morning.

All those who knew about Crisóstomo's father started or winked, as if to say: 'Come now! Out the first time at bat!' but others were more charitable.

'He must be rather tired,' they said.

'Rather tired!' cried the lieutenant. 'He must be worn out, or, as they say, out on his feet, and no wonder, after that marathon sermon.'

'A superb, a colossal sermon!' said the notary.

'Magnificent, profound!' added the correspondent.

'To be able to orate like that, one needs the kind of lungs he has,' remarked Father Martin.

The Augustinian conceded nothing to his rival except a pair of lungs.

'And that facility of expression!' added Father Salví.

'Do you know,' interposed the Governor, cutting the conversation short, 'I do believe Mr. Ibarra has the best cook in the province.'

'Just what I was saying,' one of the employees chimed in, 'but his beautiful table companion is not doing honour to the meal. She has scarcely had a bite to eat.'

María Clara blushed.

'The gentleman is too kind,' she stammered shyly. 'But...'

'But her presence is honour enough,' the gallant Governor finished the sentence for her. Then, turning to Father Salvi, he continued in a loud voice:

'I see Your Reverence has been silent and full of his own thoughts the whole day.'

'The Governor sees a terrible lot of things,' Father Sibyla exclaimed significantly.

'It's a habit of mine,' mumbled the Franciscan. 'I would rather listen than talk.'

'Your Reverence is always out to win,' the lieutenant joked.

But Father Salvi did not take it as a joke. His eyes flashed when he replied:

'The Lieutenant knows very well that, if anyone is winning or losing these days, it is not myself.'

The commanding officer tried to disguise this hit with a forced laugh, and refused to recognise the allusion to the gambling tolerated in town during the fiesta.

'But, gentlemen,' the Governor intervened, 'I do not understand how we can be talking here of wins and losses. What will these kind and proper young ladies, who honour us with their company, think of us? For me a girl is like an Aeolian harp heard at midnight; one must listen to it with eager ear so that its ineffable harmonies may raise the soul to the celestial spheres of the infinite and ideal...'

'Your Excellency is a poet!' the notary chuckled, and they both emptied their glasses.

'I cannot be less,' said the Governor, wiping his lips. 'Opportunity, if it does not always make the thief, makes the poet. In my youth I used to write verses, and not bad ones either.'

'So Your Excellency forsook the Muses for the Law,' chided the correspondent.

'Well, what can you do? I have always dreamed of doing everything once. Yesterday I was picking flowers and singing songs; today I hold the scales of justice and serve humanity; tomorrow...'

'Tomorrow,' suggested Father Sibyla, 'you will throw the scales into the fire to warm the winter of your life, and take up a minister's portfolio in the cabinet.'

'Well, now, yes... no... to be a member of the cabinet is not exactly my dream. Any upstart can get that far. But a summer villa in the north of Spain, a town house in Madrid and a few estates in Andalucia for the winter... We shall pass the days remembering our beloved Philippines. Voltaire would not have said of us that we lived among these peoples only to enrich ourselves and to slander them.'

The Governor had quoted Voltaire in French, and the employees broke into laughter, believing he had made a joke; the friars followed suit because they did not realise that the Voltaire the Governor had quoted was the same Voltaire whom they had so often cursed and consigned to hell. But Father Sibyla did, and put on a serious face, assuming that the Governor had given expression either to heresy or to impiety.

The schoolchildren were eating in the other pavilion under the supervision of the schoolmaster. Filipino children in those days were shy rather than boisterous at table and in the presence of strangers, but these managed to make their share of noise. What to use to eat this or that led to corrections and arguments; some argued for a spoon, others for a fork, still others for a knife, and as they recognised no authority who could decide it for them, the discussion acquired the proportions of a theological disputation.

Their parents winked and nudged one another happily.

'There! That settles it,' a peasant woman was telling an old man as he mashed up betel-nut for his chew. 'Whether my husband likes it or not, my Andoy is going to be a priest. All right, so we haven't any money. But we can work. If necessary, we can beg. There are always people who will give money so that poor boys can be priests.

Brother Mateo, and you know he isn't given to telling lies, says that Pope Sixtus was just a herdsman of carabaos in Batangas. Well, look at my Andoy, doesn't he look like St. Vincent?'

And the good woman felt her mouth water as she watched her boy take a fork in both hands.

'God help us,' said the old man, chewing his cud. 'If Andoy gets to be Pope, we can all go to Rome, heh heh! I've still got a good pair of legs. And if I don't live that long, well, heh heh!'

'Don't worry, grandfather! Andoy won't forget you taught him to weave baskets.'

'You're right, Petra, I too think your son will make something of himself. An auxiliary bishop at least. I haven't seen anybody learn quicker. Well, when he's Pope or bishop, he'll remember me when he has a bit of fun making baskets for his cook. He'll say a Mass or two for my soul, heh heh!'

The old man, buoyed up by this hope, started working on a fresh mouthful of betel-nut.

'If God hears my prayers, and my wishes come true, I am going to tell Andoy: "Now, son, take away all our sins and send us straight to Heaven." Then we won't have to pray or fast or buy indulgences. Why, you can commit all the sins you want if you have a Pope for a son!'

'Tell you what, Petra,' said the old man in a fit of enthusiasm, 'send him along to my place tomorrow and I'll teach him how to weave a really good cigar-case.'

'Now, really, grandfather! What do you think? Do you think a Pope has to work with his hands? The parish priest, who is a mere priest, works only at Mass, and all he does is turn about. The Archbishop does not even have to turn about; he says Mass sitting down. So the Pope—well, the Pope must say Mass in bed, fanning himself. What did you think?'

'He won't lose anything, Petra, by knowing how to weave straw hats and wallets; then he can sell them, and not have to go begging, like the parish priest does here every year in the name of the Pope. It breaks my heart to see a saint so poor, and I always give him all my savings.'

Another peasant came up, saying:

'It's all settled, your godson is going to be a doctor. Nothing like being a doctor.'

'Doctor? Go on!' answered Petra. 'Nothing like being a priest!'

'Priest? Nonsense! A doctor makes a lot of money, and his patients treat him like a saint.'

'Please! All the priest has to do is to turn about three or four times, say *deminos pabiscum*, and he eats God and gets paid for it. All of us, even the women, tell him our secrets.'

'And the doctor? What do you think of the doctor? The doctor sees everything you women have; he can hold hands with young girls. I'd like to be a doctor, just for one week!'

'And the priest? Doesn't the priest get to see everything the doctor sees? Even more! You know the saying, Plump hen and woman fair are priestly fare.'

'So what? Do you think doctors eat dry sardines? Do you think they get salt on their fingers?'

'And do you think the priest gets his hands dirty like your doctors? He hasn't got big estates for nothing, and when he works, he works to music, and with the help of sacristans.'

'How about hearing Confessions? Don't tell me that isn't work.'

'Work is it? What you would give to hear everybody's secrets! We have to work ourselves into a sweat to find out what our neighbours are doing; all the priest has to do is to sit in the confessional and everybody tells him everything; he may doze off once in a while, but then he blesses us two or three times, and we are again children of God. What I would give to be a priest just one afternoon in Lent!'

'And what about preaching? Don't tell me that isn't work. Look how the big priest was sweating this morning!' objected the man, who felt he was getting the worst of the argument.

'Preaching? Preaching, work? Where are your brains? What I would give to be talking half the day from the pulpit, scolding and nagging at everyone, with nobody daring to talk back, and getting paid for it besides! What I would give to be a parish priest just one morning when all my debtors are hearing Mass! Look at Father Dámaso himself, how he puts on weight with all this scolding and beating up people.'

Father Dámaso, in fact, had put in an appearance, rolling along with a fat man's gait, half-smiling, but in such a malignant way that on seeing him Ibarra lost the thread of the speech he was making.

The friar was greeted merrily, although with a certain constraint, by all those present except Ibarra. They were already at dessert, and champagne foamed in the wine glasses.

Father Dámaso's smile grew nervous when he saw María Clara seated at Ibarra's right, but, taking a chair beside the Governor, said in the midst of a pregnant silence:

'Don't let me interrupt you, gentlemen.'

'We were proposing toasts,' said the Governor. 'Mr. Ibarra was speaking of those who had helped him in his philantrophic enterprise, and was speaking of the architect, when Your Reverence—'

'Well, I don't understand architecture,' Father Dámaso interrupted. 'But I laugh at architects and all the boobs who employ them. Look here, I drew up the plans for the town church myself, and it's perfectly made; that is what an English jeweller told me when he stayed a day at the parish house. All you need to draw up a plan is a pinch of brains!'

'However,' the Governor objected, seeing that Ibarra did not reply, 'when it comes to certain buildings, for example, this school house, we need the know-how . . .'

'Know-how, bow-wow!' scoffed Father Dámaso. 'Only a know nothing needs know-how! One has to be a greater barbarian than the natives, who build their own houses, not to know how to put up four walls and slap on a roof—that's all a school is!'

All looked at Ibarra but the latter, although he had turned pale, continued conversing with María Clara.

'But Your Reverence should consider

'Look here,' the Franciscan went on, cutting the Governor short, 'One of our lay brothers, the most stupid one we have at that, has built a hospital, good and cheap. He knew how to get work done, and he didn't pay more than eight coppers a day even to those who had to come from other towns. That chap knew how to treat the natives, not like many know-it-alls and second-class half-breeds who spoil them by paying three or four sovereigns.'

'Your Reverence says that they were only paid eight coppers?'

'Impossible!' The Governor was trying to change the trend of the conversation.

'Yes, sir, and that is an example for all who pride themselves on being good Spaniards. It's plain to see: ever since the Suez Canal was opened, we have been corrupted. Before, when we had to go round the Cape, we didn't get so many lost souls here, nor did so many go abroad to lose their souls.'

'But Father Dámaso!'

'You know what the native's like. Let him learn a few letters of the alphabet and he passes himself off as a doctor. All these chaps who go off to Europe without having learned to wipe their noses!'

'But listen, Your Reverence...,' interrupted the Governor, whom such aggressive sentiments made uneasy.

'They will all end up as they deserve,' the friar went on. 'The hand of God is in the business; you would have to be blind not to see it. Even in this life the fathers of such vipers get their punishment: they die in gaol, heh heh, and so to speak, don't have—'

But he was not allowed to finish. Ibarra, vivid with rage, had been following him with his eyes, and, on hearing this allusion to his father, leaped up and struck the friar on the head, knocking him back stunned.

Surprised and horrified, no one dared to intervene.

'Stay back!' the young man cried in a terrible voice, and reached for a sharp knife as he kept a foot on the neck of the friar, who was regaining consciousness. 'Stay back if you don't want to get hurt!'

Ibarra was beside himself. His body was trembling, and his eyes rolled threateningly. Father Dámaso pulled himself up with an effort, but Ibarra seized him by the neck and shook him, forcing him to his knees.

'Mr. Ibarra! Mr. Ibarra!' pleaded some.

But nobody, not even the commanding officer, dared to come near, seeing the flashing knife, and the strength and state of mind of the young man. All seemed paralysed.

'Stay where you are, all of you! You have kept your mouths shut in the past. Now it's my turn. I have avoided him; God has placed him before me. Let God be the judge.'

The young man was breathing heavily, but he held the Franciscan, who was vainly struggling to free himself, with an iron arm.

'My heart is calm, my hand is sure,' he said, and looking round: 'Is there anyone among you who did not love his father, anyone who now hates his memory, anyone born in shame and humiliation? Do you see that? Do you hear the silence? Priest of a God of peace, whose mouth is full of holiness and religion, and whose heart is filled with avarice, you cannot have known a father, or you would have remembered your own! Do you see? In all this crowd that you despise, there is none so low as you. You are condemned.'

The people who had gathered round him, thinking he was about to commit murder, moved forward.

'Stand back!' he shouted again with threatening voice. 'Are you afraid that I shall stain my hand with impure blood? Haven't I told you that my heart was calm? Leave us alone. Listen to me, priests and judges, who believe you are different from other men and have other rights! My father was an honest man; ask these people who bless his memory. My father was a good citizen; he sacrificed himself for me and for the good of the country. His house was open, his table laid, for the stranger and the exile who sought him in their misery. He was a good Christian, who always did good and never oppressed the destitute or harassed the afflicted. To this man he opened the doors of his house, seated him at his table, called him friend. How was he repaid? This man slandered him, persecuted him, mustered the forces of ignorance against him, and, under cover of a holy office, profaned his grave, dishonoured his memory, and persecuted him even in the very peace of death. And now, not content with all this, he persecutes his son! I have avoided him, fled from any contact with him. You heard him this morning desecrate the pulpit and mark me out to the fanaticism of the people. I held my peace. He came here to pick a quarrel with me. Again, to your surprise, I suffered in silence. But when he once again insults the memory that is most sacred to all sons . . . You who are here, priests and judges, have you ever seen your old father go sleepless for your sake, part from you for your own good, die in gaol of a broken heart, sighing for your embrace, vainly seeking consolation in his loneliness and sickness while you were abroad—and afterwards, have you heard his name dishonoured, have you found his grave empty when you sought to pray over it? No? You are silent, and therefore you condemn this man.'

He raised his arm, but a girl, swift as light, flew between them and with her soft hands stopped the avenging arm. It was María Clara. Ibarra stared at her with the eyes of a madman. Slowly the clenched fingers of his hands loosened, dropping the knife and releasing the Franciscan. Then, covering his face, he fled through the crowd.

36 • *Reactions*

NEWS of what had happened soon spread throughout the town. At first nobody wanted to believe it, but, forced to face the facts, they were all shocked into making the comments that could be expected of their character.

'Father Dámaso is dead,' some said. 'When they picked him up his whole face was covered with blood and he had stopped breathing.'

'May he rest in peace, but he had it coming to him,' a young man exclaimed. 'Look, there are really no words for what he did this morning in the parish house.'

'What did he do? Beat up his vicar again?'

'What was it? Come on, tell us.'

'Did you see a Spanish half-breed this morning leave the sacristy during the sermon?'

'Yes, yes, indeed we did. Father Dámaso noticed it too.'

'Well, after the sermon he had the fellow called and asked him why he had left the church. "I do not understand Tagalog," he answered. "Then why did you try to be funny and say it was Greek to you?" Father Dámaso shouted, dealing him a blow. The young man made some rejoinder and the two went for each other with their fists until they were pulled apart.'

'If it had happened to me!' a student muttered.

'I do not approve of the Franciscan's action,' said another, 'for religion should not be forced on anyone as a punishment or as a penance. But I am almost glad he did it because I know that young man; he is from San Pedro Makati and he speaks Tagalog well. Now, he wants to be taken for someone fresh from Russia and puffs himself up by pretending not to know the language of his parents.'

'Birds of a feather flock together.'

'Nevertheless we should protest at what Father Dámaso did,' cried another student. 'Silence would be consent, and what happened to that fellow can happen again to any one of us. We are back in the days of Nero!'

'You are wrong,' countered another. 'Nero was a great artist while Father Dámaso is a rotten preacher.'

The comments of the elderly were of a different sort. While they awaited the arrival of the Governor General in a little house on the outskirts of the town, the Mayor was saying: 'To say who was right and who was wrong is not easy; however, if Mr. Ibarra had been more prudent . . .'

'You probably meant if Father Dámaso had been half as prudent as Mr. Ibarra,' Don Filipo interrupted him. 'The trouble is that they changed places; the young man acted like an old one, and the old man like a youngster.'

'And you say that nobody lifted a finger or tried to separate them except the daughter of Capitan Tiago?' asked Capitan Martín. 'None of the friars or even the Mayor? Hm. Worse and worse. I shouldn't like to be in that young man's shoes. They were afraid of him, and they'll never be able to forgive him that. Worse and worse. Hm.'

'Do you really think so?' asked Capitan Basilio with real interest..

'I hope,' said Don Filipo exchanging a look with him, 'that the people will not abandon him. We should think of what his family has done for us and is still doing. And if the people are too afraid to say anything, his friends at least...'

'But, sirs,' interrupted the Mayor, 'what can we do? What can the people do?'

'You mean they are always right because we always start by admitting they are right,' Don Filipo answered impatiently. 'Let us start on equal terms for once, and then we can talk.'

The Mayor scratched his head and, his eyes on the ceiling, replied sourly: 'Ah, these hotbloods! You don't seem to know yet the kind of country we're living in; you don't know our own people. The friars are rich and united; we are divided and poor. All right, try to defend Mr. Ibarra; you'll soon find yourself alone in the lurch.'

'I know,' sighed Don Filipo bitterly. 'That is indeed what will happen as long as that is the way we think, as long as fear and prudence mean the same thing. We give more importance to a possible evil than to an essential good. We meet an emergency with panic, not self-confidence. Everyone thinks of himself alone, nobody thinks of others, that is why we are all helpless.'

'Well then, look out for others before looking our for yourself, and you'll find out soon enough that they have left you out on a limb. Have you never heard the saying, charity begins at home?'

'You would better to say that cowardice begins with selfishness and ends in shame,' countered the Vice Mayor, who had reached the end of his patience. 'I resign, effective immediately; I am sick and tired of making myself ridiculous and not doing anybody any good. Goodbye.'

The women had opinions of another kind.

'Oh, the young are always like that,' sighed a kindly-looking one. 'If his saintly mother were alive, what would she say to all this? Dear God, when I think that the same thing might happen to my boy, who has a temper of his own! Jesus, I almost envy the dear departed – I would die of sorrow!'

'Not I,' another lady replied. 'I would not be sad if it happened to my two sons.'

'What are you saying, Capitana María?' the first woman cried out, clasping her hands.

'It pleases me to hear sons defending the memory of their fathers, Capitana Tinay. What would you say if you were a widow, and one day should hear someone speak ill of your dead husband while your son Antonio lowered his head and kept his tongue?'

'I would deny him my blessing,' Sister Rufa exclaimed, joining the conversation. 'But...'

'Deny him my blessing? Oh no, I could never do that,' broke in the good-hearted Capitana Tinay. 'No mother should say that. But I don't know what I could possibly do. I just don't know. I think I would die. I would—oh no, dear God! But I would not want to see him ever again. But why do you think of such things, Capitana María?'

'Taking all that into account,' added Sister Rufa, 'we should not forget that it is a grave sin to lay hands upon the sacred person of a priest.'

'The memory of one's father is even more sacred,' Capitana María replied. 'No one, not the Pope himself, and even less Father Dámaso, can profane a memory so sacred.'

'That's true, too,' Capitana Tinay murmured, admiring the wisdom of both. 'How ever do you think up such fine arguments?'

'Ah, but what do you say to excommunication and damnation?' countered Sister Rufa. 'What do honours and reputation profit us in this life if we are damned in the next? Everything passes, and passes quickly, but excommunication—to do violence to a minister of Jesus Christ—only the Pope himself can forgive that!'

'God will forgive it who commands us to honour our father and out mother. God will not excommunicate him. I will say this to you. If this young man comes to my house, I shall receive him and speak with him. If I had a daughter, I should like him for a son-in-law. A good son will be a good husband and a good father, believe me, Sister Rufa.'

'Oh, what do you want me to say? You are both right, the parish priest is right, but God should be right too. I don't know. I am only a little silly.

'But I know what I am going to do; I shall tell my son to give up his studies. They say wise men die on the gallows. Holy Mother of God! And my son wanted to go to Europe!'

'What do you plan to do? 'Tell him to stay with me. Why try to learn more? Tomorrow or the day after we shall die, learned and ignorant alike. The point is to have a peaceful life.' And the good woman sighed and raised her eyes to Heaven.

'But I,' said Capitana Maria gravely, 'if I were as rich as you are, would let my sons go travelling. They are young, and one day they must be men. I have not long to live but we would see each other in the next life. Sons must aspire to be greater than their fathers, but at our apron-strings we only teach them to be children.'

'You think of such odd things,' Capitana Tinay exclaimed, wringing her hands in dismay. 'One would think you had not borne your twins in pain.'

'Just because I bore them in pain, and brought them up and sent them to school, poor as we were, I should not like them, after all my toil and trouble, to be no more than half men.'

'It seems to me,' Sister Rufa said in rather a severe tone, 'that you do not love your children in the manner that God commands.'

'Forgive me; every mother loves her children after her own fashion; some love them because they love themselves; others, because they want to keep their children for themselves; and some love their children for their own sake. I was taught by my husband to be one of the last.'

'Your thoughts, Capitana María,' said Rufa sententiously, 'are not at all pious. I suggest you should become a sister of the Holy Rosary, of St. Francis, St. Rita, or St. Clare.'

'Sister Rufa,' Capitana María answered with a smile, ' when I have become a worthy sister of men, I shall try to be a sister of the saints.'

To end this summary of comments, and give an inkling of the reactions of the simple peasants to the events of the day, it would perhaps be useful to overhear their conversation under the awning in the town square. One of them was the man who had dreamed of physicians.

'What bothers me most,' he was saying, 'is that now they'll never finish the school.'

'What? Why?' those around him asked him eagerly.

My son won't be a doctor after all! He's just going to drive a car, after all. It's all over. No more school.'

'Who said no more school? Asked a rough and hardy villager with broad jaws and a narrow skull.

'I say so. The white friars have called Don Crisostomo *sabarsiv*. That means no more school.'

All exchanged glances. The name was new to them.

'Is that bad?' the rough villager finally got up enough courage to ask.

'The worst thing one Christian could say to another.'

'Worse than *dampul* and *bambraun?*'

'Only that! They've called me that more times than I can think of, and it didn't even give me a stomach-ache.'

'Come on, it can't be worse than *nigger*, the way the lieutenant says it.'

The peasant who had dreamed of turning his son into a physician grew even more dejected. The other scratched his head and plunged into deep thought.

'Then it must be as bad as *sanamabits* the way the lieutenant's old woman says it. Anything worse than that is spitting on the Host.'

'Well,' the fellow answered gravely, 'it's worse than spitting on the Host on Good Friday. You remember that word *saspek*. Calling anybody that was enough to bring on the Villa-Abrille Combat Team to take him to exile or gaol. Well, *sabarsiv* is much worse. According to the telegraph operator and the municipal clerk, when a Christian, a priest, or a Spaniard calls another Christian like us *sabarsiv* it is like giving us the last blessing and a "Rest in Peace". If you are ever called *sabarsiv* you might just as well go to Confession right away and pay off your debts and wait for them to put the noose around your neck. You know the telegraph operator and the municipal clerk know what they are talking about. One can talk with wires, and the other speaks

Spanish and never has anything in his hand except a pen.'

All were terror-stricken.

'I'll put on shoes and drink only that horse-piss they call beer the rest of my life if I ever let anyone call me *sabarsiv*,' a villager swore, clenching his fists. 'If I were as rich as Don Crisostomo, and knew Spanish like him and how to eat fast with knife and spoon, I would take on even five priests.'

On the other hand, a peasant, leaving the group, muttered to himself: 'The next time I see a policeman stealing chickens, I'm going to call him *sabarsiv*.'

37 • *First Effects*

CONFUSION reigned in the house of Capitan Tiago. María Clara did nothing but weep, refusing to listen to the words of solace offered by her aunt and her foster-sister Andeng. Her father had forbidden her to speak to Ibarra until the priests had lifted the excommunication he had automatically incurred by his attack on one in Holy Orders.

Meantime Capitan Tiago, who was busy enough as it was preparing his house for a worthy reception of the Governor General, had been summoned to the parish house.

'Don't cry, my child,' said Aunt Isabel, polishing the gleaming mirrorplates with chamois skin, 'the excommunication will be lifted. We shall write the Holy Father . . . give a big donation. Father Dámaso only fainted . . . he's not dead.'

'Don't cry,' whispered Andeng, I'll see to it that you can speak to him. What is Confession for if not for sinning? Everything is forgiven by telling it to the priest.'

Capitan Tiago returned at last. They sought the answers to many questions in his face, but his face only showed discouragement. The poor man was in a sweat; he drew his hand across his brow and found it impossible to say a word.

'What is it, Santiago?' Aunt Isabel asked anxiously.

For answer he sighed, and wiped away a tear.

'For God's sake, say something. What's the matter?'

'Just what I feared,' he exclaimed at last, midway to tears. 'Father Dámaso orders me to break off the engagement; otherwise I am doomed in this life and the next! Everybody tells me the same thing, even Father Sibyla. I am to close the doors of my house to Ibarra. And I owe him more than fifty thousand pesos which I shall have to pay back immediately if I break with him! I told them that but they did not want to listen to me. Which would you rather lose, they asked me, fifty thousand pesos or your life and soul? Ah, St. Anthony, if I had only known, if I had only known! Don't cry, my child,' Capitan Tiago added, turning to the sobbing María Clara. 'You're not like your mother; she never cried. She cried only when she was in the family way. Father Dámaso has told me that a relative of his has just come from Spain, and he will be your betrothed.'

María Clara put her hands over her ears.

'But, Santiago, are you mad?' screamed Aunt Isabel. 'To talk of another engagement at this time! Do you think your daughter changes fiancés like dresses?'

'That's what I thought too, Isabel. Don Crisostomo is rich in his own right, while these Spaniards only get married for money. But what do you want me to do? They have threatened to excommunicate me too. They say I am in great danger, not only to my soul but also to my body. To my body, do you hear, my body!'

'But all you do is torment your daughter. Isn't the Archbishop a friend of yours? Why don't you write to him?'

'The Archbishop is a friar himself. The Archbishop only does what the friars tell him. But don't cry, María, the Governor General is coming, and he will want to see you, and your eyes will be all red. Oh, and I thought I would spend such a happy afternoon! If it weren't for this misfortune I would spend such a happy afternoon! If it weren't for this misfortune I would be the happiest of men and all would envy me. Calm yourself, my child, I am more unfortunate than you and I am not crying. You can find another fiancé, a better one, but I, I am losing fifty thousand pesos! Oh Virgin of Antipolo, if at least I could be lucky tonight.'

The sound of salvoes, carriages and galloping horses, and the strains of the Royal March now announced the arrival of His Excellency the Governor General of the Philippine Islands.

María Clara ran off to shut herself up in her bedroom: poor girl, coarse insensitive hands were playing with her heart! While the house was filling up with people, and heavy footsteps, loud commands, and the ring of sabres and spurs echoed everywhere, the distressed girl lay slumped, half-kneeling, before a picture of the Virgin that showed her in an attitude of heart-broken loneliness, as if surprised on the way back from the sepulchre of her Son.

But María Clara was thinking not of that Mother's sorrow but her own. Her head drooping, her hands flat against the floor, she looked like a lilystem broken in a storm. How was a future dreamt of lovingly for years, the fond hopes formed in childhood and nourished through adolescence until they were become part of her self, to be now erased from her mind and heart at a single command! As well stop the one from beating and the other from all thought.

Yet María Clara was as good and pious a Christian as she was a loving daughter. It was not only excommunication that frightened her, the threats of the friars which imperiled her father's peace and safety also seemed to require the sacrifice of her love, whose full strength, how little suspected till then, she was now feeling. It had been a quiet stream running along banks of fragrant flowers on a bed of silken sand, its surface so little ruffled by the wind that the passing eye might have believed the waters to be still. Now suddenly, the channel had narrowed, harsh rocks had opposed the passage, ancient logs had become entangled in a dike, and the brook turned river had roared and risen, boiling with waves and angry foam, and, hurling itself against the barriers, seemed about to plunge into an abyss.

She wanted to pray, but who prays in the hour of despair? Prayers are said in hope; otherwise the invocation to God becomes a reproach. So it was that in her heart she cried out and complained that this one man had been singled out to be cut off from the love of others, and asked why he was not denied sun and air and the sight of the skies, when one could live without these, but not without love. She wondered if these recriminations, unheard by men, would reach the Throne of Heaven, or be heard by the Mother of the unfortunate. The grief-stricken girl had never known a human mother, and now she confided these sorrows born of human loves to that purest of hearts that had only known the love felt by a daughter and a mother; in her anguish she had recourse to that goddess-like epitome of Woman, the most lovely idealisation of the most ideal of creatures, that poetical creation of Christianity who combines in herself the fairest conditions of women, virginity and motherhood, without their faults; she who is called Mary.

She was moaning for her mother when her aunt came in to distract her from her wretchedness. It appeared that some of her friends had arrived; the Governor General himself wished to speak with her.

'Please tell them I am not at all well,' the panic-stricken girl pleaded. 'They'll make me play the piano and sing.'

'Your father promised you would. You are not going to embarrass him, are you?'

María Clara got up. She looked at her aunt, wrung her hands, and whispered: 'Oh, if only I really had...'

But she did not finish her sentence, and began instead to fix herself up.

38 • *His Excellency*

'I WANT to see that young man,' His Excellency was telling an aide. 'He interests me greatly.'

'They are looking for him now, General. Meantime there is another young man here, from Manila, who insists that he be allowed to see you. He has been told that Your Excellency just has no time for him, that you have not come to hear petitions, but he replies that Your Excellency always has time to do justice.'

His Excellency turned to the Provincial Governor with a quizzical look. 'If I am not mistaken,' the latter answered with a slight bow, 'it is the young man who had a difference of opinion this morning with Father Dámaso on account of the sermon.'

'What, again? Does this friar propose to set this province by the ears, or does he think that he is in control here? Tell that young man to come in.' His Excellency was striding irritably up and down the hall.

Outside in the antechamber a number of Spaniards were to be found, together with the military and civil authorities of San Diego and neighbouring towns, conversing or arguing in little groups. All the friars were also present except for Father Dámaso. They desired to pay their respects to His Excellency.

'His Excellency the Governor General begs Your Reverences to wait a while,' said the aide. Then he gestured the young man to enter.

The Manilan, who had confused Tagalog with Greek, went in pale and shaky.

The rest were dumbfounded; His Excellency must be exasperated indeed when he made friars wait.

'I have nothing to say to him, anyway,' said Father Sibyla. 'I am wasting my time.'

'I say so too,' an Augustinian chimed in. 'Shall we go?'

'Would it not be better to find out how his mind is working?' asked Father Salví. 'We would avoid making a scene, and then, too, we could remind him of his duties towards the Church...'

At this point the aide emerged, leading the young man who had not understood Greek and who was now beaming with satisfaction.

'Your Reverences may enter now, if you wish.'

Father Sibyla went in first, followed by Father Salví, Father Manuel Martín, and the other friars. All greeted the Governor General deferentially, except for Father Sibyla, who invested his bow with a certain air of superiority; Father Salví, on the contrary, bent from the waist.

'Which of your Reverences is Father Dámaso?' His Excellency demanded abruptly, without asking them to take a seat, inquiring about their health, or addressing to them the little flatteries to which these high personages were accustomed.

'Father Dámaso, sir, is not with us,' replied Father Sibyla almost as curtly.

'Your Excellency's servant lies ill in bed,' Father Salví added humbly. 'After having the pleasure of greeting Your Excellency and inquiring about your health, as befits all good subjects of the King and all persons of breeding, we had come also, in the name of Your Excellency's respectful servant, who has the misfortune...' 'Ah,' interrupted the Governor General, one foot playing with a chair, ' if all the servants of my Excellency were like His Reverence Father Dámaso, I would prefer to serve my own Excellency.'

Their reverences, who were already at a standstill physically, were now sharply brought up psychologically as well by this interruption.

'Pray be seated, Your Reverences,' the Governor General added after a brief pause and in a more pleasant tone.

At this point Capitan Tiago, who was in his frock-coat and walking on tiptoe, came in, leading María Clara by the hand. She entered the room shyly and hesitantly, but nevertheless made a gracious and courtly curtsy.

'Is the young lady your daughter?' the Governor General asked, taken unawares.

'And yours, Your Excellency,' Capitan Tiago replied, using the customary formula of politeness in all seriousness.

The Provincial Governor and the General's aides stared, but His Excellency, without losing his composure, stretched out his hand to the girl and told her affably:

'Happy the fathers who have daughters like you. They have spoken to me about you in terms of respect and admiration. I wanted to see you to thank you for what you did today. I am informed of everything, and when I write to His Majesty's Government I shall not forget that you acted today without regard to your own safety. Meantime, permit me, in the name of His Majesty the King, whom I represent here, and who cherishes the peace and tranquillity of his faithful subjects, as well as on my own behalf, on behalf of a father who also has daughters of your age, to give you my most sincere thanks and to nominate you for a reward!'

'Sir...' María Clara began in a trembling voice.

His Excellency guessed what she wanted to say and continued:

'It is all very well for you to be satisfied with the consciousness of having done a good deed and with the esteem of your fellow citizens; in truth that is the best reward and we should not ask for more. But do not deprive me of an excellent opportunity to show that Justice knows how to reward as well as to punish, and is not always blind.'

'Don Juan Crisóstomo Ibarra awaits Your Excellency's pleasure,' an aide announced in a loud voice.

María Clara started.

'Ah,' exclaimed the Governor General. 'Now then, permit me to express the desire to see you again before leaving this town. I still have some very important things to tell you. Governor, Your Honour will accompany me while I inspect the town, which I want to do on foot, after a private conference with Mr. Ibarra.'

'Your Excellency will allow us,' said Father Salví humbly, ' to call your attention to the fact that Mr. Ibarra is under excommunication.'

His Excellency interrupted him.

'I am very glad that I have to deplore nothing more than Father Dámaso's state of health. I sincerely wish him a complete recovery, because at his age a trip to Spain for reasons of health could not be very agreeable. But that depends on him. Meantime, God keep Your Reverences in good health.'

All now withdrew.

'Of course it depends on him, and how!' muttered Father Salví as he left.

'We'll see who makes that trip to Spain first," added another Franciscan.

'I'm leaving right now,' said father Sibyla resentfully.

'And we're going back to our province,' said the Augustinians.

None of the friars could stomach the cold reception that His Excellency had given them—all because of a Franciscan.

In the anteroom they met Ibarra. He had been their host only a few hours before, but now they did not exchange greetings, only looks that were pregnant with meaning.

The Provincial Governor, on the other hand, once the friars had gone, greeted Ibarra and stretched out his hand in a gesture of intimacy. But the arrival of an aide in search of the young man did not allow them to engage in conversation.

At the door of the hall he met María Clara. The looks they exchanged were also significant, but rather different from those the friars had given.

Ibarra was dressed in strict mourning. Although the visit of the friars did not seem a good omen for him, he presented himself serenely and gave a deep bow.

The Governor General took several steps toward him.

'I take the greatest pleasure in shaking your hand, Mr. Ibarra. Allow me to receive you in this intimate fashion.'

His Excellency, in fact, gazed thoughtfully at the young man with marked pleasure.

'Sir, you are too kind...'

'Your surprise offends me. It means that you did not expect a good reception from me. This is to doubt my fairness.'

'A friendly reception for such an insignificant subject of His Majesty as myself is not fairness, sir, but a favour.'

'Good, good,' said His Excellency, seating himself and gesturing Ibarra to another chair. 'Let me enjoy a moment of relaxation. I am very satisfied with your conduct, and I have proposed to His Majesty's Government that you be given a decoration for the philanthropic plan of constructing a schoolhouse here. If you had asked me to, I would have been happy to attend the ceremony and perhaps you would have avoided an embarrassing incident.'

'It seemed to me that the project was not important enough,' answered the young man, ' to make it worth distracting Your Excellency's attention from your numerous tasks. Besides, it was my duty to address myself first to the chief authority in my province.'

His Excellency nodded with satisfaction, and adopting more and more a tone of familiarity continued: 'With regard to the trouble you have had with Father Damaso, have neither fear nor resentment. As long as I govern these islands, not a hair on your head will be touched, and, as far as the excommunication is concerned, I shall speak to the Archbishop about it. We must, after all, adjust ourselves to our situation; we cannot laugh at these things in public here as we would do in Spain or in civilised Europe. However, be more prudent in the future. You have pitted yourself against the religious Orders which, because of their importance and their wealth, must be respected. But I shall protect you because I like good sons; I want the memory of our parents respected. I also have loved mine, and, by God, I do not know what I would have done in your place.'

Then, changing the subject quickly, he asked:

'They tell me you have just arrived from Europe. Were you in Madrid?'

'Yes, sir, several months.'

'Did you come across my family?'

'Your Excellency had just left for this post when I had the honour of making their acquaintance.'

'Then how is it that you came back without a letter of recommendation to me?'

'Sir,' answered Ibarra with a slight bow, 'I did not return directly from Spain. Besides, having been told of Your Excellency's character, I thought that a letter of recommendation would not only be useless but even offensive. All of us Filipinos are commended to your care.'

The old soldier smiled, and he replied slowly, as if measuring and weighing his words:

'It flatters me that you think that, and that is how it should be! However, young man, you should know the burdens that rest on our shoulders in the Philippines. Here, we old soldiers must do everything and be everything: King, Ministers of State, of War, of the Interior, of Economic Development, of Justice and all that. What is worse, we must consult the home government on every point, and that distant government, according to the circumstances, approves or disapproves our proposals, sometimes without knowing anything about them. And we Spaniards say: jack of all trades, master of none! Furthermore we come, usually knowing little about the country, and leave it just when we are getting to know it. I can be frank with you; it would be useless to pretend that things are otherwise. So, if in Spain itself, where every branch of the Government has its own Minister, born and bred in the country, where there is a Press and public opinion, where a forthright opposition opens the eyes of the Administration and enlightens it, everything is still run imperfectly and defectively, it is a miracle that everything is not topsy-turvy here, where those advantages are lacking and where a more powerful opposition exists and plots under cover. We in the Government do not lack good intentions, but we are compelled to make use of the eyes and arms of others, whom we usually do not know, and who perhaps, instead of serving the interests of the country, only serve their own. That is not our fault but that of circumstances. The friars help us not a little out of our difficulties, but they are no longer enough. You interest me, and I would not want the imperfections of the present governmental system to do you any harm. But I cannot stand guard over everybody, and not everybody can appeal to me. Can I be of use to you in anything? Do you have anything to ask?'

Ibarra reflected.

'Sir,' he answered, 'my greatest desire is the happiness of my country, a happiness which I would wish to be due to the Motherland and to the efforts of my fellow citizens, one united to the others with eternal ties of common ideals and common interests. What I ask can only be given by the Government after many years of continuous work and the correct measures of reform.'

His Excellency looked him in the eyes for a few seconds, and Ibarra returned the look unaffectedly.

'You are the first in this country who has talked to me like a man,' the Governor General exclaimed, shaking Ibarra's hand.

'Your Excellency has only met the opportunists who infest the capital. You have not visited the huts of our villages, on which so many calumnies have been poured. There Your Excellency would meet true men, if to be a man it is enough to have a generous heart and simple habits.'

The Governor General rose to his feet and paced up and down the hall.

'Mr. Ibarra,' he said, stopping suddenly.

The young man stood up.

'I'm leaving this country, perhaps within a month. Your breeding and your way of thinking are not for this country. Sell what you have, pack up your things, and come with me to Europe. The climate will be healthier for you.'

'I will remember Your Excellency's kindness as long as I live,' answered Ibarra who was rather touched. 'But I must live in this country where my parents lived...'

'Where they died, would be more accurate. Believe me, perhaps I know your country better than you do. Ah, now I remember,' he cried, changing his tone, ' you are marrying that adorably young lady, and I am keeping you here. Off with you now, go to her, and for your greater ease send her father to me,' he added with a smile. 'But don't forget that I want you to accompany me when I inspect the town.'

Ibarra bowed and left.

His Excellency summoned his aide.

'I am happy,' he said, patting him on the shoulder. 'Today I have seen for the first time how one can be a good Spaniard and still be a good Filipino who loves his country. Today I have at last shown Their Reverences that we are not all their puppets. That young man has given me the opportunity; and soon I shall have settled all my accounts with the friars. Pity that that young man, some day or other... But call the Provincial Governor.'

The latter immediately presented himself.

'Mr. Governor,' His Excellency said, 'to avoid the repetition of incidents like the one witnessed by Your Honour this noon, incidents which I deplore because they undermine the prestige of the Government and of all Spaniards, I allow myself to recommend Mr. Ibarra to you strongly, not only so that you may furnish to him the means to carry out his patriotic plans, but also so that hereafter you may prevent persons of whatever category from interfering with him under any pretext.'

The Provincial Governor understood the reprimand and bowed to hide his discomposure.

'Your Honour will be good enough to say as much to the commanding officer of the local garrison, and to investigate whether or not this gentleman has notions peculiar to himself which are not in the Regulations. I have heard more than one complaint about this.'

Capitan Tiago was next, erect and well-ironed.

'Don Santiago,' His Excellency told him affectionately, ' not so long ago I was congratulating you on having a daughter like Miss de los Santos. Now I congratulate you on your future son-in-law. The most virtuous of daughters surely deserves to have the best citizen in the Philippines for her husband. May I know when the wedding will take place?'

'Sir,' stammered Capitan Tiago, wiping the sweat from his brow.

'Come now, I see that there is nothing definite. If you lack sponsors, I shall have the greatest pleasure in being one of them.' Turning to the Provincial Governor he added: 'I want to take away the bad taste left in my mouth by the kind of weddings at which I have been sponsor so far!'

'Yes, sir,' answered Capitan Tiago with a pitiful smile.

Ibarra went looking for María Clara almost at a run; he had so many things to say to her, and so many stories to tell. He heard merry voices in one of the rooms and knocked lightly on the door.

'Who is it?' asked María Clara.

'It's me.'

The voices fell silent but the door remained shut.

'It's me; can I come in?' asked Ibarra, whose heart was beating furiously.

The silence continued. After a few seconds he heard light footsteps approach the door, and the lilting voice of Sinang whispered through the keyhole: 'Crisostomo, we are going to the stage-show tonight. Whatever you want to tell María Clara, put it in a letter.'

The footsteps went away, as swiftly as they had come.

Ibarra slowly walked away from the closed door, wondering what it all could mean.

39 • *The Procession*

WHEN night fell and the festive lanterns at the windows had all been lighted, there was a fourth religious procession which set out amid the pealing of church bells and the usual fireworks.

The Governor General, who had been inspecting the town on foot, accompanied by his two aides, Capitan Tiago, the Provincial Governor, the commanding officer, and Ibarra, preceded by Constabulary soldiers and municipal policemen who opened and cleared a way for them, was invited to watch the procession from the house of the Mayor, who had put up a small stage in front of it from which an ode would be recited in praise of the patron saint.

Ibarra would have gladly forgone hearing this poetical composition and would have preferred to watch the procession from the house of Capitan Tiago, where María Clara had remained with her friends, but His Excellency was bent on hearing the ode and Ibarra had no other recourse but to console himself with the thought of seeing her at the stage-show.

Three gloved acolytes bearing silver candle-sticks opened the procession. They were followed by the schoolchildren escorted by their teacher; then came boys with paper lanterns of various shapes and colours dangling from bamboo poles and decorated according to the fancies of the barrio youngsters, who had paid for these lights out of their own pockets. They had performed this duty, imposed on them by their barrio chiefs, with pleasure; each of them had designed and made his own lantern decorated with tassels and pennants in accordance with his individual fancy and the state of his finances, and lighted with a candle-stub if he had a friend or relative who worked for the parish priest, or with the little red candle that the Chinese use at their altars.

In between the two parallel files of the procession Constabulary soldiers and policemen went up and down, keeping the lines even and moving with the judicious and well-calculated use of rods, endeavouring thus to contribute to the glory and magnificence of the procession for the edification of souls and the greater splendour of the religious ritual. While some soldiers were distributing these sanctifying blows freely, others, to console the recipients, were simultaneously passing out candles large and small, equally free of charge.

Mr. Governor,' Ibarra asked in a whisper, 'are these blows being given in punishment for sin or only for pleasure?'

'You're quite right, Mr. Ibarra, put in the Governor General, who had overheard the question. 'This exhibition of barbarity scandalises all foreigners.

We would do well to prohibit it.'

For no apparent reason the first image to be carried in the procession was that of St. John the Baptist. One look at him and it was clear that Our Lord's cousin did not enjoy much of a reputation among the people; true he had been given the feet and legs of a maiden and the face of a hermit, but he was being carried on an old wooden palanquin, and concealed rather than illumined by a handful of youngsters, who had not bothered to light their lanterns and were instead pummeling one another under cover.

'Wretch,' Tasio the scholar mused, as he watched the procession from the side of the street. 'It avails you nothing that you were the bearer of good tidings or that Jesus humbled Himself before you; nothing, your deep faith and self-denial, or your dying for the truth and your beliefs; all these count for nothing among men when one stands on his own merits. It profits a man more to preach badly in the churches than to be the eloquent voice crying in the wilderness — the Philippines should teach you that. If you had eaten turkey instead of locusts, worn silk instead of the skins of wild animals, if you had joined a religious Order...'

But the old man interrupted his harangue; St. Francis was coming along.

'Just what I was saying,' he continued with an ironic smile. 'This chap comes riding on a float with wheels, and, God bless us, what a float! So many candles, such precious crystal globes! You were never so well lighted, Giovanni Bernardone that was, before you became Francis! And such music! Your sons made other music after your death. Venerable and humble Founder of their Order, if you were to come back to earth now, you would see only degenerate counterparts of your excommunicated vicar, Elias of Cortona, and would perhaps share the fate of Caesarious of Speyer, who was murdered in his prison cell by a brother in the Order for daring to call for reforms!'

After the brass band came a standard with an effigy of the same saint, but sprouting seven wings, born aloft by Tertiaries of the Order clad in their denim habits and praying aloud in mournful voices.

Next, again for no apparent reason, followed a very beautiful image of St. Mary Magdalen with flowing hair, an embroidered handkerchief of the finest pineapple cloth held between her ring-covered fingers, and a silken gown decorated with gold insets. She was surrounded by lights and incense, and the glass tears on her cheeks reflected the colours of the Bengal lights that gave the procession an air of fantasy, so that the saint wept tears that were sometimes green, sometimes red, or yet again blue. These Bengal lights were not burned at the houses along the route until the arrival of St. Francis; St. John the Baptist did not enjoy these honours and passed by hurriedly, ashamed perhaps to be the only one dressed in skins among so many gentry covered with gold and precious stones.

'There comes our saint!' the daughter of the Mayor, who had the image of the Magdalen in his care, pointed out to her guests. 'I have lent her my rings that I may go to Heaven.'

The participants in the procession were grouping about the stage in front of the house for the ode of praise; the saints were doing the same; they or their bearers wanted to hear verses. Those who were carrying St. John, tired of waiting, squatted on their heels and left St. John, by common agreement, on the ground.

'The soldiers may not like it,' one of them protested.

'Nonsense, in the sacristy they leave this chap in a corner with the cobwebs.'

So St. John, left standing on the ground, came to be one of the common people.

The women had started to appear in the procession after the image of the Magdalen, but, unlike the men, the oldest, not the youngest, came first, with the unmarried girls closing the procession in front of the float that carried the image of the Virgin; this in turn was followed by the parish priest under his canopy.

This arrangement had been made originally by father Dámaso who used to say: 'The Virgin likes young women, not old ones.' This put sour faces on the pious old spinsters, who did not thereby change the Virgin's tastes.

St. Diego came in the Magdalen's wake, although he did not seem too pleased about it, for he had an expression of self-reproach every whit as pronounced as that he had had in the morning procession when he had followed St. Francis. His float was being pulled by six female Tertiaries, who were no doubt fulfilling some unknown vow made in illness; whatever it was, they were pulling, and pulling hard. St. Diego too finally came to rest in front of the platform and there awaited the verses to be recited in his honour.

But before that the float carrying the image of the Virgin had to arrive. It was preceded by a group of people that by their costumes could only be described as ghostly, which scared the children and set up a weeping and wailing among the more imprudent babes in arms; however, in the midst of that dark massing of habits, cowls, cordons, and hoods, and of the monotonous nasal praying, there stood out, like white lilies, like fresh *sampagas* among old rags, twelve little girls dressed in white, their curled hair crowned with flowers, their eyes as sparkling as their necklaces: fairies kidnapped by ogres. Clutching two wide blue ribbons leading to the Virgin's float, they recalled the doves that pull the magic chariot of Spring.

Now, then, when all the images were all ears, pressed one against the other to listen to the verses, when all eyes were on the half-open curtain of the stage, a little boy, winged, in riding boots, chest band, rich belt, and plumed hat appeared, to a well-merited exclamation of admiration from all lips.

'It's the Governor!' a voice cried out, but the prodigy did not seem to mind the comparison and in fact began to recite a poem in the exact manner of the Governor.

There would be no point in transcribing what the Mayor's poor puppet said in Latin, Tagalog, and Spanish, all in verse; Father Dámaso's sermon of the morning should provide enough of marvels and the Franciscan might not relish a competitor.

The procession went on its way, for St. John a way of sorrow.

When the image of the Virgin was passing in front of the house of Capitan Tiago, a lovely song greeted her in the words of the Archangel. It was sung by a voice that was tender, melodious, pleading, that put tears in Gounod's *Ave María*; and the piano that accompanied the song seemed to pray with the singer. The brass bands in the procession fell silent; the loud prayers came to a stop; Father Salvi himself was given pause. The voice trembled and it moistened the eyes of those who listened; it gave more than a greeting, it spoke a plea and a lamentation.

Ibarra heard the voice from the window by which he stood, and its fear and melancholy entered his heart. He felt the sorrow that was being poured out into the song, and was afraid to ask himself its cause.

The Governor General found him sombre and thoughtful.

'Come in with me to dinner,' he told Ibarra, and we can talk there about those boys who can't be found.'

Ibarra looked at His Excellency without seeing him, and followed him mechanically, saying to himself: 'Am I to blame?'

40 • *Doña Consolación*

WHY were the windows shuttered in the commanding officer's house? Where, when the procession was passing by, were the masculine face and the flannel blouse of the Medusa, the Muse, of the Constabulary? Had Doña Consolación realised how disagreeable was the sight of her temples with their thick veins that seemed to carry not blood but vinegar and bile, the big cigar that was a fit adornment of her purple lips, and her look of rancorous envy, and yielding to a generous impulse, had not wished to spoil the merriment of the crowds with her sinister aspect?

Alas, for her all generous impulses had died with the Golden Age!

The house looked sad because the town was glad, as Sinang had pointed out. It displayed neither lanterns nor hangings. But for the sentry pacing before its door it might have been uninhabited.

A weak flame lighted its untidy main room, showing up the grime and cobwebs on the shell-panes of the windows. The lady of the house, in whom laziness had become a habit, dozed in a great arm chair. She was dressed as always, that is to say, badly, even weirdly. The most she had done to her hair was to tie a scarf around her head which did not quite hold a number of short and sparse handfuls of tangled hair. She wore a blue flannel blouse over another one which must have once been white, and a faded skirt which clung to her thin thighs, now crossed one over the other and jiggling restlessly. From her mouth she expelled clouds of smoke toward that empty space on which her eyes were fixed when they were open. If a typical Spanish correspondent of that time had seen her, he would have taken her for the cacique of the town or its magician and would have embroidered his report with commentaries in his customary pidgin language.

That morning Doña Consolación had not gone to Mass, not because she had not wanted to; on the contrary, she had been eager to show herself off to the crowd and hear the sermon; but because her husband had not allowed her, and had supplemented the order as usual with two or three insults, oaths, and threatened kicks. The lieutenant realised that his woman's clothes were a joke, that she had the air of a camp follower, and that it would not be at all convenient to let her be seen by important persons from the provincial capital or by strangers. But she did not look at it that way. She was convinced she was beautiful and attractive, that she had the carriage of a queen, and that she was better and more elegantly dressed than María Clara herself, who after all wore an overskirt while she for her part did not need one. The lieutenant had to tell her: 'Shut up or I'll kick you all the way back to your goddam home town.'

Doña Consolación was not prepared to go home on the tip of her husband's boots, but she planned on getting her own back.

The lady's saturnine face, even when it was made up, was never one to inspire confidence, but that morning it was particularly disquieting especially when she was seen roaming the house from one end to the other, wordless, and apparently brooding on some terrible and evil thing. Her look had the gleam in a serpent's eye when it has been caught and is about to be crushed underfoot: it was cold, bright, piercing, and had something about it that was slimy, loathsome, cruel.

The smallest mistake, an unusual noise, no matter how insignificant, drew from her a coarse and foul insult that turned ones' stomach; but nobody dared answer back; an explanation would have compounded the crime.

So the day wore on. Unable to vent her temper on anyone—her husband was eating out—she soaked herself in her own spleen; one might have thought that the cells of her body were being charged with electricity and that they were threatening to explode into some unspeakable outrage. Everything round her bowed like rice-stalks at the first whiff of a typhoon; she found no point of resistance on which to discharge her bad temper; soldiers and servants slunk by her.

She had the windows of her house closed so she would not hear the merriment of the fiesta outside, and commanded the sentry not to let anybody in. Wrapping up her head in a scarf, as if to prevent it from bursting, she called for lights although the sun was shining.

Sisa had been arrested for disturbing public order during the fiesta and had been taken to the barracks. In the absence of the commanding officer the wretched woman had spent the night under arrest, seated on a bench and staring vacantly before her. The lieutenant had found her the next day. Fearing for her safety at such a time of confusion and wishing to spare the town a disagreeable sight, he ordered his soldiers to keep her in custody, but to treat her kindly and give her something to eat. So the madwoman had spent two days.

That night, either because she had heard María Clara's moving song from the house of Capitan Tiago nearby, or because other strains of music made her recall the songs that she herself had known, she began, whatever the reason, to sing the *kundiman* of her youth in a sweet and melancholy voice. The soldiers listened to her in silence. Those melodies awakened old memories, memories of a time of innocence.

In her bedroom Doña Consolación heard her too, and asked who was singing. 'Send her up at once,' she ordered after a few moments' thought. Something like a smile played on her withered lips.

Sisa was taken up. She showed herself without embarrassment, anxiety, or fear; she did not seem to feel herself in the presence of a social superior. This hurt the pride of the lieutenant's wife, who wanted to inspire obsequiousness and even panic in those who saw her.

Doña Consolación cleared her throat, signalled the soldiers to go, and, taking her husband's whip, told the madwoman viciously:

'Come on, *mag-singing* ka!'

Sisa did not understand even garbled Spanish, and her incomprehension mollified Doña Consolación. Indeed, one of this lady's lovable qualities was to try to unlearn her Tagalog, or at least to pretend she did not understand it, speaking it as badly as possible, thus giving herself the air of a true 'Yorofean', as she put it. It was just as well; if her Tagalog was deliberately tortured, her Spanish was no better, either grammatically or in pronunciation, for all that her husband, with the aid of his boots and a handy chair or two, had done his best to teach her.

One of the word she had had the most trouble with, even more trouble than hieroglyphics had given the most eminent Egyptologists, was *Philippines*.

It is said that the day after her wedding, conversing with her husband, who was then a corporal, she had pronounced it *Pehleefeens*.

The corporal thought it his duty to correct her and admonished her with a cuff: 'Say *Feeleepines*, girl! Don't be so stupid. Don't you even know your goddam country is named after King Philip?'

His wife, who was still wrapped in honeymoon dreams, did her best to obey him and made it *Feeleefeens*.

The corporal thought she was getting closer, gave her a few more cuffs, and upbraided her: 'Can't you even say Philip, woman? Don't forget King Philip the ... fifth... anyway, say Philip, add pines, which in Latin means nigger islands, and you have the name of your goddam country!'

Doña Consolación, who was then a laundress, gingerly felt with her fingers the effects of her husband's cuffings, and repeated, almost at the end of her patience: 'Peeleep—Peeleep... pines—*Peeleepines*. Is that it?'

'Not *Peeleep*, with a *p!*' roared the corporal. '*Feeleep*, with an *f!*'

'Why? How do you spell *Peeleep?* With a *p* or an *f?*'

The corporal thought it the better part of wisdom to change the subject that day, and meantime to consult a dictionary. Here his wonder reached its highest pitch. He rubbed his eyes. Let's see... slowly now... but there was no doubt about it. P-h-i-l-i-p-p-i-n-e-s: he and his wife were both wrong; it was neither *p* nor *f* but *ph*.

How now, he muttered to himself. Could the dictionary be wrong? Or was this dictionary written by some stupid native?

He took his doubts to Sergeant Gómez, who in his youth had aspired to the priesthood. The latter, without deigning to give him even a look, blew out a mouthful of smoke, and replied magisterially: 'In ancient times Philip was spelled with an *f* simply because that it is the way it is pronounced. But we are much too sophisticated for that now, and so it is spelled with a *p*, but with an *h* following to show that is pronounced like an *f*. Furthermore the best people in Madrid— haven't you been to Madrid, by the way?—well, as I was saying, the best people in Madrid now all use what is known as the British or Oxford accent, and say Philippines with a long *i* at the end, like pine-trees, you understand.'

The poor corporal had never been in Madrid; so that's why he had been confused by all this business! The things one learned in Madrid!

'So, nowadays one should say...'

'Here one should use the old-fashioned pronunciation. This country is not yet civilised, man! And, of course, there are no pines here. Philip-*peens*— that's good enough here,' said Gómez scornfully.

The corporal may have been a bad speller but he was a good husband, and he wanted his wife to know what he had just learned. He took up the lessons where he had left off.

'Consola, how do you call your goddam country?'

'How else? The way you said: *Peeleepeens*.'

'You're getting worse and worse! Yesterday you were a little better; at least you were using the modern Oxford accent. Well, now you have to go back to the old-fashioned way. Pee—I mean, *Feeleepeens*.'

'Now look here, I'm not old-fashioned. What do you think I am?'

'Never mind, just say *Feeleepeens*.'

'Not me! I'm no back number. I'm not even thirty!' she retorted, rolling up her sleeves and getting ready for a fight.

'Say it, goddam you, or I'll break this chair on your thick head!'

Consolacion saw her husband pick up a chair, thought better of it, and stammered between gasps: '*Peelee—Feeli—Fili—*'

The chair broke up the lesson, which ended in a flurry of blows, slaps, and scratches. The corporal seized her by the hair; she could not bite him—all her teeth were loose so she in turn caught him by a tuft of hair on his chin and by another portion of his anatomy. The corporal gave out a yell, let her go and begged her pardon; one eye grew rapidly larger than its mate; a shirt was torn to pieces; many other parts of the anatomy emerged from their hiding-places, but Feeleepeens did not see the light of day.

Similar outbreaks occurred whenever the question of language came up. The corporal, in view of the rate of his wife's progress in linguistics, reckoned sadly that in ten years she would lose the power of speech completely. That was what in fact happened. When they were married, she still understood Tagalog and managed to make herself understood in Spanish. Soon she no longer spoke any known language; she had grown so fond of the language of gestures and among these she had chosen the most spectacular and crushing—that she could well challenge the inventor of Esperanto.

Sisa, then, was lucky not to understand her. Doña Consolacion's brow cleared; a smile of satisfaction lighted up her face; undoubtedly she had forgotten Tagalog, she was already a 'Yorofean'.

'Tell her in Tagalog to sing!' she ordered one of the soldiers. 'She doesn't understand me. Doesn't know a word of Spanish.'

Sisa understood the soldier and sang the *Song of the Night*.

At first Doña Consolación listened with a mocking smile, but it slowly faded, and she became attentive, and afterwards serious and rather thoughtful. The voice, the meaning of the words, the melody itself, were making an impression on her: perhaps that dry and withered heart felt the need of rain.

> *The cheerless clammy cold*
> *That night-time skies enfold*
> *In their descending cloak*

—in the words of the *kundiman*—seemed to her to be enfolding her own heart.

> *The sear and withered flower*
> *That in the daytime bower*
> *Made wanton with her beauty*
> *And thought that all had duty*
> *To give her their applause*

> *Contrite and broken-hearted*
> *Now that evening's started*
> *Her wilted petals raises*
> *And on the heavens gazes*
> *For pity on her cause:*

> *She asks the dark to hide her*
> *That sunlight might not chide her*
> *As pride's pretentious daughter,*
> *And asks the dew to water*
> *Her lonely grave with tears...*

'Stop it!' cried Doña Consolación in perfect Tagalog, rising to her feet. 'Stop singing! Your song upsets me.'

The madwoman obeyed, and the soldier, staring at his mistress with admiration exclaimed:

'So she knows Tagalog after all!'

Doña Consolación realised she had betrayed herself. She was overcome with shame, and, being far from feminine, shame took the form of rage and hatred. She showed the imprudent soldier the door, and closed it after him with a kick. She took a few turns about the room, twisting the whip in her nervous hands, and then, stopping suddenly before the madwoman, commanded her in Spanish:

'Dance!'

Sisa did not move.

'Dance, dance!' Doña Consolación repeated in a sinister voice.

The madwoman looked at her with vague and expressionless eyes. Doña Consolación lifted one of Sisa's arms, then the other, shaking them; it was useless; Sisa did not understand.

Then Doña Consolación started jumping up and down, shaking herself, and urging Sisa to imitate her. From far away came the strains of a grave and solemn march played by one of the brass bands in the religious procession, but Doña Consolación was cavorting about in a frenzy, following another rhythm, another melody, within herself.

Sisa watched her motionless; something like curiosity brightened her eyes and a weak smile moved her pale lips. She found the lady's dance amusing.

The latter stopped as if in embarrassment and, raising the whip, that terrible whip known to both outlaws and soldiers, made by specialists and perfected by the lieutenant with twisted wires, said:

'Now it's your turn! Dance!'

And she began, slowly at first, to whip the naked feet of the madwoman, compelling her, with a grimace of pain, to protect herself with her hands.

'Aha! You're making a start!' Doña Consolación exclaimed with savage glee, and raised the beat of her whip from *lento* to an *allegro* vivace. The wretched Sisa gave a cry of pain and jerked up on one foot.

'Are you going to dance or not, you native bitch?' Doña Consolación screamed as the whip whistled.

Sisa let herself fall to the floor, covering her legs with her hands and staring at her tormentor with panic-stricken eyes. Two strong blows of the whip on her back made her get up; what the unfortunate woman gave now were not mere cries but howls of pain. Her thin bodice had been torn, the skin broken, the blood drawn.

The sight of blood excites the tiger; the sight of her victim's blood enraptured Doña Consolación.

'Dance, damn you! Dance! Damned was the womb that bore You!' she screamed. 'Dance or I'll whip you to death!'

And she herself, leading Sisa by one hand and whipping her with the other, began to leap and dance.

The madwoman understood at last and followed her, moving her arms about at random. Her dancing mistress gave a smile of satisfaction, the smile of a female Mephisto who has trained a great disciple; it had hatred in it, contempt, mockery, cruelty; a howl of laughter could not have said more.

Absorbed in the pleasure of this spectacle, she did not hear her husband coming until he had kicked the door of the room open. The commanding officer was pale and sullen; he saw what was taking place, and gave his wife a terrible look. She did not stir and smiled cynically.

He placed his hand as gently as he could on the weird dancer's shoulder and made her stop. The madwoman sighed and fell slowly on her haunches to the floor, which was stained with her own blood.

The lull continued. The lieutenant was breathing noisily. His woman, watching him with questioning eyes, picked up the whip and asked him in a calm deliberate voice:

'And what's the matter with you? You haven't even said good evening.'

He did not answer and called a soldier.

'Take away this woman,' he ordered. 'Tell Marta to give her another bodice and treat her wounds.. Give her a good meal and a good bed. Make sure she is well treated. Tomorrow she is to be taken to the house of Mr. Ibarra.'

Then he carefully shut the door, locked it, and went up to his wife.

'You're asking for it, you're just asking for a really good beating,' he said, clenching his fists.

'What's the matter with you?' she asked, scrambling to her feet and backing away.

'What's the matter with me?' he roared with an oath, and brandishing a sheet of paper covered with a clumsy scrawl, he continued: 'It was you, wasn't it, you slut, who wrote this letter to the Provincial Governor, saying I was taking bribes to allow gambling here? I can't understand why I don't kick your guts out!'

'All right, I'd like to see you try it,' she laughed sarcastically. 'It will take more of a man than you are to do that.'

He flinched at the gibe, but saw the whip in her hand. He seized one of the plates on the table and threw it at her head. She was used to these combats and quickly ducked; the plate shattered itself against the wall, and was followed by a cup and a knife.

'Coward!' she screamed. 'You're too scared to come any closer.'

She spat at him to provoke him and blinded by rage he threw himself upon
her with a roar. But with amazing swiftness she whipped him across the face
and then rushed to her room, slamming and locking the door. Screaming
with anger and pain the lieutenant pursued her but succeeded only in flinging
himself with blasphemies against the door.

'Goddam your whole tribe, you dirty sow! Open, you bitch, you goddam
whore, or I'll break your neck!' he howled, pummeling the door with his fists
and feet.

Doña Consolacion did not answer. Noises could be heard of chairs and
trunks being dragged and piled up to form a barricade. The house trembled
under the kicks and oaths of her husband.

'Keep out,' she warned acidly. 'Just try poking your nose in here and I'll
shoot it off.'

He seemed to simmer down slowly and to content himself with pacing up
and down the room like a caged beast.

'Go out and cool off,' his wife continued mockingly. She had, to all
appearances, completed her defences.

'I swear that if ever I lay hands on you, not God Himself will save you, you
dirty bitch!'

'You can say that again! You didn't want me to go to church and do my
duty to God,' she retorted with a sarcasm that was all her own.

The Lieutenant seized his helmet, tidied himself up, and stamped out of
the room. But after a few minutes he tiptoed back silently: he had taken off
his boots. The servants, accustomed to these exhibitions, were usually bored
by them, but the novelty of their C.O. in his stockings caught their interest,
and they exchanged winks.

He seated himself beside the Heavenly Gate and waited patiently for more
than half an hour.

'Have you really gone out or are you still there, you old goat?' Doña
Consolación would scream from time to time, with a change of names and
ever higher pitch.

At last she decided to take down her barricade of furniture piece by piece;
he heard the telltale movements and smiled to himself.

'Corporal, did the C.O. go out?' she shouted.

The corporal, at a signal from the lieutenant, answered: 'Yes, ma'am, he went out.'

She was heard to laugh merrily and to unbolt the door.

Her husband rose slowly; the door was ajar.

A scream, the sound of a body hitting the floor, oaths, howls, maledictions, blows, hoarse cries—how can the events in the darkness of the bedroom be described?

The corporal went out to the kitchen and made a significant gesture to the cook.

'You're going to pay for it,' said the latter.

'Me? The poor civilians, maybe, not me. She asked me if he had gone out, not if he had come back.'

41 • Right and Might

AT about ten o'clock that night the last rockets were rising lazily toward the dark sky where great paper balloons, filled with smoke and heated air, shone like new planets. A number of these balloons carried fireworks and had been bursting into flames, threatening the houses of the town. To guard against this danger men could still be seen on the rooftops, equipped with pails of water and wet rags at the end of long poles. Their silhouettes, black against the vague reflections in the sky, gave them the appearance of phantoms descended from above to witness the pleasures of mankind.

A great number of firewheels and other kinds of fireworks had also been set off, some in the shape of towers; others, of bulls and buffaloes; and one, which had surpassed in beauty and grandeur any other ever seen by the people of San Diego, in the shape of a volcano.

Now the people were crowding into the town square to see the last performance of the stage show. Here and there Bengal lights gave a fantastical illumination to the merry company; boys searched in the grass with torches for rockets that had failed to explode and might still be used; but a burst of music gave the signal that the show was about to begin, and everyone left the empty lots.

The great stage was splendidly illuminated; countless lights surrounded its supports, were hung from its ceiling, and strewn generously along the edges of its floor. The constable who looked after them was hissed good-naturedly by the public every time he showed his face.

'Here he is again!'

In front of the stage the orchestra tuned its instruments and essayed snatches of its repertoire. Facing them were the reserved seats to which the Manila newspaper correspondent had referred in his dispatches; the authorities of the municipality, the Spaniards, and the rich from out of town were filling up the rows of chairs. The common people, those with neither titles nor dignities, occupied the rest of the square.

Some had come carrying benches on their shoulders, more to supply their defects in height than to provide themselves with a seat. But no sooner did they attempt to stand on these benches than those behind them broke out into noisy complaints; they got down immediately but were soon on top of the benches again as if nothing had been said or done.

Comings and goings, screams, exclamations, roars of laughter, a belated firecracker, all added to the hullaballoo. Here a bench lost a leg and threw to the ground, to the laughter of the crowd, those who had come far to be spectators, and now made a spectacle of themselves. There a quarrel broke out over a seat. A little farther off there was the crash of bottles and glasses; it was Andeng bearing refreshments and drinks on a large tray with both hands; she had met her sweetheart, who had tried to take advantage of the situation.

The Vice Mayor, Don Filipo, presided over the affair; the Mayor himself preferred the gambling.

'What can I do?' he asked old Tasio. 'The Mayor has refused to accept my resignation. Do you feel powerless to do your duty, he asked me.'

'And what was your reply?'

'Mr. Mayor, I replied, the powers of a Vice Mayor, however insignificant, are like the powers of anyone in authority; they come from above. The King himself derives them from the people, and the people from God. It is such powers precisely which I lack, Mr. Mayor. But the Mayor refused to listen to me, and said we would talk it over after the fiesta.'

'Then God help you,' said the old man and started to move away.

'Don't you want to see the show?'

'No, thank you. I can make up my own dreams and nonsense,' replied the scholar with a sarcastic chuckle. 'But, come to think of it, hasn't it ever struck you that our people, peaceful by nature, love warlike spectacles and bloody battles; that, being democratic, they yet adore emperors, kings, and princes; that, while irreligious, they cheerfully ruin themselves over pompous rites; that our women, so gentle by nature, scream with joy when a princess brandishes a spear? Do you know why this is so? Well, I'll tell you...'

But the arrival of María Clara and her friends cut the conversation short. Don Filipo went to make them welcome and escorted them to their seats. Behind them came the parish priest with another Franciscan and a number of Spaniards. The priest was also accompanied by those who make it their business to dance attendance on any affair at hand.

'May God reward them in the next life as well as they are rewarded in this one,' muttered old Tasio as he walked away.

The show began with a short skit featuring two well-known players from Manila. All eyes and ears were on the stage except Father Salvi's. To all appearances he had come only to watch over María Clara, whose sadness gave her beauty an air so ethereal and fascinating that his ecstatic contemplation was understandable. But the Franciscan's eyes, hidden deep in their sockets, showed no ecstasy; in that desolate look could be read a desperate sorrow— with such eyes Cain must have looked from afar on that Paradise of whose delights his mother had told him.

The skit was about over when Ibarra arrived; his coming gave rise to a wave of whispering; all eyes were on him and the parish priest. But the young man did not appear to notice it. He greeted María Clara and her friends with composure and seated himself beside them. Only Sinang talked to him.

'Did you go and see the volcano?' she asked.

'No, dear, I had to accompany the Governor General.'

'What a pity! The parish priest was with us and he kept telling us stories about the damned. What do you think of that? Scaring the life out of us so we wouldn't enjoy ourselves. Fancy!'

The parish priest had left his seat and approached Don Filipo, with whom he was apparently engaged in a lively argument. The friar was speaking heatedly; Don Filipo calmly and quietly.

'I am sorry I cannot oblige your Reverence,' said the latter. 'Mr. Ibarra is one of the most generous contributors to the festivities, and he has a right to be here so long as he does not disturb the public order.'

'Is it not a disturbance of the public order to give scandal to good Christians? It is to let the wolf loose among the fold. You shall answer for this before God and the authorities!'

'I am always ready to answer for whatever I do of my own free will, Father,' replied Don Filipo with a slight bow. 'However, my small measure of authority does not empower me to meddle in religious affairs. Whoever wants to avoid him has only to ignore him; Mr. Ibarra is not forcing himself on anyone.'

'But it gives occasion to danger, and whoever loves danger shall perish in it.'

'I see no danger, Father. The Provincial Governor and the Governor General, my superiors, have been conversing with him all afternoon, and I am not the one to correct them.'

'If you don't throw him out here, we are walking out.'

'I am extremely sorry, but I cannot throw anybody out.'

The parish priest had second thoughts, but they came too late. He gave his fellow Franciscan a signal; the latter rose reluctantly; and both left, followed by their partisans, though not without sending looks of hatred in Ibarra's direction.

The whispers and murmurs rose abruptly in volume. Several approached and greeted Ibarra and assured him:

'We're with you. Don't pay any attention to them.'

'Who are *they?*' he asked, with a puzzled frown.

'Those who have just left to avoid any contact with you.'

'To avoid any contact? With me?'

'Yes, they say you are excommunicated.'

Ibarra was so taken aback that he did not know what to say, and looked round him. He saw that María Clara was hiding her face behind her fan.

'But is it possible!' he exclaimed at last. 'Are we still in the Middle Ages?

So that...'

He returned to the group of young ladies and, changing his tone, he told them: 'I beg you to excuse me. I had forgotten an appointment. I shall be back to see you home.'

'Stay,' said Sinang. 'The star of the next number is a divine dancer.'

'I can't, dear, but I'll be back.'

The whispering grew even stronger.

While the dance was being performed, two Constabulary soldiers approached Don Filipo and asked that the show be stopped.

'But why?' the surprised Vice mayor demanded.

'Because our C.O. and his wife have had a fight, and they can't get to sleep.'

'Tell your C.O. that we have a permit from the Provincial Governor, and that nobody here can countermand it, not even the Mayor himself, who is my only superior.'

'Anyway, the show can't go on,' the soldiers insisted.

Don Filipo turned his back on them and the soldiers went off. The Vice Mayor kept the incident to himself to avoid causing alarm.

After a scene from a musical comedy, which was loudly applauded, an actor in the role of 'Prince Villardo' strode on to the stage, challenging to mortal combat the Moors who held his father prisoner, and threatening to cut off all their heads at one blow and send them straight to the moon. Fortunately for the 'Moors', who were girding themselves for battle to the lively tune of the March of Riego, a different type of trouble now broke out. The members of the orchestra suddenly stopped playing, threw down their instruments, and scrambled on to the stage. The brave Villardo, who was certainly not expecting them, apparently took them for allies of the Moors, cast aside sword and shield in his turn, and took to his heels. The Moors, beholding the flight of the terrible Christian, had no objection to following him. Amid screams, shouts, curses, and blasphemies people ran to and fro, stumbling over one another, as the lights went out and lamps flew through the air.

'Bandits! The bandits are here!' cried some.

'Fire! Fire on the highwaymen!' cried others.

Women and children screamed as benches and spectators rolled on the ground in an uproar.

What had happened?

Two soldiers of the Constabulary had set the musicians to flight with blows in order to stop the show; the Vice Mayor and the municipal policemen, armed with their ancient sabres, had managed to stop them in spite of their resistance.

'Take them to the court-house!' shouted Don Filipo. 'Don't let them get away!'

Ibarra had rushed back in search of María Clara. The frightened girls clung to him, pale and shaken; Aunt Isabel recited the Litany of the Saints in Latin.

When the people had recovered sufficiently from their fright and learned what had happened, there was general indignation. The two soldiers were stoned as they were led away by the municipal policemen; there was even a proposal made to burn the barracks and roast Doña Consolación and the lieutenant alive.

'That's all they're good for!' cried a woman, rolling up her sleeves and waving her arms in the air. 'To terrorise honest folk! They only go after law-abiding citizens. What about the bandits and the gamblers? Burn the barracks!'

One man, feeling himself all over, pleaded for a confessor; the sound of whimpering came from below one of the upset benches; it was a poor musician. The stage was full of actors and spectators, all speaking at the same time. There was the famous singer from Manila, still in an operatic costume, chatting in pidgin Spanish with another performer, dressed as a schoolmaster. The much applauded dancer, wrapped up in a silk shawl, was discussing matters with 'Prince Villardo.' The Moors tried to console the musicians, who had been more or less beaten up. Some Spaniards went from one side to another, haranguing anyone they met.

A group of men was gathering and Don Filipo, guessing their intentions, ran to forestall them.

'Don't disturb the public order!' he cried. 'Tomorrow we shall demand redress. Justice will be done to us. I guarantee we shall have justice.'

'No,' some replied. 'They did the same in Kalamba' the same things were promised; but the Provincial Governor did nothing. We want to do justice with out own hands. To the barracks!'

The Vice Mayor argued with them in vain. The group persisted in its attitude. Don Filipo looked around him for help and saw Ibarra.

'Mr. Ibarra, please stop them while I go and call the municipal police.'

'What can I do?' asked the young man, perplexed, but the Vice Mayor was already out of hearing.

Ibarra in turn looked round him, for he knew not whom. Fortunately he thought he saw Elias, impassively watching developments. Ibarra ran to him, caught him by the arm, and told him in Spanish:

'For God's sake, do something if you can. I can do nothing.'

Elias must have understood him, for he lost himself in the group.

Heated discussions and sharp exclamations were heard; then the group began to break up gradually, with its members taking a less hostile attitude.

It was about time; the soldiers were moving out of their barracks with fixed bayonets.

Meantime what was the parish priest doing?

Father Salví had not gone to bed. Standing, his forehead pressed against the shutters, he had been looking out toward the square, motionless except for an occasional sigh. If the light of the lamp had not been so feeble, his eyes might have been seen filling with tears. He spent almost an hour in this way.

The tumult in the square shook him from this state. He followed with surprised eyes the confused comings and goings of the people, whose shouts and clamouring vaguely reached him. A breathless servant soon informed him of what was going on.

A thought crossed his mind. Libertines are quick to take advantage of feminine fright and weakness in the midst of any disturbance and riot; when it is every man for himself, the screams of outraged virtue remain unheard; women faint, stumble, fall; terror and fear overcome chastity; and, worst of all, at night —when a couple are in love—he imagined Crisóstomo carrying an unconscious María Clara in his arms and disappearing into the darkness.

He ran downstairs without his hat and cane, and rushed in a frenzy to the square.

There he found the Spaniards reprimanding the soldiers; he looked for the seats which María Clara and her friends had occupied, and found them empty.

'Father! Father!' the Spaniards called out to him, but he ran off unheeding towards the house of Capitan Tiago. There he finally drew breath; he discerned through the transparent blinds the adorable silhouette, the graceful and gently formed silhouette, of María Clara, and that of her aunt carrying cups and glasses.

'Well, now,' he muttered, 'it seems she was just upset, that's all.'

Then Aunt Isabel pulled the shutters to and the graceful shadow was no longer to be seen.

The parish priest left the place without seeing those he passed by. He had before his eyes the sweet fall and rise of a sleeping virgin's lovely bosom; her eyelids fringed with long lashes, gracefully curved like those of Raphael's Virgins; her small slightly smiling mouth; a face that breathed virginity, purity, innocence, a sweet vision that lay on the bed-linen like the head of a cherub in the clouds.

His imagination went on to other things, but who is to write all that a feverish mind can imagine?

Perhaps the Manila newspaper correspondent, who ended his account of the fiesta and all its happenings in the following language:

'A thousand thanks, countless thanks, to the opportune and active intervention of the Very Reverend Father Bernardo Salví, who, defying every danger in the infuriated town, hatless and caneless in the midst of a mob let loose, calmed down the anger of the crowd using only the persuasive power of his speech and the majesty and authority which are never lacking in a priest of the Religion of Peace. The virtuous friar, with unparalleled abnegation, left the delights of sleep, which are the prize of all good consciences like his, to protect his flock from the slightest misfortune. The citizens of San Diego will surely never forget this sublime deed of their heroic Shepherd and will know how to be grateful to him forever.'

42 • Two Callers

FINDING it impossible to fall asleep in his state of mind, Ibarra set to work in his study in order to distract himself from the brooding fears that night-time exaggerates. Dawn found him making various chemical mixtures into which he inserted fragments of bamboo and other materials, which he afterwards put away in sealed and numbered containers.

A servant interrupted him to say that a peasant wanted to see him.

'Send him in,' said Ibarra, without turning his head.

Elias entered the room and remained standing without a word.

'Ah, it's you,' said Ibarra in Tagalog on recognising him. 'I'm sorry I made you wait. I didn't notice. I was making an important experiment.'

'Don't let me bother you. I have come, first to ask you if I could do anything for you in Batangas province—I am leaving now—and then to give you some bad news.'

Ibarra looked inquiringly at the pilot.

'Capitan Tiago's daughter is ill,' Elias added in an even tone, 'but not seriously.'

'I was afraid of that,' muttered Ibarra. 'What is wrong with her, do you know?'

'A fever. Now, then, if you have nothing you want me to do..."

'Thank you, my friend, no, I wish you a happy trip. But, before you leave, let me ask you a question. If it is indiscreet, you need not answer.'

Elias nodded.

'How were you able to stop the riot last night?' Ibarra asked, looking him in the eye.

'Very simply,' answered Elias with the greatest composure. 'The leaders of the movement were two brothers whose father had died after being beaten up by the Constabulary. One day I had the good fortune of rescuing them from the same fate as their father's, and they are both grateful to me for this. I appealed to them last night, and they took care of the others.'

'And these two brothers whose father was killed in this manner...'

'Will end up like their father,' murmured Elias. 'When bad luck has marked out a family, all it's members must perish. A tree struck by lightning falls to pieces.'

Ibarra fell silent and Elias took his leave.

The former, on finding himself alone, lost the serenity which he had maintained in the presence of the helmsman, and his face grew sorrowful. 'It was I, I who have made her suffer,' he murmured.

He dressed himself hurriedly and went downstairs.

A short man in mourning clothes, with a great scar on his left cheek, greeted him humbly and stopped him on his way.

'What do you want?' asked Ibarra.

'Sir, my name is Lucas. I am the brother of the man who was killed yesterday at the site of the schoolhouse.'

'Oh, I'm sorry. Well?'

'Sir, I would like to know how much money you are prepared to give in compensation to my brother's family.'

'Money?' the young man echoed, unable to hide his disgust. 'We'll talk about that some other time. Come back this afternoon. I'm in a hurry.'

'Just tell me how much you're ready to give,' Lucas insisted.

'I have told you we'll talk about it another day. I have no time now,' said Ibarra impatiently.

'No time, sir?' Lucas asked bitterly, barring his way. 'No time for the dead?'

'Come this afternoon, my good man,' said Ibarra with an effort. 'Now I have to visit a sick friend.'

'Ah, you prefer the sick to the dead. You think that because we're poor...'

Ibarra cut him short with a look.

'Don't try my patience,' he said and went on his way.

Lucas stared after him with a grimace full of hatred.

'I can tell you are the grandson of the man who staked out my father in the sun,' he muttered between clenched teeth. 'The same blood still!'

Then, changing his tone, he added: 'But if you pay well...we can be friends!'

43 • *The Espadañas*

THE town fiesta was over, and once again, as in other years, the townspeople found themselves that much the poorer; they had slaved, sweated, and lost their sleep without very much enjoyment, without even making new friends; to be brief, they had paid dearly for all the excitement and its hangover. No matter, it would be the same the next year, and the next century; it was the custom of the country.

Capitan Tiago's household was downcast enough; all the windows were shut, everyone walked on tiptoe, and it was only in the kitchen that anyone spoke out loud. María Clara, the life of the house, lay sick in bed, and the state of her health could be read in every face as a spiritual illness can be described in a man's features.

'What do you think, Isabel,' María Clara's troubled father asked in a hushed voice, 'shall I make my donation to the Holy Cross of Tunasan or the Holy Cross of Matahong? The Holy Cross of Tunasan grows like a tree, but, on the other hand, the one in Matahong sweats like a man. Which, in your opinion, is the more miraculous?'

Aunt Isabel pondered the question, shook her head, and murmured: 'To grow...surely to grow is a greater miracle than to sweat. All of us sweat, but we don't all grow .'

'That's true, Isabel, quite true. But consider that sweating... for a piece of lumber you usually make into a bench to sweat, that's no two-for-a-penny miracle either. Oh well, the thing to do is to give donations to both; that way, no one's feelings are hurt, and María Clara will get well all the sooner. Are the rooms prepared? You know that some relative of Father Dámaso whom we don't know is coming with the doctor. Nothing must be out of place.'

At the other end of the dining-room, the two cousins, Sinang and Victoria, who were keeping María Clara company in her illness, were cleaning a silver tea-set with the help of Andeng.

'Do you know Dr. Espadaña?' María Clara's foster-sister asked Victoria with interest.

'No,' she answered. All I know is that his fees are high, according to Capitan Tiago.'

'Then he must be very good, said Andeng. 'The one who opened up Doña María's belly charged a lot of money, he must have been a good doctor.'

'Silly!' cried Sinang. 'An expensive doctor is not necessarily a good one. Take Dr. Guevara. He botched that last childbirth completely, just about wrenched off the poor baby's head, and then charged the widower fifty pesos. All a doctor like that knows is how to collect.'

'What do you know about things like that?' her cousin asked her, digging an elbow into her ribs.

'As if I didn't know! The husband, a logger, lost not only his wife but even his house, because the Provincial Governor, who is a friend of the doctor, made him pay the bill. Of course I know what I am talking about! My own father lent him the money for the trip to the provincial capital.'

The arrival of a coach before the house broke up the conversation.

Capitan Tiago, followed by Aunt Isabel, went running downstairs to receive the new arrivals. They were Doctor Don Tiburcio de Espadaña, his wife the Madam Doctor Doña Victorina de los Reyes de *de* Espadaña, and a young Spaniard with an attractive face and an engaging presence.

Doña Victorina wore a loose silk gown, embroidered with flowers, and a hat with a huge cluster of tricoloured leaves half crushed by red and blue ribbons. The dust from the roads, mixing with the rice-powder on her cheeks, emphasised her wrinkles. As in Manila, she had her lame husband on her arm.

'Please to meet our cousin, Don Alfonso Linares de Espadaña,' said Doña Victorina with a nod towards the young man. 'The sir is a godson of a relative of Father Dámaso, and private secretary yet to cabinet members...'

The young man bowed gracefully. Capitan Tiago was on the point of kissing his hand.

Doña Victorina had seen forty-five summers, the equivalent, according to her own arithmetic, of thirty-two springs. She had been in her youth, with a good figure—she used to say so herself—but, engrossed in self-admiration, she had looked with great disdain on her many Filipino admirers; her aspirations were towards another race. She had refused to bestow her small white hand on any man, but not out of distrust, for not seldom had she yielded jewels beyond price to a number of adventurers from local and foreign parts.

Six months before these events she had seen her most beautiful dream come true, a lifelong dream, for which she had scorned the blandishments of youth, and even the promises of love that in another time Capitan Tiago had whispered in her ears or had had sung in serenades. Her dream had come true rather late, it had to be admitted. But although Doña Victorina spoke Spanish badly, she was more Spanish than that Agustina who was the heroine of the siege of Zaragoza by Napoleon's troops, and knowing the saying, 'Better late than never', she found solace in repeating it to herself. 'There is no perfect happiness on earth', was her other favourite saying: but she kept them both to herself and never quoted them to other people.

Doña Victorina, who had spent her first, second, third, and fourth youth fishing in worldly waters for the object of her sleepless nights, had at last to be satisfied with what luck had thrown her way. If the poor lady had only seen thirty-one, instead of thirty-two, springs—the difference was very great, according to her arithmetical views—she would have thrown back what luck offered her, to await another more in conformity with her tastes.

But man proposes, and necessity disposes; she now needed a husband very badly indeed, and was compelled to make do with a poor man, who discarded by his own native province of Extremadura in Spain, had roamed about the world, a modern Ulysses, for six or seven years, and had finally found on the island of Luzon hospitality, money, and a shopsoiled Calypso, the other half of his orange—and how sour an orange!

The wretch was called Tiburcio Espadaña, and, although he was thirty-five years old and looked older, he was yet younger than Doña Victorina, who was only thirty-two. The reason for this is easy to gather but dangerous to express. He had gone to the Philippines as a Customs official of the fifth rank, but, aside from being seasick and breaking a leg during the trip, he had the ill fortune within fifteen days of his arrival and when he had spent his last copper, of finding that the latest ship from Spain had brought his notice of dismissal.

Having had enough of the sea, he did not want to return to Spain without having made good, and cast about for something to do. Spanish pride did not permit him any manual labour. The poor man would willingly have done any honest work in order to keep alive, but considerations of Spanish prestige would not have allowed it although these considerations did not fill his stomach.

In the beginning he lived at the expense of some of his country men, but Tiburcio was an honest man, and the bread of charity was bitter. Instead of putting on weight, he lost it. Since he had neither skill nor money nor connections, his countrymen, to get rid of him, advised him to go to the provinces and pass himself off as a physician. He was reluctant at first, for, although he had been an attendant in the hospital of San Carlos in Madrid, he had learned nothing of medicine: his job had been merely to dust the benches and light the fires, and this only for a short while. But pressed by necessity and by his friends, who dismissed his scruples, he finally gave way and went to the provinces, calling on a number of patients and charging the moderate fees which were dictated by his conscience. But he ended up by charging more and more heavily for his calls, which soon gave him the reputation of being a great doctor and would probably have made his fortune, if the Board of Medical Examiners in Manila had not heard of his exorbitant fees and of the competition he was offering his colleagues.

Private persons and professors interceded on his behalf. 'Let him make a little money, man,' they told the jealous Dr. C. 'As soon as he has put aside six or seven thousand pesos, he can go home and live in peace. Anyway, what does it matter to you? So he fools the gullible natives—well, they should be smarter! Don't snatch the food away from his mouth, the poor devil. Be a good Spaniard!'

The members of the Board were all good Spaniards, and agreed to close their eyes to what was happening, but the news spread, people began to lose confidence, and soon Don Tiburcio Espadaña lost his clientele and found himself obliged anew almost to beg for his daily bread. At about that time he learned from a friend of his, who was also an intimate friend of Doña Victorina, of this lady's predicament, as well as of her patriotism and good heart. Don Tiburcio saw a rift in the clouds, and asked for an introduction to her.

Doña Victorina and Don Tiburcio met. *Tarde venientibus ossa*—'for latecomers, bones', he would have exclaimed if he had known Latin. She was more than blowzy; she was overblown. Her abundant hair had dwindled down to a bun the size, according to her maidservant, of a head of garlic; her face was furrowed with wrinkles, and her teeth were growing loose. Her eyes had also suffered considerably, she had to screw them up frequently to be able to see a certain distance away. Only her character remained.

After half an hour's conversation they understood each other and were engaged. She would have preferred a Spaniard who was not so lame, who did not stutter so, who had more hair and teeth, and who sprayed less saliva when he talked; she would have preferred a Spaniard who had, as she used to say, more brío and more class, but this type of Spaniard never asked her for her hand.

She had heard it said more than once that 'no grass grows on a busy street' and she honestly grew to believe that Don Tiburcio was a man of intelligence, for, thanks to his nights of despair, he suffered from premature baldness. What woman can be careless of her opportunities at thirty-two?

Don Tiburcio, for his part, felt a vague melancholy when he thought of the honeymoon to come. He smiled with resignation and called to his aid the spectre of hunger. He had never been ambitious or pretentious. His tastes were simple, his thoughts limited, but his heart, virgin until then, had dreamed of a different divinity. In his youth when, tired out by the day's work, he lay down on his poor bed to digest his frugal peasant's soup, he had dreamed of a girl with a caressing smile. Afterwards, with the increase of disappointments and privations and the passing of the years, the romantic image no longer came to him, and he thought simply of some good, hardworking housewife with a tidy dowry, who would comfort him after the day's work and scold him from time to time. Even a scolding would have been a measure of happiness. But when he had to wander from one country to another in search no longer of a fortune but of a modicum of comfort for the rest of his days, and when, dazzled by the stories of his countrymen back from overseas, he had taken passage to the Philippines, realism had given way to the hope of a proud half-breed or some beautiful native with huge black eyes, covered in silks and transparent veils, loaded with gold and diamonds, who would offer him her love, her carriages, and all that she possessed. He arrived in the Philippines and thought that his dreams had come true, for the young ladies who rode in the Luneta and the Boulevard in their silver-coloured carriages had looked at him with a certain curiosity but, once unemployed, the dream of the half-breed and the native girl vanished, and with great effort he conjured up another image, that of a widow, but an attractive widow. So, when he saw these dreams take flesh, at least in part, he was depressed, but having a share of natural philosophy, told himself: 'Those were dreams, and in this world one cannot live on dreams!'

He had his own way of resolving his doubts. Doña Victorina put on too much rice-powder—well, once married, he would make her scrub it off. She was wrinkled—but his jacket was torn and mended. She was a pretentious, domineering, masculine old woman—but hunger was even more overbearing, nagging, and demanding, and anyway he had been born with a mild disposition, perhaps precisely for this purpose, and one never knew, love had been known to change temperaments. She spoke Spanish very badly but he did not speak it very well either, as his division chief had observed in giving him notice; at any rate, what did it matter? Was she ugly, ridiculous, and old? He was lame, toothless, and bald. Don Tiburcio preferred to be the doctor rather than the patient when it came to hunger. When some friend made fun of him, he answered: 'Fill my stomach and you can call me fool.' Don Tiburcio was the kind of a man that is commonly described as one who would not hurt a fly. Modest and incapable of an evil thought he would have made a good missionary in the old days. His stay in the Philippines had not given him that superiority complex, that conviction of his own high worth and importance, that the greater part of his countrymen acquired in a few weeks. There had never been any room for hatred in his heart; he still had to think of anyone as a subversive agitator, he only saw unfortunates whom he had to fleece so as not to be more unfortunate than they were. When the attempt was made to bring charges against him for pretending to be a physician, he had not resented it or complained; he realised the justice of it, and only answered: 'But one has to live!'

So Doña Victorina married Don Tiburcio or vice versa, and they went to the suburb of Santa Ana for their honeymoon. She had a terrible stomachache on the wedding night, and he, giving thanks to God, showed himself to be solicitous and considerate. The second night, however, he did his duty as an honourable man, and the morning after gave himself a melancholy smile in the mirror, displaying his toothless gums; he had aged at least ten years.

Doña Victorina was very satisfied with her husband. She had a good set of false teeth made for him, as well as clothes and accessories by the best tailor in the city. She ordered light carriages and buggies, sent to Batangas and Albay for the best teams of horses, and even made her husband keep two race horses, for the coming season.

While she was transforming her husband, she did not forget her own person. She put away silken *saya* and *piña* bodice and took up European dress; instead of the simple coiffure of the Filipinas, she put on artificial fringes, and disturbed the peace of her idle and gossiping neighbours with clothes that she wore with an inspired bad taste.

She would not allow him to go out on foot because she did not want him to be seen limping; he, for his part, took her driving in the most unfrequented places. This annoyed her because she wanted to show off her husband in the most crowded promenades, but she kept her peace because they were on their honeymoon.

The moon waned when he brought up the subject of her rice powder, saying it was artificial, unnatural; Doña Victorina turned a frowning look on his dentures. He shut up and she perceived that he was weak.

Soon she believed herself pregnant and made her condition known to her friends in these terms:

'I and de Espadaña are going to the Peninsula next month. It is not good also that our son will be born here and they will be calling him dissident.'

She had added an aristocratic 'de' to her husband's surname; it cost nothing and gave the name class. She took to signing herself Victorina de los Reyes de *de* Espadaña. The double *'de'*, one signifying her married status and the other signifying that she had married into the landed gentry, became an obsession; neither the engraver who made her calling cards nor her husband could get it out of her head.

'If I am using only one *de*, people may think also you don't have one yourself, you boob,' she explained to her husband.

She babbled incessantly of the preparations she was making for her trip, memorised the names of all the ports of call on the way, and chattered to everyone's delight: 'I must not omitting the isthmus in the Suez canal. De Espadaña thinks it is very beautiful, and you know, de Espadaña has gone already round the world... I am not coming back any more to this land of barbarians... I am not suiting to this kind of country; I am always thinking, even when I was a little girl yet, that Aden or Port Said is better for me...' In Doña Victorina's geography the world was divided into the Philippines and Spain, which was slightly different from the geography of the Spanish street urchins, who divided the world into Spain and America, otherwise known as China.

Her husband knew very well that some of the things she said were outrageous, but he said nothing, to escape being yelled at and having his stammer thrown in his face. Doña Victorina pretended to suffer from the whims of pregnancy and took to wearing vari-coloured dresses, covering herself with flowers and ribbons, and even promenading in a housecoat in the shopping district. Alas, after three months, these illusions vanished, and, without the motive of preventing her future son from being dubbed a dissident, the trip to Spain was abandoned. She then took to consulting physicians, midwives, old wives, and all other sorts of wives, but it was all to no avail. On the other hand, to Capitan Tiago's great disgust, she made fun of St. Paschal the dancer, and would not hear of appealing to any saint of either sex, which had prompted a friend of her husband to remark to her:

'Believe me, ma'am, in this boring country, your spirit is 100 proof.'

She had smiled without understanding the '100 proof,' but that night at bedtime she asked her husband.

'The only 100 proof spirits I know, dear girl,' he answered, ' are spirits of ammonia. My friend must have been speaking metaphorically.'

Ever since then she had seized every occasion to say: 'I am the spirit of annomias in this boring country, mephaturically speaking Mr. So and So is telling me, and he is a high-class Spaniard from Spain yet.'

She would not brook contradiction, and had gained complete mastery over her husband, who, for his part, offered little resistance, and ended up by becoming a kind of lapdog to her. If she was annoyed with him, she would not let him out of the house; and when she was really angry, she snatched the denture out of his mouth and left him looking ghastly for one or two days, in proportion to his crimes.

It occurred to her that her husband should be a doctor, both physician and surgeon, and told him so.

'Dear girl,' he cried out in horror. 'Do you want me to be arrested?'

'Don't be a boob,' she replied. 'I am responsible. You will not be touching anyone. I want only you will be called Doctor and myself Madam Doctor!'

The next day the city's best sign-maker received an order for a slab of black marble to be engraved with the words DR. DE ESPADAÑA, SPECIALIST IN ALL KINDS OF DISEASES.

The whole household was required to address them with the new titles, another consequence being that Doña Victorina multiplied her ringlets, ribbons, and laces, thickened the layer of rice-powder on her face, and looked down with greater disdain than ever on her poor unfortunate countrywomen whose husbands were not so distinguished. Every day she felt her rank in society rise, and at that rate of progress she would probably have believed herself of divine origin within a year.

These sublime illusions, however, did not prevent her becoming older and more ridiculous day by day. Every time Capitan Tiago ran across her and remembered having courted her without success, he straightaway sent a peso to the nearest church for a Thanksgiving Mass. Nevertheless, Capitan Tiago had a high regard for Doña Victorina's husband, whose claim to be a specialist in all kinds of diseases impressed him, and paid the closest attention to the few broken phrases that de Espadaña managed to stammer out. For this reason, and also because he was one doctor who, unlike his colleagues, was not at the beck and call of everyone, Capitan Tiago chose de Espadaña to attend his daughter in her illness.

The young Linares was another matter altogether. When the trip to Spain was still being planned, Doña Victorina had had bethought herself of the need for an administrator of their affairs in their absence; he would have to be a Spaniard from Spain; she had no confidence in Filipinos. Her husband recalled that he had a nephew in Madrid who was reading law and who was considered the smartest in the family. They wrote to him forthwith, advancing the cost of his passage. When the dream of parenthood had vanished the young man was already at sea.

These were the three new arrivals.

While they were taking a light snack before lunch, Father Salví arrived and the couple, who were already acquainted with him, introduced the young Linares with all his titles, including a blush in his cheeks.

They talked of María Clara, which was only to be expected; she, it turned out, was resting in bed. They talked also of the famous trip to Spain, and Doña Victorina exhibited the richness of her vocabulary in criticisms of the habits of the country people, their nipa huts and their bamboo bridges, without forgetting to drop, for the benefit of the parish priest, the names of the Vice Governor General, Governor This and Governor That, Justice So-and-So, and Director Such-and-Such, all persons of high rank who, of course, had the highest consideration for Doña Victorina.

'You should have been here two days ago, Doña Victorina,' Capitan Tiago ventured to remark on the occasion of a slight break in her conversation. 'You would have found yourself face to face with His Excellency the Governor General. He was seated right there.'

'What! How! His Excellency here? In your house? It is not true also!'

'I am telling you he was seated right there. If you had only come two days ago...'

'Oh, what a pity Clarita did not becoming sick more earlier!' she exclaimed with sincere regret. Then, turning to Linares, she continued: 'Are you hearing that, coz? His Excellency here already! Maybe you believe de Espadaña now! He was already telling you, you are not going to the house of just so-so native only. You know, Don Santiago, our cousin was the friend in Madrid of Ministers and Dukes and was even eating many times in the house of the Count of the Belfry—or was it the Duke of the Tower?'

'If you are referring to our former Governor General, Victoria,' returned her husband, 'he is the Duke of the Tower.'

'All the same! You're telling me!'

'I wonder if I would find Father Dámaso in his parish,' Linares interrupted, directing his question to Father Salví. 'I am told it is not far from here.'

'Father Dámaso happens to be in town. He is calling here shortly,' the parish priest replied.

'Wonderful! I have a letter for him,' said the young man. 'Were it not for the happy coincidence which brings me here, I would have made it a point to call on him.'

Madam Happy Coincidence now came to with a start.

'De Espadaña?' she said, polishing off her snack. 'Shall we see Clarita?' And to Capitan Tiago: 'For you only, Don Santiago. For you only! My husband does not give treatment except to the high-class people, and even then, even then! My husband is not like other doctors, what you think? In Madrid he would not treat anyone except people that is very high-class!'

They proceeded to the sickroom.

It was almost in pitch-darkness. The windows were closed for fear of a draught, and what little light there was coming from two candles before an image of the Virgin of Antipolo.

Her head bound in a kerchief soaked in cologne, her body carefully wrapped in white sheets whose voluminous folds concealed her virginal curves, the girl lay in her bed of black hardwood behind hangings of delicate native cloths. Her hair, framing her oval face, accented its transparent pallor to which only her great sad eyes gave life. Beside her were her two friends and

Andeng, who carried a cluster of lilies.

De Espadaña took her pulse, looked at her tongue, asked a few questions, and said, shaking his head. 'Well, she's s-s-s-sick, but she'll s-s-s-survive!' Then he prescribed lichen with milk in the morning, marshmallow syrup, and two pills of hound's tooth compound.

Linares was so fascinated by the girl's eloquent eyes, seemingly searching for an absent face, that he did not hear Doña Victorina calling him.

'Mr. Linares,' said the parish priest, interrupting his contemplation. 'Here comes Father Dámaso.'

It was indeed Father Dámaso, pale and rather downcast. His first visit on leaving his sickbed was for María Clara. He was no longer the Father Dámaso of other days, so hearty and roguish; now he walked in silence and rather uncertainly.

44 • *Plans*

IGNORING everyone else he went straight to the sickbed and took María Clara by the hand.

'María,' he said with indescribable tenderness, tears springing to his eyes, 'María, my child, you are not to die!'

She opened her eyes and gave him a puzzled look.

Father Dámaso could not go on and left the girl. Weeping like a child, he went out to the terrace where he indulged his distress under María Clara's favourite plants.

'How he loves his godchild!' all who watched him thought. Father Salví, who also had his eyes on him, was silent and motionless, slightly biting his lips.

When Father Dámaso had calmed down, Doña Victorina introduced young Linares to him. The youth approached the priest respectfully. Father Dámaso silently studied him from head to foot, and took the letter which the young man was handing to him. He read it, apparently without understanding it, for he asked:

'And who are you?'

'Alfonso Linares, the godson of your brother-in-law,' stammered the youth.

Father Dámaso drew back, scrutinised the young man again, and then, his face lighting up, rose to his feet.

'So you are the godson of Carlicos!' he cried, embracing Linares. 'Come let me hold you! I had a letter from him some days ago. So it's you! I did not recognise you. Well, of course, you hadn't even been born when I left the old country. No, I did not recognise you at all!'

Father Dámaso was clasping the young man so tightly that the latter was turning red, either from embarrassment or asphyxiation. The friar seemed to have forgotten his sorrows completely. After the first demonstrative moments and the customary questions about Carlicos and Pepa, Father Dámaso asked:

'Now, then, what does Carlicos want me to do for you?'

'I believe he has something to say in his letter.' mumbled Linares.

'In this letter? Now, let's see. You're right. He wants me to get you a job and a wife. Hmmmm. A job—that's easy. Can you read and write?'

'I have a degree in Law from the Central University of Madrid.'

'Good heavens! A shyster, are you? Well, you don't look it. You look more like a schoolgirl. But so much the better. Now, about a wife... Hmmmm. A wife!'

'I am in no hurry, Father,' said Linares in confusion.

But Father Dámaso was pacing up and down the hall, mumbling: 'A wife, a wife!' his expression was neither glum nor gay; it was deeply thoughtful.

Father Salví watched the scene from afar.

'I did not think the business would cause me so much pain,' said Father Dámaso to himself with a pang in his voice. 'But of two evils, the lesser.'

He raised his voice and called to Linares.

'Come here, my boy; let us talk to Santiago.'

Linares winced but allowed himself to be pulled along by the priest, who was deep in thought.

Now it was Father Salví's turn to pace up and down, brooding as usual.

A voice wishing him good day interrupted the monotony of his walk. He raised his head and saw Lucas, who greeted him with humility.

The parish priest looked at him inquiringly.

'Father, I am the brother of the man who was killed on the day of the fiesta,' he whimpered.

Father Salví stepped back.

'Well?' he asked in a voice that could scarcely be heard.

Lucas was trying to force tears into his eyes, dabbing them with a handkerchief.

'Father, he whined, 'I have been to the house of Don Crisóstomo to ask for an indemnity. At first he received me very badly, saying he did not want to give anything because he had almost been killed through the fault of my dear unfortunate brother. Yesterday I went back, but he had already left for Manila leaving me five hundred pesos, as if it were an act of charity, and the message never to come back. Oh, Father, five hundred pesos! Father...'

At first the parish priest had listened to him with startled interest; then slowly he smiled with such contempt and sarcasm at the sight of this farce that if Lucas had seen him he would have taken to his heels.

'And what do you want now?' Father Salví asked, turning his back.

'Oh, Father, tell me, for the love of God, what I should do. Father has always given good advice.'

'Who told you that? You're not from here.'

'Ah, Father is known all throughout the province.'

Father Salví went up to him angrily and pointing to the street told the astonished Lucas:

'Go home, and be thankful to Don Crisóstomo for not having sent you to gaol! Get out!'

Lucas forgot his pretenses and murmured:

'But I thought...'

'Get out!' Father Salví cried nervously.

'I would like to see Father Dámaso.'

'Father Dámaso is busy. Now get out of here!' the parish priest repeated his order imperiously.

Lucas went down the stairs muttering:

'Another one cut from the same cloth... If he doesn't pay well... Whoever pays more...'

All had come running, even Father Dámaso, Capitan Tiago, and Linares, at the sound of the parish priest's cries.

'An insolent tramp who wanted a hand-out, not work,' explained Father Salví, picking up his hat and walking-stick to return to the parish house.

45 • *An Examination of Conscience*

THERE were long days and depressing nights by María Clara's bed-side; she had suffered a relapse shortly after having gone to Confession, and at the height of her fever had called only on her mother, whom she had never known. But her friends, her father, and her aunt watched over her; Masses were ordered and donations sent to all miraculous images; Capitan Tiago promised to give the Virgin of Antipolo a golden sceptre; and at last the fever fell slowly but steadily.

Dr. de Espadaña was amazed by the powers of marshmallow syrup and lichen broth; he had not altered the prescription. Doña Victorina was so proud of her husband that when the latter stepped on the tail of her housecoat one day, she did not apply the usual penal sanction of yanking out his denture. Instead she limited herself to saying:

'If you are not lame, maybe you will even step on my girdle.'

But of course, she never used one!

One afternoon, while Sinang and Victoria were keeping their friend company, the parish priest, Capitan Tiago, and the family of Doña Victorina were chatting over a snack in the dining-room.

'Well, I'm very sorry to hear that,' the physician was saying. 'Father Dámaso won't like it very much either.'

'Where did you say they were transferring him to? Linares asked the parish priest.

'To the province of Tayabas,' answered the latter nonchalantly.

'María will also take it very badly when she hears of it,' said Capitan Tiago. 'She loves him like a father.'

Father Salví looked at him sharply.

'I think, Father,' Capitan Tiago continued, 'that all this illness of hers started because she was so very badly upset the day of the fiesta.'

'I agree, and you were very wise in not allowing Mr. Ibarra to see her. She would have taken a turn for the worse.'

'If not only for us,' Doña Victorina broke in, 'Clarita is already in Heaven singing Hallelujah.'

Capitan Tiago thought it his duty to say Amen.

'Good for you only that my husband did not have other patients more high-class. You will be obliged to call another doctor, and all doctors here are ignorant. My husband....'

'I still think I was right,' the parish priest interrupted her in turn. 'When María Clara went to Confession, it was a turning point that saved her life. A clean conscience is worth more than many medicines, although, mind you, I do not deny the powers of science, above all surgery! But a clean conscience... Read religious books, and you will see how many cures have been made by a good Confession alone.'

'I beg your pardon', Doña Victorina objected, somewhat in a temper. 'This power of Confession you are talking about—let us see already, you cure the wife of the C.O. with a Confession!'

'A black eye, Madam, is not a disease which is amenable to the influence of conscience,' father Salví replied coldly. 'However, a good Confession would perhaps save her in the future from the blows she received this morning.'

'She deserves them!' Doña Victorina exclaimed as if she had not followed Father Salví. 'That woman is very insulting also! In the church she is always staring at me. Of course, she is low-class. Last Sunday I was going to ask her already what's the matter, do I have a mustache? But why should I go down to her level?'

For his part the parish priest, ignoring all this chatter, continued:

'Believe me, Don Santiago, your daughter must receive Communion tomorrow if she is to make a complete recovery. I shall come myself, I don't think she has to make a new Confession; however, if there is anything on her conscience, I could come tonight.'

'I don't know, Doña Victorina said, taking immediate advantages of a light pause. I cannot understand also why some men are marrying comics like that woman! Even from far away you can tell already what kind she is; anybody can see she is very envious. Very clear. What is the matter with the C.O.?'

'That's settled then, Don Santiago. Please ask your cousin to warn our little patient about Communion tomorrow. I shall drop in tonight to hear about all her little faults.'

To Aunt Isabel, who was leaving the room, he added in Tagalog:

'Prepare your niece for Confession tonight. Tomorrow I shall give her Communion. That way she will get better all the sooner.'

'But, Father,' objected Linares timidly, ' she might think she is in danger of death.'

'Don't you worry about that,' the parish priest replied without deigning to look at him. 'I know what I'm about. I have been at a very great number of sickbeds. Anyway, it is up to her to say whether or not she wants to take Holy Communion. You'll see, she'll say yes to everything.'

For the time being it was Capitan Tiago who had to say yes to everything.

Aunt Isabel entered the sickroom. María Clara was still in bed, pale, very pale. Her two friends were beside her.

'Take one more,' whispered Sinang, offering her a white pill which she had taken from a small glass tube. 'He says you are to stop taking it only when you feel a buzzing in the ears.'

'Hasn't he written to you again?' the sick girl whispered back.

'No. He must be very busy.'

'No messages for me?'

'Only that he will try to get the Archbishop to lift the excommunication so that...'

The entry of Aunt Isabel suspended this conversation.

'Father Salví says you should prepare to make a good Confession, girl,' she said. 'Now leave her alone so she can make an examination of conscience.'

'But she went to Confession only last week!' Sinang protested. "I'm not sick and even I don't commit sins as often as that!'

'Come now, don't you remember what the parish priest said? Even the just man sins seven times a day. Well, shall I bring you the *Anchor of Salvation,* the *Bouquet of Virtues* or the *Straight and Narrow Path?*'

María Clara did not answer.

'Oh well,' good Aunt Isabel continued, to make her feel better, 'I suppose you mustn't tire yourself. I'll read the examination of conscience to you, myself, and all you will have to do is remember in what you have sinned.'

When her aunt had left the room to fetch the work of piety, María Clara whispered in Sinang's ear as they said goodbye: 'Write to him, tell him to forget me.'

'What!'

But her aunt had re-entered the room and Sinang had to leave without understanding what her friend had said.

Good Aunt Isabel placed a chair near the light, adjusted her glasses on the tip of her nose, and opening a little book, said:

'Now pay attention, child. I shall begin with the Ten Commandments. I shall go very slowly so you can gather your thoughts. If you do not hear anything well, tell me so I can repeat it. You know I shall never mind doing anything for your good.'

She began to read in a monotonous nasal voice an analysis of the situations in which sins may have been committed. At the end of every paragraph she paused for a long time to give the girl an opportunity to recall her sins and to repent.

María Clara looked vaguely out at space. Aunt Isabel, peering at her over the rim of her glasses after considering the First Commandment to love God above all things, was satisfied with the girl's air of thoughtful sadness. She gave a pious little cough, and after a long pause started on the Second Commandment. The dear old lady did the reading with reverence and, the analysis completed, looked again at her niece, who slowly turned her head away.

'Really,' Aunt Isabel said to herself. 'All this about taking the name of God in vain has nothing to do with the poor child. Let us go on to the Third.'

The Third Commandment was analyzed and commented upon, and Aunt Isabel, having finished giving the various ways in which it might be broken, looked toward the bed again and saw her niece bring a handkerchief to her eyes as if to dry her tears.

'Hm,' she thought, 'aha! The poor child must have dozed off during some sermon.' Then replacing her glasses on the end of her nose, she continued to herself: 'Now we shall see whether she has honoured her father and mother any better than she has kept holy the Sabbath day.'

She read the considerations on the Fourth Commandment even more slowly and nasally, thinking thus to lend greater solemnity to the act, as she had seen many friars doing; Aunt Isabel had never heard a preacher from the Quaker sect, else she might have imitated their holy shakes too.

The girl meantime had raised her handkerchief to her eyes a number of times and her breathing had grown louder.

'What a good soul!' the old lady thought. 'She who is so obedient and submissive to everyone! I have committed more sins but was never able to weep for them in earnest.'

She began on the Fifth Commandment with even longer pauses and all possible unction, with such enthusiasm in fact that she did not perceive her niece's muffled sobs. Only upon pausing after the considerations on homicide with a deadly weapon did she perceive the sinner's sighs. Her voice then reached a pitch higher than sublime; she read out the rest of the analysis of the Commandment in an accent which she tried to make minatory; then, seeing that her niece was still weeping, she urged, leaning over the bed:

'That's right, child, weep, the more you weep the sooner you will win God's forgiveness. Be sorry for your sins out of the love of God, not only in fear of Hell. Weep, child, weep, you don't know how happy it makes me to see you cry. You might also strike your breast, but mind, not too strongly, you're not very well yet.'

But, as if her sorrow had had need of mystery and privacy in order to grow, María Clara, seeing herself surprised, gradually ceased to sigh and dried her eyes without saying a word or replying to her aunt.

The latter continued with her reading but, since the weeping of her audience had ceased, she lost her enthusiasm. The last Commandments bored her so that she started to yawn, to the great detriment of the monotony of her nasal accent which was thus periodically interrupted.

'I wouldn't have believed it if I hadn't seen it with my own eyes,' the old lady thought later. 'This girl sins like a veteran against the first five Commandments, but not a venial sin from the sixth to the tenth, all the opposite from the rest of us! How the world changes!'

She lighted a great taper before the Virgin of Antipolo, and others, rather smaller, before Our Lady of the Holy Rosary and Our Lady of the Pillar, taking the precaution of putting aside in a corner an ivory crucifix so as to make it quite clear that the candles had not been lighted for it. The Virgin of Delaroche likewise had no share; she was an unknown foreigner and Aunt Isabel had yet to hear of any miracle performed by her.

The secrets of the Confession that night must be respected. It was a long one, and the aunt, who watched over her niece from afar, observed that the parish priest, instead of turning his ear to the word of the sick girl, had, on the contrary, turned squarely to face her, as if he wanted to read or guess her thoughts in her lovely eyes.

Father Salví was pale, his lips wet, when he left the room. His clouded

brow, covered with sweat, would have suggested that it was he who had made
his Confession and that he had been refused absolution.

'Jesus, Mary, Joseph!' exclaimed the aunt crossing herself to conjure away
an evil thought. 'Who can understand young people nowadays?'

46 • The Oppressed

BY the feeble moonlight that filtered through the treetops a man walked
slowly and calmly in the forest. From time to time, as if to find his bearings,
he whistled a tune. When it was repeated in the distance by another whistle,
he listened attentively and then went towards it.

At last, after the thousand obstacles that were to be encountered in a virgin
forest at night, he reached a small clearing bathed by the light of a crescent
moon. Tall rocks crowned with trees rose round, forming a kind of ravaged
ampitheatre, its centre filled with newly felled trees, burned trunks, and huge
boulders, only half-covered with a mantle of green foliage.

He had scarcely arrived when a man appeared suddenly from behind a great
rock and advanced towards him, drawing a revolver.

'Who are you?' he demanded in Tagalog, cocking his gun.

'Is old Pablo with you?' the new arrival asked calmly, without answering
the question or appearing cowed.

'You mean the commander? Yes, he is.'

'Then tell him that Elias is looking for him.'

'Are you Elias?' the other asked with a certain respect and approached him,
without lowering his gun. 'In that case, come on.'

Elias followed him.

They entered a cave which sank down into the depths of the earth. The
guide, who knew the way, warned Elias when they were on an incline, or
when he was to stoop or crawl on his belly. For all that they did not take
long to reach a kind of hall, lighted meanly by pitch torches, and occupied
by twelve or fifteen armed men with unwashed faces and wretched clothes,
some seated, others on their backs, scarcely speaking to one another.

A melancholy old man, his head wrapped in a bloodstained bandage, sat
with his elbows on a rocky slab which served him for a table, lost in thought
as he watched the torches that gave so little light amid so much gloom. So

deep was the despair in his face that he might have been taken for Dante's Ugolino, the treacherous Count of Pisa, cast into a tower with his two sons and two grand sons, there to starve to death.

When Elias and his guide entered, the men half rose, but a sign from the latter reassured them and they were content to keep their eyes on the unarmed boatman.

The old man slowly turned his head toward Elias, who gazed at him gravely, uncovered, and in evident distress.

'It's you, is it?' asked the old man whose spirits, on recognising the youth, seemed to rally.

'I never thought I would see you like this,' murmured Elias, shaking his head.

The old man nodded silently and gave his men a signal. They rose and moved away, not without measuring with looks Elias's height and strength.

'Yes,' the old man told Elias once they found themselves alone, 'six months ago, when I gave you shelter in my house, it was I who pitied you. Now our luck has changed, and it is you who pity me. But sit down, and tell me how you got here.'

'I was told about your misfortunes about fifteen days ago. I set out at once and looked for you from mountain to mountain. I have searched almost two whole provinces.'

'I had to flee to avoid the shedding of innocent blood. My enemies were afraid to face me themselves, and only sent against me poor wretches who had never done me the slightest injury.'

After a short pause, which Elias used to read the thoughts in the old man's sombre face, he said:

'I have come to make you a proposition. I have searched in vain for any surviving members of the family that was the cause of the misfortunes of my own, and now I have decided to emigrate to the North and live among the free pagan tribes. Would you leave the life you have only just now taken up, and come with me instead? I shall be your son, for you have lost the ones you had, while I, who have no family, will have you for a father.'

The old man shook his head and said:

'At my age, desperate decisions are taken only because there is no alternative. A man like myself, who has spent his youth and his maturity working for his own future and that of his sons, who has submitted to all the wishes of his superiors, who has conscientiously performed the most difficult tasks, and endured everything so as to live in peace and tranquility as long as possible— when such a man, whose blood has been cooled by age, renounces all his past and all his future on the very brink of the grave, it is because he has come to the deliberate conclusion that peace neither exists nor is supreme good. Why live miserably in a strange land? I had two sons, a daughter, a home, money of my own; I enjoyed general respect and esteem. Now I am like a tree shorn of its branches; I am a fugitive, hunted like a beast in the forest. Why? Because a man dishonoured my daughter, because her brothers called upon him to settle the accounts of this infamy, and because this man is placed above the rest with the title of a minister of God. For all that, I, the father, dishonoured in my old age, forgave the wrong, and was lenient towards youthful passion and the weakness of the flesh. What could I do in the face of an irreparable injury except keep my peace and try to salvage what remained?

But the wrong-doer was afraid of retribution sooner or later and sought the ruin of my sons. Do you know what he did? A fake robbery was staged in the parish house, and one of my sons was among those accused of it. The other could not be included because he happened to be out of town. You know the tortures to which they were subjected, because they are the same in all the towns. I saw my son hanging by his hair, I heard his screams, I heard him call for me, and I, cowardly and over-fond of peace, had the courage neither to kill nor be killed. The robbery could not be proven, and the calumny was exposed. The parish priest was punished by being transferred to another town. But my son died as the result of the torture he had suffered. My remaining son was not a coward like his father, and the murderer feared that he would avenge the death of his brother. So, on the pretext that he was not carrying an identity card—he had simply forgotten to take it with him – he was seized by the Constabulary, beaten up, and goaded and hounded by torture into taking his own life! I have survived all this shame, but, if I did not have a father's courage to defend my sons, I can still avenge them, and I shall! The discontented are gathering under my command, and my enemies themselves create new recruits for me with their excesses. The day I judge myself strong enough, I shall go down to the plains and consummate in fire both my vengeance and my own life. That day will come, or there is no God!'

The old man sprang to his feet in a passion.

'It was I,' he cried with an oath, 'who sent my sons to their death. If I had allowed them to kill the guilty, if I had believed less in the justice of God and men, I would now have my sons with me; we would be fugitives, true, but they would now be at my side, they would not have died in torture. I was not born to be a father, that is why I have lost them. With all my years I failed to understand the world in which I lived. But I shall know how to avenge them in fire and blood and my own death.'

In his frenzy the unfortunate father had torn the bandage from his head, and reopened a wound on his forehead from which the blood flowed once more.

'I respect your sorrow,' replied Elias, 'and I understand your desire for revenge. I am in the same situation, but, for fear of doing the innocent an injury, I prefer to forget my misfortunes.'

'You can afford to forget because you are young, and because you have not lost a son or one last hope. But I can assure you, I shall not harm the innocent. Do you see this wound? I received it rather than kill a poor municipal policeman who was only doing his duty.'

'But consider,' said Elias after a moment's silence, consider to what a holocaust you propose to consign our unfortunate towns. If you take vengeance with your own hand, your enemies will take terrible reprisals, not against you, not against those who are armed, but against the common people on whom it is their usual practice to put all the blame. And then, how many injustices will be done!'

'Let the people learn to defend themselves! Let every man defend himself!'

'You know that is impossible. Sir, I have known you in another time, when you were happy. Then you gave me good advice. Now, will you allow me to offer you the same?'

The old man crossed his arms and seemed prepared to listen.

'Sir,' Elias continued, measuring his words, 'I have the good fortune of rendering a service to a rich young man of good heart, a noble young man who seeks the welfare of the country. It is said that he has friends in Madrid; I do not know whether that is true or not, but I can assure you that he is a friend of the Governor General. Why not arouse his interest in the cause of the oppressed and make him the spokesman of the grievances of the people?'

The old man shook his head.

'You say he is rich? The rich think only of becoming richer, they are blinded by pride and pomp; and since as a rule they have a good life, especially when they have powerful friends, none of them troubles himself with the unfortunate. I know it all because once I was rich myself.'

'But the man I am talking about is not like the others. The memory of his father has been desecrated, and, since he will soon start a family of his own, he thinks also of the future, a good future for his sons.'

'Then he will be a happy man, and our cause is not for happy men.'

'But it is a cause for men of good heart.'

'Very well,' replied the old man, sitting down, ' supposing he consents to be our spokesman before the Governor General, supposing that he finds in the Spanish Parliament deputies who will be our advocates, even then, do you think they will do us justice?'

'Let us try it before using force,' answered Elias. 'You must find it strange that I, one more unfortunate like the rest, but young and strong, should propose peaceful measures to you, who are old and weak, but it is because I have seen so much misery, caused as much by ourselves as by our oppressors. The unarmed always pay.'

'And if we get nothing?'

'Believe me, we shall get something; not all of those who govern are unjust. And if we get nothing, if a deaf ear is turned to our complaints, if man has grown so indifferent to the sorrows of his fellow-men, then you will have me at your orders.'

The old man stood up enthusiastically and embraced Elias.

'I accept your proposition; I know that you keep your word. You shall come to me, and I will help you to avenge your forefathers, as you will help me to avenge my sons. They were so much like you!'

'And you, sir, will avoid all violence in the meantime?'

'You will explain the grievances of the people; you know them already. When shall I know the answer?'

'In four days send one of your men to meet me on the beach at San Diego, and I shall tell him the answer of the man in whom I have placed my hopes. If he accepts, then they will do us justice. If not, I shall be the first to fall in the struggle we shall begin.'

'Elias will not die. When Capitan Pablo falls, happy in his revenge, Elias will be the head!' exclaimed the old man, and personally escorted Elias out of the cave.

47 • *The Cockpit*

THE Sabbath day is generally kept holy in the Philippines by going to the cockpit in the afternoon, just as in Spain it is kept by going to the bullring. Introduced and exploited for a century, cockfighting was at the time one of the vices of the people, even more widespread than opium-smoking among the Chinese. To the cockpit went the poor man to risk what little he had in order to make money without working, as well as the rich man who went to amuse himself with the money left over from his parties and thanksgiving Masses; but at least the latter was staking his own money and his cock was trained with great care, perhaps with even greater care than his own son, his successor in the cockpit, so this was no ground for complaint.

Since the Government of that day allowed and even promoted cockfighting with the regulation that it should be held only in the public squares on holidays (to give everyone a chance to see, and to encourage by example?) from the end of High Mass until nightfall, the faces in the cockpit in San Diego this Sunday were familiar.

It was no different from those in other towns except in minor details. It had three main divisions. The entrance was a large rectangle approximately twenty metres by fourteen. There was a door in one of its sides, usually in the charge of a woman who collected the entrance fees. The Government took a proportion of these fees, amounting to some hundreds of thousands of pesos a year, and it was said that the money vice thus paid for its freedom was used to build magnificent schools, bridges, and highways, and to institute awards for the development of agriculture and commerce. Blessed the vice that produced such excellent results!

In this compartment of the cockpit might be found the peddlers of betel-nut, cigars, sweetmeats, and other eatables; here also were many young boys with their fathers or uncles, who were thus solicitously introducing them to the secrets of adult life.

This enclosure led to another slightly larger one, a kind of lobby where the public gathered before an actual cockfight. Here were to be found the majority of the fighting cocks, held to the ground by a cord fastened to a bone or wooden nail; here were the gamblers, fanciers, and gaffers. Here bets were crossed, form studied, money borrowed amid oaths, promises, and loud laughter. In one corner a sportsman handled his favourite cock, stroking its brilliant plumage; elsewhere, another counted and studied the scales on a game cock's legs; still others recounted the feats of past victors. But there were also to be seen many crestfallen gamblers, holding a plucked carcass by its legs; the bird that had been its master's favourite for months, fondled, watched over day and night, the centre of so many dazzling hopes, was now only a carcass to be sold for a peseta and cooked with ginger and eaten that very night. *Sic transit gloria mundi!* So doth the glory of the world pass away! The loser returned home to his anxiously waiting wife and ragged children, both penniless and cockless. Of all those golden dreams, the solicitude of months from daybreak to nightfall, of all the work and hardship, there only remained a peseta, ashes after so much smoke.

In this lobby there was no one so stupid that he did not have a voice, or so careless that he did not consider matters conscientiously, feeling the weight of the rival cocks, examining their every aspect, stretching out their wings, fingering their muscles. Some men were fashionably dressed and were followed and surrounded by those who fancied their fighting cocks. Others, dirty, their gaunt faces marked by vice, anxiously attended the movements of the wealthy and placed bets for them; pockets can be emptied of their money but not the heart of its passions. Here were no long faces; the indolent, apathetic, taciturn Filipino was not to be found here; all was movement, passionate, eager, driven by a thirst only sharpened by the muddy waters with which one thought to slake it.

This place led to the pit proper or ring, whose floor, surrounded by a bamboo fence, was higher than the other two compartments. In its upper part, almost reaching the roof, were stands for the spectators or, for they came to the same thing, the gamblers. During the fights these stands were filled with men and boys, shouting, cheering, sweating, quarreling, swearing: fortunately there were almost never women there. In the ring itself were the men of distinction, the wealthy, the famous gamblers, the concessionaire and the referee. The birds fought on the perfectly leveled ground, from which

Destiny distributed laughter or tears, plenty or want.

This Sunday the Mayor, Capitan Pablo, Capitan Basilio, and Lucas, the scar-faced man who had felt the death of his brother so keenly, were early at the cockpit.

Capitan Basilio approached one of the townsmen and asked:

'Do you know which bird Capitan Tiago is fighting today?'

'I don't know, sir, but two were delivered to him this morning. One of them is the red and white cock that defeated the Consul's green one.'

'Do you think my black and white can fight him?'

'Of course. I'll bet my house and shirt on it.'

Capitan Tiago arrived at this point. Like all the big gamblers, he was wearing a Chinese linen shirt, woolen trousers, and a straw hat. Two servants followed him, carrying the red and white bird and a huge white cock.

'Sinang tells me María is getting better and better every day,' said Capitan Basilio.

'Her fever's gone, but she hasn't got her strength back yet.'

'Did you lose last night?'

'A little. I know you won. Shall we see if I can get it back from you?'

'Do you want to fight the red and white?' asked Capitan Basilio, taking the bird from its handler and studying it.

'It depends. Depends on the betting.'

'How much will you bet?'

'Nothing less than two.'

'Have you seen my black and white?' asked Capitan Basilio and signalled a man, who brought a small bird over.

Capitan Tiago looked it over, and after weighing it and studying its leg scales, returned it to the handler.

'How much would you put on it?' he asked.

'Anything you say.'

'Two and a half?'

'Three?'

'Three it is.'

'For the next one.'

'The circle of gamblers and onlookers quickly spread the news that two famous birds would be fighting each other; each had its own history and merited fame. Everyone wanted to see and examine the two celebrities; opinions were given and prophecies made.

Voices were raised in the increasing hubbub; the ring was filling up and the stands were being taken by storm. The handlers were carrying two birds to the pit, one red, the other white, already armed but with the gaffs still sheathed. Shouts were heard for the white and one or two for the red. The white was obviously the favourite.

Constabulary soldiers were moving about in the crowd. They were not in uniform but neither were they in civilian clothes. Denim trousers with red stripes, shirts stained blue from their jackets, fatigue caps: this was a disguise in keeping with their manner. They gambled as they policed, and disturbed the order which they were said to keep.

Amid the shouts, the waving hands jingling coins, the last minute searches for money, the pledges of a carabao or the next harvest, two young men, who appeared to be brothers, looked enviously at the gamblers. They approached some with embarrassed whispers, but nobody paid any attention to them and they grew more downcast with every rebuff, exchanging looks of chagrin and despair. Lucas observed them shyly with a malignant smile. Jingling some silver pesos in his hand he walked by the two brothers, shouting in the direction of the pit:

'Fifty to twenty on the white!'

The two brothers exchanged looks.

'I told you not to bet all our money the last time,' the elder brother muttered. 'If you had listened to me, we would have some money left now to bet on the red.'

The younger brother approached Lucas timidly and touched him on the arm.

'Oh, it's you, is it?' the latter exclaimed, turning and feigning surprise. 'Well, does your brother accept my proposition, or have you come to make a bet?'

'How do you expect us to be? We've lost everything.'

'Then you accept?' He doesn't want to. If you could give us a loan... you yourself said you know us...'

Lucas scratched his head, smoothed down his shirt, and answered:

'Of course I know you. You are Tarsilo and Bruno, a pair of strong young men. I know also that your brave father died because the soldiers were giving him a hundred strokes of the lash a day. And I know that you have no intention of avenging him.'

'Don't meddle in our affairs,' interrupted Tarsilo, the elder brother. 'That's unlucky. If we didn't have a sister, we'd have been sent to the gallows long before this.'

'Gallows? Only cowards, only those who have neither money nor influence, get sent to the gallows. Anyway, the mountains aren't too far away.'

'A hundred to twenty on the white!' cried a passer-by.

'Lend us four pesos... three... two,' pleaded the younger brother. 'We'll pay you back double. The fight is about to start.'

Lucas scratched his head again.

'Well, the money isn't mine. Don Crisóstomo gave it to me for those who want to fight for him, but I can see that you are not like your father. Now where was a man with guts. Well, no guts, no fun.'

And he walked away, though not too far.

'Come on, let's take him up. What difference does it make?' argued Bruno. 'Hanged or shot, it doesn't matter; we poor people are good for nothing else.'

'You're right, but think of our sister.'

Meantime the pit had been cleared; the cockfight was about to start. The shouting was dying down. Only the two handlers and the gaffer remained in the centre of the arena. At a signal from the referee, the gaffer unsheathed the spurs, and the fine razor gleamed bright and threatening.

The two brothers went up to the fence, downcast and silent, leaning their foreheads against the bamboo. A man approached them and said in their ear:

'Hundred to ten in the white, friend!'

Tarsilo stared at him stupidly. Bruno dug his elbow into his brother's side, and the latter replied with a grunt.

The handlers held the birds with subtle skill so as not to be slashed by the razors. A breathless silence fell; one might have thought that all present, except for the two handlers, were dolls out of some nightmare waxworks. The gamecocks were brought together, the head of one held tight while the other pecked at it and infuriated it, afterwards the reverse. Every duel must be fought on equal terms, be it between Parisian cocks o' the walk or between Filipino gamecocks. Then the birds were brought face to face, nearer and nearer, so that each wretched fowl might recognize the enemy that had plucked out its feathers and which it now must fight. Their hackles rose and their small round eyes met, vibrant with hatred. The moment had come: they were placed on the ground at a certain distance from each other and left alone.

They advanced slowly, their steps audible on the hard ground; no one in the cockpit spoke or breathed. Raising and lowering their heads as if measuring each other with their eyes, the gamecocks uttered sounds, threatening or perhaps scornful. They caught sight of the razor blades, gleaming with a cold blue light; danger stimulated them, and they approached each other with determination. But a step apart, they stopped, and with fixed eyes lowered their heads and raised their hackles. At that moment blood rushed into their tiny brains, their anger flashed like lightning and with all their natural courage they hurled themselves impetuously upon each other, beak against beak, breast against breast, steel spur against its fellow, wing to wing: but the blows were parried masterfully, and only a few feathers fell. They sized each other up once again. Suddenly the white cock leapt up, slashing with the deadly razor, but the red cock had bent its legs and lowered its head and the white cock hit only the empty air. As it landed it turned quickly to protect its back and faced the red cock. The latter attacked it furiously, but it defended itself with complete self-control. It was not the favourite for nothing. Everyone followed the ups and downs of the duel with the first drawing of blood; for the Filipino, following the laws of his Government, it was a duel that only death or flight could end. Blood soaked the ground of the pit; the brave encounters were repeated again and again; but victory remained uncertain. At last, in a supreme effort, the white cock hurled itself forward to give a final blow; it nailed its spur in one of the red cock's wings, where it was caught in the bones; but the white cock had itself been hit in the breast, and the two birds, panting, exhausted, drained of their life's' blood, one joined to the other, were still, until the white cock fell, blood spurting out of its beak, its legs jerking in its last agony. The red cock, bound to it by the wing, remained standing beside it, but little by little its own legs crumpled and its eyes closed.

The referee, in accordance with official regulations, declared the red cock the winner. A savage roar greeted the verdict, a roar heard through the town, sustained and long drawn out. Whoever heard it from afar would have understood that the favourite had lost. So it is among nations. The small nation that achieves a victory over a larger one tells and sings of it forever after.

'Did you see that?' Bruno asked his brother sulkily, when the white cock, the favourite, had lost. 'If you had believed me, we would have a hundred pesos by now. It's your fault we haven't a penny.'

Tarsilo did not answer but stared about him, as if looking for someone.

'There he is, talking to Pedro,' added Bruno. 'He's giving him money , a lot of money.'

It was true. Lucas was counting out silver coins into the hand of Pedro, Sisa's husband. They exchanged some words in secret and parted, apparently satisfied with themselves.

'Pedro has joined. Now that's a man who gets what he wants.'

Tarsilo remained grim and lost in thought, wiping the sweat from his forehead with his shirt-sleeve.

'Brother,' said Bruno, 'I'm joining up if you don't make up your mind. Our system is working, Capitan Tiago's cock must win the next fight, and we shouldn't throw away our chances. I want to place a bet in the next fight. What's the difference? We shall be avenging our father in any case.'

'Wait,' Tarsilo pleaded. They were both pale. 'I'm coming with you. You're right. We'll avenge our father.'

But he hesitated and again wiped away his sweat.

'What are you waiting for?' asked Bruno impatiently.

'Do you know what cocks are fighting in the next one? Is it worth it?'

'But haven't you heard? It is Capitan Basilio's against Capitan Tiago's. According to our system Capitan Tiago's bird can't lose.'

'Ah, well, I would bet on it too, but let's make sure.'

Bruno made a gesture of impatience, but followed his brother as the latter studies Capitan Tiago's gamecock, analyzing, thinking it over, reflecting, asking questions. The wretch was in a frenzy of doubt.

Bruno nervously harangued him:

'But don't you see that broad scale near its spur? Look at those claws — what more do you want? Look at the legs. Pull out the wings. And that split scale over the broad one—and that double scale!'

Tarsilo was not listening. He continued examining the bird. The tinkle of gold and silver was in his ears.

'Now let us look at Capitan Basilio's fighting cock,' he said in a strangled voice. Bruno tapped his foot, ground his teeth, but obeyed his brother.

They went to another group. There the fighting cock was being armed. A choice of spurs was being made, and the red silken binding cords waxed and rubbed.

Tarsilo covered the bird with a brooding and inscrutable look; he did not seem to see the gamecock but something else in the future. He drew his hand across his brow and asked his brother huskily:

'Ready?'

'Me? Long ago. I wouldn't have bothered to look at the damned birds.'

'It's because... because of our poor sister.'

'But haven't they told you that Don Crisóstomo will be our leader? Haven't you seen him going round with the Governor General himself? What chances are we taking?'

'And if we're killed?'

'What's the difference? Our father was killed under the whip.'

'You're right.'

The two brothers looked for Lucas among the various groups. As soon as they caught sight of him Tarsilo stopped.

'No, let's get out of here. This is ruin,' he cried.

'You go if you want to. I'm going to join.'

'Bruno!'

Unfortunately, a man came up to them and asked:

'Want to bet? I am for Capitan Basilio's.'

The two brothers did not reply.

'I'll give you odds.'

'How much?' asked Bruno.

The man counted his money; Bruno watched him breathlessly.

'I have two hundred pesos—fifty to forty.'

'No,' said Bruno firmly, 'make it...'

'All right, fifty to thirty..'

'Double it.'

'All right, it's my boss's cock, and I have just won. One hundred to sixty.'

'Done. Wait here, I'll get the money.'

'But I'll hold the stakes,' said the other, who did not put too much trust in Bruno's looks.

'It's all the same to me,' answered the latter, who put his trust in his fists. Turning to his brother he said: 'If you're staying, I'm going.'

Tarsilo reflected: he loved his brother and he loved gambling. He could not leave Bruno alone and he murmured: 'All right.'

They approached Lucas; the latter saw them coming and smiled.

'Sir,' said Tarsilo.

'What is it?'

'How much are you giving us?' asked the brothers.

'I've told you. If you get others to join in the surprise attack on the barracks, thirty pesos for each of you, and ten pesos for every one who joins you. If all goes well, a hundred pesos for each and every one, and double that for yourselves. Don Crisóstomo has a lot of money.'

'It's a deal,' said Bruno. 'Give us the money.'

' I knew you were as brave as your father. Come over here, so his killers won't hear us,' said Lucas, pointing to some Constabulary soldiers. In a corner, while he counted out the money to them, he said:

'Tomorrow Don Crisóstomo arrives with weapons. Day after tomorrow, about eight o'clock at night, go to the cemetery and I'll give you your last instructions. You still have time to look for others to join us.'

They parted. The two brothers seemed to have changed roles. Now Tarsilo was calm, Bruno pale.

48 • *Two Ladies*

WHILE Capitan Tiago was fighting his red and white gamecock, Doña Victorina was taking a walk through the town for the purpose of seeing for herself how indolent natives kept their houses and their fields. She had dressed herself as elegantly as possible, adorning her housecoat with all her ribbons and artificial flowers, so as to impress these provincials and show them how far they were below her sacrosanct person. On her lame husband's arm she strutted like a peacock along the streets of the town, to the amazement and wonder of its inhabitants. Cousin Linares had stayed behind.

'How ugly also the houses of these natives,' Doña Victorina began making a face. 'How can they live there already? Really, you must be a native to do it. And how bad manners, how proud yet! They meet us and they are not also taking off the hat. Come on, hit them on the hat already like the friars and the officers of the Constabulary are doing. Teach them good manners!'

'But suppose they hit me back?' Asked Dr. de Espadaña.

'That is why also you are a man!'

'But-b-b-but I'm lame!'

Doña Victorina was beginning to lose her temper. The streets were unpaved and the tail of her housecoat was growing dusty. Moreover the young girls she met along the way, and there were quite a number of them, lowered their eyes and failed to exclaim, as they should have done, over her elegant costume. Sinang's coachman, who was driving her and her cousin in an elegant open carriage, had the nerve to shout to Doña Victorina to get out of his way in such an imposing voice that she had actually done so, and could not protest: 'Look at that bum brown driver! I will complaining to his boss to educate his servants!'

Then she commanded her husband: 'Home!'

The latter, who feared a storm was brewing, wheeled round obediently on his crutch.

They met the lieutenant and exchanged greetings, but this only sharpened Doña Victorina's discontents. The officer had not only failed to compliment her on her dress but had eyed it almost mockingly.

'You must not shake hands with a lieutenant only,' she told her husband when he was out of earshot. 'Besides he only touched his helmet and you are already taking off your hat. You do not know protocol!'

'But he is the c-c-c-c-commanding officer here!'

'Never mind. What about us, are we natives?'

'I suppose you're right,' he agreed, anxious to avoid a quarrel.

They were passing in front of the officer's house. Doña Consolación was at her window as usual, dressed in her flannel shirt and smoking a cigar. The house was rather low; they exchanged looks. Doña Victorina had a good eyeful; the Muse of the Constabulary in turn looked her over coolly from head to foot, and then, sticking out her lower lip, turned her face away and spat. This brought Doña Victorina's patience to an end and, leaving her husband with nothing to lean on, she drew herself up before Doña Consolación, in such a rage that she was unable to say a word. Doña Consolación slowly turned her head again, coolly looked her over once more, and spat a second time with even greater contempt.

'What's eating you Doña?' she asked.

'Can you telling me, Madam, why you looking at me like that?' Doña Victorina finally managed to demand. 'Are you jealous?'

'Me? Jealous? With you?' asked Doña Consolación scornfully. 'Yes, I am jealous with your ringlets!'

'Come, my dear,' said the doctor, 'don't pay her any attention.'

'Let me only teaching a lesson to this low-class-no-good,' replied his wife, giving her husband such a push that he almost fell flat on his face. Then turning back to Doña Consolación, she warned:

'Be careful only with whom you are talking! Maybe you think I am from the province or a hootchie-kootchie of the soldiers! In my house in Manila, if only lieutenant, no entrance, but must waiting by the door!'

'Excuse me, Your Excellency Madame *Sanamabits!* Maybe lieutenants are not entering, but physically unfit like that can entering!' And Doña Consolación let out a roar of laughter.

Had it not been for the rouge on her cheeks, Doña Victorina might have been seen to blush; she attempted to bring the matter to blows, but the sentry at the house door stopped her. Meantime a crowd had been gathering in the street.

'Pay attention to me only, I am going down, a high-class person talking to you. Do you want to wash my cloths? I give you money. Maybe you are thinking I do not know you are only laundrywoman!'

Doña Consolación drew herself up angrily. That bit about the laundry hurt!

'Are you thinking also we do not know what kind of people you are and your companion? Never mind, my husband told me already. Madam, maybe I have one man only, and you how many already? Somebody was too hungry to eat the left-overs of everybody else!'

Doña Victorina had been hit in the bulls-eye; she rolled up her sleeves, closed up her fists, clenched her teeth, and cried:

'All right, you dirty sow, come down and I am going to smack your stinking mouth! You are sleeping with a battalion! You are already born a whore!'

Doña Consolación suddenly disappeared from the window and was soon seen running downstairs, brandishing her husband's whip.

Don Tiburcio tearfully placed himself between them, but they would have come to blows if the lieutenant had not arrived.

'Ladies, Don Tiburcio!'

'You are better education your wife, buying her more better cloths, and if you are not having money yet, you are better stealing from the peoples because you have soldiers!' Doña Victorina shouted.

'Here I am already, Madam, why are you not smacking my mouth? You are having only saliva and tongue, Madam Excellency!'

'Madam!' cried the furious lieutenant. 'Be thankful that I remember you are a woman, otherwise I would kick you to Kingdom Come with all your ringlets and ribbons!'

'Lieu-t-t-t-tenant!'

'Go away, sawbones, and get your pants back!'

It would be indiscreet to describe the ensuing hubbub of words and gestures, the screams, insults, and name-calling; skeletons were dragged out of cupboards; four people speaking at once and saying such truths that the prestige of their class was irreparably damaged. The onlookers did not understand all that was said, but they enjoyed it nevertheless, and waited for everything to be settled with blows. Unfortunately, the parish priest entered the scene and imposed a truce.

'Gentlemen, ladies, shame! Lieutenant!'

'None of your business, you sneaking rebel!'

'Don Tiburcio, please take your wife home. Madam, please, some discretion!'

'Tell it to those racketeers!'

'But gradually the dictionary of epithets was exhausted, the history of each pair's shamelessness came to an end, and they began to withdraw amid threats and insults. Father Salví livened up the show even more by dashing from one side to the other. If the newspaper correspondent had only been present!

'We are returning already to Manila and will consulting the Governor General!' Doña Victorina told her husband in a perfect fury. 'You are not a man, waste only your trousers!'

'B-b-b-but, my dear, what about the s-s-s-soldiers? I am lame!'

'You must challenging to a duel the C.O. Maybe pistols, maybe sabres. If not, if not...'

And she looked threateningly at his denture.

'Ch-ch-ch-child, I have never even had my hand on a p-p-p—.' Doña Victorina didn't allow him to finish. With a superb gesture she snatched out his denture, threw it down on the street, and stamped it shapeless. He, midway to tears, and she, flashing with rage, arrived in Capitan Tiago's house as Linares was chatting with María Clara, Sinang, and Victoria; knowing nothing of the quarrel, he was upset no little by the appearance of his cousins. María Clara, who was reclining in an armchair in a confusion of pillows and blankets, was no less surprised by the extraordinary expression on the doctor's face.

'Cousin,' began Doña Victorina, 'you must challenging the C.O. to the duel or else...'

'But why?' asked the surprised Linares.

'You must challenging him already because or else I am telling everybody who you are only.'

'But, Doña Victorina!'

The three friends exchanged looks.

'What do you think? The C.O. is insulting us, and is saying what you are. The old *sanamabits* is coming down with whip, and this also, this is allowing more insultings. He is a man, yet!'

'Oh, they've had a fight and we've missed it!' cried Sinang.

'The lieutenant knocked the doctor's teeth in,' added Victoria.

'We are already going to Manila, and you are stay here to challenge the C.O. or else. Or else I am telling Don Santiago that it is lying only what you are telling him.'

'But, Doña Victorina, Doña Victorina,' the distraught Linares cut her short, coming closer, 'do please calm yourself, and do not please make me recall...' he added in a whisper: 'Don't be imprudent, now of all times.'

It was at this point that Capitan Tiago returned from the cockpit, tired and sighing, his gamecock had been defeated.

Doña Victorina did not give him much time for sighing; she told him what had happened in few words and many insults, placing herself, of course, in a good light.

'Linares is challenge him, you know? Or else, you must not also let him marry your daughter. If he is not more braver, he does not deserving Clarita.'

'So you are getting married to that gentleman?' asked Sinang, her bright eyes filling up with tears. 'I knew you were discreet, I did not know you were so fickle.'

María Clara, pale as a wax, half raised herself and stared with horror at her father, Doña Victorina, and Linares. The latter blushed, Capitan Tiago lowered his eyes, and the lady added:

'Clarita, remember only, do not get married to a man who has no pants. Maybe even the dogs are insulting you.'

The girl did not reply and asked her friends to take her to her room; she did not feel she had the strength to go there by herself. They helped her to her feet, and their round arms about her waist, her head on the shoulder of the lovely Victoria, she retired to her bedroom.

That same night the Espadañas packed up their things, presented Capitan Tiago with the bill, amounting to several thousands of pesos, and the next day, very early, set out for Manila in their host's coach. To the bashful Linares they assigned the role of avenger.

49 • A Puzzle

The dark swallows will come flying back....

—Becquer

AS Lucas had foretold, Ibarra arrived the following day. His first call was on the family of Capitan Tiago; he wanted to see María Clara to tell her that His Most Illustrious Excellency the Archbishop had restored him to the good graces of the Church, and had indeed written in his own hand a letter of recommendation to the parish priest, which Ibarra carried with him. Aunt Isabel was overjoyed; she had a great liking for Ibarra and did not look with favour on the marriage of her niece to Linares. Capitan Tiago was not at home.

'Come in, come in,' she urged Ibarra. 'María, Don Crisóstomo is again in a state of grace, the Archbishop has ex-excommunicated him.'

But the young man stood as if paralysed, the smile vanished from his lips, and he was unable to say a word: Linares was standing by the balcony at María Clara's side, weaving wreaths with flowers and leaves from the climbing vines; roses and *sampagas* lay scattered on the floor. María Clara, reclining in an armchair, wan, pensive, with a despondent look, was toying with an ivory fan not one bit whiter than her slender fingers.

On seeing Ibarra Linares paled, while María Clara blushed crimson. She tried to rise, but her strength failed her, and she lowered her eyes and dropped her fan.

An embarrassing silence lasted for a few seconds. Finally, Ibarra managed to step forward and to mumble uncertainly:

'I have just arrived. I hurried over to see you. I find you better than I thought.'

María Clara seemed to have been struck dumb; she said not a word and kept her eyes lowered.

Ibarra looked Linares over from head to foot, a look which the shy young man met with dignity.

'Well, now, I see that my coming was not expected,' said Ibarra slowly. 'Forgive me, María, for not letting you know I was calling. I shall explain myself some other time. We shall see each other again, surely.'

The final words were accompanied by a glance at Linares. María Clara raised her beautiful eyes to him; they seemed to him so pure and sad, so eloquent and pleading that he stopped in confusion.

'Can I call tomorrow?'

'You know that, where I am concerned, you are always welcome,' she whispered.

Ibarra left, outwardly calm, but with his head awhirl and a cold fear in his heart. What he had just seen and felt was incomprehensible. What was it, fickleness, a slight, a betrayal?

'She's a woman, after all,' he muttered.

Almost inadvertently he reached the school site. The work was very far advanced. Master Juan, still with his metre-stick and plumbstring, went to and fro among the work-gangs. He came running when he saw Ibarra.

Don Crisóstomo,' he said, 'so you are here at last. We were all waiting for you. Look at the walls now; they are already up one metre ten. In two days they will be a man's height. And I have used only the best hardwood; I have ordered only the best also for the woodwork upstairs. Do you want to inspect the basement?'

The laborers greeted the young man respectfully and stepped up their work when he was around. For this part Ibarra tried to show as much satisfaction as was possible for him in his state of mind.

'Now here I have taken the liberty of digging a sewer system,' added Master Juan. 'It will lead to a tank thirty paces away, which will serve to fertilise the garden. There was nothing about this in the plans. Does it displease you?'

'On the contrary, I approve, and I congratulate you on the idea. You are a real architect. From whom did you learn your trade?'

'From myself, sir,' the old man answered modestly.

'Oh, before I forget. Just in case anybody has any scruples about working for me, but does not dare bring it up, let them know I am no longer excommunicated. The Archbishop has even asked me to dinner.'

'Well, sir, we don't pay much attention to these excommunications. We have all been excommunicated, even Father Damaso himself, and he does not seem to have lost any weight over it.'

'How's that?'

'No doubt about it. A year ago he beat up his vicar, and his vicar is just as much a priest as he is. Who bothers about these excommunications?'

Ibarra caught sight of Elias among the workers. The latter touched his forelock to him like the others, but gave him a look as if to warn him that he had something to say.

'Master Juan,' said Ibarra, 'could you bring me the payroll?'

When the master-builder went off to fetch it, Ibarra approached Elias, who was lifting a heavy stone block single-handed and placing it on a wheel-barrow.

'If you can let me have a few hours of your time, take a walk this evening along the lake and get into my boat. I have to talk to you about important matters,' said Elias, moving away when he saw Ibarra nod.

The overseer brought the payroll, but Ibarra read and re-read it in vain; it did not carry the name of Elias.

Ibarra took his leave and went to see the schoolmaster.

50 • *Spokesman of the Oppressed*

THE sun had not yet set when Ibarra stepped into the boat of Elias along the lake shore. He looked annoyed.

'I am sorry, sir,' said Elias with a certain discouragement; 'forgive me for daring to make this appointment with you. I wanted to speak to you freely and here we shall not be overheard. We can be back in an hour.'

'You are wrong, my friend,' answered Ibarra, essaying a smile, 'you must take me to that town; you can see its church steeple from here. Fate sends me there.'

'Fate?'

'Yes. Fancy, on my way here I met the lieutenant, and he insisted on keeping me company. I thought of you: I am aware that he knows you; and so, to get rid of him, I told him I was going to that town. Now I shall have to spend the whole of tomorrow there because the fellow said he would look me up there tomorrow afternoon. He is really being much too friendly with me.'

'I appreciate your thoughtfulness,' answered Elias impassively, 'but you should have simply let him come along.'

'But what about you?'

'He would not have recognised me. The only time he saw me, he was not in a position to describe me for the military register.'

'What rotten luck I have today,' sighed Ibarra, thinking of María Clara. After a few seconds he asked: 'What did you have to tell me?'

Elias looked round him. Already they were far from shore; the sun had set and since there is scarcely any twilight in the tropics, the darkness of the night was spreading, lending brightness to the full moon.

'Sir,' began Elias in grave accents, 'I am the bearer of the wishes of many unfortunates.'

'Can I do anything for them?'

'A lot, sir, more than anybody else.'

Elias told him in a few words the conversation he had had with the commander of the outlaws, omitting the doubts and threats expressed by the latter. Ibarra heard him attentively. When Elias had finished, a long silence fell which Ibarra was the first to break.

'So they ask for...'

'Radical reforms in the armed forces, in the clergy, in the administration of justice, that is to say, a more paternal approach from the Government.'

'Reforms? In what sense?'

'For example, more respect for human dignity, greater security for the individual, less strength in the armed forces, less privileges for an organisation which so easily abuses them.'

'Elias,' replied the young man, 'I do not know who you are, but I have the feeling that you are not an ordinary man. You do not think and act like the others. You will understand me if I tell you that, although the present state of things has its defects, it would have even more should it be changed. I could get the friends I have in Madrid to make speeches, by paying them; I myself could speak to the Governor General; but my friends would accomplish nothing, the Governor General has not enough power to introduce such innovations and I myself would never take a step in that direction because I know very well that, while these institutions have their defects, they are necessary now; they are what is called necessary evil.'

Elias, astonished, raised his head and stared at Ibarra aghast.

'You too believe in necessary evils? You believe that to do good it is necessary to do evil?'

'No, I believe in the necessary evil as I believe in those drastic treatments we use when we want to cure a disease. Now, then, the country is an organism which suffers from a chronic sickness, and to cure it the Government feels compelled to use means which, if you wish, are harsh and violent but useful and necessary.'

'It's a bad doctor, sir, who only seeks to correct and suppress symptoms without trying to determine the cause of the illness, or knowing it, fears to go after it. The Constabulary has only one purpose: to repress crime by force and terror, a purpose which is not achieved except by chance. Furthermore, you must consider, sir, that society can only be hard on individuals when it has first furnished them with the means necessary for their moral improvement. In our country there is no organised society as such since the people and the Government are not united; the latter therefore should be lenient, not only because it wants to be judged leniently, but also because the individual, neglected and abandoned by the Government, is less responsible precisely because he has received so little instruction in his duties. Moreover, using your own comparison, the treatment applied to the country's ills is so destructive that it makes itself felt only in those parts of the organism which are healthy, weakening their vitality and preparing the way for the spread of the disease. Would it not be more reasonable instead to strengthen those parts of the organism that are sick and to lessen the violence of the treatment?'

'To weaken the Constabulary would be to endanger the security of the towns.'

'The security of the towns!' cried Elias bitterly. 'It will soon be fifteen years that those towns have had the protection of the Constabulary, and look: we still have outlaws, we still hear that they sack towns and hold people up on the highways; robberies still take place and the robbers are not discovered; crime exists, and the real criminal goes about freely, but not the peaceful inhabitants of the town. Ask any honest citizen if he looks upon the Constabulary as a good thing, as a means of protection furnished by the Government and not as an imposition, a despotism whose excesses are more harmful than the depredations of the outlaws. True, these depredations are usually on a great scale, but they do not happen often, and a man is allowed to defend himself against them. But one cannot even protest against the impositions of the forces of law and order, and if these impositions are sometimes not so great in extent, they are on the other hand continuous and sanctioned by society. What is the effect of this organisation on the life of our towns? It paralyses communications because everybody is afraid of being harassed for petty causes. It is concerned with appearances rather than with fundamentals—one of the first symptoms of incapacity. A man is tied and beaten up because he has forgotten his identity card, no matter if he is a decent person with a good reputation. The officers think it is their first duty to exact a salute, willing or unwilling, even at night, and they are imitated in this by their subordinates, who use it as an excuse—although an excuse is never lacking —to man-handle and fleece the peasants. The sanctity of the home does not exist for them; not long ago they entered a house in Kalamba through the window and beat up a peaceful inhabitant to whom their commanding officer owed money and favours. There is no security for the individual: when they want their barracks or their houses cleaned, they go out and seize anyone who does not resist and make him work the whole day. Do you want to hear more? During these days of the fiesta they have permitted gambling, but have brutally disturbed the celebrations which were duly authorised. You saw yourself what the people think about them. What good has it done them to swallow their anger and place their hopes on human justice? If this, sir, is what you call maintaining peace and order...'

'I agree that there are evils,' replied Ibarra, 'but let us accept the evils for the sake of the good things that go with them. The Constabulary may not be perfect, but, believe me, the fear it inspires prevents an increase in the number of criminals.'

'Say rather that this fear increases their number,' Elias corrected him. 'Before the creation of this organisation almost all criminals, with the exception of a very few, were driven to crime by hunger; they looted and robbed to stay alive, but when times were easier, the highways were once more safe. Outlaws could be scared away even by the municipal policemen and their primitive weapons – those poor brave policemen, so libeled by writers about our country, whose right is to die, whose duty is to fight, and whose reward is a sneer. Now outlaws are outlaws for life. One misdemeanour, one felony punished with inhumanity, one gesture of resistance against the excesses of authority, is enough, with the fear of atrocious tortures, to exile them forever from society, and condemn them to kill or be killed. The Constabulary's terrorism shuts the doors of repentance, and, since an outlaw fights and defends himself in the mountains better than the soldier whom he flouts, the result is that we cannot extinguish the evil we have created. Remember what was accomplished by the prudence of Governor General de la Torre; the amnesty which he granted to these unfortunates proved that the outlaws in the mountains are still human beings, and are only waiting for an amnesty. A regime of terror is useful when a people are enslaved, when there are no caves in the mountains, when the ruling power can place a sentry behind every tree, and when the body of the slave has only a stomach and intestines! But when a desperate man fighting for his life feels his arm stiffen, his heart beat, and his whole body fill up with spleen, can terrorism extinguish the fire on which it pours more fuel?'

'When you talk like that, Elias, you confuse me. I would believe you were right had I not my own convictions. But note one fact—do not take offence because I make an exception of you. Who asks for these reforms? Almost all of them felons or those who are very close to it.'

'Present or prospective felons—but why are they what they are? Because their peace has been broken, their happiness torn up by the roots, their most cherished affections outraged, and because, when they thought to seek protection from the law, they were convinced that they could depend only on themselves. But you are wrong, sir, if you believe that only felons ask for reforms; go from town to town, from house to house, listen to the hidden complaints of every family, and you will be convinced that the evils which the Constabulary prevents are not greater, perhaps less, than those which it inflicts continuously. Shall we conclude from this that all these citizens are felons? Then why defend them from other felons? Why not destroy them all?'

'There is an error in your reasoning which escapes me at this moment, some error of principle which can be refuted by experience, for in Spain, our Motherland, this organisation renders and has rendered very great services..'

'I do not doubt it. Perhaps its organisation is better there, its personnel more carefully selected. Perhaps, also, Spain needs it, but not the Philippines. Our customs, our character, which are always used as arguments when it is a question of denying us a right, are wholly forgotten when it is wanted to impose something on us. Tell me, sir, why have other countries, which, more than the Philippines, should resemble Spain because they are her neighbours, not imitated this institution? And is this the reason why they have even less train robberies, less riots, less murders, and why less people knife one another in the streets of their capitals?'

'My friend,' said Ibarra thoughtfully, ' this should be studied with great care. If I find after investigation that these grievances are justified, I shall write to my friends in Madrid, since we have no official representatives in Parliament there. Meantime, do believe that the Government has need of a body of men with that unlimited power and authority which it needs to make itself respected.'

'That, sir, would be true if the Government were at war with the people, but for the Government's own good we should not lead the people to believe that they and the Government are on opposite sides. But if such is the case, if we prefer force to a good name, we should consider well to whom we give such unlimited power and authority. So much power placed in human hands, the hands of ignorant and willful men, without moral training, without proven honesty, is a weapon placed in the hands of a madman let loose in unarmed crowd. I admit, and I want to believe like you, that the Government needs this strong right arm, but it should choose it well, from among the most worthy, and since it prefers to confer authority on itself rather than receive it from the people, let it at least show that it knows how to do so.'

Elias was speaking with passion and enthusiasm; his eyes were flashing and his voice vibrant. An impressive pause followed. The boat, undisturbed by the paddle, seemed to float motionless on the water; the moon shone splendidly in the dark blue sky; on the distant shore a few lights gleamed.

'And what else do they ask?' Ibarra wanted to know.

'The reformation of the clergy,' replied Elias with glum discouragement. 'The unfortunate ask for greater protection from...'

'From the religious Orders?'

'From their oppressors.'

'Has the Philippines forgotten what she owes to these Orders? Has she forgotten her immense debt of gratitude to those who redeemed her from error and gave her the True Faith, to those who shielded her from the tyranny of civil power? This is the evil result of not teaching the history of our country.'

Elias, surprised, could scarcely believe what he heard.

'Sir,' he answered gravely, 'you accuse the people of ingratitude. Permit me, one of the suffering people, to defend them. If favours are to be acknowledged, they should be disinterested. We need not talk about such commonplaces as duty or Christian charity. Let us put history aside and forbear from asking what Spain did to the Jews who gave all Europe one Book, one Faith, and one God, or what she did to the Arabs who gave her culture, who themselves tolerated her religion, and who awakened her national self-consciousness, dormant, almost dead, under Roman and Visigothic rule. But you say that the religious Orders gave us the True Faith and redeemed us from error. Do you call external practices the True Faith, or the commerce in girdles and scapulars, religion; or the stories of miracles and other fairy tales that we hear every day, the truth? Is this the law of Jesus Christ? God did not have to be crucified for this, nor we assume the obligation of eternal gratitude, superstition existed long before this, all that was needed was to organise it and raise the price of the merchandise. You will tell me that imperfect as our present religion may be, it is preferable to the one we had before; I believe you and I agree with you, but it is too expensive, for we have paid for it with our national identity, with our independence. For its sake we have given to its priests our best towns, our fields, and even our savings, which are spent on the purchase of religious trinkets. A product of foreign manufacture has been imported here; we have paid for it; and we are even. You speak to me of the protection given to our people by the religious Orders against the early Spanish conquerors who were given full dominion over the lives and possessions of the natives in lands assigned to them. I could answer you that it was precisely because of the religious Orders that we fell into the power of these men. But I admit that a genuine faith and a true love of humanity inspired those first missionaries who came to our shores; I recognise our debt of gratitude to those noble-hearted men; I know that the Spain of that age abounded in heroes of all kinds, religious, political, civil, and military. But because the forerunners were virtuous, are we to submit to the abuses of their degenerate descendants? Because we received great benefits, are we committing a crime in protecting ourselves against great injuries? The people do not ask for the abolition of the religious Orders, but only for the reforms required by new circumstances and necessities.'

'I love our country, Elias, as you may love her; I understand somewhat of what is wanted; I have listened attentively to what you have said. Yet, my friend, for all that, I think we have been rather carried away by emotion. I see less need for reforms in this field than anywhere else.'

'Is it possible?' asked Elias throwing up his hands despondently. 'You do not see the need for reforms, you, whose family misfortunes...'

'I do not consider myself and my own misfortunes when it comes to the security of the Philippines and the interests of Spain,' Ibarra interrupted him hotly. 'To keep the Philippines for Spain it is necessary for the friars to continue as they are, and the good of our country lies in her union with Spain.'

Elias seemed to be listening still even when Ibarra had stopped; his face was grim, and his eyes had lost their brightness.

'Is it true that the missionaries won this country for Spain,' he answered. 'But do you believe that Spain will keep it because of the friars?'

'Yes, and only because of them; all those who have written about the Philippines are of the same opinion.'

'Oh,' cried Elias, throwing down his paddle into the boat dejectedly. 'I would not have believed you had such a poor opinion of the Government and of the people. Why don't you come out and say you despise them both? What would you say of a family that lives in peace because of the intervention of a stranger? A people that obey because they are deceived; a Government that rules by deceit; a Government that does not know how to make itself loved and respected for its own sake. Forgive me, sir, but I believe that your Government is stupid and suicidal when it is glad that such things are believed. I thank you for your kindness in listening to me. Now, where do you want me to take you?'

'No,' answered Ibarra, 'we must thrash it out. We must know who is right on such an important matter.'

'Forgive me, sir,' answered Elias, shaking his head. 'I am not eloquent enough to convince you. Although I have had a little schooling, I am only a native. You will always doubt my right to say anything, and whatever I may say will always be suspect. Those who have given a contrary opinion are Spaniards, and, as such, although they may spout trivialities and stupidities, their accent, their titles, and their race make what they say sacred, and give them such authority that I shall never try again to argue with them. Then again, when I see that you, who love our country, whose own father rests beneath these quiet waters, who have found yourself provoked, insulted, and persecuted, maintain such opinions in spite of everything, in spite of your education, I begin to doubt my own convictions and to admit the possibility that the people may be wrong. I must tell those unfortunates who have placed their faith in men to place it in God and their own strength. I thank you again; tell me where you want me to take you.'

'Elias,' said Ibarra, 'your bitter words touch my heart and make me doubt in turn. Well, how can I help it? I was not brought up among the people, and perhaps I do not know what they need. I spent my childhood in the Jesuit school and grew up in Europe. My opinions were formed by books, and I know only what men have brought to light; I know nothing of the things that remain hidden, that have not been written about. For all that, I love our country like you do, not only because it is the duty of every man to love the country that gave them life and which will perhaps be his last refuge, not only because all my most beautiful memories are alive in it, but also because I owe it and will owe it my happiness.'

'And I, because I owe it my misfortunes', Elias murmured.

'Yes, my friend, I know you suffer, that you are unfortunate. That is why
you see the future so dark; that is what influences your way of thinking. It
makes me listen to your grievances with certain reservations. If I could only
gauge your motives, know some of your experiences in the past...'

'My misfortunes have another source. If I were sure that it would have
some useful purpose, I would tell you about them; I have never made a secret
of them, and besides they are well known to many.'

'Perhaps if I knew them I might change my mind. You know that I distrust
theories; I prefer to be guided by facts.'

Elias remained silent for a few moments.

'In that case,' he replied, 'I shall tell you my story in a few words.'

51 • *The Story of Elias*

'ABOUT sixty years ago my grandfather lived in Manila, working as a
book-keeper in the offices of a Spanish merchant. My grandfather was then
very young but was already married and had a son. One night the merchant's
warehouse caught fire from an unknown cause; the fire spread through-out
the entire establishment, and then to many others. The losses were very
heavy; a scapegoat had to be found; and the merchant brought charges against
my grandfather. He protested his innocence in vain; he was poor and could
not retain eminent counsel, and so he was condemned to be paraded along
the streets of Manila and publicly flogged. This degrading punishment, a
thousand times worse than death, was still in use until not so long ago. My
grandfather, forsaken by all except his young wife, found himself bound to
a horse, followed by a sadistic crowd, and flogged at every street corner, before
the men who were his brothers and near the many temples of a God of Love.
When the wretch, condemned to perpetual infamy, had sated the vengeance
of men with his blood, his sufferings, and his screams, they had to cut him
loose from the horse for he had lost consciousness —would he had lost his
life! In a refinement of cruelty, they set him free. His wife, who was then
pregnant, went from door to door begging in vain for work or alms for her
sick husband and helpless child. But who would trust the wife of a convicted
arsonist? So she became a whore.'

Ibarra started.

'Oh, don't let it disturb you. Prostitution was no longer dishonourable either for her or for her husband; honour and shame were no longer for the likes of them. The husband's wounds healed, and he came with his wife and child to hide in the mountains of this province. Here his wife gave birth to a deformed and diseased foetus that was fortunately dead. Here they lived a few months longer, miserable, isolated, hated and avoided by all. My grandfather, unable to bear his misfortunes, and less courageous than his wife, hanged himself; seeing his wife sick and deprived of all help and care drove him to despair. The corpse rotted before the very eyes of the son, who could scarcely take care of his ailing mother. The stench revealed it to the authorities. Charges were brought against my grandmother and she was found guilty of not notifying the police; the death of her husband was also blamed on her, and the charge was believed, for a felon's wife who had turned whore was thought to be capable of anything. If she said anything under oath, she was only perjuring herself; if she wept, she lied; if she called on God, she blasphemed. However, they took pity on her because she was pregnant again, and did not have her flogged until she had given birth. You know the friars propagate the belief that the only way to treat the natives is by beating them up; read what Father Gaspar de San Agustin has to say about it.

'Under such a judgment, a woman will curse the day her son is born; which is not only to lengthen her torment, but also to do violence to motherly love. Unfortunately, she was safely delivered of a son who, just as unfortunately, was born strong. Two months later the judgment was executed to the great satisfaction of men, who thus thought they had done their duty. No longer at peace in the mountains, she fled with her two sons to the neighbouring province, and there they lived like wild beasts, hating and hated. The elder of the two brothers, who could still remember his happy childhood in the midst of such misery, turned bandit as soon as he was strong enough. Soon the sanguinary name of Bálat ran from province to province, the terror of the towns, for in his desire for vengeance he put everything to the torch and to the sword. The younger brother, who had a naturally good heart, had resigned himself to living in opprobrium beside his mother; they lived on what the forest yielded, and clothed themselves in the rags that were thrown to them by travellers. Her name had been forgotten, and she was known only as a slut and a convict who had been publicly flogged. He was known only as his mother's son, because the gentleness of his character made people doubt that he was the son of the arsonist, and because the morals of the natives were always subject to suspicion. In the end the famous Bálat fell into the hands of the law, and human justice, which had done nothing to teach him virtue, demanded a strict accounting of his crimes. One morning the younger brother was looking for his mother, who had gone into the forest to look for mushrooms and had not returned. He found her stretched out on the ground by the highway, under a cotton tree, her face turned to the sky, her eyes staring out of their sockets, her fingers dug convulsively into the bloodstained earth. He glanced upward following the dead woman's eyes and saw, hanging from a branch of the tree, a basket, and inside the basket the bloody head of his brother.'

'My God!' exclaimed Ibarra.

'That is what my father said,' continued Elias coldly. 'Human society had dismembered the bandit's corpse; the trunk had been buried, but the limbs had been hung up in different towns. If you go some time from Kalamba to Santo Tomas you will still find the miserable *lomboy* tree where one of my uncle's legs hung rotting. Nature has cursed it and the tree neither grows nor gives fruit. The same thing was done with the other limbs, but the head, a man's best part, and the one most easily recognised, was hung near his mother's hut.'

Ibarra lowered his head.

'The young man fled like one accursed,' continued Elias. 'He fled from town to town, over mountains and valleys, and when he thought that he would no longer be recognized, went to work in the house of a rich man in the province of Tayabas. His industry, and the sweetness of his character, won him the esteem of all those who did not know his past. By dint of hard work and thrift he managed to accumulate a little capital, and, since the bad days had gone, and he was young, he dreamed of happiness. His good looks, his youth, and his now comfortable means, won him the love of a girl in the town. He did not dare to ask her hand in marriage for fear that his past should be discovered. But love was stronger, and they succumbed to passion. To save the girl's honour, he risked everything and asked for her hand; and everything was discovered when the necessary documents were looked up. The girl's father was rich; he succeeded in having charges brought against the young man; the latter did not try to defend himself, but admitted everything and was sent to prison. The girl gave birth to a boy and a girl, who were brought up secretly in the belief that their father had died, which was not difficult since at a tender age they had seen their mother die, and did not bother much with looking into their parentage. Since our grandfather was rich our childhood was very happy. My sister and I started our schooling together. We loved each other as only twins can before they know other kinds of love. While still very young I went to study in the Jesuit school, and my sister was sent to board in the convent school of La Concordia so that we should not be wholly parted. Our brief schooling over—we only wanted to be farmers—we went home to take possession of our grandfather's estate. We lived happily for some time; the future smiled on us. We had many servants; our fields were fruitful; and my sister was on the eve of marrying a young man whom she adored, and who returned her love. Then, on some money matter, and because of my then arrogant character, I antagonised a distant relative and one day he taunted me with my illegitimacy and my criminal descent. I thought it a calumny, and demanded satisfaction. Then the sepulchre in which lay so much rottenness was reopened, and the truth emerged to confound me. To our greater misfortune, we had had for years an old servant who endured all my caprices without ever leaving us, finding it enough to weep and sigh amid the scoffing of the other servants. I do not know how my relative found it out; the thing is that he had the old man haled into court and interrogated. The servant was our own father, who had clung to his beloved children. And I had beaten him up more than once! Our happiness vanished. I renounced our wealth; my sister lost her betrothed; and together with our father we left town. The thought that he had contributed to our misfortune shortened my father's days. I learned the sorrowful past from him. My sister and I were left alone.

'She wept much. In the midst of all the sorrows that piled up on us, she could not forget her love. Without a word of complaint she saw her betrothed marry another. I saw her waste away from day to day without being able to console her. One day she disappeared. I looked everywhere in vain for her; in vain made inquiries. Only six months later I learned that about that time, after a flood, the body of a girl, drowned or murdered, had been found on the beach of Kalamba. There was, it was said, a knife buried in her bosom. The town authorities issued notices of this discovery in the neighbouring towns, but nobody came forward to claim the body. No girl was missing. But by the description they gave me afterwards, of her dress, her jewels, the beauty of her face, and her abundant hair, I recognised my poor sister. Since then I go from province to province. My name and my story are known to many. I am said to do many things, and sometimes it is not true. But I do not pay much heed to human society, and I go my way. Such is my story in a few words, and the story of one of society's judgments.'

Elias stopped, and silently plied his paddle.

'I am beginning to believe you are not wrong when you say that the law should seek the common good by rewarding virtue and reforming the criminal,' Crisóstomo murmured. 'Only, such a thing is impossible. Utopian. Where would all the money come from, and all the officials?'

'What then is the use of all these priests who proclaim their mission of peace and charity? Is it more meritorious to pour water on a baby's head and touch his lips with salt in Baptism than awaken in the darkened conscience of the criminal that spark given by God to every man to guide him to virtue? Is it more human to accompany the condemned man to the gallows than to accompany him along the straight path that leads from vice to virtue? Is there no money for informers, executioners, and soldiers? These things are not only degrading but also expensive.'

'My friend, even though we wanted to do it, neither you nor I could achieve it.'

'It is true that by ourselves we are nothing. But take up the cause of the people, join them, do not turn a deaf ear to their voice, give an example to the rest, give us an idea of what it is to have a country.'

'What the people ask is impossible. It is necessary to wait.'

'Wait! To wait is to suffer.'

'If I were to ask for these reforms, they would laugh in my face.'

'And if the people were behind you?'

'Never! I would never be the one to lead the mob to take by force what the Government believes inopportune. If I should ever see the mob in arms, I would take the side of the Government and fight against it because I would not recognise my country in such a mob. I want my country's good, that is why I am building the schoolhouse, but I seek it through education, through progress. We cannot find our way without the light of knowledge.'

'Neither can freedom be won without a fight!' answered Elias.

'But I do not want that kind of freedom.'

'Without freedom, there can be no light,' retorted the boatman with spirit. 'You say you know little about your country. I believe it. You see nothing of the struggle that is being prepated, or the clouds on the horizon; the struggle begins in the field of ideas, but will end in the blood-stained arena of action. I hear the voice of God: woe to those who would resist Him, history has not been written for them.'

Elias was transfigured; he had stood up in the boat, and his manly face, uncovered and lighted by the moon, had some extraordinary quality. He shook his long hair and continued:

'Do you not see how everything awakens? Our people slept for centuries, but one day the lightning struck, and, even as it killed Burgos, Gómez, and Zamora, it called our nation to life. Since then new aspirations work on our minds, and these aspirations, now scattered, will one day unite under the guidance of God. God has not failed other peoples; He will not fail ours, their cause is the cause of freedom.'

A solemn silence followed these words. Meantime, the boat, carried imperceptibly by the current, neared the shore, Elias was the first to break the silence.

What shall I say to those who sent me?' he asked in a different tone.

'I have told you: that I deplore their condition, but that they should wait, for wrongs are not righted by other wrongs, and for our misfortunes all of us have a share of the blame.'

Elias did not reply. He lowered his head, continued paddling and, having reached the shore, said goodbye to Ibarra:

'I thank you, sir, for your consideration to myself. In your own interest I ask you to forget me from now on and not to recognise me in whatever circumstances you may find me.'

Having said this, he set out again, paddling towards a thicket further on along the shore. During the long passage he remained silent; he seemed to see nothing but the thousands of diamonds that with his paddle he raised from and returned to the lake, where they vanished in mystery among the blue waves.

He arrived at his destination at last. A man left the thicket and approached him.

'What shall I tell the commander?' he asked.

'Tell him that Elias will keep his word,' Elias answered sadly, 'if he does not die sooner.'

'When will you join us then?'

'When your commander believes that the hour of danger has come.'

'Very well. Goodbye.'

52 • Changes

THE diffident Linares was seriously worried; he had just received the following letter from Doña Victorina:

'Dere casin: In tree days I expecting to here from you dat de C.O. has kiling you or you him I do not want one more day to gobay without dat animal recib his panisment ifnot orelse and you do not chalenching him I am olready teling Don Santiago you ar neber praibet secretary op Praim Minister or joking-joking with him or meking whupi with Gobernor General also me teling Clarita you are ol blaf and I olso not gibing you one penny mor bat if you chalenching him I promise you everiting so meibi you are olredi chalenching him bat I warn you no alabais.

Yur labing casin

Victorina de los Reyes de de Espadaña

Sampaloc Mondey, 7 p.m.'

Matters were taking a grave turn. Linares knew Doña Victorina's character and what she was capable of doing; to ask her to be reasonable would be like asking a Customs inspector to be honest when he was determined to discover smuggled goods where there were none; to plead with her would be useless; to deceive her, worse; there was nothing left to do but to challenge the lieutenant.

'But how?' he mumbled to himself as he paced up and down. 'Supposing he is in an ugly mood when I call on him? Supposing I meet his wife? And who will want to be my second? The parish priest? Capitan Tiago? Why did I ever listen to that bore! Whose idea was it anyway to make me put on the dog, put up a bluff, make up those fairy stories? Whatever will this dear young lady think of me! This is what I get for being private secretary to all the members of the cabinet!'

Linares was immersed in these lugubrious meditations when Father Salví arrived. The Franciscan, to tell the truth, was thinner and paler than usual, but his eyes glittered with a singular light and a strange smile played about his mouth.

'All alone, Mr. Linares?' he greeted the young Spaniard, walking towards the living-room through whose half-opened door could be heard the sound of the piano.

Linares tried to smile.

'And Don Santiago?' added the parish priest.

Capitan Tiago made an appearance just at this moment, kissed the friar's hand, and relieved him of his hat and cane, smiling the smile of the blessed.

'Come, come,' said the parish priest as he entered the living-room followed by Linares and Capitan Tiago. 'I have good news for all of you. I have received letters from Manila which confirm the one Mr. Ibarra brought me yesterday. So, Don Santiago, the excommunication has been lifted and the impediment to the marriage is gone.'

María Clara, who was seated at the piano between her two friends, half rose, but her strength failed her and she fell back. Linares paled and looked at Capitan Tiago, who lowered his eyes.

'I am more and more attracted to that young Ibarra,' the parish priest continued. 'At first I misjudged him. He is rather hot-tempered, but afterwards he knows so well how to make amends that it is impossible to hold a grudge against him. If it were not for Father Dámaso!'

The parish priest shot a glance at María Clara, who was listening without taking her eyes off the music sheets, in spite of Sinang, who was pinching her under cover to express her delight, and who, if she had been alone, would have danced for joy.

'Father Dámaso?' asked Linares.

'Yes, Father Dámaso has said,' the parish priest continued without taking his eyes off Maria Clara, 'that as María Clara's godfather, he could not allow... but anyway, I think that if Mr. Ibarra asks his forgiveness, and I do not doubt he will, everything will be all right.'

María Clara stood up, gave an excuse, and went to her room, accompanied by Victoria.

'And if Father Dámaso does not forgive him?' Capitan Tiago asked in a hushed voice.

'Then... María Clara will understand... Father Dámaso is her spiritual father, after all. But I believe they will come to some understanding.' At this point footsteps were heard and Ibarra entered, followed by Aunt Isabel. His appearance had a very varied effect. He greeted Capitan Tiago affably, and the latter hesitated between a smile and tear. To Linares he gave a deep bow. Father Salví rose to his feet and stretched out his hand so cordially that Ibarra was unable to repress a look of wonder.

Don't be surprised, Father Salví told him. 'I was just singing your praises, as a matter of fact.'

Ibarra thanked him and went to Sinang's side.

'Where have you been all day?' she asked in her adolescent flow of chatter. 'We kept asking ourselves and wondering where that poor soul snatched from Purgatory could have gone to? And, of course, each of us had her own version.'

'May I know what they were?'

'No, it's secret, but I'll tell you anyway when we are by ourselves. Now tell us where you really were so we can see who was right.'

'No, that's a secret too, but I'll tell you alone if the gentlemen will excuse us.'

'Of course, of course,' said Father Salví. 'That's only to be expected.'

Sinang led Crisóstomo to one end of the living-room; she was delighted that she was going to learn a secret.

'Tell me, dear, is María angry with me?'

'I don't know, but she keeps saying it would be better for you to forget her, and then breaking down into tears. Capitan Tiago wants her to marry that gentleman over there, Father Dámaso too, but she doesn't say yes or no. This morning when we were asking after you, and I wondered if you had gone to pay court to somebody else she said she hoped so and burst into tears.'

Ibarra turned serious.

'Tell María I want to talk to her alone.'

'Alone?' Sinang asked with a frown and a quizzical look.

'All by ourselves, no, but I don't want that man around.'

'It will be difficult to arrange, but don't worry, I'll tell her.'

'And when shall I know the answer?'

'Tomorrow. Come to my house tomorrow. María never wants to be alone, so we are always with her. Victoria sleeps with her one night, and I the next. Tomorrow it's my turn. But listen, what's your secret? Are you going without telling me the most important thing of all?'

'That's true! Well, I was in Los Baños. I am going to set up an oil mill to make better use of the coconut groves there. Your father is to be my partner.'

'Is that all! What a secret!' cried Sinang out loud, in the tone of a money-lender who has been swindled. 'I thought...'

'Careful now, I don't want you to spread it round...'

'As if I'd want to,' replied Sinang wrinkling her nose. 'If it had been anything important I would have told my friends, but really, a mill for coconuts! Who cares about coconuts?'

And she scurried off to look for her friends.

Shortly afterward Ibarra took his leave; conversation in that group was obviously going to languish. Capitan Tiago had a sweet sour expression; Linares was silent and watchful; the parish priest was talking strangely with an air of false gaiety, and none of the young ladies had put in another appearance.

53 • *The Lucky Card*

THE moon was hidden in the cloudy sky. A cold wind, harbinger of the coming December, swept dry leaves and dust along the narrow path to the graveyard.

Three shadows were whispering to one another at the gate.

'Have you talked to Elias?' asked one voice.

'No. You know how strange and tight-lipped he is. But he must be one of us. Don Crisóstomo saved his life.'

'That is why I joined,' said the first voice. 'Don Crisóstomo has placed my wife for treatment in a doctor's clinic in Manila. I am going after the parish priest to settle my accounts with the priest.'

'And we're going after the barracks to show the soldiers that our father had sons.'

'How many will you be?'

'Five. Five will be enough. Don Crisóstomo's agent says we'll be twenty in all.'

'And if you don't succeed?'

'Quiet!' said one and all fell silent.

Another shadow could be seen approaching in the half-light, gliding along the cemetery wall. From time to time it stopped as if turning to look back; with reason, because twenty paces behind, another shadow followed, larger and somehow even more of a shadow, so lightly did it move and so swiftly disappear, as if the earth had swallowed it, every time the first shadow stopped and turned.

'I am being followed,' thought Lucas. 'Can it be the Constabulary? Did the head sexton lie to me?'

'They said they would meet here,' Elias thought. 'They must be up to no good when the two brothers hide it from me.'

The first shadow reached the cemetery gate at last and the three who were waiting there joined him.

'Is that you?'

'And you?'

'Let us split up. I have been followed. You will have the weapons tomorrow. It is for tomorrow night. Remember the rallying cry is Long live Don Crisóstomo! Now go.'

The three shadows disappeared behind the mud-walls. Lucas hid himself in the gate and waited in silence.

'Now let's see who has been following me,' he said to himself.

Elias advanced with the utmost care and then stopped to look round him.

'I'm too late. But maybe they'll be back.'

It was beginning to drizzle persistently and Elias in turn decided to take shelter inside the gate, thus coming face to face with Lucas in the pitch dark.

'Who are you?' asked Elias.

'And you?' countered Lucas coolly.

They paused, trying to recognise each other's voice and features.

'What are you waiting for here?' asked Elias.

'For the stroke of eight. I want the dead to pick a lucky card for me; I want to make money when I gamble tonight,' Lucas replied evenly. 'What about you?'

'Same thing.'

'I'm glad. I'll have company. I have a deck with me. On the first stroke of eight I'll deal out two cards, and two more on the second. The cards that move will be those chosen by the dead, and we must fight the spirits for them. Have you brought your pack of cards too?'

'No.'

'Well, then?'

'You're dealing for the dead, and I expect the dead to deal for me.'

'And if they don't?'

'Can't be helped. They haven't made gambling compulsory for the dead yet.'

There was a moment of silence.

'Have you come armed? How are you going to fight the spirits?'

'With my fists,' replied Elias.

'Oh damn, I remember now. The spirits won't choose lucky cards when there is more than one living person present, and there are two of us.'

'Really? Well, I'm not going.'

'Nor I. I need the money,' answered Lucas. 'But we can do one thing. Let's have a game between the two of us; the loser leaves.'

'All right,' agreed Elias with some reluctance.

'Then let's go in. Do you have matches?'

They entered the graveyard and searched in the darkness for a suitable place; soon enough they found a tombstone, on which they sat. Lucas took a deck of cards from his straw hat and Elias struck a match.

They stared at each other by its light, but made no sign of recognition.

'Cut,' said Lucas without taking his eyes off Elias.

Then he brushed away some bones which were on the tombstone, and laid down an ace and a queen. Elias kept striking one match after another.

'I bet on the queen,' he said, and marked his card by placing a vertebra on top of it.

'Call,' said Lucas, and after four or five cards drew a second ace. 'You lose,' he said. 'Now leave me alone to my business.'

Elias, without replying, went off into the darkness.

Some minutes later the church clock struck eight, and the bells rang out the hour of the Holy Souls, but Lucas made no move to gamble with the dead or call upon the spirits in accordance with superstition; instead he uncovered himself and muttered a few prayers, crossing himself repeatedly with the same fervour as that which undoubtedly filled the prefect of the Confraternity of the Most Holy Rosary in those moments.

It rained all night. By nine o'clock the streets were already dark and deserted. The oil lamps which every householder was bound to hang outside his windows scarcely illumined a radius of one metre; they seemed to have been lit merely to emphasise the darkness of the night.

Two Constabulary soldiers paced up and down a street near the church.

'It's chilly,' said one in Tagalog with a Visayan accent. 'We haven't caught any of the priest's servants yet, and there's that chicken coop of the lieutenant to repair. Ever since that other chap died, they haven't dared stick their noses out into the street. I'm bored.'

'Me too,' agreed the other. 'No robberies, no riots. Thank God, they say that fellow Elias is in town. The C.O. says that whoever catches him will not be whipped for three months.'

'Ah! Have you learned his description by heart?' asked the Visayan.

'Of course. Height: tall, according to the C.O., medium, according to Father Dámaso. Complexion: brown. Eyes: black. Hair: black. Nose: medium. Mouth: medium. Beard: none.'

'And distinguishing marks?'

'Black shirt, black trousers, woodcutter.'

'He won't get away. I can almost see him.'

'I won't mix him up with anybody else, even if they look alike.'

The two soldiers continued their patrol.

Once again two shadows were to be seen by the light of the street lamps, one following the other with great caution. A sharp 'Who goes there!' stopped them both. The first shadow answered in a shaking voice: 'Long live Spain!'

The soldiers took him by the arm to a street lamp in order to identify him. It was Lucas, but the soldiers exchanged doubtful looks.

'The C.O. said nothing about a scar,' said the Visayan. 'Where are you going?'

'To commission a Mass for tomorrow.'

'Have you seen Elias?'

'I don't know him, sir,' Lucas answered.

'I'm not asking you if you know him, stupid, we don't know him either. What we want to know is whether you have seen him.'

'No, sir.'

'Now, listen well, and I'll describe him to you. Height: sometimes tall, sometimes medium. Eyes and hair: black. All the rest, medium. Now,' said the Visayan, 'do you know him?'

'No, sir,' answered Lucas in a daze.

'Then get going, stupid!'

'Do you know why Elias is tall according to the C.O., and of medium height according to the priest?' the Tagalog asked the Visayan reflectively.

'No.'

'Because the C.O. was flat on his back in the mud when he saw Elias.'

'Why, that's right!' exclaimed the Visayan. 'You're smart. How come you are in the Constabulary?'

'I wasn't always a soldier. I used to be a smuggler,' replied the Tagalog smugly.

But the other shadow now caught their eye. They challenged him and took him to the light. This time it was Elias himself.

'Where do you think you're going?'

'I'm going after a man, sir, who insulted and beat up my brother. He has a scar on his face. Name of Elias.'

'What!' the soldiers exclaimed, looking at one another openmouthed and dashed to the church into which Lucas had vanished a few minutes earlier.

54 • *A Good Day can be Foretold by the Morning*

IT did not take long for the news to spread round town that many lights had been seen in the graveyard the night before.

The head of the Tertiaries spoke of lighted candles, and described their shapes and sizes but could not say how many there were for certain, although he had counted up to twenty. Sister Sipa, of the Confraternity of the Most Holy Rosary, could not bear it that a member of the rival brotherhood should boast of having alone witnessed this mark of heavenly grace, and, although she did not live near the graveyard, spoke of having heard weeping and sighing, and even thought she recognised the voices of certain persons with whom in other times she... But out of Christian charity she declared that she had not only forgiven them, but even prayed for them and kept their names to herself. This was saintliness beyond dispute, everyone agreed. Sister Rufa, it is true, did not have so sharp an ear, but she could not allow that Sister Sipa had heard what she herself had not, and so she had had a dream, she declared, in which many souls had passed before her eyes, and souls not only of the dead but even of some who were still alive; the souls in torment had begged her for some of the indulgences which she had so carefully accumulated and registered. She could give their names to the families concerned and only asked in return a small donation to help the Pope out in his daily needs.

A little boy, who looked after a herd of carabaos, and was foolish enough to assert that he had seen only one light and two men in the wide straw hats of peasants, scarcely escaped being beaten up. He swore he was telling the truth and called upon his carabaos to witness, but it was all in vain.

'Do you think you know more than the prefect of the Confraternity and the Sisters, you Freemason, you heretic?' they upbraided him with sharp suspicious looks.

The parish priest took to the pulpit and preached once more on Purgatory; and the pesos once more emerged from their hiding places to pay for Masses for the dead.

Meantime, oblivious of the souls in torment, Don Filipo was conversing with old Tasio, who was sick abed in his isolated house. The scholar— philosopher or fool—had been confined to his bed for quite some time past, laid low by a general debility that was rapidly increasing.

'Really, I don't know whether or not to congratulate you now that your resignation has been accepted. Before, when the Mayor so shamelessly overrode the wishes of the majority, it was right to resign. But now that you are in open conflict with the Constabulary, it is not so proper. In wartime one should remain at his post.'

'Perhaps, but not when the commanding general is the first to go over to the enemy,' objected Don Filipo. 'As you know, the very next day after the fiesta the Mayor released the soldiers whom I had managed to arrest, and since then he has refused to take a single step in the matter. I can do nothing without the consent of my superior.'

'You, by yourself, can do nothing, but together with the others, a lot. You should have used this opportunity to give the other towns an example. The rights of the people are superior to the ridiculous authority of the Mayor; it could have been a good lesson for a start, but you lost your chance.'

'And what could I have done against the representative of vested interests? Take Mr. Ibarra; he has bowed to the beliefs of the crowd; but do you think he really believes in excommunication?'

'You are not in the same situation. Mr. Ibarra wants to sow ideas, and to do that he must bend low and adjust himself to his material; your mission was to give the social structure a good shaking-up, and that requires strength and self-confidence. Moreover, the fight was not against the Mayor personally, but rather against any public officials who had abused their powers, disturbed the public order, and failed to do their duty, and if you had presented it in those terms, you would not have left without support; our country today is not what it was twenty years ago.'

'Do you really believe that?' asked Don Filipo.

'Don't you feel it to be true?' countered the old man, propping himself up in bed. That is because you did not know the old days; you have not studied the effects of the new immigration from Spain, of the coming of new books, and of the exodus of our youth to Europe ever since the opening of the Suez Canal. Observe and compare. It is true that the Royal and Pontifical University of Santo Tomas still exists with its most learned faculties, and that there are still a number of intellects that are active in making distinctions and carrying the subtleties of scholastic philosophy to their ultimate conclusions. But where will you find now that youth of our own day, engrossed in metaphysics under a prehistoric system of instruction, who, racking their brains to formulate sophistries in obscure provincial corners, died without ever really understanding the attributes of being or solving the problem of essence and existence, concepts so rarefied that they made us forget what was truly essential: our own existence and our own identity? Look at our youth nowadays. Full of enthusiasm at the sight of broader horizons, they study history, mathematics, geography, literature, physics, languages, all of them subjects which we regarded with as much horror as if they had been heresies. The most advanced intellectual of my time pronounced these subjects inferior to the categories of Aristotle and to the laws of the syllogism. But man has at last realised that he is man; he has given up analysing his God, scrutinising the immaterial and what he never saw with his own eyes, and laying down laws for his cerebral fancies. Man at last understands that his heritage is the vast world whose dominion is now within his reach, weary of a fruitless and presumptuous task, he now lowers his head and looks round him. See how our poets now blossom forth; the Muses of Nature open up their treasures to us, little by little, and begin to smile encouragement on our labours. The experimental Sciences have already yielded their first fruits; only time is needed to ripen them. The new lawyers are being shaped in the novel disciplines of the Philosophy of Law; some already begin to shine in the midst of the darkness that surrounds our judicial benches, and mark a change in the progress of our times. Hear the youth talk; visit the schools; other names echo along the walls of those schoolrooms where we, in our own times, heard only the names of St. Thomas, Suarez, Amat, Sanchez, and other scholastic philosophers. It is useless for the friars in their pulpits to complain about demoralisation, as fishmongers might complain about the stinginess of their customers without realising that their wares are spoiled and worthless. The convents push out their roots and branches farther afield in order to hold back in the towns the flood of new ideas, but in vain; the gods are on the way out; the roots of a tree can strangle its parasitic plants, but cannot kill other living things that, like birds, take flight for the skies.'

The scholar spoke excitedly, his eyes flashing.

'However,' the sceptical Don Filipo objected, 'these new springs of knowledge are not yet so abundant; if we all draw from them, we may exhaust the progress for which we have paid so high a price.' 'Exhaust it? Who? This sickly dwarf, man, exhaust Progress, the powerful son of Time and Action? When did he ever do it? Dogma, the scaffold, the fires of the Inquisition, trying to stop Progress, only helped it on. *E pur si muove*, nevertheless it moves, said Galileo when the Dominicans tried to make him admit that the earth did not move around the sun; human progress too, in spite of everything, moves on. A few wills may be broken, a few individuals sacrificed, it will not matter, Progress will go on its way, and from the blood of those who fall new and strong shoots will sprout. See how even the Press itself, no matter how reactionary it may wish to be, is compelled to take a step forward. The

Dominicans themselves are not exempt from this law and imitate the Jesuits, their irreconcilable foes; now they too entertain in their convents, build little theatres, compose poems, all this because they are not stupid even if they are still living in the Middle Ages, and they realise that the Jesuits are right and will have a part to play in the future.'

'You say that the Jesuits go with Progress?' the admiring Don Filipo asked. 'But why then are they opposed in Europe?'

'I shall answer you,' said the scholar, leaning back and assuming anew his sardonic smile, in the language of one trained in scholastic philosophy. There are three ways of going with Progress: ahead of it, alongside it, and behind it. Those who go ahead guide Progress; the second group go along with Progress; and the third group are dragged forward by Progress. The Jesuits belong to this last group. They would be glad enough to guide it but they realise that Progress is too strong for them and seeks its own roads; so they give in, they follow rather than be trampled underfoot or left behind the chariot of Progress; we are scarcely emerging from the Middle Ages. That is why the Jesuits, who are reactionaries in Europe, represent Progress from our viewpoint. The Philippines owes them the beginnings of the Natural Sciences, soul of the nineteenth century, just as we owe to the Dominicans Scholastic Philosophy, now dead for all that Pope Leo XIII may say or do. No Pope can bring back to life what common sense has condemned to death.

But, he asked, changing his tone, 'where have we gone off to? Oh yes, we were speaking of the present state of the Philippines. We are now entering into the period of struggle, or rather you are. My generation belongs to the night, and we must take our leave. The struggle is between the Past, which crying maledictions clings to the crumbling feudal castle, and the Future, whose triumphant song can be heard from afar amid the splendours of the dawn, bearing the good tidings from other lands. Who are to fall and be buried in the ruins of the crumbling Past?'

The old man fell silent and, observing Don Filipo's thoughtful look, smiled and continued:

'I can almost guess what you are thinking.'

'Really?'

'You are thinking that I might well be wrong,' he said with a sad smile. 'Today I have a fever and I am not infallible. *Homo sum et nihil humani a me alienum puto,* said Terence, I am a man and I believe that nothing that concerns humanity is alien to me. But if it is ever allowed to dream, then why not have pleasant dreams in life's last hours? Besides, I have lived only on dreams. You are right; our young people think only of love affairs and pleasures; they spend more time and effort on seducing and dishonouring a girl than on planning the good of their country; our women are so devoted to the care of God's house and household that they neglect their own; our men are energetic only in the pursuit of vice and heroic only in dishonouring themselves. Childhood awakens in meaningless routine; youth lives its best years without an ideal; and maturity, sterile maturity, serves no other purpose than to corrupt youth by its example. I am glad I'm dying. *Claudite jam rivos, pueri.* Ring down the curtain, boys.'

'Shall I get you some medicine?' asked Don Filipo to change the conversation, which had cast a shadow on the sick man's face.

'The dying need no medicines; only those who stay behind. Tell Don Crisóstomo to visit me tomorrow. I have something important to tell him. In a few days I shall be gone.'

After a few more snatches of conversation Don Filipo left the sickroom, grave and thoughtful.

55 • *The Conspiracy*

What is veiled will be revealed.
What is hidden will all be known.
—Luke xii, 2
(Knox Translation)

THE church bells were ringing the Angelus, and everyone, on hearing the traditional call, uncovered himself and put aside whatever he was doing; the ploughman, going home from the fields, stopped the rhythmic walk of the carabao he was riding and said his prayers; the women in the streets crossed themselves and moved their lips affectedly so as to leave no doubt of their piety; the gambler stopped caressing his gamecock and said the Angelus for luck; in the houses it was said out loud, and any sound that was not the Hail Mary was stilled.

The parish priest, however, his hat on his head, was striding across the street to the scandal of many old women, and, worse scandal still, was seen heading for the commanding officer's house. Nor did Father Salví pay any heed to the devout women who thought it time to suspend their mouthings in order to kiss the hand of the parish priest. This time he derived no pleasure from his usual practice of pressing his bony hand against some Christian nose and from there sliding it downward inconspicuously (as Doña Consolación had observed) to the bosom of some attractive young girl leaning forward to ask his blessing. He must have had important things on his mind indeed, thus to forget his own interests and those of the Church!

He scrambled up the stairs of the lieutenant's house and knocked impatiently on his door. The latter appeared with a frown on his face, accompanied by his spouse who was grinning like the damned.

'Ah, Father! I was just going over to see you. That goat of yours...'

'I have something of the utmost importance...'

'I really cannot allow your animals to keep breaking down my fence. The next time I see that goat I'll shoot him.'

'That is, if you're still alive tomorrow,' said the friar, breathing heavily and leading the way toward the officer's living-room.

'What! Do you think a seven-months baby is capable of killing me? I'll kick his guts out.'

Father Salví fell back and looked instinctively at the lieutenant's boot.

'Who else but that silly billy who has challenged me to a duel with pistols at a hundred paces?'

'Ah, Linares,' sighted the priest with relief, adding: 'I have come to speak to you about a most urgent matter.'

'Don't bother me with your matters. It's probably another story like that of the two boys.'

If the light in the room had not come from an oil lamp, and if the lamp's globe had not been so dirty, the lieutenant might have noticed the priest's pallor.

'This time,' he replied in a hushed voice, 'it is a serious matter affecting our very lives.'

'Serious?' the lieutenant repeated, losing colour. 'Is that young man such a good shot?'

'I am not speaking about him.'

'Then?'

The friar looked towards the door, and the officer closed it, as was his practice, with a kick. The lieutenant found hands superfluous, and would scarcely have been handicapped if he had turned into a quadruped. An oath and an angry roar came from behind the door.

'Brute! You have breaking my head!' screamed Doña Consolación.

'Now,' said the lieutenant nonchalantly to the parish priest, 'spill it.'

The latter gave him a long look, and then, in the nasal monotone of a preacher, asked:

'Did you see how I came running?'

'Of course, dammit, I thought you had diarrhoea.'

'Well, then,' said the priest, ignoring the officer's coarseness, 'when I forget myself so far it is only for the most serious of reasons.'

'Anything else?' asked the lieutenant, bringing down his boot heavily to the floor.

'Don't get excited.'

'Then why come running so fast?'

The friar leaned closer and asked with an air of mystery:

'Have you... heard nothing... new?'

'Do you want to talk to me about Elias, whom your head sacristan sheltered last night?' asked the lieutenant.

'No, I am not speaking of fairy tales,' replied the parish priest peevishly. 'I am speaking of a great danger.'

'Well, damn it, open up then!'

'Come now,' said the friar slowly and with a certain contempt, 'you'll see once again how important we religious are; the lowliest lay brother is worth a regiment, so that a parish priest...'

Then lowering his voice and with a heavy air of mystery: 'I have discovered a great conspiracy.'

The lieutenant started and stared dumbfounded at the friar.

'A terrible and well planned conspiracy which is to strike this very night.'

'This very night!' cried the lieutenant, leaping up to the friar, and then running for his revolver and sabre, which were hanging on the wall.

'Whom do I arrest?' he shouted. 'Whom?'

'Calm yourself. There is still time, thanks to my promptness. Until eight o'clock...'

I'll shoot them all!'

'Listen, this afternoon a woman whose name I am forbidden to reveal (it is a secret of Confession) came to me and told me all. At eight they take the barracks by surprise, sack the convent, seize the patrol boat, and murder all of us Spaniards.'

The commanding officer was in a daze.

'The woman did not tell me any more than that,' the friar added.

'Didn't tell you more? Then I'll arrest her.'

'I cannot consent to that. The confession is the throne of the God of mercy.'

'I don't care about God or mercy. I'm going to arrest her.'

'You are losing your head. What you should do is prepare yourself. Quietly put your men under arms and in ambush. Give me four soldiers to guard the parish house, and warn the crew of the patrol boat.'

'The patrol boat isn't here! I'll call for help from the other garrisons!'

'No, don't do that; it will be noticed, and then they won't go through with what they are planning. The important thing is to catch them alive and make them talk, or rather, you'll make them talk; I, as a priest, should not be mixed up in these matters. Be on the lookout! This is a chance for you to win a promotion and a citation. All I ask is that you put it on record that it was I who warned you.'

'It'll be on record, Father, and perhaps you'll find yourself with a mitre on your head,' replied the beaming lieutenant, looking speculatively at the sleeves of his uniform.

'So, then, you are to send me four soldiers in disguise, eh? Be discreet. Tonight at eight, promotions and citations!'

While this was going on, a man went running to Crisóstomo's house and hurried up the stairs.

'Is your master in?' Elias was heard asking a servant.

'He is working in his study.'

Ibarra, to distract himself as he waited impatiently for the hour of his appointment with María Clara, had set himself to working in his laboratory. 'Ah, it's you, Elias', he exclaimed. 'I was just thinking about you. Yesterday I forgot to ask you the name of that Spaniard in whose house your grandfather lived.'

'Sir, this has nothing to do with me.'

'Look,' Ibarra continued, not noticing the young man's excitement, and placing a piece of bamboo near the flame, 'I have made a great discovery. This bamboo does not burn...'

'It is not a question of the bamboo now. You must get your papers together and get away at once.'

Ibarra gave Elias an astonished look, and then, seeing the seriousness of his aspect, dropped what he had in his hands.

'Burn anything that can compromise you, and be in a safer place within the hour. Put away all your valuables. Burn every paper written by you or to you; the most harmless may be used against you.'

'But why?'

'Because I have just discovered that a rising is being planned and that you will be blamed for it and ruined.'

'A rising? By whom?'

'It was impossible for me to find out who is behind the whole thing. Just a moment ago I was talking to one of the wretches who were paid to have a part in it, and whom I have not been able to convince to give it up.'

'And didn't he tell you who was paying him?'

'Yes. He made me promise to keep it secret, and he said that it was you.'

'My God!' Ibarra exclaimed, terrified.

'Sir, do not hesitate; let us not lose time; the uprising may take place this very night.'

Ibarra, his eyes staring, and his head in his hands, did not seem to hear him.

'The attack cannot be stopped,' Elias continued. 'I was too late; I don't know the leaders. Save yourself, sir, keep yourself for your country!'

'Where shall I go?' asked Ibarra, and, thinking of María Clara: 'I have an appointment tonight.'

'Go to some other town, to Manila, to the house of some official, anywhere but here, so it can't be said that you were leading the movement.'

'And if I should denounce the conspiracy myself?'

'You an informer?' Elias cried, stepping back appalled. 'You would be considered a traitor and a coward by the conspirators and faintheart by everybody else. It will be said that you trapped them for your own advancement; it will be said...'

'But what am I to do?'

'I've told you. Destroy all your papers which may implicate you, get away, and wait for developments.'

'And María Clara?' cried the young man. 'No, I'd sooner die!' Elias wrung his hands in despair.

'Well, then, at least protect yourself from the blow; prepare yourself against the charges they are going to make.'

Ibarra looked round him dazedly.

'Then help me. My family letters are in those portfolios. Pick out my father's letters; they are the ones that may compromise me. Read the signatures.'

And the young man, bewildered, stunned, opened and shut drawers, gathered up papers, read letters hurriedly, tore up some and kept others, took down books and leafed through them. Elias was doing the same thing, in less confusion but with equal zeal. Then he stopped, staring at a paper in his hands, and asked hoarsely:

'Did your family know Don Pedro Eibarramendía?'

'Of course,' Ibarra answered, opening a drawer and taking out a bundle of papers, 'he was my great-grandfather.'

'Your great-grandfather, Don Pedro Eibarramendía?' Elias asked again, livid, his face distorted.

'Yes,' Ibarra replied off-handedly. 'We shortened the name; it was too long.'

'Was he a Basque?'

'A Basque? But what's the matter with you?' Ibarra asked, surprised.

Elias pressed his fists against his brow and glared at Ibarra, who fell back at the expression on his face.

'You know who Don Pedro Eibarramendía was?' he asked between clenched teeth. 'Don Pedro Eibarramendía was the scoundrel who falsely accused my grandfather and was the cause of all our misfortunes. It was his name I sought. God has delivered you unto me. Render me an accounting of our misfortunes!'

Crisóstomo looked at him terrified, but Elias shook him by the arm and said in a bitter voice burning with hatred:

'Look at me well; judge whether I have suffered; and you are alive, you love, you have wealth, a home, honours—you live, you live!'

Beside himself, he ran to a small collection of arms, but he had scarcely seized two daggers when he dropped them and stared like a madman at Ibarra, who remained motionless.

'What was I going to do?' he muttered and fled from the house.

56 • Ruin

CAPITAN TIAGO, Linares, and Aunt Isabel were having dinner, and the sound of china and silver could be heard from the living-room. María Clara had said she was not hungry, and had sat down at the piano, with the gay Sinang by her side whispering mysteriously into her ear while Father Salví paced up and down the room.

Not that the convalescent had really not been hungry; but she was awaiting Ibarra and had decided to take advantage of the one time when her hundred-eyed guard would not be present: Linares's dinner-time.

'I bet you that ghost stays till eight,' whispered Sinang, nodding towards the priest. 'Crisóstomo is supposed to come at eight, but that friar is just as much in love as Linares.'

María stared at her friend with horror, but the latter continued unheeding the terrible flow of her chatter:

'Oh, I know why he doesn't go home in spite of all my hints. He wants to save on oil in the parish house! Do you know, ever since you fell ill, those two special lamps which he had had lighted have been allowed to go out. But look at him, look at his eyes, his face!'

At that moment the clock struck eight. The parish priest shivered and seated himself in a corner.

'He's coming,' said Sinang, pinching María Clara. 'Hear him?' Now the church bells pealed the hour and all rose to pray. Father Salví led the prayer for the Holy Souls in a weak and trembling voice, but nobody noticed it; everyone was absorbed in own thoughts.

The prayers were scarcely over when Ibarra made his appearance. The young man was in mourning, not only in his clothes but also in countenance, so that María Clara, when she saw him, rose to her feet as if to ask him what ailed him, but on this instant a volley of shots was heard. Ibarra stopped, whirled round, and lost his voice. The parish priest hid himself behind a post. More explosions and shots were heard coming from the direction of the parish house, followed by shouts and the sound of running feet. Capitan Tiago, Aunt Isabel, and Linares stumbled into the room shouting: 'Bandits, bandits!' Andeng followed them, brandishing a roasting-spit and running protectively to the side of her foster sister.

Aunt Isabel fell to her knees, weeping, and said the *Kyrie eléison;* Capitan Tiago, pale and trembling, tearfully offered the Virgin of Antipolo the chicken liver on his folk; Linares had his mouth full and was armed with a spoon; Sinang and María Clara were in each other's arms; only Crisóstomo was motionless, as if turned to stone, his face pale beyond description.

The sound of cries and blows continued; windows were being slammed shut all round; whistles were heard, and once in a while a shot. '*Christe eléison!* Christ, have mercy! Santiago, the prophecies are being fulfilled—shut the windows!' sobbed Aunt Isabel.

'Fifty giant rockets and two Thanksgiving Masses,' replied Capitan Tiago. *Ora pro nobis!* Pray for us!'

Little by little a terrible silence fell.

The voice of the commanding officer was heard, crying out as he ran:

'Father! Father Salví! Come here!'

'*Miserere!* Have mercy! The lieutenant wants to go to Confession!' Aunt Isabel cried.

'Is the lieutenant wounded?' Linares asked with an exclamation of relief, noticing at last that he had not yet swallowed the food in his mouth.

'Father Salví, come on,' the commanding officer kept calling. 'There's nothing more to be afraid of!'

Father Salví, still ashen, made up his mind at last, left his hiding place, and went down the stairs.

'The bandits have killed the lieutenant! María, Sinang, to your room, lock yourselves in! *Kyrie eléison!* God the Father, have mercy!' cried Aunt Isabel, and then to Ibarra, who was following the parish priest:

'Don't go out! You haven't been to Confession! Don't go out!'

The good lady had been his mother's dearest friend.

But Ibarra left the house. He felt everything in a whirl round him; he scarcely felt the ground he stepped on; his ears were ringing; his legs were heavy and moved spasmodically; waves of blood, light, and darkness followed one another in his eyes. Despite the moon which shone in splendour in the skies, the young man stumbled over odds and ends in the deserted street. Near the barracks he saw soldiers with fixed bayonets, who were talking so excitedly that he passed by unnoticed. From the townhouse could be heard blows, cries, curses, and lamentations. The lieutenant's voice was the most prominent. 'This one to the stocks! Handcuffs for that one! Shoot anyone who makes a move! Sergeant, you will be in charge of the guard! Nobody has leave tonight, not even God! And you can't go to bed, Mayor!' Ibarra hastened to his house. His servants awaited him easily. 'Saddle my best horse, and go to bed,' he told them.

He went to his study to pack as quickly as possible. He opened a safe, took all the money there, and put it in a sack. He gathered up all his jewels, took a portrait of María Clara from the wall, armed himself with a dagger and two revolvers, and was going towards a cupboard where he kept some tools when three sharp strong blows were heard on the door.

'Who goes there?' asked Ibarra in a desolate voice.

'Open in the name of the King! Open immediately or we'll smash down the door!' an imperious voice answered in Spanish.

Ibarra looked at the window; his eyes gleamed and he cocked his revolver; but, changing his mind, he put the arms aside and opened the door himself just as his servants were coming up.

Three soldiers seized him immediately.

'Consider yourself under arrest, in the name of the King!' said the sergeant.

'On what grounds?'

'They'll let you know when you get where you're going. We are not allowed to tell you.'

The young man thought it over for a moment and then, perhaps so that the soldiers would not discover what preparations he had for flight, took his hat and said:

'I am at your service. I suppose it will be only for a few hours.'

'If you give us your word you won't try to escape, sir, we won't tie you up. It's a favour from the C.O. But if you try to get away...'

Ibarra followed, leaving his servants aghast.

When Elias had run away from the house of Crisóstomo, like one insane, he did not know where he was going and crossed the fields until he had reached the forest. He was in the grip of a violent frenzy; he was running away from human habitations, away from the light; even the light of the moon unsettled him, and he plunged into the thick and mysterious shadows of the wood. There, now stopping, now moving on by unknown paths, clasping aged trunks, entangling himself in the underbrush, he could now and again look down on the town, which lay at his feet bathed in moonlight, stretching back into the plain by the shores of the lake. Night birds, or those awakened by his passage, flew above him; giant bats and owls darted from branch to branch, screaming and staring at him with their round eyes. Elias neither heard nor saw them.

He fancied himself pursued by the angry shades of his forbears; saw hanging on every branch the sinister basket with the bloody head of *Balát*, as in his father's tale; he thought to stumble on the corpse of the bandit's old mother at the foot of every tree; every shadow seemed to be swinging like the rotting skeleton of the condemned grandfather, and skeleton, corpse, and trunkless head cried out to him: 'Coward, avenge us!'

Elias left the mountain, fleeing down to the lake, and ran frenziedly along its shore; and there, far away, in the middle of the waters, where the moonlight seemed like mist, he thought he saw another shadow rise and sway, the shadow of his sister, her breast all bloody, her hair streaming in the wind.

Falling to his knees on the sand, he cried, stretching out his arms: 'You too!'

Then, his staring eyes on the patch of mist, he rose slowly and stepped forward into the water as if he were following someone. He walked down the slow incline of the bank; soon he was far from shore, the water up to his waist, and still he went on as if hypnotised by some seductive spirit. The water was up to his breast when, with the volley of shots in town, the vision vanished and he returned to reality. Thanks to the tranquility of the night and the heaviness of the air the sound of the firing reached him clearly and distinctly. He paused, gathered his thoughts together, and saw that he was in the water; the lake was calm and he could still see the lights in the fishermen's huts.

He went back to shore and set off dazedly towards the town.

It appeared uninhabited; the houses were all shut up, and even the animals, the dogs that barked in the night, had hidden themselves in fright. The silvery light of the moon only increased the effect of sadness and solitude.

Fearing to meet the patrols, he plunged into groves and gardens; he thought he saw two people in one of them, but he went on, leaping over walls and fences until, at the other end of town, he reached Ibarra's house. The servants were at the gate, recounting and bewailing their master's arrest.

Having learned what had happened, Elias walked away, round to the back of the house, and leaped over the wall. Entering the house through a window he went into the study where the candle Ibarra had lit still burned.

Elias saw the papers and the books, and found the weapons and the sacks which held Ibarra's money and jewels. He thought back over what had happened, and, seeing so many compromising papers he thought of gathering them together, throwing them out of the window, and afterwards burying them.

But a glance at the garden showed him, under the light of the moon, soldiers, their bayonets and helmets gleaming in the moonlight, accompanied by a civilian.

Making a decision, he piled up clothes and papers in the middle of the study, emptied an oil lamp on them, and set them on fire. He buckled on the weapons, kissed María Clara's portrait, and then put it in one of the sacks. Carrying them, he jumped out through the window.

It was just about time. The soldiers were breaking down the door.

'Let us go upstairs to seize the papers of your master,' the Municipal Secretary was saying.

'Have you his permission?' an old servant asked. 'If not, you cannot go up.'

The soldiers smashed the door open with the butts of their guns and went up the stairs. But the house was already full of thick smoke, and giant tongues of fire burst out of the living-room, licking at the doors and windows.

'Fire! Fire!'

Everyone went into action to save what he could, but the fire had already reached the small laboratory and the chemicals and other inflammables now exploded. The soldiers were forced to retreat; the way was barred to them by the roaring fire which swept everything before it. Water was drawn from the well, but in vain. There were loud cries for help, but the isolated house, was a long way from the town. The fire reached the other rooms and lifted up to the sky thick spirals of smoke. Now all the house was in flames, whipped on by the hot winds; a few peasants had finally come, but they were in time only to see the terrible bonfire, the end of the old house that the elements had for so long respected.

57 • *Rumours*

DAWN came at last to the terror-stricken town.

The street where the barracks and the courthouse were situated was still deserted and empty; the houses gave no signs of life. Then a wooden shutter was opened noisily and a boy put out his head, turning it round in all directions, stretching out his neck everywhere. Leather slapped human hide, the boy made a grimace, shut his eyes, and disappeared; and the shutter was pulled to again.

But the example had been given; that opening and closing of shutters had obviously been heard, for another was now opened slowly and the head of an old woman, wrinkled and toothless, peeped out: it was the same Sister Pute who had made such an uproar during Father Dámaso's sermon. Children and old women are truly the embodiment of curiosity on earth: the first because they want to know, the second because they want to gossip.

Apparently nobody was prepared to hit the old woman's behind with a slipper, for she for one remained at the window. She peered out with a frown, washed out her mouth, spat noisily, and crossed herself. The house across the street now, in turn, had a window opened, revealing Sister Rufa, she who would neither fool nor be fooled. The two exchanged a quick look, smiled, made signs to each other, and crossed themselves all over again.

'Jesús,' exclaimed Sister Rufa. 'Wasn't it like a Thanksgiving Mass though? All the fireworks!'

'Haven't seen a night like it since *Bálat* sacked the town,' said Sister Pute.

'So many shots! They say it was old Pablo's gang.'

'Bandits? Can't be. They say it was the municipal policemen against the Constabulary. That is why Don Filipo is in gaol.'

'*Sanctus Deus!* Holy God! And they say there are at least fourteen dead.'

Other windows were now being opened and different faces emerged to exchange greetings and comments.

In the full light of what promised to be a glorious day the grey figures of soldiers could be seen coming and going in confusion.

'There goes another corpse,' said one from a window.

'One? I see two.'

'Well, I... anyway, I bet you don't know what it was all about,' said a man with a sly face.

'The municipal policemen, of course.'

'No, sir. Mutiny in the barracks.'

'Mutiny nothing! It was a fight between the parish priest and the commanding officer.'

'Oh no, nothing like that at all,' said the man who had proposed the question. 'It was the Chinese, an uprising of the Chinese.'

And he closed his window.

'The Chinese!' everyone echoed with the greatest surprise.

'That's why you can't see one anywhere.'

'Probably all killed.'

'I thought they were up to something funny. Why, just yesterday...'

'I could see it coming. Last night...'

'What a pity!' exclaimed Sister Rufa. 'All the Chinese dead before Christmas, when they send us such nice gifts. They should have waited for New Year's Day.'

The street was slowly growing livelier. The dogs, chickens, pigs, and pigeons were the first to essay normal traffic; these animals were followed by some ragged boys, arm in arm, who sidled up timidly towards the barracks; then came a number of old women, kerchiefs tied under their chins, heavy rosaries in their hands, pretending to pray to get past the sentries. When it became clear that it was safe to walk in the streets without risk of getting shot, the men began to come out, pretending indifference; at first they only paced up and down in front of their houses, caressing their gamecocks; later they walked a little farther on, tentatively, with many a pause in between, until they had reached the courthouse.

In a quarter of an hour other versions of the night's events were in circulation. Ibarra had tried to abduct María Clara with the help of his servants, and Capitan Tiago had defended her with the help of the Constabulary... The number of the dead had risen from fourteen to thirty; Capitan Tiago had been wounded, and was leaving for Manila immediately with his family.

The appearance of two municipal policemen carrying what seemed to be a dead man on a litter and followed by a soldier caused a great sensation. It was learned that they had come from the parish house; someone tried to guess the identity of the man from the feet that swung from the stretcher; a little farther along the street the guess became a certainty; farther on the dead man grew in numbers and the mystery of the Holy Trinity found a counterpart; later, the miracle of the loaves and fishes was repeated, and the number of the dead reached thirty-eight.

By half-past seven, when Constabulary reinforcement arrived from the neighbouring towns, the current version of the night's events had become clearer and more detailed.

'I have just come from the courthouse,' a man said to Sister Pute,' and saw Don Filipo and Don Crisóstomo under arrest. I talked to one of the policemen on guard. It seems Bruno, whose father, you will recall, was beaten to death, told the whole story last night. As you know, Capitan Tiago is marrying off his daughter to that young Spaniard. Don Crisóstomo felt insulted and in revenge tried to kill all the Spaniards, including the parish priest. Last night they attacked the barracks and the parish house. Fortunately, by the mercy of God, the parish priest was in Capitan Tiago's house; otherwise they would have killed him. A lot of them got away, they say. The Constabulary soldiers burned down Don Crisóstomo's house, and, if they hadn't arrested him earlier, they would have burned him too.'

'They burnt his house?'

'And arrested all the servants. Look, you can still see the smoke from here,' said the narrator, going over to the window. 'Those who come from there have many sad stories to tell.'

All eyes were turned toward a slight column of smoke that was still rising to the skies. There were comments from everyone, comments that were more or less pious, more or less hostile.

'Poor fellow,' exclaimed Sister Pute's husband.

'Yes,' she answered, 'but remember that yesterday he failed to have Mass said for the soul of his father, who undoubtedly needs it more than anybody else.'

'But, dear, have you no pity?'

'Pity for an excommunicated man? The parish priest says it is a sin to have pity on the enemies of God. Remember how he walked about on consecrated ground in the cemetery as if it were a poultry yard.'

'But it does look like one,' retorted the old man. 'The only difference is that only one kind of animal enters the poultry yard.'

'Now stop it!' cried Sister Pute. 'You're going so far as to defend someone whom very clearly God has punished. Watch out you're not arrested too. Prop up a falling house and it will crush you.'

The argument shut up her husband.

'There!' she continued. 'After assaulting Father Dámaso, there was nothing left for him to do, of course, but kill Father Salví.'

'You can't deny he was a good little boy.'

'All right, he may have been a good little boy, but then he went to Spain, and those who go to Spain come back heretics. That's what the friars all say.'

'Oho!' cried her husband, who saw how he could turn the tables on her. 'What about the parish priest, and all the other priests, and the Archbishop, and the Pope, and the Virgin, aren't they all from Spain? So they're all heretics too, hey? Hey?'

Luckily for Sister Pute the discussion was cut short by the appearance of a maidservant, who came running, pale and panic-stricken.

'There's a man hanging in the neighbour's kitchen-garden!' she panted.

'Hanging!' they cried out, dumbfounded.

The women crossed themselves but nobody seemed capable of any other movement.

'Yes, sir,' continued the trembling maidservant. 'I was going to pick some peas... I looked over to the neighbour's kitchen garden to see if I could find... I saw a man swinging in the air and I thought it was Teo, the neighbour's servant, who always gives me... I came nearer to... pick peas, and then I saw that it wasn't Teo at all but a dead man, so I ran and ran and...'

'Let's have a look at him,' said Sister Pute's husband, getting up. 'Lead the way.'

'Don't go!' screamed his wife, seizing the tail of his shirts. 'Something terrible might happen to you! So he's hung himself! Well, that's his funeral!'

'Let me see him, woman. Now, you, Juan, go to the courthouse and notify the authorities. Maybe he isn't dead yet.'

The old man went off to the kitchen-garden, followed by the maidservant, who was hiding behind his back. The women, including Sister Pute herself, came behind them, full of fear and curiosity.

'Now I shan't be able to come again in the afternoons to speak with Teo,' thought the maidservant to herself.

Aloud she said: 'There he is, sir,' stopping and pointing with her finger.

The commission of inspectors stopped at a respectable distance, leaving the old man to go on by himself.

A body, hanging from a branch of a *santol* tree, swung slightly in the wind. The old man stared at it for some time: the stiff feet, the arms, the stained clothing, the broken back.

'We should not touch him until the police arrive,' he said aloud. 'He is quite stiff; he has been dead for quite some time.'

The women approached step by step.

'It's the fellow who lived in the other orchard, in the little hut, the one who arrived two weeks ago. See that scar on his face?'

'Holy Mary!' exclaimed some of the women.

'Shall we say a prayer for his soul?' asked a young girl after she had looked him over.

'Silly!' Sister Pute scolded her. 'You're talking like a heretic. Don't you know what Father Dámaso said? To pray for the damned is to tempt God, and suicides are hopelessly damned; that is why they cannot be buried in consecrated ground.'

And she added:

'I had a feeling this man would end up badly; I never could find out where he lived.'

'I saw him twice speaking to the head sacristan,' observed another young girl.

'It wasn't to go to Confession or to have a Mass said, you can be sure of that.'

The neighbours had now put in an appearance and there were quite a number of people round the body, which continued swaying above them. A sheriff, the Municipal Secretary, and two policemen arrived after half an hour, and the body was cut down and placed on a litter.

'People are in a hurry to die today,' giggled the Municipal Secretary taking down the pen which he had over his ear.

He took down the maidservant's statement, putting misleading questions, trying to trip her up, now looking at her suspiciously, now threatening her, attributing to her things she had never said, until she thought she would be sent to gaol and, bursting into tears, confessed she had not gone to pick peas at all, calling on Teo as witness.

Meantime a peasant in a typical wide straw hat and a great patch on his neck was examining the body and the rope.

The face was no more livid than the rest of the body; above the mark of the rope two scratches and two small bruises could be seen; the bruises caused by the rope were white and bloodless. The curious peasant also examined carefully the dead man's shirt and trousers, and observed that they were dusty and recently torn in various places; but what attracted his attention most were the deeds of a local weed which clung even to the neck of the shirt.

'What are you looking at?' asked the Municipal Secretary.

'I was trying to see if I recognised him, sir,' stammered the peasant, half uncovering himself but contriving in so doing to lower his hat over his face.

'But haven't you heard it was a certain Lucas? Asleep on your feet, are you?'

Everyone burst into laughter. The peasant, seemingly abashed, stammered a few words and walked away slowly, head bent.

'Hey, where are you going?' shouted Sister Pute's husband after him. 'You can't get out that way; that's the way to the dead man's hut.'

'The fellow's still asleep,' sneered the Municipal Secretary. 'We'll have to empty a bucket over his head.'

There was another burst of laughter.

The peasant left the place where he had played such a sorry part and went to the church. In the sacristy he asked for the head sacristan.

'He's still sleeping,' they told him roughly. 'Don't you know they sacked the parish house last night?'

'I can wait till he gets up.'

The church servants looked at him with the bad temper to be expected from those who are themselves ill-treated.

The one-eyed head sacristan was sleeping in a long armchair in a dark corner. His eyeglasses had been pushed upward to his forehead amid his long tangled hair; his thin narrow chest was bare, and rose and fell regularly.

The peasant seated himself nearby, seemingly ready to wait patiently, but a coin fell from his fingers and he searched for it, with the help of a candle, under the head sacristan's armchair. He was thus able to observe the seeds of the same weed on the trousers and shirt sleeves of the sleeping man. The latter finally awoke, rubbed his one healthy eye, and began to scold the peasant in rather a temper 'I wanted a Mass said, sir,' the latter said ingratiatingly.

'No more Masses today,' the one-eyed man replied, changing his tone slightly for the better. 'Now, if you want, tomorrow... Is it for the Holy Souls in Purgatory?'

'No, sir,' answered the peasant, handling over a peso, and adding with a look into the solitary eye: 'It is for someone who is about to die.'

Then he left the sacristy.

'I could have fixed him last night,' he sighed as he unstuck the patch on his neck and straightened himself to recover the face and height of Elias.

58 • *Woe to the Vanquished*

My joys fell
Down the well.

CONSTABULARY soldiers paced with sinister air in the front of the courthouse door, threatening with their rifle butts the daring children who tried to see through the barred windows on tiptoe or on one another's backs.

The courthouse hall no longer had the festive air it had when the programme for the town fiesta had been discussed; now it gave a sombre and disquieting impression. The Constabulary soldiers and municipal policemen who occupied it scarcely talked, and when they did, said only a few words in a hushed voice. The Municipal Secretary, two clerks, and a number of soldiers were writing at the main table, the commanding officer walked to and fro, every so often glaring fiercely at the door. Themistocles could not have borne himself so proudly when he appeared at the Olympic Games after the battle of Salamis. Doña Consolacíon was yawning in a corner, showing her blackened gums and jagged teeth; her eyes were fixed with a cold and sinister look on the door to the detention cells which was covered with indecent scrawls. She had persuaded her husband, whom victory had made generous, to allow her to witness the investigation and perhaps the accompanying tortures. The hyena in her had already had a whiff of the corpse and licked its chops. The delay before the tortures began bored her.

The Mayor looked depressed; his armchair under the portrait of the King was empty, and seemed to be reserved for somebody else.

At about nine o'clock the parish priest arrived, pale and frowning.

'Well, you didn't half keep us waiting, did you?' the lieutenant said.

'I would rather not have been present at all,' Father Salví replied in a low voice, ignoring the officer's sarcasm. 'I have a nervous temperament.'

'Since nobody else could leave his post to come, I thought your presence here... You know that they are being taken away this afternoon.'

'Young Ibarra and the Vice Mayor...?'

The lieutenant cocked a thumb towards the cells.

'There are eight of them there,' he said. 'Bruno died at midnight but his statement is on record.'

The parish priest greeted Doña Consolacíon, who replied with a yawn and a sigh, and then took the armchair under the King's portrait.

'We can begin,' he said.

'Bring out the two who are in the stocks,' ordered the lieutenant in a voice which he tried to make as terrifying as he could. Changing his tone he added to the parish priest: 'They're in the stocks skipping two holes.'

The holes in the stocks through which the legs of arrested persons were put were usually only about a hand's breadth apart; skipping two holes, however, meant that the prisoner found himself in a rather unnatural position, with a singular discomfort in his ankles and with legs almost a yard apart, although, as can be very well imagined, it was not the sort of thing to cause instant death.

The warden, followed by four soldiers, unbolted the door to the cells. A nauseating stench, a thick and damp atmosphere, rose from the deep darkness within; a few cries and sobs were heard. A soldier struck a match, but the flame flickered out in the charged and heavy air, and it was necessary to wait for a little more fresh air.

By the weak light of a candle some human figures could be made out vaguely: men clasping their knees and hiding their faces between them, others lying on their stomachs, still others standing and facing the walls. A hammering and squeaking could be heard, accompanied by oaths, as the stocks were opened.

Doña Consolacíon was leaning forward, the muscles of her neck tensed, her staring eyes fixed on the half-open door.

A sombre figure appeared between two soldiers; it was Társilo, Bruno's brother. He was handcuffed. His torn clothes revealed a well-muscled body. He gave the lieutenant's wife an insolent look.

'He is the one who fought best, and ordered his companions to save themselves first,' the lieutenant told Father Salví.

Behind Társilo came a wretch who complained and wept like a child; he was limping and his trousers were bloodstained.

'Mercy, sir, have mercy!' he screamed. 'I'll never go into the barracks yard again!'

'He's a scoundrel,' the lieutenant commented to the parish priest.

'He tried to run away but was wounded in the thigh. They are the only two we have alive.'

'What's your name?' the lieutenant asked Társilo.

'Társilo Alasigan.'

'What did Don Crisóstomo promise you if you attacked the barracks?'

'Don Crisóstomo never had any communications with us.'

'Don't deny it! That's why you made your surprise attack.'

'You're wrong. You beat our father to death, and we were avenging him. That's all. Ask our two companions.'

The lieutenant gave the sergeant a look of surprise.

'They're down a precipice; we threw them there yesterday, and there they'll rot. Now kill me too; you won't know anything more.'

There was general silence and surprise.

'You are going to tell us who your other accomplices are,' the lieutenant threatened, brandishing a whip.

The prisoner smiled scornfully.

The lieutenant conferred briefly with the parish priest, and then, turning to the soldiers, ordered:

'Show him the bodies!'

In a corner of the courtyard, in an old cart, five corpses were piled up, half covered by a piece of filthy and torn matting. A soldier paced up and down, spitting.

'Do you know them?' the lieutenant asked, lifting the mat.

Társilo did not answer. He recognised the husband of the madwoman, and two others, his brother, covered with bayonet wounds, and Lucas, still with the halter round his neck. He seemed dejected and sighed.

'Do you know them?' he was asked again.

Társilo remained silent. The whip whistled through the air and struck his shoulders. He shuddered as his muscles reacted. The whip fell again and again but Társilo remained impassive.

'Beat him until he talks or is busted!' shouted the exasperated lieutenant.

'Come on, talk,' the Municipal Secretary urged Társilo. 'They're going to kill you anyway.'

Társilo was taken to the courthouse hall, where the other prisoner was calling on all the saints, his teeth chattering and his knees shaking.

'Do you know this man?' asked Father Salví.

'It's the first time I've seen him,' Társilo answered, looking at the other man with a certain pity.

The lieutenant hit Társilo with his fist and kicked him.

'Tie him up to the bench!'

Társilo, the bloodstained handcuffs still on his wrists, was tied to a wooden bench. The unfortunate looked round him as if searching for something and saw Doña Consolacíon. He laughed sardonically. His laugh surprised those present and following his eyes they saw the lady, who was biting her lips slightly.

'I've never seen an uglier woman,' Társilo exclaimed amid the general silence. 'I would rather lie down on a bench like this than beside her, like the lieutenant.'

Doña Consolacíon blanched.

'You are going to beat me to death, Lieutenant,' Társilo continued, 'but this night your wife will avenge me when she takes you in her arms.'

'Gag him!' screamed the furious commanding officer, shaking with anger, 'Beat him to death!'

It would have seemed that a gag was precisely what Társilo wanted, when he was muzzled, his eyes gleamed with satisfaction.

At a sign from the lieutenant, a soldier, armed with the whip, began his grisly task. Társilo's whole body shook; a long muffled roar was heard through the gag that covered his mouth; he lowered his mouth; he lowered his head, the bloodstains spreading through his clothes.

Father Salví, pale, with wandering look, rose painfully to his feet, and with a gesture stumbled our of the room. In the street he saw a young woman, leaning back against the wall, rigid, motionless, listening avidly, looking into space, her hands stretching convulsively on the old wall. The sun poured its heat on her as she counted, apparently without drawing breath, the sharp blows of the whip and the heartbreaking sobs. She was the sister of Társilo.

Meanwhile, in the courthouse hall, the unfortunate Társilo exhausted by pain, could groan no longer and seemed only to wait for his torturers to tire. At last the panting soldier let his arm fall. The lieutenant, pale with rage and amazement, gave the signal to untie Társilo.

At this point Doña Consolacíon stood up and whispered a few words in her husband's ear. He nodded and said:

'Take him to the well.'

Any Filipino would have known what this meant. The inventor of the torture is unknown, but it must be of considerable antiquity; perhaps the saying that truth comes from a well is a sarcastic commentary on it.

The picturesque mouth of the well rose in the middle of the courtyard, made roughly of unpolished stone. A primitive arrangement of bamboo forming a lever served to draw water from it, slimy, dirty, and evil-smelling. Broken pottery, garbage, and other liquids ended up in the well, for it was like a prison; whatever society discarded or gave up as useless ended up there, and whatever fell into it was lost, no matter how good it was. However, it was never closed up; sometimes prisoners were set to deepening it, not because such a punishment was expected to serve some useful purpose, but because of the difficulties of the task. Any prisoner who ever went down the well caught a fever of which he inevitably died.

Társilo watched the preparations being made by the soldiers fixedly; he was very pale and his face twitched; perhaps he was mumbling a prayer. The pride which despair had given him seemed to have vanished, or at least to have weakened. Many times he bent the neck he had held so high and lowered his eyes to the ground in resignation.

They took him beside the well-mouth, followed by a grinning Doña Consolacíon. The unfortunate man looked enviously at the pile of corpses and a sigh escaped him.

'Come on, talk now,' the Municipal Secretary urged him again. 'They'll hang you anyway. At least die without having suffered so much.'

'You'll leave here for the gallows, friend,' a municipal policeman told him.

They took off his gag and hung him up by the feet. He would be lowered head first and kept some time under the water, like a bucket, only a man is given more time.

The commanding officer went off to look for a watch by which to time the process.

Meantime Társilo hung by his feet, his long hair waving in the air, his eyes half closed.

'If you're Christians, if you have hearts,' he pleaded in a low voice, 'lower me fast or hit my head against the wall and kill me. God will reward you for this good deed. Think, maybe some day you will find yourselves where I am.'

The lieutenant returned and, watch in hand, supervised the lowering.

'Slowly, slowly!' screamed Doña Consolacíon, following the unfortunate man's progress with her eyes. 'Be careful!'

The pulley lowered Társilo slowly; his head grazed against the protruding stones and filthy growths. Then the lever ceased to move, and the lieutenant started counting the seconds.

'Up!' he ordered after half a minute.

The silvery and harmonious sound of water dropping on water announced the return of the prisoner to daylight. This time, since the counterbalancing weight was greater, he went up more quickly. Pebbles and shingles fell noisily.

His forehead and hair covered with muck, his face full of wounds and bruises, his body wet and dripping, he re-appeared before the silent crowd. A wind made him shiver with cold.

'Do you want to talk?' the lieutenant asked him hoarsely.

'Take care of my sister,' Társilo murmured, looking pleadingly at a policeman.

The bamboo lever creaked again and the doomed man was lost to sight once more. Doña Consolacíon watched to see if the water at the bottom of the well was undisturbed. The lieutenant counted off a full minute.

When Társilo was raised again, his features were contracted and empurpled. He looked round at the spectators, keeping his bloodshot eyes open.

'Are you going to talk?' the lieutenant asked again in a discouraged tone.

Társilo shook his head and they lowered him again. His eyelids were beginning to close; the pupils of his eyes searched as long as possible for the sky where white clouds floated; he bent his neck forward to snatch a last glimpse of daylight but was soon submerged; a damnable curtain fell and closed for him the spectacle of the world.

A minute passed. Doña Consolacíon, watching, saw great bubbles of air rising to the surface of the water.

'He's thirsty!' she cackled.

Then the water was again unbroken.

This time the lieutenant did not give the signal until after a minute and a half.

Társilo's features were no longer contorted; half-opened lids revealed the white eyeballs; muddy blood-streaked water ran from his mouth. The cold wind blew but his body no longer shivered.

All looked at one another in silence, pale and in consternation. The lieutenant ordered Társilo to be unhung, and left deep in thought. Doña Consolacíon pressed the lighted end of her cigarette a number of times against the naked legs, but the body did not react, and the cigarette went out.

'He strangled himself,' a policeman muttered. 'See how he turned his tongue in as if trying to swallow it.'

The other prisoner had watched the scene, trembling and sweating; he looked round him like a madman.

The lieutenant assigned the Municipal Secretary to question him.

'Sir, sir,' he sobbed, 'I will say anything you like.'

'Good. Let's see. What's your name?'

'Andong, sir.'

'Bernardo... Leonardo... Ricardo... Eduardo... Gerardo... which?'

'Put down Bernardo or whatever you want,' the lieutenant decided. 'Surname?'

The prisoner looked at the Municipal Secretary as if scared out of his wits.

'What name do you have in addition to that of Andong?'

'Ah, sir, Andong Halfwit, sir.'

The onlookers could not repress their laughter; the lieutenant himself stopped in his tracks.

'Occupation?'

'A pruner of coconut trees, sir, and servant of my mother-in-law.'

'Who ordered you to attack the barracks?'

'Nobody, sir.'

'What do you mean nobody? Don't lie or they'll lower you down the well.'

'Now, then, who gave you the orders? Tell the truth.'

'The truth, sir?'

'Who?'

'Who, sir?'

'I am asking you who gave you the orders for the revolution.'

'What revolution, sir?'

'That for which you were in the barracks yard last night.'

'Ah, sir,' exclaimed Andong blushing.

'Who was to blame for that?'

'My mother-in-law, sir.'

Laughter and surprise followed these words. The lieutenant stopped again and looked sternly at the wretch, who, believing that his words had had a good effect, continued with more spirit.

'Yes, sir, my mother-in-law, sir, she lets me eat only what is rotten and no good, sir, so, last night when I was near here, sir, I had a stomach-ache, sir, and I saw the yard of the barracks, sir, and I said, anyway, it is dark, nobody will see me, so I entered, sir, and then, sir, and then, when I was finished, sir, there were many shootings, but I was only pulling up my pants, sir.'

The whip cut him short.

'To the cells,' ordered the lieutenant. 'This afternoon, to the provincial capital!'

59 • *The One to Blame*

THE news that the detainees were being taken away soon spread throughout the town; at first it was heard with fear, then came the weeping and the lamentations.

The families of the detainees ran about like mad; they went from the parish house to the barracks, from the barracks to the courthouse, and finding consolation nowhere, filled the air with screams and moans. The parish priest had shut himself up on the excuse of illness; the commanding officer had increased his sentries, who received the suppliant women with rifle butts; the useless Mayor seemed to be more stupid and useless than ever before. Those who still had the strength for it ran here and there in front of the prison cells; others squatted wearily, calling out the names of their dear ones.

There was a burning sun, but none of those unfortunates thought of taking shelter. Doray, the merry and happy wife of Don Filipo, the Vice Mayor, wandered about anxiously, carrying her babe in arms, both weeping.

'Go home,' they told her. 'Your son will catch a fever.'

'Why live if he won't have a father to bring him up?' answered the disconsolate woman.

'Your husband is innocent. Perhaps he'll come back.'

'Yes, when we're all dead.'

Capitana Tinay wept and called for her son Antonio. The courageous Capitana María stared at the barred window behind which lay her twin sons, her only children.

The mother-in-law of the pruner of coconut trees was also there; she did not weep; she paced to and fro, gesticulating in her rolled-up sleeves, haranguing passers-by.

'Have you seen anything like it? Arresting my Andong, shooting him, putting him in the stocks, taking him to the provincial capital, and only because... only because he did not want to dirty his pants! This calls for revenge! The Constabulary is committing abuses! I swear that if I ever find one of them again in my orchard, looking for some place where he can be by himself, and it's happened many times, I'll mutilate him, mutilate him, otherwise... they can mutilate me!'

But few people were to be found to agree with this Moslem mother-in-law.

'Don Crisóstomo is to blame for all this,' sighed one woman.

The schoolmaster mingled with the crowd. The master-builder, without his plumbstring and metrestick, and no longer rubbing his hands, was dressed in black because he had heard bad news and, true to his way of looking at the future as something that had already happened, he was already in mourning for the death of Ibarra.

At two o'clock in the afternoon an open cart pulled by two bullocks stopped before the courthouse.

The cart was surrounded by the crowd, which wanted to unhitch and destroy it.

'Don't do it,' said Capitana María. 'Do you want them to go on foot?'

This stopped the families of the prisoners. Twenty soldiers marched out and surrounded the vehicle. Then the prisoners emerged.

The first was Don Filipo, tied up. He greeted his wife with a smile; Doray broke down into bitter tears and two soldiers had to struggle to keep her from embracing her husband. Antonio, the son of Capitana Tinay, appeared weeping like a child, which only increased the lamentations of his family. The halfwit Andong broke into tears on seeing his mother-in-law, cause of his misfortunes. Albino, the ex-seminarian, was also tied up like Capitana María's twins. These three young men seemed serious and determined. The last one to emerge was Ibarra, untied but between two soldiers. The young man was pale; he looked round for a friendly face.

'That's the one to blame!' cried many voices. 'He's the guilty one, and yet they haven't tied him up!'

'My son-in-law did nothing and yet he's handcuffed!'

Ibarra turned to his guards. 'Tie me up, but well, elbow to elbow,' he said.

'We have no orders to do so.'

'Tie me up or I'll make a run for it.'

The soldiers obeyed.

The commanding officer appeared on horseback, armed to the teeth, followed by ten of fifteen more soldiers.

Every prisoner had his family pleading for him, weeping for him, calling him the most endearing names. Only Ibarra had nobody; Master Juan himself and the schoolmaster had disappeared.

'What have my husband and my son done to you?' the weeping

Doray reproached him. 'Look at my poor son, you have taken his father away from him.'

The sorrow of the families turned into anger against the young man, who was charged with having instigated the rising. The lieutenant gave the order to start.

'You're a coward!' shouted the mother-in-law of Andong. 'While the others were fighting for you, you were in hiding! Coward!'

An old man followed running after the cart, cursing Ibarra and his family wealth, which had brought such disasters to the town.

'I hope they hang you, you heretic!' a relative of Albino screamed, and unable to control herself she pitched up a stone and hurled it at him.

Her example was quickly followed and a rain of dirt and stone fell on the unfortunate youth.

Ibarra endured impassively, without anger, without complaint, the just revenge of so many wounded hearts. This was the leavetaking, the farewell, to him of the town where he had all his loves.

He bowed his head, thinking perhaps of a man who had once been flogged through the streets of Manila, of an old mother struck dead at the sight of her son's head; perhaps the story of Elias was unfolding before his eyes.

The lieutenant deemed it necessary to keep the crowd at a distance, but the stones and the insults did not stop. Only one mother did not avenge her sorrows on him, Capitana María. Motionless, her eyes full of silent tears, she saw her two sons being taken away; Niobe herself, the inconsolable mother of the Grecian fable, who wept so much upon the loss of her twelve children that she was turned into a stone running tears, could not have matched her impassivity and silent sorrow.

The contingent moved on.

Among the persons at the few open windows only the indifferent or the merely curious had shown pity for Ibarra. His friends had all gone into hiding, even Capitan Basilio himself, who had forbidden his daughter Sinang to weep.

Ibarra saw the smoking ruins of his house, his ancestral home, where he had been born and which had kept alive for him the sweetest memories of his childhood and adolescence. The tears which he had so long kept back now poured forth; he bent his head and, his arms tied, wept without the measure of relief which he might have had if he had been able to conceal his tears, or if his sorrow had moved anyone to pity. Now he had neither country nor home, neither loves nor friends nor a future.

From a height a man watched the sombre caravan. He was an old man, pale, emaciated, wrapped in a woolen blanket, who leaned tiredly on a cane. It was old Tasio the scholar who, hearing the news, had left his sickbed to be present at the event. He had lacked the strength to reach the courthouse. The old man followed the cart with his eyes until it disappeared in the distance. Still he remained at his vantage point for some time, thoughtful and melancholy; then he pulled himself up and with great effort took the way back to his house, resting at every step.

Next day some herdsmen found him dead on the very threshold of his solitary retreat.

60 • *Patriotism and Self-Interest*

NEWS of the rising had been secretly telegraphed to Manila, and thirty-six hours later the newspapers of the capital contained some references to it, veiled, coupled with many warnings, and in versions embroidered, corrected, and mutilated by the censor. Meantime private accounts had circulated from the convents of the religious Orders by word of mouth, in secret, and to the panic of those who heard them. People were inclined to believe, with more or less readiness, the countless versions which distorted the real happenings, depending on whether this version or that one suited or offended their feelings and beliefs.

Although on the surface public peace had not been disturbed, the peace of many homes was in a turmoil, just as in a pond the surface may appear to be smooth and motionless while underneath it the silent fish dart about, chasing one another incessantly. Medals, crosses and epaulettes, jobs, prestige, power, influence, and dignities, began to flutter like butterflies in a golden atmosphere for a part of the population. For others, a dark cloud had risen on the horizon, from whose grey depths emerged the black shadows of prison bars, chains, and even the sinister scaffold. Interrogations, the screams of the tortured, verdicts of guilty, were in the air; and the affrighted eye glimpsed, as if through a tattered and bloodstained veil, the vision of exile to the

Marianas or death upon the scaffold in Bagumbayan. Fish and fishermen were in troubled waters. Destiny showed the events in San Diego to the imagination of the people of Manila in the manner of certain Chinese fans, which are all black on one face and on the other all gilded and covered with birds and flowers in brilliant colours.

The greatest excitement was to be found in the convents. Carriages were hastily hitched as Fathers Provincial called on one another for secret conferences or presented themselves in administration buildings to offer their support to the Government, which was said to be in the direst peril. There was talk of comets, pinpricks, and other mysterious allusions.

'A *Te Deum*, a *Te Deum!*' a friar was saying in one of the convents. 'We must give thanks to God, and this time let no one be absent from the choir. It is no little grace from God that He should make it plain now, precisely during these irreligious times, how valuable we are!'

'I bet this little lesson is making our little General Bad-Omen bite his lips,' said another, referring to the Governor General.

'Where would he have been without the religious Orders?'

'And to make the celebration really great, I move that suitable instructions be given to Brother Cook and the Father Administrator. *Gaudeamus*, let us rejoice, for three days.'

'Amen! Amen! Long live Salví! Long live!'

The conversation took another turn in another convent.

'What did I tell you? The man was brought up by the Jesuits. All the dissidents come from the Ateneo,' said one friar.

'And the anti-clericals.'

'I have said it time and again. The Jesuits are ruining the country. They corrupt the youth, but they are tolerated just because they make a few squiggles on paper in their Observatory whenever there is an earthquake.'

'And God only knows how that is done!'

'That's right. They're quite safe from contradiction. When everything is shaking and moving about, who's going to have time to make silly drawings? Don't tell me that this so-called astronomer of theirs...'

And they exchanged smiles of supreme disdain.

'But how about predicting storms and typhoons?' asked another friar ironically. 'Would that not suggest divine powers, now?'

'Any fisherman can predict a storm.'

'When the head of the Government is a fool... Well, tell me how your head is, and I'll tell you how your leg is. But just watch how our friends the Franciscans are taking care of themselves. The newspapers are just about asking a bishop's mitre for Father Salví!'

'And he'll get it!'

'You think so?'

'Why not? They make you a bishop for anything these days. I know one who got his mitre for less; he wrote a silly little book showing that the natives were incapable of anything higher than manual labour—you know, all the old stuff!'

'That's true. So many injustices injure the Church!' exclaimed another friar. 'If mitres had eyes and could see the kind of skulls they're placed on!'

'If mitres were only like Nature,' added another, 'which abhors a vacuum.'

'On the contrary,' countered a third. 'The vacuum sucks in the mitre and holds it fast!'

These and other things more were said in the convents, comments which ranged from the political and metaphysical to the merely spicy. Meantime there was quite a different atmosphere in the house of Capitan Tinong, the hospitable man who had so insistently pressed an invitation to dine on Ibarra.

Now, in the spacious and richly furnished living-room of his house in Tondo, he was seated in a great armchair, slapping his brow and neck in a gesture of affliction while his wife, Capitana Tinchang, tearfully lectured him. Their two daughters were in a corner listening, half dazed and half affrighted.

'Oh, Virgin of Antipolo!' the wife was crying. 'Oh Virgin of the Most Holy Rosary and of the Girdle! Oh, oh, oh Blessed Lady of Novaliches.'

'Mummy!' interjected the younger daughter.

'What did I tell you!' scolded Capitana Tinchang. 'I warned you! Oh, Virgin of the Carmel!'

'But you told me nothing!' Capitan Tinong ventured to object in a tearful voice. 'On the contrary, you used to tell me that I was right to call at the house of Capitan Tiago, and cultivate his friendship because... because he was rich... and you told me...'

'What? What was it I told you? I never told you that. I never told you anything. Oh, if you had only listened to me!'

'Now you're blaming me!' said Capitan Tinong bitterly, slapping the arm of his chair. 'Didn't you always tell me that I was right to invite Mr. Ibarra to dine with us because he was rich, and you said we should make friends only with the rich? Well, really!'

'It's true I said so but it was only because... well, because I had no choice. You were always talking about him. Mr. Ibarra here, Mr. Ibarra there, Mr. Ibarra everywhere. Well? But I never told you to see him or talk to him at that dinner party; you can't deny that.'

'How did I know he was going to be there?'

'Well, you should have known!'

'How? I didn't even know him!'

'Well, you should have known him!'

'But, Tinchang, it was the very first time I had seen him or heard about him!'

'Well, you should have seen him before, you should have heard about him, that's why you're a man, wear trousers, and read the Manila Daily!' his wife continued undeterred, and giving him a terrible look.

Capitan Tinong was unable to reply.

Capitana Tinchang, not satisfied with this victory, wanted to complete his rout and, closing her fists, came up to him and upbraided him:

'Is this what I have worked and scrimped for, year after year, so that you could throw away the fruits of my labours with your stupidity? Now they'll come and take you away to exile; they'll strip us of everything we have, as they did to the wife of... Oh, if only I were a man! If only I were a man!'

And observing that her husband had lowered his head, she started sobbing again, repeating over and over:

'If only I were a man!'

'Well, if you were a man,' her husband asked at length in a burst of annoyance, 'just what would you do?'

'What? Well... well... well, I would go to the Governor General this very minute and offer to fight the rebels, right now!'

'But haven't you read the Daily? Read what is says. *The infamous and illegitimate rebellion has been suppressed with energy, strength, and vigour; and soon the rebellious enemies of the Motherland and their accomplices will feel the weight and severity of the laws.* Well, you see? The rising is over.'

'Never mind, you should offer your services anyway; those who did so in 1872, saved themselves.'

'But so did Father Bur—'

But he was unable to finish uttering the name of Father Burgos, who had in fact been executed for alleged complicity in the events of 1872. His wife leaped on him to cover his mouth with her hand.

'Go on! That's right! Say his name so they'll string you up in Bagumbayan tomorrow morning! Don't you know it's enough to pronounce his name to get yourself condemned without trial? Go on, say it!'

Even if Capitan Tinong had wanted to obey her, he could not very well have done so, since his wife had both her hands on his mouth, pushing back his little head against the back of the armchair, so that the poor man would probably have choked to death if a new arrival had not intervened.

This was a cousin of the family, Don Primitivo by name, who knew by heart the standard philosophical work in Latin, a man in his forties, neatly dressed, rather stocky and full-bellied.

'*Quid video?* That is to say, what do I see?' he exclaimed upon entering.

'What goes on here? *Quaere?* Meaning, why?'

'Ah, dear cousin,' said Capitana Tinchang, running to him in tears. 'I had you called because I do not know what is to become of us. What do you advice? Tell me, you have studied Latin, you know how to argue...'

'But first, *quid quaeretis? Nihil est in intellectu quod prius non fuerit in sensu; nibil volitum quin praecognitum.* I translate for your benefit. What do you want? There is nothing in the mind which is not first perceived by the senses, and what is unknown cannot be desired. So tell me first what the trouble is.'

He chose a chair deliberately. As if the Latin phrases had been endowed with tranquillising powers, husband and wife ceased their lamentations and approached him to listen to the words of wisdom fall from his lips as in another time the Greeks had awaited the saving phrases of the Oracle that would free them from the Persian invaders.

'Why are you crying? *Ubinam gentium sumus?* Meaning, where do you think we are?'

'You have heard about the rising...'

'*Alzaementum,* that's rising, *Ibarrae ab lieutenento Constabuleriae destructum.* That's clear enough, isn't it? *Et nunc?* Now what? Does Don Crisóstomo owe you any money?'

'No, but you know, Tinong asked him to dinner, and greeted him on the Bridge of Spain in broad daylight! They'll say he's a friend of his.'

'A friend!' exclaimed the surprised Latinist jumping up. '*Amice, amicus Plato sed magis amica veritas.* Friend, Plato is my friend but truth is even more my friend. Birds of a feather flock together! *Malum est negotium*; looks bad to me; I'm afraid it's going to end very badly indeed. *Est tirmendum rerum istarum horrendisimum resultatum!*'

Capitan Tinong turned dreadfully pale when he heard so many words ending in *um*; it had such an ominous sound. His wife clasped her hands pleadingly and said:

'Cousin, please do not talk Latin to us now. You know we are not scholars like you are; speak to us in Tagalog, in Spanish, but give us your advice.'

'Pity you don't know Latin, coz. What is true in Latin is false in Tagalog. For instance. *Contra principia negantem fustibus est arguendum.* That is to say, you have to argue with your fists with someone who doesn't accept first principles. Now in Latin that is as true as that Noah built the Ark. But I tried putting it into practice in Tagalog, and the result was that I got beaten up. That is why it's a pity you don't know Latin. You could fix everything in Latin.'

'Well, we know how to say *oremus, parce nobis,* and *Agnus Dei quitolis,* but right now we wouldn't understand one another. Give Tinong a reason why they shouldn't hang him!'

'You were wrong, very wrong, coz, in making friends with that young man,' replied the Latinist. 'The just always suffer for the sinners. I would almost advice you to make your last will and testament. *Vae illis!* Woe be to them. Where there's smoke there's fire. *Ubi est fumus ibi est ignis.*'

And he shook his head in disgust.

'Saturnino!' screamed Capitana Tinchang, suddenly terror-stricken. 'Oh, my God, he's dead! Doctor! Call a doctor! Tinong! Sweet little Tinong!'

The two daughters came running and the three broke into lamentations.

'He's only fainted, coz. I would have been happier if... if... unfortunately, he has only fainted. Better to die in bed than on the scaffold in Bagumbayan.

Non timeo mortem in catre super espaldonem Bagumbayanis. Bring some water!'

'Don't die!' wept Capitana Tinchang. 'Don't die; they're coming to arrest you and if the soldiers come and you're dead, whatever shall I do? Oh!'

Don Primitivo splashed Capitan Tinong's face with water and the latter revived.

'Come now, stop crying. *Inveni remedium!* I've got the solution. Take him to bed. Come now, courage. I am with you, together with all the wisdom of the ancients. Have a doctor called. And right now, cousin, you must go to the Governor General with a present, a gold chain, a ring—gifts will move the hardest rocks. *Dadivas movant rockas.* Tell him it's a Christmas gift. Now, close the windows, shut the doors, and tell anyone who asks after him that Tinong is seriously ill. Meantime I shall be burning all his papers, letters and books, so they can find nothing against him; that is what Don Crisóstomo did. Any letters can be used against you. *Scripti testes sunt.* However, *quod mediccamenta non sanat, ferrum sanat, quodferrum non sanat, ignis sanat.* What drugs won't cure, iron will, and what iron won't, fire will.'

'Oh yes, cousin, here, burn it all,' said Capitana Tinchang. 'Here are the keys to the house, and here Capitan Tiago's letters: burn them! There mustn't be a trace left of newspapers from Europe; they are very dangerous. Oh, and here are the copies of *The Times* of London which I was keeping to wrap up soap and skirts. Here are the books.'

'On your way now, cousin, to the Governor General,' said Don Primitivo. 'Leave me alone. In *extremis extrema.* In desperate times, desperate measures. Give me the powers of a Roman dictator and you'll see how I get... get dear cousin out of it.'

He gave order after order, turned drawers upside down, tore up papers, books, letters. Soon there was a bonfire in the kitchen; some old guns were broken up with hatchets; rusty pistols were thrown into the cesspool, and a maidservant who wanted to keep the barrel of one to use as a blower, was sharply told off.

'*Conservare etiam sperasti, perfida?* So you thought you were getting away with that, did you, you wretch? Into the fire with it.'

And the *auto da fe* went on.

He caught sight of an old tome in parchment and read out the title: Revolution of Celestial Bodies by Copernicus. 'Pfui!' he exclaimed, throwing it into the fire. 'Into the stove with ye, accursed! *Ite maledicti in ignem kalanis* Revolutions! Copernicus! Really, this is one crime after another! If I hadn't got here on time! Now, what's this? *Freedom in the Philippines!* Tarara! What books! Into the fire!'

Harmless books by unsophisticated authors thus found their way into the fire. Not even the most naive work was saved. Yet Cousin Primitivo was right. The just suffer for the sinners.

Four or five hours later, at a pretentious gathering in the Spanish walled city, the events of the day were the subject of conversation. There were a great number of old women, spinsters, the wives and daughters of Spanish officials or employees, all dressed in housecoats, yawning and fanning themselves. Among the men whose faces, like those of their women, betrayed their origin and breeding, there was a small elderly one-armed gentleman to whom they showed great consideration and who in turn treated the rest with a disdainful silence.

'To tell the truth, up to now I couldn't bear friars and Constabulary officers; they're so ill bred,' a fat lady was saying. 'But now that I have seen how useful and valuable they are, I'd almost marry any one of them with pleasure. I'm a patriot.'

'Those are my sentiments,' agreed a thin lady. 'Pity we don't have the former Governor General. That one would leave the country as clean as a whistle.'

'And wipe out all this subversive breed.'

'Don't they say there are still many islands which are uninhabited? Why don't they deport all these stuck-up natives there? If I were the Governor General...'

'Ladies,' said the one-armed man, 'the Governor General knows his duty. I have heard that he is very annoyed because he had heaped so many favours on this Ibarra.'

'Heaped favours,' echoed the thin lady fanning herself vigorously. 'See how ungrateful these natives are! How can one treat them like human beings? *Jesús!*'

'And do you know what I've heard? asked an officer.

'What? Come on, what do they say?'

'Reliable sources,' said the officer in the midst of a profound silence, 'assert that all that business of building a schoolhouse was a fairy tale.'

'*Jesús,* what do you think of that?' exclaimed the ladies, ready to believe a newer fairy tale.

'The school was just a blind. What he really planned to build was a fortress where he could defend himself once we went after him.'

'*Jesus,* what infamy! Only a native could have such cowardly thoughts,' cried the fat lady. 'If I were Governor General, they'd see... they'd see soon enough.'

'Those are my sentiments,' agreed the thin lady once more. 'I would arrest every native shyster, every native priestling, every native buy-and-sell rascal, and off to exile or deportation with them, without benefit of trial. We must pull up the evil by the roots.'

'Well, they say that our little agitator is the son of Spaniards,' observed the one-armed man distantly.

'Ah, obviously, it had to be a half-breed!' exclaimed the fat lady unperturbed. 'No native knows anything about revolutions. Breed crows and they'll pluck your eyes out.'

'Do you know what I've heard?' a half-breed' girl interrupted. 'The wife of Capitan Tinong—remember him? We dined and danced in his house during the town fiesta of Tondo...'

'The one with two daughters? What about him?'

'Well, his wife has just this afternoon given the Governor General a present, a ring worth a thousand pesos!'

The one-armed man turned.

'Really? What for?' he asked, a gleam in his eyes.

'The wife said it was a Christmas present.'

'Christmas is a month away.'

'Probably afraid they would be caught in the storm,' observed the fat lady.

'And taking shelter beforehand,' added the thin lady.

'The wicked flee where no man pursueth.'

'Those are my sentiments. You have hit the nail on the head.'

'It will be necessary to look into this,' said the one-armed man thoughtfully. 'There is more here than meets the eye.'

'More than meets the eye. Just my sentiments,' echoed the thin lady.

'Mine too,' chimed in a third. 'The wife of Capitan Tinong is a skinflint;

fancy, we've called on her and she still hasn't sent us a present. So when a woman as tight-fisted and money-minded as she is starts giving away presents worth a thousand pesos...'

'But are you sure of this?' asked the one-armed man.

'As sure as anything,' said the half-breed. 'His Excellency's own aide is engaged to a cousin of mine, and it was he who told her. And I am almost sure it is the same ring the older of Capitan Tinong's daughters was wearing the day of the fiesta. She's always loaded with diamonds!'

'A walking shop-window!'

'Just another form of advertising: instead of buying a dummy or renting a shopfront...'

The one-armed man found an excuse to take his leave.

Some two hours later, when all were already asleep, soldiers delivered invitations to a number of residents of Tondo. The authorities could not allow certain persons of rank and property to sleep in houses which were so badly ventilated and guarded; they would find sleep more peaceful and refreshing in Fort Santiago and other government buildings. Among these favoured individuals was included poor Capitan Tinong.

61 • *A Wedding for María Clara*

CAPITAN TIAGO was very happy. In all this terrible time nobody had bothered with him; he had not been arrested; he had not been subjected to solitary confinement, interrogations, electric machines, perpetual foot baths in underground cells, and other deviltries well known to men who consider themselves civilized. His friends, or rather his former friends (for he had renounced his Filipino friends the minute they had become suspect to the Government), had for their part returned to their houses after a few days' vacation in the state buildings. The Governor General himself had ordered them out, perhaps judging them unfit to remain inside Government property, to the great disappointment of the one-armed official who had hoped to spend the coming Christmas in their rich and lavish company.

Capitan Tinong returned home sick, pale, and bloated; the excursion had not turned out at all well for him. He was such a changed man that he said not a word, even of greeting, to his family, who wept, laughed, chattered, and went wild with joy. The poor wretch no longer dared step out of his house, to avoid the danger of greeting a subversive character. Cousin Primitivo himself, for all the wisdom of the ancients, could not shake him out of his silence.

'Believe me, cousin,' he said,' if I had not been able to burn your papers, they would have strung you up; as it is, if I had only burned down the whole house, they would not have touched a hair on your head. But what's done is done, *quod eventum, eventum. Gratias agamus Domino Deo*, let us give thanks to the Lord our God that you are not in *Marianis insulis camotes plantando.*'

Capitan Tiago was not unaware of stories like Capitan Tinong's and he was overflowing with gratitude, without knowing for sure to whom he should be grateful for the signal favours he had received. Aunt Isabel gave the credit for the miracle to the Virgin of Antipolo, the Virgin of the Most Holy Rosary, the Virgin of the Carmel at least, or at the very very least, and this was as far as she would go, to Our Lady of the Girdle. According to her the miracle could not go farther than that. Capitan Tiago did not deny the miracle but added:

'I believe it, Isabel, but the Virgin of Antipolo could not have done it all by herself. She must have been helped by my future-son-in-law, Mr. Linares, who, as you know, is on joking terms with the Prime Minister himself, the very same one whose picture was in the illustrated weekly the other day. He is so important he shows only half his face to the public.'

The good fellow could not suppress a smile of self-congratulation every time he heard a significant piece of news regarding the events in San Diego. And no wonder: it was rumoured confidentially that Ibarra would be sent to the gallows; that, although there had not been enough evidence to find him guilty, proof of the charges against him had only lately been discovered; that experts had declared that the schoolhouse under construction could well have been used as a stronghold, a fort, although rather defective, since nothing better could be expected from ignorant natives. These rumours reassured Capitan Tiago and made him smile.

Like Capitan Tiago and his cousin, the friends of the family were divided into two factions: one which attributed Capitan Tiago's good fortune to a miracle, and another which attributed it to political influence. But the latter school was insignificant. Those who believed in a miracle were in turn subdivided: the head sacristan of the Binondo church, a candle pedlar, and the prefect of a certain confraternity, saw the hand of God moved by Our Lady of the Most Holy Rosary. On the other hand the Chinese candlemaker, who provided Capitan Tiago with candles when he went to Antipolo, said as he fanned himself and swung a leg:

'Donbee clazy; Bilgen Anipolo issy wan; she stlongeh evelybody; donbee clazy!'

Capitan Tiago held this Chinese in high esteem, for he passed himself off as prophet, physician, and all the rest. Reading the palm of Capitan Tiago's deceased wife in her sixth month of pregnancy, he had foretold:

'Ifen no man chile and ifen no dead, velly good man.'

And María Clara had seen the light of day to fulfill the infidel's prophecy.

A prudent and fearful man, Capitan Tiago was therefore unable to make up his mind as easily as the Trojan Paris when he was asked to pick the most beautiful of the goddesses; he could not give preference to one of the two Virgins for fear of offending the other with what might be grave consequences.

'Prudence,' he told himself. 'Let's not ruin it all now.'

He was in the midst of these doubts when the faction upholding the theory of political influence called on him: Doña Victorina, Don Tiburcio, and Linares.

Doña Victorina spoke for the two men and for herself; she spoke of the visits which Linares had made to the Governor General, suggesting repeatedly the advantages of being related to persons of influence.

'Nebbah mind only,' she concluded, 'if you-all are takin' sheltah under a biggah tree, you are gettin'a biggah beatin'.'

'J-j-just the other way round,' the doctor corrected her.

For some time now Doña Victorina had assumed a 'southern accent' by dint of lengthening her vowels and suppressing her final consonants, and nobody could get the idea out of her head; she would have sooner suffered her artificial fringe to be stripped from her forehead.

'Yas, suh,' she added, speaking of Ibarra. 'He only deservin' what he is gettin'. I seen him only the fust time, and I already concludin', he is a subversive elements. What is the General tellin'you-all, cuzzin? And what did you-all tellin' the General? Come on, you tell us already, what li'l ole things you telling him about Ibarra.'

Seeing that her cousin was slow in answering, she went on, turning to Captain Tiago:

'You believe, believe me only, if they shoot him, and that is maybe very shouah, it is the work of my cuzzin already.'

'Madam, Madam!' Linares started to protest.

But she did not give him time.

'Why you-all are so diplomatic also? You are the right-ahm man of the General, he cannot be livin' without you, we know that! Ah, Clarita, my deah, it shore is a pleasure to seein' you!'

María Clara was still rather off-colour, although she had recovered considerably from her illness. Her long hair was gathered with a light blue silk ribbon. She greeted them shyly, with a sad smile, and offered her cheek to Doña Victorina for the customary kiss.

After the usual exchanges the pseudo-Southerner continued:

'We are only visitin' you-all, now that you are already saved because of good connections!' She cast a significant look in the direction of Linares.

'God saved my father,' the girl answered quietly.

'Mebbe, mebbe, Clarita, but miracles are not happening any moah. We Spaniards are sayin', nevah mind the Virgin, bettah you trust youah laigs.'

'J-j-just the other way round!'

'Pahdon me only. Don't trusting youah laigs.'

Captain Tiago, who had until then found no opening for a contribution to the conversation, got up enough courage to ask a question, the reply to which engaged all his attention.

'Do I understand, Doña Victorina, that you believe that the Virgin...'

'It is already the virgin we are comin' to speak to you about,' she answered enigmatically, jerking her head towards María Clara. 'Already we must be talkin' about business is business.'

The girl understood that she was expected to withdraw, and found a pretext to do so, leaning weakly on chairbacks and tables on her way.

What was said and discussed at this conference is too despicable and mean to be recorded. Suffice it to say that when the visitors took their leave, everyone was in high spirits, and that afterwards Capitan Tiago told Aunt Isabel:

'Notify the restaurant that tomorrow we are having a celebration. And start breaking it to María that we are marrying her off soon.'

Aunt Isabel looked horrified.

'You'll see! When Mr. Linares is our son-in-law, we'll go in and out of all the Government buildings. Everybody will envy us; they'll all die of envy!'

That was why at eight o'clock the next evening the house of Capitan Tiago was crowded once again, only this time his guests were exclusively Spaniards and Chinese, the women only local Spaniards and Spaniards from the Peninsula.

Father Sibyla and Father Salví were among a number of other Franciscans and Dominicans. Also present were old Lieutenant Guevara of the Constabulary, looking even more grim; the former commanding officer of San Diego, looking over his shoulder at everyone with an air of importance, in the belief that he was a second Don John of Austria, the victor of Lepanto (he now had the provisional rank of major); de Espadaña, who gazed on him with respect and fear and avoided his eyes; and a disgusted Doña Victorina. Linares had not yet arrived; as a personage of some importance, he would arrive later than the other. There are beings so naive that they believe arriving an hour late everywhere they go is a sign of importance.

Among the ladies was María Clara, who was the subject of much gossip. She has greeted her guests punctiliously but without losing her air of melancholy.

'Psh,' said a young lady. 'Rather conceited, isn't she?'

'Quite attractive,' replied another. 'But he could have picked somebody who looked less stupid.'

'Money, darling. Eligible bachelors are for sale.'

Elsewhere it was said:

'Really, now, getting married when her first fiancé is just about on the gallows!'

'That's what I call foresight, having a substitute handy.'

'Well, when I lose my dearly beloved...'

Perhaps María Clara heard these conversations, for as she sat arranging flowers on a tray, her hand trembled noticeably, and she was often seen to lose colour and bite her lips.

Among the men the conversation was held in a loud voice, and naturally turned on the latest events. All were speaking, even Don Tiburcio, with the exception of Father Sibyla, who maintained his contemptuous silence.

'I have heard it said that Your Reverence is leaving the town of San Diego, Father Salví,' remarked the new Acting Major whom the additional stars of his new rank had turned amiable.

'I have nothing more to do there. I am to have a permanent assignment in Manila. And you?'

'I too am leaving the town,' he answered, stretching himself. 'The Government needs me to disinfect the provinces of dissidents with a combat team.'

Father Sibyla looked him up and down quickly and turned his back completely.

'Is anything definite known about what is to be done with the ring-leader, that would-be dissident?' inquired an employee.

'Do you speak of Crisóstomo Ibarra?' asked another. 'Probably, and it is only just, he will be sent to the gallows like those rascals in 1872.'

'He is being exiled,' said old Lieutenant Guevara drily.

'Exiled, only exiled! But surely it will be exile for life,' a number of voices protested simultaneously.

'If that young man,' continued Lieutenant Guevara in a loud stern voice, 'had been more prudent; if he had put less trust in certain persons with whom he was in correspondence; if our prosecuting attorneys were not so excessively clever in reading meanings into documents, he would surely have been acquitted.'

The old lieutenant's assertion and his manner of making it caused great surprise among those who heard him, and they did not know what to say. Father Salví looked elsewhere, perhaps to avoid the lowering look which the old man turned on him. María Clara dropped her flowers and sat frozen. Father Sibyla, who knew how to keep his mouth shut, now seemed to be also the only one who could open it.

'Do you speak of letters, Lieutenant Guevara?'

'I am only repeating what I was told by his defence counsel, who took up his case with zeal and interest. There was nothing that could be used against him except for a few ambiguous lines which Ibarra wrote to a girl before leaving for Europe. The prosecuting attorney claimed that these words revealed a plan and a threat against the Government, and Ibarra admitted that he had indeed written them.'

'What about the *ante-mortem* statement by one of the outlaws?'

'Defence counsel destroyed its effectiveness, for, according to the outlaw himself, he and his companions had never had any communications with Mr. Ibarra, but only with a certain Lucas, who, it was established, was Mr. Ibarra's enemy, and who committed suicide, driven perhaps by remorse. It was proved that the papers found on the corpse were forgeries, for the handwriting was similar to that of Mr. Ibarra seven years ago, but not to his present handwriting. The supposition is that the model for the forgeries was the letter to the girl. Moreover, defense counsel said that, if Mr. Ibarra had not admitted the letter to be his, much more could have been done on his behalf, but when he saw it, he blanched, lost spirit, and confirmed all that he had written.'

'You were saying,' asked a Franciscan, 'that the letter was addressed to a girl—how did it get to the hands of the prosecuting attorney?'

Lieutenant Guevara did not reply. He glanced briefly at Father Salví and moved away, striding across the room, as the others exchanged opinions.

'You can see the hand of God there!' said one. 'Even the women hate him.'

'He had his house burned, thinking that would save him, but he did not reckon with the lady guest, that is to say, with the mistress, the little bitch,' another one added with a laugh. 'God wills it! Cry Santiago, and up Spain!'

Meantime the old officer had paused beside María Clara, who was listening to the conversation, motionless in her chair, her flowers at her feet.

'You are a very prudent young lady,' the old lieutenant whispered. 'You did well in handing the letter over. That way you and your family are sure of an untroubled future.'

She saw him move away with vacant eyes, biting her lips. Fortunately Aunt Isabel passed by. María Clara had enough strength to snatch at her dress.

'Aunt,' she murmured.

'What's come over you?' Aunt Isabel answered, horrified by the girl's expression.

'Take me to my room,' she pleaded, clutching at the old lady's arm to raise herself.

'Are you ill, darling? You don't seem to have a bone in your body! What is it?'

'I feel faint... so many people... so much light... I need a rest. Tell Papa I've gone to bed.'

'You're like ice. Would you like some tea?'

María Clara shook her head. Once in her room she locked the door and, feeling all her strength leave her, let herself fall on the floor at the foot of an image, calling to her mother.

Moonlight streamed in through the window and the door leading to the porch.

The orchestra went on playing merry waltzes. The sound of laughter and the murmur of conversation seeped into the bedroom. Her father, Aunt Isabel, Doña Victorina, even Linares, knocked at the door at various times, but María Clara did not reply.

The hours passed; the pleasures of the table came to an end; there was the sound of dancing. The taper in the room went out. The girl remained motionless on the floor, lighted by the moon, at the foot of the image of the Mother of Jesus.

Gradually the house fell silent; the lights were put out. Aunt Isabel knocked again on the bedroom door.

'Well, now, she's fallen asleep,' she said aloud. 'She's young and has nothing to worry about. She's dead to the world.'

When all was silent María Clara rose slowly and looking round her was attracted by the porch and its little trellises bathed in the melancholy light of the moon.

'An untroubled future! Dead to the world!' she murmured, and went out on the porch.

The city slept. Only the clatter of a carriage could be heard from time to time as it crossed the wooden bridge over the river whose lonely waters tranquilly reflected the lights of the moon.

The girl lifted her eyes to the deep blue sky, and slowly took off her rings, earrings, hairpins, and comb. She placed them on the balustrade and looked down into the river.

A boat loaded with horse-fodder was stopping at the foot of the landing which each house had on the river bank. One of the two men in it went up the stone steps, and climbed the wall. In a few seconds his steps were heard going up the staircase to the porch.

María Clara saw him stop when he saw her, but it was only for a moment, for the man went on and did not stop until he was barely three steps away. María Clara started back.

'Crisóstomo!' she whispered, full of terror.

'Yes, it is I, Crisóstomo,' the young man replied gravely. 'An enemy, a man who had reason to hate me, Elias, has rescued me from the prison where I was flung by my friends.'

A rueful silence followed these words. María Clara lowered her head and let both hands fall.

Ibarra continued:

'By my dead mother's coffin I swore to make you happy, no matter what happened to me. You could break your own pledge; she was not your mother. But I am her son, and I hold her memory sacred, and I have braved a thousand perils to come here and keep mine. By the grace of God I can speak to you in person. María, we shall never see each other again. You are still young, but perhaps some day your conscience may trouble you. I have come to say, before we part, that I forgive you. And now, be happy, farewell.'

Ibarra tried to leave, but María Clara found the strength to stop him.

'Crisóstomo,' she said, 'God has sent you to save me from despair. Hear me and judge.'

Ibarra gently tried to disengage himself.

'I have not come for an accounting, but to give you peace of mind.'

'I don't want that peace of mind you're offering me. If I am ever to have it, I must give it to myself. You despise me, and your contempt would make even death bitter.'

Ibarra saw her sorrow and despair and asked her what she wanted.

'I want you to believe that I have always loved you.'

Crisóstomo smiled bitterly.

'You doubt me, you doubt your childhood friend who never had any secrets from you,' she exclaimed sadly. 'But when you know the story of my life, the tragic story they told me when I was ill, you will take pity on me; you will not then have that smile for my sorrow. Why didn't you leave me to die at the hands of that ignorant doctor? You and I would have been happier!

'But you wanted it this way. And then you doubted my love. So be it; may my mother forgive me! One night when I was sick and in pain someone told me the name of my real father, and he forbade me to love you... unless my real father forgave you the injury you had done him.'

Ibarra drew back aghast.

'He told me that he could not allow our union because it would be against his conscience, and he would feel compelled to proclaim, at the risk of grave scandal, that my father is...'

And she whispered a name in the young man's ear that only he could have heard.

'What was I to do? Was I sacrifice to my love for you my mother's memory, my pretended father's honour, my real father's good name? Could I have done that without you yourself despising me?'

'But proofs, did you have them? You should have asked for proofs!' cried Crisóstomo in a frenzy.

The girl drew two papers from her bosom.

'Two letters from my mother, written in remorse, when she was carrying me in her womb. Take them and read them, and you will see that she curses me and wishes I were dead, as dead as I would have been if my real father had found the right drugs. He forgot these letters in the house where he was living; someone found them and kept them. They were given to me only in exchange for your letter to me... as a pledge, he said, that I would not marry you without the consent of my real father. Since I have carried them on me, instead of your letter, I have felt a chill on my heart. I gave you up; I gave up love. What would we not do for one dead mother and two live fathers? How could I suspect what they would do with your letter?'

Ibarra was appalled.

'What was there left for me to do? Do you think I could have told you— at the time—who my real father was? Could I have asked you to beg his forgiveness when he had caused your own father so much suffering? Could I have asked my own father to forgive you, because I was his daughter, when he had wanted so much to see me dead? I could only suffer, keep my secret, and die with it. And now, my friend, now that you know the sad story of your poor María, do you still have for her that smile of contempt?'

'María, you are a saint!'

'I'm happy because you believe me...'

'But,' said Ibarra changing his tone, 'I hear you are getting married...'

'Yes,' she hastened to explain. 'My father requires this sacrifice from me. He gave me a home and affection when it was not his duty to do so. I repay this debt of gratitude assuring him peace by means of this new relationship, but...'

'But what?'

'I will not forget that I swore to be faithful.'

'What do you mean to do?' Ibarra asked, trying to read her eyes.

'The future is dark. Our fate is hidden. I do not know what I am going to do. But I love only once, and I shall never belong to anyone without love. And you, what's to become of you?'

'I am only a man on the run. Soon they will discover my escape.'

María Clara held the young man's head in her hands, kissed his lips again and again, embraced him, and then pushed him away.

'Go! Go quickly! Goodbye!'

Ibarra looked at her with gleaming eyes, but at her gesture he left, uncertain, beside himself.

He jumped over the wall again, and boarded the boat. María Clara leaned over the balustrade and watched him go.

Elias uncovered himself as they passed by and gave her a deep bow.

62 • *The Chase on the Lake*

LISTEN,' said Elias thoughtfully as they went towards San Gabriel, 'this is what I have in mind. You are to hide out for now in the house of a friend of mine in Mandaluyong. There I shall take you all your money; I saved it from the fire and cached it at the foot of the *bálete* tree where your grandfather's grave is. Then you are to leave the country...'

'To go abroad?' interrupted Ibarra.

'To live out in peace the remaining days of your life. You have friends in Spain; you are rich; you can get a pardon. Anyway, a foreign country is for us a better home than our own.'

Crisóstomo did not answer, deep in thought.

They were entering the Pasig river, and the boat began to move upstream. A horseman galloped along the Bridge of Spain, and a sharp and long-drawn-out whistle was heard.

'Elias,' Ibarra countered, 'you owe your misfortunes to my family; twice you have saved my life; and I owe you not only gratitude but also the restitution of your wealth. You advice me to live abroad; come with me and we shall live together like brothers. Here you too are unfortunate.'

Elias sadly shook his head and answered:

'Impossible. It is true that I cannot love or be happy in my country, but

I can suffer and die in it, and perhaps for it; that is always something. Let the misfortunes of my country be my own, and since our people are not all united by a noble ideal, since our hearts do not beat faster to the same name, at least our common unhappiness may unite me with them. I shall weep with them over our sorrows, and let the same misfortunes oppress all our hearts.'

'Then why do you advice me to leave?'

'Because you can be happy elsewhere, because you are not made for suffering, because you would hate your country if some day you were to find yourself outcast for her sake, and to hate one's own country is the greatest of misfortunes.'

'You are being unfair to me,' Ibarra complained bitterly. 'You forget that, as soon as I returned, I dedicated myself to seeking the good of the country.'

'Do not take it amiss, sir, I am not reproaching you. I wish all could imitate you. But I do not ask the impossible of you, and do not be offended if I say that your heart misleads you. You loved your country because that is what your father taught you to do. You loved her because you had love, wealth, youth, and fortune here. Your country had not been unjust to you; and you loved her as we love all that makes us happy. But the day you find yourself poor, hungry, hunted, and delivered to your enemies for a price by your own countrymen, that day you will disown yourself, your country, and humanity itself.'

'I am hurt by what you say, my friend,' said Ibarra resentfully.

Elias lowered his head briefly and replied:

'I want to disillusion you, sir, and save you from future disappointments. Remember when I was speaking to you in this very boat, under the light of this same moon, about a month ago: you were happy then. The pleas of the oppressed did not touch you; you scorned to hear their complaints because they were the complaints of criminals; you gave greater heed to their enemies, and, in spite of my arguments and pleas, you placed yourself at the side of their oppressors. It depended on you then whether I should become a criminal myself or allow myself to be killed to keep a sacred promise. God did not allow it; the old commander of the outlaws died. A month has passed, and now you think differently!'

'You are right, Elias, but man is a creature of circumstance. At that time I was blind, disgusted—I don't know what. Now misfortune has snatched away the blindfold from my eyes. Now I see the horrible cancer that is gnawing away at our society, that seizes on the flesh of our country, and must be torn out. They have opened my eyes to our social cancer. They have compelled me to become a criminal. And since that is how they want it, I shall become an agitator, but a true agitator, I shall call to all the oppressed, all those who feel a heart beat in their breasts, all those who sent you to me. No, that will not be a crime; it is never a crime to fight for one's own country. On the contrary! For three centuries we have stretched out our hands to them; we have asked them for love; we wanted to call them brothers. What has been their answer? Insults, sarcasm, a denial that we are even fellow-men! But God, as you once said, will not forsake us. He has given His helping hand to all peoples that fought for their independence.'

Ibarra was in a passion; his whole body trembled.

They were passing in front of the Governor General's palace, and thought they observed an unusual activity and excitement among the sentries.

'I wonder if they have discovered your escape,' muttered Elias. 'Lie down, sir, and I'll cover you with grass; we are passing by the powder magazine and the sentry may think it odd that there are two of us in this boat.'

The boat was one of those sheer and slender canoes that glide over the surface of the water rather than move through it.

As Elias had foreseen the sentry hailed him and asked him where he came from.

'From Manila, delivering horse-fodder to the judges and the priests,' he answered, imitating the local accent of the grass-growing region in Pandacan.

A sergeant came out to find out what was going on.

'You can go,' he told Elias. 'But I warn you; take no one aboard; a prisoner has just escaped. If you catch and bring him to me, I'll give you a good reward.'

'Very good, sir. What is he like?'

'He is in a frock-coat and speaks Spanish. So keep your eyes open!'

The boat moved away. Elias turned his head and saw the silhouette of the sentry, still standing at the river bank.

'We shall lose a few minutes,' he whispered. 'We must enter the Beata river to make it appear that I am from Peñafrancia. You will see the river of Francisco Baltazar's poems.'

The town slept in the moonlight. Crisóstomo pulled himself up to savour

the peace of Nature. The river was narrow, running through a plain sown
with grass.

Elias threw his load ashore, and with a bamboo pole picked up some empty
sacks from under the grass. They went on.

'You are your own master, sir, and you must decide your own future,' he
told Crisóstomo, who remained silent. 'But if you would permit me to make
an observation, I would tell you to think well about what you are going to
do. You are going to start a war, for you have money and brains, and will
easily find many helping hands; unfortunately many are disconnected. But
in this fight which you propose to start, the defenceless and the innocent will
suffer most. The same sentiments which a month ago led me to ask you for
reforms, lead me now to ask you to reflect further. Our country does not
think of independence from the Motherland; she asks nothing more than a
small measure of liberty, of justice, and of love. The discontented, the criminal
and the desperate will follow you, but the people will stand apart. I would
not follow you myself: I would never resort to these extreme measures while
I could see some hope in men.'

'Then I shall go on without you,' replied Crisóstomo resolutely.

'Is that your firm decision?'

'My firm and only decision. God and my father be my witnesses! I do not
allow peace and happiness to be snatched away from me with impunity. I
have only sought what was good. I have respected and endured everything
for love of religion, for love of country. How have they repaid me? By
burying me in a foul prison and degrading my future wife. Not to avenge
this would be itself a crime; it would be to encourage my enemies to commit
fresh injustices. Let there be an end to cowardice, weakness, to sighing and
weeping, as long as there is blood and life, and when derision is heaped on
top of insult and challenge, I shall call on this people in their ignorance; I
shall make them see their wretchedness. Let them not think of brothers;
there are only wolves that devour one another. I shall tell them that man's
eternal right to freedom rises and protests against this oppression.'

Elias bowed his head with a sigh.

'Can you take me to the mountains?'

'Until you are in safety,' Elias answered.

They went out again into the Pasig. They speak once in a while about inconsequential things.

'Santa Ana!' murmured Ibarra. 'Would you know that house?'

They were passing by the country house of the Jesuits.

'I spent many happy days there,' sighed Elias. 'In my time we went there once a month. I was like the others then: I was wealthy, I had a family, dreams, a future. In those days I would visit my sister in the neighbouring college; she had a friend, a pretty girl. That's over now. It was a dream.'

They remained silent until they reached Malapad-na-bato, their thoughts familiar to anyone who has ever gone down the Pasig river on one of those magic Philippine nights when the moon pours forlorn poetry from the deep blue sky, when shadows conceal the wretchedness of men and their pretty voices are muffled by the silence, and only Nature speaks.

The guard at Malapad-na-bato was sleepy, and, seeing that the boat was empty and there was nothing to loot from it in accordance with the traditions of his organisation and the usages of that particular check-point, he let them go without objection.

The Constabulary soldier at Pasig suspected nothing either, and they were not molested.

It was beginning to dawn when they reached the lake, tame and tranquil like a gigantic mirror. The moon was paling, and the East was rosy. Some distance away they made out a grey mass that was moving slowly.

'The patrol launch is coming,' whispered Elias. 'Lie down and I'll cover you with these sacks.'

The launch was now becoming clearer and more distinct.

'It is placing itself between us and the shore,' Elias observed uneasily.

He gradually changed their own course, paddling toward Binangonan. To his great dismay he saw the patrol launch following suit.

A voice hailed them.

Elias stopped to think. The shore was still far away, and soon they would be within range of the patrol launch's rifles. He thought of turning back to Pasig; his boat was faster than the launch. But fate was against them; another boat was coming from that direction, gleaming with the helmets and bayonets of Constabulary soldiers.

'We're caught,' he whispered, losing colour.

He studied his muscled arms briefly, and taking the only course left began to paddle with all his strength toward the island of Talim. Meantime the sun was coming up.

The boat glided swiftly over the waters. Elias saw men standing, signalling to him, aboard the turning patrol launch.

'Do you know how to handle a boat?' he asked Ibarra.

'Yes, why?'

'Because we're lost unless I jump out and lead them away. They'll go after me, but I am a good swimmer and diver. I'll lead them away from you; then you must try and save yourself.'

'No, stay, and we'll sell our lives dearly!'

'Useless. We are unarmed, and with their rifles they can pick us off like birds.'

At that instant there was a hiss of hot lead in the water, followed immediately by the sound of a shot.

'See?' said Elias, placing the paddle inside the boat. 'We shall see each other on Christmas Eve by your grandfather's grave. Save yourself.'

'And you?'

'God has delivered me from greater dangers.'

Elias took off his shirt. A bullet tore it from his hands and two shots were heard. Undisturbed he clasped the hand of Ibarra, who was still lying at the bottom of the boat. Then he rose and dived into the lake, pushing the boat aside with his foot.

Several shouts were heard, and soon the head of Elias, coming up for air, appeared some distance away, disappearing in an instant.

'There, there he is!' shouted several voices, and the bullets whistled again.

The patrol launch and the Constabulary boat went off in pursuit; Elias left a slight wake that grew farther and farther away from Ibarra's boat, which floated as if abandoned. Every time the swimmer came up for air, the Constabulary soldiers and the crew of the launch fired on him.

The chase was taking a long time. Ibarra's boat was now far away. The swimmer was nearing the shore, only fifty fathoms away. The men paddling the pursuing craft were tiring, but so was Elias, because he came up more and more often, although in different directions to confuse his pursuers. The telltale wake no longer betrayed the way he was going under water. They saw him for the last time about ten fathoms from shore. They fired. Minutes passed; but nothing broke the smooth and deserted surface of the lake.

Half an hour later one of the rowers claimed to have discovered signs of blood in the water near the shore, but his companions shook their heads doubtfully.

63 • *Father Dámaso Explains Himself*

IN vain were valuable wedding gifts piled up on a table; neither diamonds in blue velvet cases nor embroidered pineapple cloth nor bolts of silk attracted the eyes of María Clara.

Suddenly she felt two hands covering her eyes and holding her fast, and heard a teasing voice, Father Dámaso's, ask:

'Who am I? Guess who I am!'

María Clara jumped from her chair and looked at him with dread.

'You were scared, weren't you, you little goose? Didn't expect me; did you? Well, I have come all the way from the provinces for your wedding.'

Approaching her again with a happy smile, he stretched out his hand to be kissed. Trembling, María Clara raised his hand respectfully to her lips.

'What is the matter with you, María?' the Franciscan asked, losing his merry smile and growing uneasy. 'Your hand is like ice, you are pale. Are you ill, child?'

Father Dámaso drew her to him with a tenderness of which he would have seemed incapable, caught both her hands, and looked at her searchingly.

'Don't you trust your godfather any more?' he asked reproachfully. 'Come, sit down here, and tell me all your little troubles, as you used to do when you were a little girl and wanted the drippings from the candles to make wax dolls. You know I have always loved you... never scolded you...'

Father Dámaso's voice was no longer rough and had tender overtones. María Clara broke into tears.

'Why are you crying, my child? Have you quarrelled with Linares?'

María Clara covered her ears.

'Not a word about him! Not now!' she cried out in agony.

Father Dámaso looked at her with surprise.

Don't you want to confide in me? Haven't I always tried to satisfy every whim of yours?'

The girl raised her tear-filled eyes to him and burst again into bitter weeping.

'Don't cry like that, my child, it hurts me to see you cry. Tell me what's wrong, and you'll see how much your godfather loves you.'

María Clara knelt at his feet, and, raising her tear-stained face, whispered in almost imperceptible accents:

'Do you still love me?'

'Child!'

'Then, protect my father, but stop my marriage. Otherwise, I swear by the memory of my mother, I'll kill myself!'

Father Dámaso could scarcely believe what he heard.

'While Crisóstomo lived,' she continued, 'I could fight, hope, be confident. I wanted to live to hear about him. But now that they have killed him, there is no longer any reason why I should go on living without happiness.'

She said this slowly, in a low voice, calmly and without tears.

'But, silly, isn't Linares a thousand times better than...'

'When he was alive, I could go through with the marriage. I planned to run away and look for him after the ceremony... My father wants only good connections. Now that he is dead, I'll kill myself before marrying anybody else. When he was alive I could degrade myself; I still had the consolation of knowing that he lived and perhaps might think of me. Now that he is dead, I would rather be a nun or be dead myself.'

The girl's voice was so determined that Father Dámaso lost his festive air completely and fell into deep thought.

'Did you love him so much?' he mumbled.

María Clara did not answer. Father Dámaso lowered his head to his breast and fell silent.

'My child,' he cried with a broken voice, 'forgive me for having unwittingly made you so unhappy. I was only thinking of your future, I wanted you to be happy. Could I allow you to marry a Filipino, and see you unhappy as a wife and wretched as a mother? But I could not put your love out of your head. I opposed it with all my strength, I abused all my powers, for your sake, only for yours. If you had been his wife, you would have wept afterwards to see your husband's condition, exposed to all manner of persecution without means of defence. As a mother, you would have wept over the fate of your children, for if you had given them an education, you would have only prepared a tragic future for them; they would have become enemies of the Church, and you would have seen them on the gallows or in exile; and if you had kept them in ignorance, you would have seen them oppressed and degraded. That is why I sought for you a husband who could make you the happy mother of children who would command, not obey, who would have the power to inflict punishment, not endure it. I knew that your childhood friend was a good man; I loved him as I loved his father; but I hated them from the day I saw they were going to make you unhappy, because I love you, I idolise you, I love you like my own daughter; I have no other love but yours. I saw you grow up; no hour passes but I think of you; I dream of you; you are my only joy.'

Father Dámaso wept like a child.

'Then, if you love me, do not make me unhappy all my life. He is no longer alive. I want to die or be a nun.'

The old priest leaned his brow on his hand.

'A nun, a nun!' he repeated. 'My child, you have no idea of the life, of the hidden mysteries, behind the walls of a nunnery. You have no idea. I would rather a thousand times see you unhappy in the world than in the cloister. Here you can make your grievances heard; there, you will have only the walls to listen to you. You are beautiful, very beautiful, and you were not born for Him, to be the spouse of Christ! Believe me, my child, time wipes away everything; sooner or later you will forget Crisóstomo, and you will grow to love your husband, Linares.'

'The nunnery or death,' said María Clara.

'The nunnery, the nunnery or death!' exclaimed Father Dámaso. 'I am old, María, I shall not be here much longer to watch over you and your happiness... ask me for something else. Fall in love with somebody else, another young man, whoever he is. But not the nunnery.'

'The nunnery or death.'

'My God, my God,' cried the priest, covering his face with his hands, 'You punish me, and I accept it. But watch over my daughter!' Then, turning to the girl: 'Do you want to be a nun? So you shall be. I will not have you die.' María Clara fell to her knees, seized his hands, and pressed and kissed them.

'Godfather, godfather!'

Father Dámaso left soon afterwards, gloomy, spiritless, sighing: 'Oh, God, You must exist since we are witness to Your punishments, but let Your vengeance be wreaked on me; do not wound the innocent; spare my daughter!'

64 • *Christmas Eve*

BESIDE a spring in the mountain near San Diego, on the banks of a stream, there was a hut raised on some twisted stumps. A squash vine, laden with fruits and flowers, crept over its grass roof. Inside, the rustic dwelling was decorated with antlers and the skulls of wild boar, some with exceptionally long tusks. It was the house of a Tagalog family of hunters and woodcutters.

In the shade of a tree Grandfather was making brooms with the stems of palm leaves while two of his grandsons husked rice to the tune of a song and a girl arranged eggs, lemons, and vegetables in a basket. Two children, a boy and a girl, were playing beside another child, wan, listless, with great deep-set eyes, who was seated on a tree trunk. His thin features were those of Sisa's son, Basilio, the brother of Crispín.

'When your foot is all right,' the girl told him, 'we can play hopscotch and hide-and-seek. I'll be it.'

'And you can climb with us to the top of the mountain,' added the boy. 'You can drink deer's blood there with lemon juice, and you will get fat.'

Basilio smiled sadly and stared at the wound in his foot. Then he gazed at the glorious sun.

'Peddle these brooms,' said the grandfather to the young girl, 'and buy some sandals for the children. It's Christmas Eve.'

'Firecrackers!' shouted the little boy. 'I want firecrackers!'

'And I want a new head for my doll!' shrieked the little girl, tugging at her sister's skirt.

'And you,' the grandfather asked Basilio, 'what do you want for Christmas?'

Basilio rose painfully to his feet and went limping to the old man's side.

'Sir,' he asked, 'have I really been ill for more than a month?'

'Two full moons have passed since we found you unconscious and wounded. We thought you were going to die.'

'God reward you. We are very poor,' replied Basilio. 'But since it's Christmas I should like to go to town to see my mother and my brother.

They must be looking for me.'

'But, son, you are still not well enough. Your town is quite a distance away; you won't make it by midnight.'

'Never mind, sir. My mother and my brother must be very sad; we spend the holidays together every year. Last year we had one fish for the three of us; mother had been crying, looking for me.'

'You won't reach the town alive,' boy! Tonight we are having chicken and smoked boar. My sons will be looking for you when they come back from the fields.'

'You have many sons and my mother has only two of us; maybe she thinks me dead already. Tonight I want to make her happy, I want to give her a present, a son.'

The old man felt his eyes moisten, put his hand on the boy's head and told him with emotion:

'You speak like a grown-up. Go then, look for your mother, give her her present... from God, as you say. If I had known the name of your town I would have gone there when you were ill... Go, my child, may God and the Lord Jesus go with you. Lucia will go with you to the next town.'

'What! You're not going, are you?' the little boy asked. 'Down below there are soldiers and many bandits. Don't you want to hear my firecrackers? Bang, bang, bang!'

'Don't you want to play blind man's buff?' asked the little girl in turn. 'Or hide-in-seek? Really nothing is more fun than hiding!'

Basilio smiled, took up his cane, and told them with tears in his eyes:

'I'll come back soon. I'll bring my brother along, and you can play with him. He's your age.'

'Does he limp too?' asked the little girl. 'Then he can be it.'

'Don't forget us,' said the grandfather. 'Here, take this smoked boar for your mother.'

'We'll visit you when we go to town,' said the boys who were husking rice.

The children accompanied him to a bamboo bridge, which crossed the turbulent stream.

Lucia placed her hand on his shoulder, and he leaned on her arm. The two were soon out of sight.

Basilio walked quickly in spite of his bandaged leg.

A northern wind whistled and the inhabitants of San Diego shivered with cold.

It was Christmas Eve but the town was sad. Not one paper lantern hung from the windows; no bustle in the houses promised the rejoicing of other years.

In the ground floor of his house, Capitan Basilio and Don Filipo (the latter's misfortunes had made them friends) were chatting by a barred window while at another one Sinang, her cousin Victoria, and the beautiful Iday looked out into the street.

The waning moon was beginning to shine on the horizon and gilded the clouds, trees, and houses, throwing long fantastic shadows.

'You were more than a little lucky to have been acquitted in these times,' Capitan Basilio told Don Filipo. 'They have burned your books, it is true, but others have lost more than that.'

A woman approached the window and looked in. Her eyes glittered, her face was gaunt, her hair loose and unkempt. The moonlight gave her a peculiar aspect.

'Sisa!' Don Filipo exclaimed with surprise. As the madwoman walked away he turned to Capitan Basilio and asked:

'Was she not under a doctor's care? Has she recovered?'

Capitan Basilio smiled bitterly.

'The doctor was afraid he would be charged with being a friend of Don Crisóstomo, and turned her out of his house. Now she is wandering about again, singing, as mad as ever. But she does no harm. She lives in the forest.'

'What else has happened in town since we left? I know we have a new parish priest and a new commanding officer.'

'What terrible times! Humanity goes from bad to worse,' murmured Capitan Basilio thinking on the past. 'Let us see now. The day after you were taken away they found the head sacristan dead, hanging from the ceiling of his house. The curious thing is that, according to the medical findings, he had been poisoned, like Lucas. Father Salví felt his death very much and seized all his papers. Oh yes, Tasio the scholar died too, and was buried in the Chinese cemetery.'

'Poor Don Anastasio,' sighed Don Filipo. 'And his books?'

'They were burned by the pious, who thus thought to please God. I could save nothing, not even the works of Cicero. The Mayor did nothing to prevent it.'

Both fell silent.

The madwoman could be heard singing a sad and melancholy song.

'Do you know when María Clara is getting married?' Iday asked Sinang.

'I don't,' answered the latter. 'I had a letter from her, but I don't dare open it; I would rather not know. Poor Crisóstomo!'

'They say that, if it had not been for Linares, Capitan Tiago would have gone to the gallows. What was María Clara to do?' commented Victoria.

A boy passed limping by; he was running towards the town square where Sisa's song was coming from. It was Basilio. He had found his mother's house deserted and in ruins; after many questions all he had gathered was that his mother had gone out of her mind and was wandering about the town. He had not heard a word about Crispín.

Basilio swallowed his tears, put his emotions under control, and went to look for his mother without stopping to rest. Arrived in town, he was asking after her when he heard her song in the distance. The poor boy controlled the shaking of his knees and ran after his mother to throw himself in her arms.

The madwoman left the town square and went on to the house of the new commanding officer. Now as before there was a sentry at the door, and a woman's head at the window, but it was not that of Medusa but of a young woman; after all, commanding officers are not necessarily unfortunate in marriage.

Sisa began to sing in front of the house, her eyes on the moon which swayed majestically in the blue sky among golden clouds. Basilio could see her but did not dare approach her, and waited for her to leave the place. He walked to and fro but avoided coming nearer to the barracks.

The young woman at the window listened attentively to the madwoman's song, and ordered the sentry to take her upstairs.

But on seeing the soldier approach and on hearing his voice the terror-stricken Sisa ran away, and God knows how fast a madwoman runs. Basilio went after her, fearing to lose her, and forgetting the pain in his feet.

'Look how that boy is chasing the madwoman,' a servant-girl in the street cried indignantly. Seeing that he kept running after Sisa, the girl picked up a stone and threw it at him:

'Take that! Pity our dog is tied up.'

Basilio felt the blow on his head, but kept running without giving heed. Dogs barked at him, geese honked, some windows were opened by the curious, others were shut by those who feared another night of tumult.

When they were out of the town Sisa began to slow down her pace, but there was still a great distance between her and her pursuer, despite all his efforts.

'Mother!' he cried when he caught sight of her.

But the madwoman began her flight anew when she heard the voice.

'Mother, it's me!' screamed the desperate boy.

She seemed not to hear him and he ran panting after her. They had left behind the cultivated fields and were nearing the forest.

Basilio saw his mother enter it, and followed. The shrubs and bushes, the thorny canes, the protruding roots of trees made running difficult for both of them. He followed her by the light of the moon which, falling through the branches on the clearings, drew her in silhouette from time to time. It was the mysterious wood of the Ibarra family.

The boy stumbled and fell several times, but rose again, feeling no pain; all his soul came to a focus in his eyes, which followed the beloved figure of his mother.

They went across the sweetly murmuring brook. The thorns in the bamboo fallen into the muddy bank buried themselves in Basilio's naked feet, but he did not stop to pluck them out.

To his great surprise he saw his mother was going deeper into the thicket. When she came to the tomb of the old Spaniard at the foot of the *balete* tree, she opened the wooden door and entered.

Basilio tried to do the same but he found the door locked. The madwoman was denying him entrance, keeping the door closed with all the strength of her gaunt arms, even pushing against it with her dishevelled head.

'Mother, it's me, Basilio, your son,' the exhausted boy cried, letting himself fall to the ground.

But she would not yield, and planting her feet on the ground offered energetic resistance.

Basilio hammered at the door with his fist, with his bloodstained head; he wept; but in vain. He rose painfully, looked at the encircling wall of the tomb, and thought of climbing it, but could find no foothold. He went round it and saw one of the branches of the ill-omened *balete* crossing the branch of another tree. He climbed; his filial love wrought miracles, and from one branch to the other, he got to the *balete* tree and saw his mother still pressing her head against the door.

The noise he made in the branches attracted Sisa's attention; she turned to flee, but her son, dropping from the tree, embraced her and covered her with kisses. Then he fainted.

Sisa saw the bloodstained forehead. She leaned over him, her eyes starting out of their sockets. She started at his face, and those pale features shook the dormant cells in her brain awake. Something like a spark was struck in her mind, and she recognised her son at last. With a cry she fell on the unconscious boy, embracing and kissing him.

Mother and son were motionless for a long time.

When Basilio had recovered from his faint he found his mother unconscious. He shook her, called her the most tender names, and, seeing that she neither wakened nor breathed, rose and went to the brook. He gathered a little water in a cone of banana leaves, and washed his mother's bloodless face. But she did not make the slightest movement, her eyes remained closed.

Basilio looked at her horror-stricken. He placed his ear against her heart but the thin and withered bosom was cold and the heart did not beat; he put his lips on hers and felt no breath. The unfortunate boy threw his arms round the corpse and wept bitterly.

The majestic moon shone in the sky, there was a vagrant breeze and the crickets chirped in the grass.

This night of lights and merriment for so many children who in the warm bosom of their families observed the most sweetly remembered of all holidays, the holy day which commemorates Heaven's first look of love on earth; this night when all good Christian families ate, drank, danced, sang, laughed, played games, made love and kissed one another; this night, so magical for childhood in cold climates with its traditional pine tree loaded with lights, dolls, sweetmeats, and tinsel dazzling the round eyes of innocence—this night brought Basilio nothing but the death of his mother. Perhaps even in the home of the taciturn Father Salví other children were playing, singing perhaps the old Spanish carol:

> *Christmas is coming,*
> *Christmas is gone,*
> *We too are going,*
> *Not to return anon.*

When Basilio raised his head he saw a man standing before him, silently watching him. The man came nearer and asked him in a hushed voice:

'Are you her son?'

The boy nodded.

'What do you plan to do?'

'Bury her.'

'In the cemetery?'

'I have no money, and besides the parish priest wouldn't allow it.'

'So?'

'If you would help me...'

'I am very weak,' answered the unknown, letting himself fall gradually to the ground until he was leaning on both hands. 'I am wounded. I have not eaten or slept for two days. Has nobody else come tonight?'

The man studied the boy's interesting face speculatively.

'Listen,' he continued in a weakening voice, 'I shall be dead too before daybreak. Twenty paces from here, on the other bank of the creek, there is a great pile of firewood. Bring it here, make a pyre, put our bodies on it, cover us, and set the wood on fire, a great fire, until we are turned to ashes.'

Basilio listened.

'Then, if nobody else comes, dig here. You will find much gold. It will all be yours. Study!'

The voice of the unknown was growing ever more unintelligible.

'Go and look for the firewood. I want to help you.'

Basilio went away. The unknown turned his face to the East and whispered as if in prayer:

'Nothing will remain of me... I die without seeing the sun rise on my country. You who are to see the dawn, welcome it, and do not forget those who fell during the night!'

He raised his eyes to the sky, his lips moved as if to say a prayer, then he lowered his head and fell slowly to the ground...

Two hours later Sister Rufa was at her kitchen window washing up before going to Mass. Looking out towards the forest the pious woman saw a thick column of smoke rising; she frowned and, with holy anger, exclaimed:

'Now who is that heretic making a forest clearing on a holiday of obligation? That is why we have so many misfortunes! May God spare you Purgatory, you barbarian, you'll have none of my indulgences to get you out of it.'

Epilogue

SINCE many of the characters in this story are still alive while others have dropped out of sight, a real epilogue is out of the question. Nevertheless one may be essayed after a fashion. After María Clara entered the nunnery Father Dámaso left the town where he was parish priest to live in Manila. Father Salví did the same and, while waiting for his mitre, preached often in the chapel of the nunnery of St. Clare, where he held an important post. After a few months Father Dámaso was ordered by his Very Reverend Father Provincial to take up a parish in a very distant province. He took it so badly, it was said, that they found him dead in bed the next day. Some said he had died of a stroke; others, of a nightmare; but the attending physician resolved all doubts by giving it as his opinion that Father Dámaso had died all of a sudden.

None of his acquaintances would have recognised Capitan Tiago. Weeks before María Clara made her vows he had fallen into such a deep state of depression that he began to lose weight and grew morose, brooding, and as suspicious as his former friend, the wretched Capitan Tinong. As soon as the gates of the nunnery had closed on María Clara he ordered his disconsolate cousin Aunt Isabel to pack up everything that had ever belonged to his daughter and his deceased wife and to go and live in Malabon or San Diego; he wanted to live by himself from then on. He dedicated himself frenziedly to card-playing and the cockpit and took up opium smoking. No longer did he go on pilgrimage to Antipolo or commission Masses; Doña Patrocinio, his old rival, piously celebrated this triumph by snoring throughout the sermons in church. The casual passer-by along the first street in Chinatown of an evening was likely to see, seated in a Chinese store, a small jaundiced man, thin, bent, with sunken dreamy eyes and muddy lips and nails, staring out at the people without seeing them. At nightfall he would struggle to his feet and, leaning on a cane, head for a narrow alley and enter a disreputable hut over whose door a sign in large red letters said: *Opium Smoking. Open to the Public.* This was what was left of the famous Capitan Tiago, now utterly forgotten even by the head sacristans.

Doña Victorina, not content with her artificial ringlets and her Southern accent, developed a passion for driving her carriage herself, with Don Tiburcio rigid at her side. Her short-sightedness caused so many accidents that she took to wearing a pair of pincenez, which gave her a formidable aspect. Nobody ever called the doctor again, and his servants saw him toothless—a very bad sign—many days of the week.

Linares, the poor man's only defender, had gone to his grave some time before, the victim of a dysentery and of maltreatment by his cousin.

The victorious commanding officer returned to Spain as an acting major, leaving his wife behind in her flannel shirt whose colour was by then indescribable. The poor woman, forsaken by her husband like the Ariadne of Greek mythology, followed the example of her fabled predecessor and took up the cult of Bacchus, the god of wine, and the cultivation of tobacco. She drank and smoked with such fervour that soon she was feared not only by young girls but also by old women and children.

The characters in this story from the town of San Diego are probably still alive, those at least who were not killed in the explosion of the *Lipa* which was the steamship service to those parts. Nobody ever bothered to identify the unhappy victims of that catastrophe in 1883, or to sort out the arms and legs scattered all over the Island of Convalescence on the outskirts of Manila and on the banks of the Pasig River. Still, the Government and Press of the time were content, and so should everyone be, to ascertain that the single friar aboard was safe and sound. What is important, after all, is the life of virtuous priests, whose dominion over the Philippines may God preserve for the good of souls.

There was nothing to be learned about María Clara other than that apparently she was in her grave. Persons of great influence in the nunnery of St. Clare had nothing to say about her, not even its most garrulous patronesses who regularly received their share of the convent's famous dish of fried chicken livers and its even more famous sauce *a la Poor Clares*, prepared by the clever cook of the Spouses of the Lord.

However, there was talk of a night in September when a storm was beating its wings against the houses in Manila. Against a running roll of thunder, lightning flashes revealed briefly the destruction wreaked by the typhoon and struck panic into the inhabitants of the city. Rain was falling in torrents. Here zigzagging lightning flashes revealed the corner of a roof; there a shutter flew through the air and fell with a terrifying crash. No carriage, no pedestrian was on the streets. When a hoarse clap of thunder, a hundred times repeated, lost itself in the distance, the sighing of the wind could be heard, a wind which the rain turned into a whirlpool beating against the shell-panes of the closed windows.

That night two sentries had taken shelter in a building under construction near the nunnery: one was an ordinary soldier, the other a soldier of noble blood.

'What are we doing here?' asked the soldier. 'There's nobody out in the streets. We should go to a proper house. My girl friend lives quite near here.'

'From here to there is quite a way and we'll get wet,' objected the blueblood.

'So what, as long as we're not struck by lightning.'

'Oh, don't worry about that, the nuns will have a lightning rod.'

'Really? Are you sure it's any good?'

As he peered at the roof of the nunnery through the darkness there was a long lightning flash followed by a shattering thunderclap.

'Oh my sainted mother! Jesus, Mary, Joseph! exclaimed the soldier crossing himself and tugging at the blueblood. 'Let's get out of here!'

'What's the matter with you?'

'Come on, let's get out of here,' the soldier repeated, his teeth chattering with fear.

'What is it?'

'I've seen a ghost!' he whispered shakily.

'A ghost?'

'On the roof!'

The blueblood stuck his head out; he wanted to see too.

There was another lightning flash; a vein of fire traced itself against the sky followed by a deafening thunderclap.

'Jesus!' he said, crossing himself.

Indeed, by the brilliant lightning, he had seen a white figure standing almost on the ridge of the roof, its arms stretched out to the sky and its face turned pleadingly upward while the heavens replied with thunder and lightning.

In the silence that followed the thunder a doleful moaning was heard.

'It isn't the wind, it's the ghost!' hissed the soldier when his companion pressed his hand.

The moaning floated in the air over the clatter of the rain; nor did the whistling wind override the sweet forlorn lament.

There was another blinding lightning flash.

'No, that's no ghost!' cried the blueblood. 'I saw her again. She is beautiful as the Virgin. Let us get away from here and notify the authorities.'

The soldier did not wait for the invitation to be repeated and they both disappeared into the night.

Who was it that grieved in the night, in wind, rain, and storm? Who was the timid virgin, the spouse of Christ, who thus defied the unloosed elements and chose that dreadful night, that open sky, that perilous height to call upon the Lord? Had God abandoned His temple in the nunnery, had He turned a deaf ear to prayer, had the convent vaults forbidden that forlorn soul to soar towards the throne of the Most Merciful?

The storm raged furiously throughout the night, a night in which no star shone; the desperate moaning, mingled with the sighing of the wind, continued, but unheard by Nature and by man.

The next day, when the sun shone once again in a sky cleared of dark clouds, a carriage drew up at the gates of the nunnery of St. Clare. A gentleman alighted and, identifying himself as a representative of the authorities, sought immediate audience with the abbess. He demanded to see all the nuns.

It is said that one of them appeared with her habit soaking wet and in tatters and, with many tales of horror, begged for the gentleman's protection against the assaults of hypocrisy. It is also said that she was very beautiful, and had the loveliest and most eloquent eyes that ever had been seen.

The representative of the authorities did not see fit to take her under his care; instead, after conferring with the abbess, he abandoned her despite her tearful pleas. She saw the gates close behind him as the damned might see the gates of Heaven close against them, if ever Heaven were as cruel and unfeeling as the world of men. The abbess said the young nun was out of her mind.

The gentleman was perhaps unaware that, if so, there was an insane asylum in Manila, or perhaps it was his opinion that the nunnery was itself a madhouse, although it is argued that in any case he was rather ignorant, and incapable of judging whether or not a person was in her right senses.

It is also said that the Governor General was of a different mind when he heard of these events, and that he sought to give shelter to the mad nun.

But this time no forlorn beauty was allowed to show herself to the authorities, the abbess refusing any inspection of the cloister on the authority of the Church and the Holy Rules of the Order.

Nothing more was said about it, nor about the unhappy María Clara.

THE END